Readers love the Hockey Ever After series by Ashlyn Kane and Morgan James

Winging It

"From the terrific world building, the endearing characters and the solid plot and timelines, this book was simply so much more than I could have hoped for."

—The Novel Approach

Scoring Position

"The pace was even faster, the characters even more lovable and the chemistry even hotter, and I loved meeting some of my favorite characters from the first book again. This book truly warmed my heart!"

—Annie's Reading Tips

Unrivaled

"I loved that they figured out how to be together even if they had to play against each other on the ice, especially since it made things hard off the ice too."

—Bayou Book Junkie

Crushed Ice

"I am not a hockey fan, but Kane and James have taught me to appreciate the elegance and nuance of the game... Without hockey, this book just wouldn't be any fun.

—Paranormal Romance Guild

By ASHLYN KANE

American Love Songs
With Claudia Mayrant & CJ Burke: Babe in the Woodshop
A Good Vintage
Hang a Shining Star
Homecoming for Beginners
The Inside Edge
The Rock Star's Guide to Getting Your Man

DREAMSPUN BEYOND
Hex and Candy

DREAMSPUN DESIRES
His Leading Man
Fake Dating the Prince

With Morgan James
Hair of the Dog
Hard Feelings
Return to Sender
String Theory

HOCKEY EVER AFTER
Winging It
The Winging It Holiday Special
Scoring Position
Unrivaled
An Unrivaled Off-Season
Crushed Ice
Textbook Defense

Published by DREAMSPINNER PRESS
www.dreamspinnerpress.com

By MORGAN JAMES

Purls of Wisdom

DREAMSPUN DESIRES
Love Conventions

With Ashlyn Kane
Hair of the Dog
Hard Feelings
Return to Sender
String Theory

HOCKEY EVER AFTER
Winging It
The Winging It Holiday Special
Scoring Position
Unrivaled
An Unrivaled Off-Season
Crushed Ice
Textbook Defense

Published by DREAMSPINNER PRESS
www.dreamspinnerpress.com

TEXTBOOK DEFENSE

ASHLYN KANE
MORGAN JAMES

Published by
DREAMSPINNER PRESS

8219 Woodville Hwy #1245
Woodville, FL 32362 USA
www.dreamspinnerpress.com

This is a work of fiction. Names, characters, places, and incidents either are the product of author imagination or are used fictitiously, and any resemblance to actual persons, living or dead, business establishments, events, or locales is entirely coincidental.

Textbook Defense
© 2025 Ashlyn Kane and Morgan James

Cover Art
© 2025 L.C. Chase
http://www.lcchase.com
Cover content is for illustrative purposes only and any person depicted on the cover is a model.

Mass Market Paperback ISBN: 978-1-64108-733-9
Trade Paperback ISBN: 978-1-64108-732-2
Digital ISBN: 978-1-64108-731-5
Trade Paperback published February 2025
v. 1.0

With special thanks to Lindsey for the assist.

Warmup

JORDY SHAW had not paid a terrible amount of attention to his high school English classes, but one concept had stuck with him. He couldn't remember the exact wording—something about the best-laid plans of mice and men going awry. And that Jordy understood.

Some days it felt like the only thing he *had* planned was his hockey career. At age five he'd told everyone he would one day play in the NHL.

But he definitely *hadn't* planned on early morning wakeup calls from a six-year-old excited about going to the library.

Jordy grunted awake as Kaira landed on the bed and snuggled onto his back like an excitable kitten. "Daddy, Daddy," she cooed in a manner that might have fooled a stranger. "It's *library* day."

He grunted and buried his face into his pillow. Maybe if he didn't talk, she'd think he was still asleep and would likewise settle in for more rest.

"Daddy." She poked him between the shoulder blades. "I know you're awake."

A lie. Jordy was pretty sure she was guessing. Mostly.

"Daddy, it's morning. You said we'd go to the library today, and I stayed in bed until the clock said six, just like you said, and it's morning and"—her tone shifted from overeager puppy to reverent apostle—"*books*, Daddy."

Jordy couldn't deny her a moment longer. But that didn't mean he wanted to get out of bed any more now than he had a few minutes ago.

In one fairly practiced move, he gently lurched upward with a roar, caught his daughter around the waist, threw her down on the mattress, and pulled her in for a cuddle. "Sleep," he groaned and snuffled his face into her neck as she shrieked and giggled.

"No, Daddy! Books, not sleep!"

"Yes, sleep." Jordy pulled the duvet over them both.

Kaira giggled and squirmed and gasped, "No! Wake up!"

Jordy laughed, pulled back from his aggressive snuggling, and stared down at her beloved, impish face. "Morning, sweetheart."

"Good morning, Daddy! Did you sleep good?"

"Hm." He settled next to her, hoping she'd let them linger just a few moments. "Yes."

She tucked her hands under her chin and asked seriously, "Did you have good dreams?"

"I dreamed about our trip to Curaçao last summer."

"You did? Did you dream about the beach? And the water? And the fishes?"

Jordy hummed. It had been a wonderful vacation—just sun, sand, water, and Kaira—and not a single person on the island knew who he was. For the first week, Kaira had flourished under his exclusive care and had nearly vibrated out of her shoes when her beloved Auntie Emma arrived to join them for their last days.

Jordy's sister was fifteen when she called him, choked up and scared to tell him she'd been stupid. He'd forever count his blessings for the NHL off-seasons and his dumb salary that let him get on a plane that same day and ride to her rescue. As scared as Emma had been, Jordy could never regret anything that brought her daughter—*his* daughter, now—into his life.

"Are we going to swim with fishes this summer?" Kaira asked.

Jordy hummed noncommittally. "Maybe." Kaira had just finished her kindergarten schoolyear, and Jordy hadn't made plans yet, mostly because he was looking forward to hanging out with his baby and enjoying some quiet days, just the two of them.

Undeterred, Kaira rambled on about sand castles and fish and playing with Jordy and Auntie Emma in the sun. It sounded good to him. And even better, her musings bought him several more minutes snuggled in bed.

STORY TIME at the library had been Kaira's favorite weekly haunt ever since Jordy's friend-slash-lawyer, Gem, introduced them, but given its timing on Sunday mornings and the NHL's love for Saturday evening and Sunday matinee games, Jordy could rarely join her. It was a treat to drive her there, even if he couldn't stay with her for the full program. Once she was settled in the children's area, he headed back out to his car for his meeting.

Conducting business from the back seat of his SUV might not have been the classiest of moves, but it worked. And at least it was a cooler June morning.

"Sorry again about the Sunday meeting, Jordy," Erika said by way of greeting.

Considering they were about to talk about his participating in an outreach program this summer, Jordy didn't protest the timing.

Almost an hour later, he headed back into the library to collect Kaira. Story time had ended, and kids and their parents were wandering away from the children's section. Jordy finger combed his hair out of his eyes and looked around for his baby.

He found her in the kids' section with the librarian. Kaira was curled up on one of the many pillows scattered on the floor. On the cushion next to her sat a gorgeous man in a polo shirt that seemed to be a size too small. The man was leaning forward with his chin propped on one hand, smiling kindly at Kaira, who was overflowing with excitement.

"Everybody knows the Shield are the best team in the league," Kaira was saying seriously as Jordy got within hearing range.

"Do they?" the man asked with a smile that appled his smooth brown cheeks. "*I* didn't know that." Jordy wasn't the best at judging accents, but he was pretty sure the stranger was from the UK.

"That's because you don't know hockey," Kaira said baldly. "You'll learn." She patted the man's arm.

Even from a distance, Jordy could make out the twinkle in the man's eye as he leaned forward to coax more information from Jordy's little chatterbox. "Thanks. So what is it that makes them so great?"

Kaira pondered the question for a split second before she started enumerating reasons on her fingers. "Daddy. Uncle Sully. They're old. Everyone says so. They win." She paused and tilted her head. "They don't have the best mascot, though. The Orcas have a better one, but that's because orcas are better than rocks."

"Naturally."

"They also have okay uniforms."

The stranger's cheeks appled as he held back a laugh. "Just okay?" If he kept holding in that laughter, he might hurt something.

"Yeah. No one has a great uniform because they're all boring colors."

"None of them are your favorite?"

"Glitter is the best color," Kaira said in the same tone she used when explaining the basics of toddler pop culture.

"Ah, of course. That makes sense." The laughter bubbled out on the edge of his otherwise sincere tone. He looked up over Kaira's shoulder, perhaps to regain some composure, and caught sight of Jordy.

Which was when Jordy realized he was looming at the edge of the children's section… without a child.

Creepy.

But the stranger—who obviously worked at the library, judging by the name badge Jordy couldn't quite read from this angle—didn't look alarmed or call for help. Instead he smiled further and asked, "Kaira dear, I don't suppose your father is a frightfully tall and horribly handsome man who has hair the same honey shade as yours?"

Kaira scrunched her nose. "He is very tall, but I don't know about handsome. Uncle Sully calls him pretty boy, though. He says if Daddy doesn't want to be called pretty, he shouldn't have shampoo-commercial flow. He also says that it's a good thing for me since I look like Daddy."

Jordy didn't cringe from embarrassment. Kaira had given him way too much practice hiding his mortified winces. Unfortunately, she *loved* to quote her Uncle Sully.

"So would I be right in guessing that gorgeous statue behind you is your daddy?" The man pointed over her shoulder.

Kaira turned around and beamed. "Daddy!" She sprang up and ran for him, and Jordy swooped her into his arms. She was getting so big, but thankfully not too big for him to do this.

She pressed her cheek against his and said a bit too loudly, "I missed you, Daddy. Rowan read a book about a unicorn and one about a train, but that one wasn't any good."

Jordy smiled into her blond pigtail and caught sight of the stranger—Rowan—who was silently laughing. He seemed to do that a lot.

"I'm sorry you didn't like the second story," Jordy said.

Kaira pulled away to look him in the eye. "I didn't like it because it was bad."

"Remember, sweetie, just because you don't like something doesn't mean that no one likes it."

Kaira wrinkled her nose, clearly not persuaded. Before she could offer a rebuttal, Rowan spoke up. "Well, maybe you could give me some good book recommendations. After all, today was my first time doing story time, and I'll need more book ideas if I'm going to do it every week."

Kaira practically leaped out of Jordy's arms. Only his quick reflexes and years of practice saved him from getting a toddler elbow to the face. "Oh yes, I could do that. I know lots of good ones. Do you like armadillos?"

"My dear, I adore armadillos," Rowan said with a straight face.

Kaira beamed and opened her mouth, no doubt to expound more on her favorite books, but Jordy cut in. He wasn't prepared to stand here all day. "Kaira, we need to get going."

She whirled on him and stared up at him suspiciously. "Why?"

"Sully said he was making us lunch today."

"He did?" Kaira spun back to Rowan and said in a polite if somewhat rushed voice, "Sorry, Mr. Rowan, I will have to help you another day, because we need to go see Uncle Sully for lunch. He makes the best hot dogs, and it's the only lunch he makes when it's not freezing-your-tits-off too cold to barbeque."

Jordy did not facepalm. He did make a mental note to yell at his liney for not keeping better control of his tongue around little ones—not that it would do much good, knowing Sully. At least he'd be reaping his own consequences soon, now that he was a father himself.

Rowan laughed. "Well, if he's making hot dogs, then you must go, though I am terribly disappointed to cut short a discussion of books with such a brilliant, well-read young lady." He gave a flourishy bow like some medieval courtier. "I will await your return, my dear, so that you can continue to educate me in the ways of picture books."

"Yes! Maybe Daddy can bring me back tomorrow now that he's out of work."

That one gave Rowan pause, and Jordy remembered that the man seemed oblivious to the world of hockey—and probably to Jordy himself. Cheeks warming, he said to his daughter, "I'm on summer vacation, honey."

"Yes," Kaira agreed.

"How delightful," Rowan said, recovering, "that your daddy gets summers off with you. I bet you two have all sorts of fun adventures."

"Last year we went to the beach! I want to go back."

The smile Rowan gave Kaira as he hummed his agreement about the joys of the beach was sweet and charming; the smile he gave Jordy next was anything but. It was secretive and a little bit dirty. His tone, though, stayed light. "Oh, I think I can picture you on the beach all too well, Daddy, and I bet everyone thoroughly enjoys it." His eyes flicked down and back up, so quickly Jordy thought maybe he imagined it.

Jordy flushed. It wasn't that he wasn't used to being flirted with—that happened all the time. Being a rich and moderately famous athlete meant no shortage of interest. And just because Jordy didn't flirt with strangers didn't mean he couldn't recognize it when it happened, but no one had ever flirted with him like this before.

For one thing, strangers didn't usually flirt with him when Kaira was around. Not once she started walking, at least—baby Kaira strapped to his chest had attracted plenty of attention—and those who did acted like she wasn't even there. No one had "flirted" with Kaira too. Or called him "Daddy" without innuendo.

And while Rowan was absolutely gorgeous and hypothetically the kind of guy Jordy wouldn't mind a date with, Jordy didn't actually know what Rowan was after.

Fortunately, Kaira made a perfect social buffer. Sully and most of their teammates thought it was hilarious that Jordy's kid was such a chatterbox, and they teased him about it regularly. They didn't understand that her talkative nature saved him from dealing with awkward social situations.

The innuendo flew right over Kaira's head, and she nodded eagerly. "Daddy and I played games and went swimming, and Daddy is the *best* at building sand castles."

Jordy just knew how to turn over a bucket. "I'm average at best."

"Oh," Rowan said lightly, "I'm sure there is nothing average about you."

Jordy huffed in amusement.

"He's the best daddy," Kaira informed Rowan seriously.

Self-conscious, Jordy stroked his daughter's hair and asked, "Are we checking out any books today?"

"My books!" Kaira ran off to gather the ones she'd chosen. The stack was as large as it always was and contained some old favorites. "Ready, Daddy!"

"So many books," Rowan said with delight. "Come along, then, Princess Kaira, and let's get you to the checkout desk so you can feed your brain with all these books."

Kaira skipped next to him as he led her to the circulation desk, and Jordy followed, bemused.

"There you go—all checked out. I hope that I'll be seeing you next week." Rowan crossed his arms and leaned over the desk, the better to look Kaira in the face. His biceps flexed and strained the fabric of his shirt. Jordy wondered if the seams would survive. "And don't forget about those recommendations for story time."

"I won't." Kaira took her books from Rowan and handed them to Jordy to carry.

"Excellent. It was lovely to meet you, Princess Kaira—and your knightly father."

Perhaps *princess* was too apt of a moniker, Jordy admitted to himself, but who could resist spoiling such a perfect child?

Kaira giggled and gave a clumsy curtsy. "You too, Mr. Rowan. Bye!" She waved with one hand and dragged Jordy out with the other.

For some reason, Jordy couldn't help one last look over his shoulder. Rowan was still leaning over the desk, his eyes locked on them as they walked out. Though if Jordy wasn't mistaken, it wasn't Kaira Rowan was watching, even if his eyes were focused down low.

"Damn," Rowan muttered to himself. If he'd had a more appreciative audience, he might have swooned. "The view might actually be better from the back."

"Hockey butt," Taylor said with a dreamy sigh. "And Jordy Shaw certainly has a fine example."

Intrigued, Rowan arched his eyebrows at his colleague. "You know him?"

"Sweetie, I know you're not of this native land, but even you can't have missed his face plastered around the city."

Now that she mentioned it, he could recall something about Jordy's face on a blue background showing up on bus shelters and tube platforms. "Huh. She mentioned he played hockey, but I hadn't realized." He paused and reviewed the conversation. "Did you say *hockey butt*? This is a documented phenomenon?" Why didn't they put *that* on the posters?

"God, yes." She perched her own behind on the corner of the circulation desk. "Although it's difficult to appreciate under all the padding they play in. Criminal."

"Someone should definitely be arrested." Probably Rowan, for the direction his thoughts had taken while he was at work, where he was around children.

Taylor fanned herself. "I still can't believe you didn't recognize him. You were flirting pretty hard for someone who had no idea."

"I thought he was just a DILF," Rowan defended, keeping his voice down. Story time was over, but several parents and their charges were still milling around, picking out reading material. "You should've heard him with his kid. The world's cutest mutual admiration society." He couldn't help that he had a weakness for that. His own parents had done everything they could to avoid being responsible for raising him. *Obviously* he had daddy issues. "Everyone in this damned country plays hockey. How was I supposed to know she meant *professionally*? I thought he was a teacher or something." At least that made sense, given his ease with his kid. And who else got summers off?

Professional hockey players, apparently.

"I mean, he *is* a DILF," Taylor allowed.

"Yeah, a *sugar* DILF."

The sound of someone clearing their throat snapped Rowan out of the conversation, and he smiled winningly at an amused-looking woman and her six-year-old twins. "No, don't tell me—it's Devante and… Thea, right?"

The twins nodded, grinning, and Mom's eyebrows went up in acknowledgment. "Not bad for your first day."

"I'll probably get worse as the week goes on," Rowan said wryly. The maternity leave he was covering would last until the end of August. Five days a week of children's programming? By Wednesday his head would be so full of kids' names that he'd be sticking labels on their foreheads. "What've you got here—oh, good choices. I love this one."

He checked out their books and slid them into their book bag—it had a sponge-painted dinosaur that Rowan happened to know was one of the crafts last year's groups had made. He wouldn't mind doing something similar. Who didn't like dinosaurs? Although maybe he could open it up a little. Surely the internet had an assortment of animal-shaped sponges to choose from. Perhaps even a set that included an armadillo?

"Did I miss the introduction of a new sparkly object?" came a familiar voice once the family had left.

"There was a formal introduction," Taylor answered seriously. "Rowan Chadha, meet hockey butts."

Rowan pulled himself out of his mental tangent but didn't bother to mount a defense. "Hello to you too, wench." He leaned across the desk and swapped cheek kisses with Gem, his *other* best friend, though on the surface their relationship looked more like frenemies. Rowan blamed their parents, who'd thrown them together on the rare occasion when both sets had been unable to pawn them off on nannies or boarding schools. "What brings you out of your crypt before noon on a Sunday?"

"I'm in search of a slut whose blood to bathe in, obviously," she answered smoothly, her perfect façade never slipping.

"Well, all of Rowan's blood is currently in his pants—"

"Oi!" Rowan protested. There could be delicate ears around. He shot Taylor a quelling look. "There will be no bathing of anything in my pants." He paused and reconsidered. "That came out wrong. Let's start over." He took a deep breath. "Gem, darling. To what do we owe the pleasure?"

He realized he should've sensed the trap when Gem lifted a dark purple envelope in her perfectly manicured fingers. "I wanted to secure your RSVP in person, of course."

Rowan felt his heart drop into his pants along with all his blood. "Another one?"

"Oh honestly, don't make that face. You know you love playing Ken for me." One of Gem's more sadistic traits was the enjoyment she got out of forcing Rowan to dress up in her dead husband's tuxedos and accompany her to various social functions. Rowan hated the clothing, but he had to admit that it was entertaining to see Gem navigate the highest echelons of Toronto society to secure funding for one social project or another, only to have her turn around once they were alone and absolutely excoriate their hypocrisy.

Besides, the food was always good. Not to mention the wine.

"What's-his-face isn't going to be there, is he?" What's-his-face was old enough to be Rowan's grandfather and richer than Midas, and he was under the mistaken impression that this made him the most interesting person in the world and that he deserved a captive audience.

Rowan had no idea why he'd been selected for this dubious honor, but inevitably he spent these social interactions devising increasingly ludicrous ways to escape, from ducking under a catering cart until a server pushed him away to leaping from the roof *Mission Impossible* style.

"Don't be ridiculous," Gem said, "he's the fourth-richest man in the city. Of course he's going to be there."

Rowan understood that funds had to be raised from people who had access to them. However—"Can't you have the third-richest challenge him to a cage match or something?"

She tutted. "Where's your sense of civic duty?"

"Hiding under my sense of self-preservation. The man could bore a tax accountant to death, Gem."

"Oh, don't be so dramatic. I know you've had plenty of practice entertaining yourself."

Ouch. He clutched his chest. "Jabs at my love life are completely uncalled-for and I won't respond to them." She was going to make *such* a good politician when she finally built up enough cachet to run for mayor. Rowan was both excited and terrified at the prospect. "What are we raising funds for this time?"

"Children's Aid Society."

Ugh. He plucked the invitation from her claws. "Fine, yes, of course I'll go." Especially since Gem was paying. Perhaps this time he could drink enough wine to make What's-his-name seem interesting. Then again, he liked his liver. "But I get to pick the tie this time."

"Absolutely not."

It was worth a try.

"You're due a lunch break, right?" Gem asked, which was how Rowan ended up a few blocks from the library, drinking an iced tea while Gem sipped on a G and T.

"So, how is it you were introduced to hockey arse?" she asked with a smirk.

"One of the parents who came to pick up a kid after story time had a spectacular example." Rowan hummed in memory. He wasn't sure he'd ever seen an arse so wonderfully peach-like in person. He wanted to take a big bite. "I was enraptured from first sight."

Gem snorted. "Of course you were, you slut."

"Gem, it was magnificent." He sighed. "I didn't even know its owner was famous until Taylor pointed out that Jordy's face is plastered all over town."

Gem arched an eyebrow. "Jordy Shaw?"

"You *know* him?" And it was at this moment that Rowan remembered that Gem knew the entire team. Somehow, through a series of events Rowan was not clear on, Gem had become the de facto contract lawyer for most of the city's professional athletes.

"We travel in the same circles," Gem said carelessly. She sipped her G and T and considered him over the top of her glass. "Does this mean you're finally cured?"

"Of what?" He lifted his glass in a toast and took a sip.

"Your appalling taste in men."

Rowan nearly choked on his drink.

"Don't give me that look. You vacillate between unemployable bums and overeducated pretentious douchebags."

"Ouch," Rowan muttered. He knew Gem had never liked any of his romantic partners—she didn't make it a secret—but she usually saved her criticism for postbreakup bitchfests.

"You know it's true. Your last dick had two master's degrees and no tact." Rowan opened his mouth to defend Darius, but Gem continued. "Darling, when I refused the lamb, he told me that Hitler was a vegetarian." Rowan winced; that sounded all too plausible. "Which, aside from being obnoxious and a completely insipid thing to say, isn't even factually correct."

"Okay, so Darius was a bit...." Rowan searched for a tactful yet fitting term but had to give up. "Fine, yes, he was a douchebag. But that doesn't mean—"

"Before Darius, there was Gary. Now you know I would never judge a man for his education or lack thereof, but I *will* judge a man for being a waste of space."

"Gem," Rowan tried to cut in, but Gem was on a roll.

"Rowan. The world needs deliverymen, but only ones who can show up on time to do deliveries. The only ambition that man had, aside from beating the next level on his video game, was to be a kept man, and he wasn't particular about who did the keeping."

Gary had been a mistake of epic proportions. Rowan's only excuse was that he'd had a mouth like a Hoover. "I know Gary was awful—"

Gem shot him a look. "The only reason I didn't stage an intervention is because you caught him with his pants down before I could send out the invitations."

"Technically, Gary wasn't the one with his pants down." Rowan wasn't the only man who appreciated Gary's skills.

"Rowan."

Rowan's shoulders slumped. "You think I need reminding of what a mistake Gary was? I'm the one he made a fool out of for two months." He gulped his iced tea and wished he could order something stronger, but unfortunately it was a bad look to show up with alcohol on your breath when you worked with children.

"Apparently you do. He only made a fool of you because you let him. Not in an *it was your fault* way, but in a *because you picked a douchebag again* way."

"Just because the last two weren't prizes—"

"The rest of them were carbon copies of the last two. Brian was another Gary, Welland another Darius…. Need I go on?"

Rowan gritted his teeth. Okay, so he didn't have the best track record, but Gem didn't have to bring out the claws. She'd better be paying for this lunch to make it up to him. "Is there a point to this embarrassing trip down memory lane?"

"Yes!" Gem snapped and then softened. "I'm hoping you've finally seen the light. You deserve better."

Rowan scowled. Thinking about his unfortunate and colorful dating history made him think about what had *led* to it. The Garys and Dariuses of the world might be completely awful boyfriends, but at least they didn't prioritize their jobs over everything else.

Of course, now Rowan was forced to admit that they could have stood to rearrange their priorities just a wee bit. "How did we even get here?"

"Your crush on Jordy Shaw and my enthusiasm for you picking a worthwhile object of your affections for once."

"I admired the man's ass, I didn't elope with him." No matter how many fantasies Rowan's overactive and slutty imagination had already created about that peach and all the other lovely muscles it was configured with, he wasn't delusional. Even if a traitorous little voice in the back of his mind pointed out that Jordy hadn't rejected his flirting.

"That doesn't mean you can't ask him out on a date."

Rowan shook his head. "I have a strong policy against sleeping with straight boys and married men." He might have terrible taste in men, but he had *some* self-respect.

Gem chuckled. "Oh, honey. Two strikes. He's single *and* bisexual."

That traitorous little voice made a friend and high-fived him. Rowan told them both to shut up. "Just because he likes a manly physique doesn't mean he'll want mine."

"True."

"And there is a world of difference between ogling and dating. Just because he's a pretty package doesn't mean I want to take it home and unwrap it."

Gem snorted and bit into the lime that came with her G and T. Rowan couldn't remember the last time he'd seen her eat something that wasn't a cocktail garnish. "I think we've established that's a lie."

Damn her. She knew him too well. "True." He thought of Jordy's perfect form, huge thighs, and yes, perfect ass again, and sighed. "It's not to be, Gem. What am I going to do, ask him out the next time he brings his daughter to the library? I'd rather not get fired for sexual harassment, thanks."

But looking was free, he reminded himself, his spirits lifting. If nothing else, the scenery this summer should be excellent.

JORDY TIGHTENED the knot on his tie, picked up his jacket, and checked himself in the mirror. He wasn't a vain man, but he didn't clean up too badly, especially in his tailored black tux. At times like this, he was glad one of the veterans years ago had convinced him it would be a worthwhile investment. A comfortable suit made all the difference during stuffy black-tie events. Well—okay, a handful of suits, each tailored to fit him at different points in the hockey season.

Satisfied, he left his bedroom and headed for the kitchen to say good night to his baby.

As expected, Kaira sat at the counter, talking a mile a minute to Janice, who was cooking dinner at the stove.

"—and then Jake said I couldn't do it, but he was totally wrong, because I did!"

"Of course you did," Janice agreed with a nod that said she hadn't doubted Kaira for a moment.

Kaira beamed and continued her story. Not for the first time, and certainly not for the last, Jordy thanked whatever trick of fate had brought Janice into their lives. Her arrival wasn't a miracle—Jordy had advertised for a nanny and she had applied—but she was a perfect fit in their household and was the only reason Jordy could be a "single" parent.

"Are you off, then?" Janice asked when she caught sight of him.

"Yes." He stepped forward to hug Kaira and kiss her silky hair. "Love you, peanut. Have fun with Janice tonight, and I'll see you tomorrow."

"We're going to eat popcorn and watch movies," Kaira chirped.

"Well, that does sound like fun."

"Doesn't it? Way more fun than a stuffy party that you have to dress up for."

Jordy chuckled. "Definitely." He gave Kaira one last kiss, and she wrapped her arms tight around his waist.

"Bye, Daddy. I love you. Try to have fun!"

"Thanks, peanut. I will."

Famous last words, he thought at the venue later as he adjusted his cuffs and looked at himself in the bathroom mirror. He looked significantly less pressed than he had at home.

He had arrived almost an hour ago, and he couldn't say he was enjoying himself. The person on the door made a fuss about Jordy's missing plus-one in a bubbling, overeager way. Then, in the main room, Jordy hoped to find a glass of water to ease his parched throat, but every time he spotted a waiter or tried to move toward the bar, someone else popped up in his space, ready to chat about the Shield's latest and most disappointing season—which was how some people categorized any season that didn't end in a Cup win, no matter that a Cupless end was the fate of over thirty teams every year.

Jordy had finally gotten his hands on some water, but the bartender turned out to be another armchair coach with the solution to all the Shield's problems.

By the time he spotted the sign for the restroom, he was desperate for a break.

Dinner wasn't for another hour. He had at least another three ahead of him before he could duck out gracefully.

Which was fine. Jordy was a big boy, and he could handle it. He took a deep breath and left the restroom… only to do an about-face when he recognized the woman walking into the ladies' room.

Fuck. Of course Alana was here.

Jordy didn't like to think himself a coward, but he had no intention of exchanging a single word with her. He took three long strides away from the restrooms to a small curtained-off alcove and stepped into it. He wasn't *hiding*. He was just taking a little time-out to get his bearings.

Except he didn't look *into* the alcove beforehand, and he stepped on someone's foot. "Ow," said a familiar voice. "What the fuck."

Jordy blinked as the man from the library—Rowan—scowled at him from a few inches away. So close together, it was hard not to notice that Rowan might actually be taller than him.

"Oh, it's you."

What was that supposed to mean? Flustered, Jordy opened his mouth and said, "What are you doing here?"

"Here as in the party?" Rowan gave a winsome smile, as if Jordy had not just accidentally caught him hiding in what amounted to a closet. "I was invited." Rowan paused, placed a finger to his lip, and amended, "Ordered at stiletto-point? Coerced? I'm here at the behest of Her Majesty Gemma Bancroft, ostensibly to entertain her every whim because the rest of the table is insufferable—"

That sure was a lot of five-dollar words.

"—just because I can't afford a thousand-dollar-a-plate dinner—"

"I meant here in this…" Jordy gestured around them. "… alcove."

"Hiding." Rowan deflated, then immediately puffed up again, a glint in his eye. "Wait—what are *you* doing here? At this dinner and also in this alcove?"

"I was invited."

Rowan tilted his head. "Because…?"

Jordy hunched his shoulders. This was going to sound conceited. "The organizers asked people from the Shield to come to sell more tickets."

To his surprise, Rowan didn't roll his eyes. "Oh. Yeah, I can see how that would be a selling point if you're going to spend this kind of money on dinner." He peeked out from behind the curtain. Then he swore and plastered himself against the wall again. "So. Why are you hiding?"

You first, Jordy wanted to say. But something about Rowan's endless talking disarmed him. Maybe he shouldn't give the man too many excuses to talk about himself. "There's a woman…."

"Does she bite?" Rowan asked. "I mean." He waved a hand in Jordy's direction. "You look like you could take her."

As if Jordy was going to get into a physical altercation with anyone off the ice. He'd be thrown in jail immediately, and he'd deserve it. "She's...." This was so hard to explain without using the word *stalker*, which felt like overkill. *Puck bunny* was pretty misogynistic. Unfortunately the alternatives, again, made him sound self-important. "Obsessed with me."

Rowan took it in stride, one corner of his mouth quirking up as he flicked his gaze up and down Jordy's body. "Ah. Well, at least she's got some taste. No restraining order?"

Jordy shook his head. "It's not dangerous or invasive or anything. Her parents have money, and she shows up to every event...." As well as some of the open practices and training-camp scrimmages. It made him uncomfortable, but she hadn't crossed any lines. If she started showing up at Kaira's school plays or something, he'd reconsider. "It's just awkward." And this conversation had become far too focused on him. "Your turn. Why are you hiding?"

Sagging against the wall, Rowan tilted his head as though to peer out from behind the curtain thing. "Same reason. Well, okay, not exactly. Do you know the fourth-richest man in Toronto? He keeps telling me his name and I keep forgetting it on purpose. Anyway, he's very talkative. *Very.* And that's coming from me, so that's saying something. He loves a captive audience."

He didn't remember the man's name but knew he was the fourth-richest man in Toronto? For a moment Jordy was perplexed, and then he remembered Rowan was here on orders from Gem. "And you're his favorite?"

If possible, Rowan slumped further. "I don't know if he's looking for a sugar baby or if I just remind him of his favorite grandchild, and I don't want to know. I am *actively avoiding* knowing."

That sounded like the best course of action. Privately Jordy was a little perturbed at Gem. Knowing her, she'd brought Rowan along to be sacrificed to the man in the name of charity. Then again, she'd done the same thing to Jordy, and he didn't *really* mind. Except for Alana being present, of course. "What if it's both?"

Rowan yelped and then covered his mouth, as though afraid he might give away their spot. "That's horrible. Gods, *why?*"

To make you laugh. It had worked too; the mirth in Rowan's eyes danced in the dim light in their cubbyhole. Sanna, his ex, would have called him *boyishly handsome*, with that slightly too-long hair that flopped over his forehead. Jordy would've bet he was older than he looked, but he couldn't say how much. "Sorry."

"Eh." Rowan waved this off. "Nothing I haven't thought before, even if I somehow had the restraint not to say so out loud." But now he was looking speculatively at Jordy. "You know, we might be able to help each other out here."

Jordy could guess where this was going. "I technically have two tickets." Because he was a softie, and knowing there were kids in the city with so much less than Kaira, and so few people in their corner, made him hate the world a little bit. "So there's an extra seat at my table. No Gem, though."

Rowan grinned. "Under the circumstances, I think she'll forgive me if I abandon her to play pretend boyfriend with you all night." He paused. "Actually, she'll probably send me a bottle of champagne. She's made her opinions on my previous actual boyfriends *very* clear."

"Subtlety isn't really her strong suit."

"Yes, that's why we get along." Rowan linked his arm through Jordy's. "So, all right, are we stepping out of this alcove with our outfits disheveled like we can't keep our hands off each other, or am I going to have to pretend subtlety as well?"

"If it won't kill you," Jordy said. "I prefer not to make a scene."

With a put-upon sigh, Rowan twitched the curtain to one side and peered out. "If you insist. Looks like the coast is clear."

"Then let's go have dinner."

Rowan led him by the hand out of the alcove. "Let's have *drinks*," he corrected. "Then dinner. And we'll make sure everyone sees we're so besotted with each other that we couldn't possibly notice them."

Bemused, Jordy allowed himself to be pulled along for the ride. "Have you done this before?"

Rowan tossed a look back at him over his shoulder. "Why? Do I seem like some kind of fake-date slut?" His eyes were dancing again. "My parents threw a lot of intolerable parties growing up."

They bellied up to the bar. "Intolerable?"

"Over-the-top. Very boring. Self-important." This time Rowan's grin was a little strained. "One learns to make the best of the situation. Sometimes that means having a little fun at Mummy and Daddy's expense. Literally and figuratively. What's your drink of choice? Since you're being a public figure, I'm assuming no hard liquor."

He just skipped from one subject to another like a fruit fly. "Safe bet," Jordy murmured.

"So, wine? Beer? Coke? The blood of your enemies?"

A smile tugged at the corner of Jordy's mouth. Something told him Rowan was far more likely to be the blood-of-his-enemies type than Jordy. "Beer."

"Great. Light, medium, dark? Any allergies?"

"Medium, and no," Jordy answered. Why was Rowan asking so many questions? Surely he knew Jordy could order his own drink?

"Lovely." Rowan fluttered his lashes at the bartender—thankfully a different one from before. She didn't seem impressed, but she did smile.

"What can I get you?"

"A couple of beers, please," Rowan said with an easy smile. He unlinked their hands and placed a finger on one of the fancy menu cards in front of him. "Amber for this one, and the light IPA for me." He leaned forward conspiratorially. "I prefer blonds."

Oh, so that was the game. Jordy smiled ruefully in spite of himself and shook his head.

The bartender laughed. "I see that. Coming right up."

"You are enjoying this," Jordy observed.

"Oh, *immensely.*" The bartender slid their beers across the bar top, and Rowan thanked her and passed Jordy his with a little bow. "Here you are, darling."

Jordy wasn't used to being doted upon. It was weird, but Rowan's enthusiasm made it easy to go along with. "Thanks." He shoved some money in the tip jar as they swept away from the bar.

"Oooh," Rowan crooned, leaning into his space. "Handsome *and* generous."

The kicker of it was that the ruse was clearly working. Jordy could see people noticing him, even looking in his direction and turning to whisper to their companions, but people kept their distance. Rowan and his feigned affection provided a perfect buffer.

"Well, with you occupied, she might be the target of the fourth-richest man in Toronto. She's earned it."

Rowan laughed and found a table for their drinks. "And he's clever and thoughtful too. I'm a lucky man."

Shaking his head, Jordy set his drink down. "Are you always like this?"

Rowan blinked at him, the picture of innocence. "Like what?"

Loud. Friendly. Flirty. Jordy gestured, hoping he didn't come across as critical. "You're very… excited. All the time. Doesn't it get tiring?"

"Does a fish tire of swimming?" The words came out teasing, but the expression on Rowan's face, the slight tension at the corners of his eyes, the crease in his forehead, told Jordy he was taking the question seriously. "I'm not, actually. Always like this, I mean. But I wouldn't let on about that to a fake boyfriend. Not when I'm here to be charming."

"Of course not," Jordy said dryly. Over Rowan's shoulder, he spotted Alana heading in their direction. He'd have to take a page from Rowan's book and try something a little less subtle. "Are you a fake boyfriend who dances?"

Rowan followed his line of sight and inclined his head in understanding. "My dear, I do whatever is required of me." He offered his hand. "Shall we?"

PLAYING PRETEND lovers with Jordy was not exactly hard, even if parts of Rowan didn't get that memo while they were pressed against each other on the dance floor. Mercifully, Jordy either didn't notice or simply had too much tact to comment. Probably the latter. After dinner, a group of intrepid fans zeroed in on him with gushing excitement, flattering him and pushing into his personal space. Jordy smiled and gave diplomatic answers, but the experience was a far cry from the ease with which he interacted with Rowan.

He was uncomfortable with the adoration, Rowan realized. Shameful. A man like that ought to be adored on the regular.

Then again, perhaps he'd misjudged this group of fans.

"Just gotta be more aggressive on the forecheck, right, Shaw? Then maybe the Shield can take home our Cup again," one of the fans said with a chuckle. Rowan might not know hockey, but he could still recognize a reductive statement from a middle-aged white guy who enjoyed believing he had answers to all the world's problems.

Rowan made an executive decision. "Babe, look who it is," he said with a gesture of his head across the room. He was sure they could find someone to talk to over in that general direction. He turned to the fans. "I'm so sorry to interrupt, but we really should go say hello. It was wonderful to meet you. I hope we get another opportunity to talk again soon."

Jordy put on a convincing sad face and made his excuses. After shaking their hands, he retook Rowan's and let himself be pulled away. "Who are we going to see?"

"Oh, someone, anyone," Rowan said vaguely. "I'm sure we can find a person willing to talk to us."

Jordy chuckled. "Thanks for that. I don't mind fans, but...."

"Yeah, no, that wasn't a fan. That was a know-it-all." Rowan sipped his beer and drank in the sight of Jordy biting back laughter. He really was ridiculously attractive, and Rowan enjoyed the look of mischief sparkling in his eyes.

"Takes one to know one?" he ribbed.

Rowan gasped theatrically. "Now that's just rude. Suggesting that I would pretend to know anything about ice hockey."

Jordy gave him an affronted look. "It's just hockey."

"You see? I don't even know what it's *called*—"

"Rowan. Jordy." The smooth, amused voice washed over him like a bucket of cold water. Gem, of course. She'd probably been waiting to pounce since the first course, and now she had her chance. When Rowan turned around, there she was in all her finery, sipping from a martini glass that seemed impervious to lipstick smudges from that smug mouth. "I see you've gotten better acquainted. Did you decide to take my advice after all?"

Abort! Rowan's brain tried to shout through his skull. If Gem ruined his evening of fun by alerting Jordy to the fact that Rowan was every bit as big a fan of his arse as his stalker was, he would die of mortification and come back as the ghost of Gem's sex life.

Before Rowan could find a smooth answer or Gem could dig him into a deeper hole of embarrassment, Jordy arched an eyebrow and said, "Yes, if your advice was to proposition a near stranger to be his fake boyfriend for the evening."

The silence hung in the air for a moment as Gem took that in. Then she burst into laughter. "Tell me he didn't." She shot Rowan an incredulous look. "Only you."

Jordy shrugged. "To be fair, it was more of a mutual thing."

"Yes," Rowan said, finding his voice again. "Actually, I'm pretty sure you were the one to suggest it first, Mr. I Have Two Tickets. Also, you have to admit that it's worked spectacularly."

Jordy tipped his head in agreement, and Gem asked, "Oh?"

"Well, it's not like we wanted to be each other's fake date for no reason."

"Of course not. That would be weird," Gem agreed dryly.

"Exactly. The thing is, we were both trying to avoid someone?"

Gem narrowed her eyes. "Are you telling me that you haven't made nice with the very rich man who is likely to double his donation tonight after hearing you talk about children in need and good public works that help improve their lives?"

Rowan groaned. This was why he always ended up talking to the man and why he let Gem talk him into these things. Because she wasn't wrong. If Rowan could get a few thousand dollars more for a good cause by suffering through a couple of hours of terrible small talk... well, shouldn't he?

"You are an evil harpy and I hate you," he sighed.

Gem patted his cheek consolingly. "I forgive you."

That was way too easy. Rowan narrowed his eyes.

"Good evening, Mr. Cornwell," she said over his shoulder. "How are you?"

Stomach dropping, Rowan turned to see the fourth-richest man in the city standing behind him.

"Oh, I'm doing just fine," he said genially to Gem. "But it sounds like Mr. Chadha isn't doing as well. What has he done to need forgiveness?" He was smiling, so Rowan doubted he'd heard any more of the conversation.

"Neglecting to tell me he'd arranged for another date this evening, leaving me without a companion for dinner," she said with a wide-eyed sincerity that fooled no one.

"Well, it was a bit of a last-minute decision," Rowan pointed out.

Gem sighed dramatically, then shifted into hostess mode. "Louis Cornwell, have you had the pleasure of meeting Jordy Shaw? He plays for the Shield."

Jordy held out a hand to shake and Louis, whose name Rowan would forget before this destined-to-be-interminable conversation ended, took it. Either he wasn't jealous of Jordy's date or he was too wise to try to use the shake as a power move against a pro athlete, because it looked normal enough.

"I don't believe I've had the pleasure, but I think you're a favorite of my granddaughters. Defense, right?"

"Yes, sir."

"You must get dragged to these sorts of things often."

Jordy shrugged. "I wouldn't say dragged is the right word. If I can help kids just by being here, I'm happy to do it." Then, in a move that earned him all the fake boyfriend brownie points, he turned his gaze to Rowan and added, "Besides, how could I say no?"

"How indeed?" Louis said. There seemed to be a smile hovering at the edges of his mouth and eyes. Maybe Rowan just reminded him of a grandson after all.

Gem excused herself to greet more people, and Louis turned to Rowan, his rich-old-man charm dialed up to eleven.

"Indulge an old man and tell me how you two met. I feel there must be a story in there."

It was a good one too—too bad they couldn't tell Louis.

Rowan's thoughts whirled as he wondered what story to spin.

"We met when I took my daughter to the library." Jordy shrugged like that was the end of it.

Yeah, no. That would not do. Jordy might not have a sense of drama and flair, but Rowan was much too gay to let that stand.

"I was hopelessly charmed by their adorable father-daughter act. Not to mention Jordy's many fine attributes." Rowan gave Jordy an over-the-top leer. It was always best to keep a lie close to the truth.

"Of course," Louis agreed, obviously amused.

"And our story might have continued as a lot of pining and sighing and longing looks—at least on my part—if not for Jordy's quick reflexes." Jordy was watching Rowan with raised eyebrows, clearly wondering where this was going.

"You probably haven't observed this about me yet," Rowan said to Louis, "but I have my clumsy moments. Weak ankles, you know. So one day at work, I trip and stumble right into a bookshelf." He mimed stumbling and flailing, gaining the chuckles from Jordy and Louis he'd been aiming for. Good. It wasn't nearly so funny when it happened to him two years before. "Now library shelves *should* be stable, but they're getting ready to move this one and it's empty, so when I stumble, the whole shelf tips."

"Oh my," Louis said with genuine concern.

"There I am, crouched on the floor, my life flashing before my eyes, when this man swoops in from nowhere and catches the shelves. I look up and there he is, standing over me." Rowan reached out and stroked a hand on Jordy's shoulder as if getting rid of some lint. "Shoulders like Atlas. They come in handy."

"I bet they do," Louis agreed warmly with a smirk.

Maybe the sugar baby theory wasn't wrong.

"Well," Jordy said dryly. "Like you said, you are clumsy."

Rowan fluttered his lashes and leaned into Jordy, hamming it up. "My hero," he swooned.

Jordy did not look moved, which only seemed to convince Louis of their act.

"It seems like you are off the market, and you found a good one." He nodded his approval.

"Oh, I definitely did." Rowan smiled, aiming for a mix of besotted and lascivious.

Louis turned to Jordy and said sternly, as a father to their child's new boyfriend, "You be sure to treat him right."

"Of course." Jordy nodded. "Though if I didn't, I think Rowan would be the first one to tell me off."

Louis chuckled, and Rowan couldn't help but smile—Jordy had him pegged well enough. Even without having pegged him. Rowan might have awful taste in men, but once he accepted the evidence of their inadequacy, he didn't mince words letting them know about it.

"Too right. You best stay on his good side, then. Treat him *well*." He winked at Rowan, not in the least subtle, before taking his leave.

"How," Jordy began after a brief pause, "is it that that conversation didn't confirm or deny our theory of both?"

"I don't know," Rowan admitted. It was unsettling.

"Jordy," drawled a singsong voice from behind him—the Atlas shoulders blocking Rowan's view.

They turned to see an attractive blond in a red wiggle dress that highlighted her many assets, which she clearly knew, given the sway in her walk as she approached them.

"Alana." Jordy did not sound excited. The woman he had been avoiding, Rowan guessed.

"I told you I'd see you here," she cooed.

Rowan manfully resisted the urge to roll his eyes. "I don't believe we've met," he cut in.

She turned to him but didn't look happy about it. "No, I don't think we have."

"Alana Woodruff, this is Rowan Chadha."

"Lovely to meet you," Rowan said cheerfully, figuring that the best defense was a good offense. "I'm Jordy's date." He smiled. "It's been so lovely meeting some of his acquaintances."

Alana's smile turned brittle. "His date?"

"Yes." Rowan powered through and Jordy shifted his weight.

"Oh. I had heard the rumors," she said to Jordy, "but I hadn't thought…. Well, anyone handsome and charming enough to capture the likes of Sanna Miller surely doesn't have to stretch to broadening their dating pool."

For a split second, Rowan was left speechless by the biphobic nonsense she'd dared to say to Jordy's face. A glance at Jordy showed he was equally dumbfounded. "I'm sorry. I must have misunderstood you," Rowan said politely. "Since I'm sure you did not just imply that bisexuals were people who were desperate to get a date."

She turned back to Rowan and her face did… something. It seemed she wasn't sure how to respond to Rowan's service-industry cheer. "I think anyone could agree that a man who can land a gorgeous and sophisticated woman wouldn't want to look elsewhere."

Ugh, this woman was intolerable. Rowan had given politeness a fair shot, but now he saw that it was a lost cause. No wonder Jordy wanted to avoid her. Rowan resolved to annoy her as much as possible without letting on that she'd gotten to him. "Beauty is a short-lived tyranny," he quoted dismissively. "And even Gemma will tell you *sophisticated* is just a euphemism for *tedious*."

In his peripheral vision, he could see Jordy bringing his hand to his face, as though to cover a smile.

"Gemma?" Alana echoed, falling haplessly into Rowan's trap despite the simmering anger he could practically smell wafting off her.

"Sorry," he breezed, "I forget not everyone knows Gemma Bancroft—the woman in the Swarovski dress? The chair of the fundraising committee for the Children's Aid Society?" Rowan wasn't above name-dropping in the noble pursuit of taking this harridan down a peg. "She always could wear a dress well, of course, though woe betide the poor nanny who tried to wrestle her into one when we were knee-high to a grasshopper together."

Alana's tone went frosty. "Am I supposed to be cowed?"

You're already a *cow*, Rowan thought. "Frankly I don't expect a homophobe to have the sense to be, so no."

At his elbow, Jordy rumbled quietly, "Rowan."

Alana narrowed her eyes. "Do you have any idea who I am?"

Rowan gave her a sharp smile. "A self-important little peacock who doesn't notice when a gentleman has indicated his polite disinterest in her pursuit?"

This time he caught Jordy's laugh, muffled and brief though it was. "Rowan, come on." He moved his hand from Rowan's and wrapped an arm around his waist instead. "I think I see someone with cake."

Belatedly, Rowan remembered Jordy wouldn't enjoy drawing undue attention, no matter how much Rowan would enjoy publicly eviscerating this woman. "I'm sure it's got nothing on yours," he said, allowing himself to be turned away. He wouldn't grope Jordy's arse in public without his permission, but he did make a show of looking at it appreciatively where Alana could see him. "But I do have a sweet tooth."

Jordy made it another two steps before he glanced over, his expression wry. "I should probably be grateful you didn't go for her throat right away."

It was like he knew Rowan already. "Sometimes it's nice to gut them subtly instead," Rowan offered. "For variety's sake."

Jordy snorted. "You think that was subtle? I can't believe Gem invites you out in public."

"Oi! I can be charming. To the right clientele, anyway." That made Rowan sound like a prostitute, but well, both of them were essentially selling themselves for charity this evening. It was just that Rowan only had one particular intended diner and Jordy was sort of a buffet.

"I don't doubt it."

Grinning, Rowan wrapped his arm around Jordy's ridiculous bicep. It did indeed appear that the time had come for the venue to serve dessert. That meant things were winding down. And the evening had gone surprisingly well. Maybe he ought to push his luck just a little.

He eyed one of the trays as a server passed by. "So, remember when I said I have a sweet tooth?"

"Thirty seconds ago?"

Rowan stuck his tongue out at him. Mature? No. Called-for? Maybe. A convenient distraction from the way the thought of asking Jordy out for a post-fake-date real date made his heart race? Absolutely. "I wasn't lying, but I don't much fancy coconut flakes. Terrible, chewy texture. Like eating semisweet soggy cardboard. However, since we've fulfilled our obligation to the betterment of child welfare... I do know a café down the street that's open late, and they have an excellent cupcake selection. We could make our excuses." Damn, he should've stopped walking and watched Jordy's face while he asked. Then he'd have some idea of his reaction. "Before I get you into trouble with any other superfans."

They stopped walking, and Rowan made himself look into Jordy's eyes—his very pretty blue eyes, which were currently crinkled in the corners with amusement. "I could've handled Alana."

Was he going to answer the question, or no? "Yes," Rowan said, trying to be patient, "but I'm not a public figure, so I can be rude to people without repercussions. Do you want to go grab coffee and cupcakes? Preferably before Gem can sic someone else on us?"

"Aren't we a bit overdressed?"

"In this part of town?" Rowan scoffed.

Jordy huffed in amusement. "I take your point. Did you bring a coat?"

"No. Lord, I know the look is unparalleled, but I'm already roasting to death in the jacket. I'd have conveniently left it on the subway if I didn't know Gem would fillet me alive." The jacket had belonged to her unlamented dead ex-husband, whom she wasn't sentimental about, but she did appreciate fashion.

"Then I think we can sneak out." He glanced to the side, and Rowan followed his gaze across the room to where Gem was holding court near her dinner table. "If we hurry."

If this went anywhere, Rowan would owe Gem a *really* expensive bottle of wine. "In that case, what are we waiting for?"

Under no circumstances would Rowan call the night *pleasant*. It was hot and sticky, and the breeze did little to make the air less oppressive. But he had a very large handsome companion who made sweating his bollocks off in a suit seem like a small price to pay.

Besides, the café really wasn't that far, and they had the air-conditioning cranked.

At this time of night there were only a handful of cupcakes left. Rowan looked forlornly at the case with its pathetic offerings and made sad eyes at the teenager behind the counter, who was looking back and forth between him and Jordy with wide eyes.

Out of the frying pan, Rowan thought. "Hello," he said. "I don't suppose you've got any pineapple upside-down cupcakes left tonight?"

They did.

A few minutes later they were settled at a table with two cupcakes, a coffee for Jordy, and a tea for Rowan. Rowan had opted for decaf—he didn't need to vibrate out of his chair while doing his best to woo the most beautiful man to ever agree to cupcakes with him.

Despite Rowan's needling, Jordy refused the pineapple cupcake and opted for lemon poppyseed. Rowan wanted to be horrified, but it was hard to stay mad at a guy who looked that blissed out sipping a cup of plain coffee with a dash of milk. He hadn't even tried the cake yet.

"I probably should have guessed you were a tea drinker," Jordy said.

Rowan smiled and leaned forward. "Don't tell anyone or they'll revoke my citizenship, but I prefer coffee in the mornings. But tea is preferable at night."

Jordy inclined his head in acknowledgment. "Something I've been wondering about. You know why I moved to Canada. What brought you here?"

Rowan sipped his tea and wondered how to answer. Did he want to give the pat answer or the honest one? "Well, to start with, I'm actually a citizen here too."

Jordy tilted his head. "International man of mystery?" he teased.

Flirt, Rowan thought. "I grew up in England, but Nan was Canadian and Mum was born here. At eighteen I filled out the paperwork and got my dual citizenship. It comes in handy."

"Yeah," Jordy agreed. "But why move here?"

"Honestly?" He pushed some crumbs around on his plate. "Because I knew my parents never would."

Jordy hummed softly but said nothing, clearly waiting for Rowan to continue.

Rowan couldn't believe he was telling Jordy this. The man was a virtual stranger. Rowan had barely told Taylor anything about his family.

"My parents—when I was growing up I would've said they had a pretty good marriage. They rarely fought, though that could be because they were too busy working to have time for it. But one of the many things they had in common was a general disinterest in children." Not typical for immigrants from Pakistan, though they were so determined in their climb up the social ladder that no one outside their families shamed them for it. If either of them had been religious, they might have put in an effort for appearances' sake, but no—the closest they got was capitalism.

Jordy winced. "Bad parents."

Rowan shrugged. "Not really? I mean, they weren't exactly *good* parents, but I was provided for and well looked after. They made sure there was always someone around to have me fed and watered and tucked into bed. They were just sort of… not there all that much."

"I'm sorry. That sounds lonely."

It was. It was also one hell of a depressing conversation for a potential first date.

"Anyway," Rowan continued in a more upbeat tone, trying to shift the mood, "the cracks started showing when I went to uni and didn't want to study medicine *or* law. And then Mum took a case against a plastic surgeon Dad worked with, and Dad thought she shouldn't, and I wouldn't take sides." *And now neither of them talks to me or each other.* But no, that was too far. Rowan couldn't say that. "Nan took me to Toronto a few times as a kid, so after I finished my bachelor's, I hopped on a plane and headed west to do my MLS." He smiled and sipped his tea.

"Sounds like you're happy to be living here."

"Yes." Rowan thought about the home he was building here. He'd managed to make ends meet working odd jobs and using the money left to him by those same grandparents. He had never asked his parents for money, and he hoped he never would. "My parents sent me to boarding schools, mostly, so I never had that sense of belonging somewhere. I've been here for just over three years, and I want to stay here, build a home, put down roots, have some sort of permanence, you know?"

Jordy nodded, his expression thoughtful.

And Rowan was suddenly very aware of how much he'd been doing all the talking. And it was a kind of depressing topic. "I can stop rambling about my poor-little-rich-boy childhood," he said with a self-deprecating smile.

"Everyone has their own story." He nudged his plate, avoiding Rowan's eyes. "I got married before I could drink—in the US. We were twenty, together since forever. Childhood sweethearts, first love. Classic Americana, you know?" He looked up again and gave Rowan his own self-deprecating smile.

"I'm guessing this doesn't have a happily ever after ending," Rowan said gently.

Jordy shook his head and cleared his throat. "Things... fizzled out. Five years later and Sanna and I are just good friends, trying to figure out who we even are as people. She's, uh, she's a model. Sanna Miller?"

Rowan blinked. He might not know much about fashion or modeling, but even he'd heard of Sanna Miller. The harpy's earlier comment clicked. "Wow."

Jordy snorted. "That's what most men say." His tone implied he was surprised by *Rowan* following the trend.

"Look, just because I'm historically gay doesn't mean that I don't have eyes."

"Historically gay?"

Rowan waved a hand. "I'm not saying I could *never* be attracted to a woman, just that it hasn't happened yet. Ergo, historically gay." Jordy's lips twitched and Rowan patted himself on the back. "So, you and Sanna split?"

"Yeah. Sanna had to put her life on hold to be with me, and moving wherever hockey took me could make it tough to find work. She needed to do her own thing." Jordy cleared his throat. "Besides, we'd realized a pretty big irreconcilable difference. Sanna never wanted to be a mom. When Emma got pregnant and I dropped everything... that was sort of the final nail in the coffin."

"Ah." Rowan wasn't sure what to say. He'd assumed Jordy's ex and Kaira's mom must be the same person, but that sounded like Kaira's mom was someone else entirely. Could he ask? He settled for something safer. "Can't be easy, doing the single parent thing." Jordy had clearly opened up to even the score, share some of his own depressing background so Rowan felt less alone, but he looked done with the conversation.

"Not always. I'm lucky, though. Kaira has an amazing nanny, and I have money to help make things easier. But long road trips are hard."

"Well, you're doing something right," Rowan said, "because Kaira adores you. And she's got the confidence of a child who's never been let down, who knows she's safe and secure and that her opinion is valued."

Jordy gave a wry smile. "You mean she talks a lot."

Rowan laughed. "Hey, that's a good thing. Kids who talk a lot usually do so because they know they can. She knows you'll listen." Rowan would know. His own upbringing had been different enough from that. Somehow he'd gathered the fortitude to talk all the time anyway, but that was because he was the human equivalent of a hardy weed.

"I'm not a saint." Jordy poked his fork into his cupcake and then leaned forward and said in a confessional whisper, "Sometimes when she goes on about armadillos I tune it out."

God, he was adorable. "Well, nobody's *perfect*." Rowan shoved a bite of cupcake in his mouth—no fork for him; cupcakes were firmly in the finger-food category—and wiped a smear of icing from his lip with his thumb. But the sentiment reminded him. "Can I ask you a personal question?"

Jordy took an exploratory bite of his poppyseed cupcake, and his eyes went wide in surprise. When he'd swallowed it, he said, "You're only asking me now? Why am I suddenly worried?"

"It just seemed polite to ask." Especially since he wanted to dig further into Jordy's romantic history.

"It's fine. Go ahead." He paused. "Though I might not answer."

"That's fair." Rowan stirred his tea while he gathered his courage. The spoon clanked against the side of his mug; his mother would be appalled. "So, professional athlete, good dad, handsome…. You're apparently a bit of a catch. I would've thought…." Surely it wouldn't be difficult for Jordy to find a partner if he wanted one, yet Rowan had the firm impression that Jordy's romantic life had been stagnant for years. "There's been no one since Sanna?"

Oh Lord, he hadn't meant to imply the man had been *celibate*—

"No one serious," Jordy said, as if Rowan hadn't just made a complete arse of himself. Rowan thought that was a pretty diplomatic and G-rated way of saying *I hooked up a couple times*. Jordy was all class.

And then Jordy dropped the truth on the conversation like a housecat delivering a decapitated mouse. "I don't date. With Kaira…. Like you said, I have a lot on my plate with my job and being a good dad. I need to put time with her first whenever I can."

Oh bollocks, Rowan had misread this whole thing. His only solace was that Jordy delivered this so matter-of-factly that he obviously hadn't realized *Rowan* thought it was a date. "Of course, that makes sense." He shook his head, hoping he hadn't telegraphed his disappointment. "I really do think that might make you a saint, though. Sorry. Saint Jordy, patron of single dads."

While he'd been fumbling through what to say, Jordy had finished his cupcake. "Mmm. I'm going to get extra points when I bring Kaira here, so I should be thanking you. Even if pineapple is an evil fruit."

"You picked *lemon*," Rowan pointed out, affronted. "You can't even *eat* a lemon without adding its weight in sugar and pastry, and you're slandering *pineapple*?"

"Anything with that many defenses on the outside isn't meant to be eaten."

Rowan narrowed his eyes. Was Jordy having him on? He couldn't tell, but he enjoyed the game. "Aren't you from Minnesota? Don't your people eat fermented shark or something? Sharks have plenty of natural defenses."

Jordy frowned. "That's Iceland."

Whoops. "Ah, you're right, I got it mixed up with the fish one." What was it called again? "Lutefisk?"

"It's just cod," Jordy said. "Not an apex predator."

"So you've never had…." Rowan searched for the most ludicrous examples he could think of. "Bear meat?" He paused. "Moose?"

Jordy picked up his mug in both hands, an absolutely charming image considering how completely even one hand covered the cup. "Moose aren't predators."

"Oh, next you'll be telling me they have no natural defenses."

Jordy chuckled and sipped his coffee. "You have a point. No, I haven't eaten moose, or bear, or, I don't know, fugu." He leaned back a bit in his chair. "I have had reindeer, though. Don't tell Kaira. She believes in Santa Claus."

"My lips are sealed," Rowan promised, crossing a finger over his heart.

Jordy favored him with a small smile over the top of his mug. "Somehow I doubt that."

"At least it wasn't armadillo."

Jordy's warm laugh filled the little café and wrapped over Rowan's shoulders like a fuzzy blanket. It was the middle of summer, but somehow sitting here with him made Rowan think of a firelit room in the winter, the two of them cozied up against the cold.

It was a silly fantasy to indulge in now that he knew Jordy wasn't interested, but Rowan was nothing if not silly, so he let himself imagine it.

Then Jordy changed the subject and the fantasy drifted away. Rowan let it go and focused on retraining his brain to see Jordy as... an acquaintance, maybe. A partner in the crime of sneaking out of one of Gemma's parties. The father of one of Rowan's library charges.

"I should probably get going," Jordy finally said when their drinks had long since been consumed. "Kaira will be up very early to ask me about my night. I think the nanny sabotages me."

Rowan stacked their plates to put into the dish return bin. "Oh?"

"I've heard her. 'The sooner you go to sleep, the sooner your daddy will be home.'" He gave a rueful snort. "Which means she goes to bed early and then gets up even earlier."

Rowan couldn't fault the nanny's logic—or Kaira's enthusiasm to see her dad. "She really is a sweet kid."

"Yes. I'm lucky." He meant that, Rowan knew—it was obvious in the way the man talked about his daughter, prioritized her. Yet now, for the first time, Rowan thought he detected a little wistfulness in the man's eyes. Maybe he was thinking about Kaira's mother, whoever she might be, and his life's empty co-pilot seat. "Thank you for tonight. It was more fun and less painful than the last three parties I went to."

"Wow, remind me not to attend any parties thrown by hockey players."

Jordy laughed and gathered their mugs, and together they stood to put the dishes in the bins. "It was good running into you again. Kaira and I will see you at story time."

Rowan made himself smile and hoped it looked sincere, but Jordy's *see you later* sounded a whole lot like *goodbye*. "I look forward to it."

Very Important Hockey News
July 22, 09:34 a.m.
ShieldMaiden

OMG Shield Nation!

Everyone's favorite walking thirst trap and adorablest single DILF Jordy Shaw was at the Children's

Aid gala last night, looking as delish as always in his formalwear.

I was flipping through all the photos totally not like a stalker and Shaw is with the SAME GUY IN EVERY PICTURE!

"But ShieldMaiden," I hear you ask, "I have not seen these pictures; do you have receipts?"

Of course, fam.

Cropped shots heeeeeere.

As you can see, Shaw stuck with the same guy all night—drinks, dinner, mingling, DANCING (did we know he danced????).

Sadly, many of the shots are background photobombs, but Mystery Man is clearly as droolworthy as Shaw. Look at those mile-long legs.

A gala date feels like a #milestone. Here's hoping we get to see lots more of this new boo!

Tags: ShieldNation, Jordy the DILF Shaw, Shield Fan Service, Rainbow NHL

Comments:

MrsShaw7:

Don't mind me. I'm just crying that my husband has a totally gorgeous boyfriend that makes him smile Like That.

Pregame

JORDY GRUNTED as he did his final push-up of the morning and, after a brief consideration of the merits of burpees, decided to transition into his cool-down instead. He wasn't hungover, as he'd stuck to his beer-and-wine-only limit. Still, he had gotten in much later than he anticipated—he'd lost track of time at the café thanks to Rowan's engaging conversation, and it had been pushing midnight by the time he got home—and he could hear Kaira stirring upstairs, so it seemed like a good morning to cut things short.

Sighing into the stretch, Jordy leaned toward his toes and thought about the night before. Dinner had actually been enjoyable. Rowan had made it almost fun—he had a true talent for talking with anyone and everyone. He'd bonded with one of the women at their table, and the two of them had chattered enough to carry the entire table through the three courses.

And then Rowan suggested they round out the evening with a proper dessert, and Jordy had surprised himself by saying yes. For the most part, Jordy spent his free time with Kaira, Sanna, and his teammates and their families. He didn't go for cupcakes with almost-strangers. It had been nice, though, to talk with Rowan, to make friends with someone outside the world of hockey.

Jordy headed for the kitchen and rustled up a protein shake. He was chugging it when Kaira shuffled into the kitchen. "Good morning, peanut."

"Hi, Daddy." Kaira walked into his legs and hugged his thigh. The first few minutes of her morning—when he could get them—were some of Jordy's favorites. She was always a cuddlebug before she woke up properly.

He scooped her up for a snuggle. She looped her arms around his neck and sighed, and for a few minutes they stood together enjoying the quiet.

When she started to pull away, Jordy hummed and asked, "Pancakes this morning?"

"Pancakes?" Kaira chirped.

"Pancakes."

Jordy put her down, and she skittered off to fetch her stepstool so they could cook together.

Several minutes later, Kaira happily made her way through a stack of pancakes loaded with fresh strawberries and whipped cream while Jordy indulged and ate his with raspberry jam and cream. He'd have extra protein with his lunch.

"Pancakes are the best," Kaira told her plate and shoved more into her mouth. She had whipped cream on her nose.

Cleanup and clothes were first up on the after-breakfast to-do list. Jordy was contemplating their moves for the day when his phone pinged with a message from Sully.

LOL Looks like you had fun last night. ;) It's all over the blogs. Tell me you got laid. It ended with a string of eggplant and peach emojis.

No one would ever accuse Sully of being classy. *What are you talking about?*

Twitter is all abuzz about your new pretty boy. He looks pretty cute on your arm. ;) Another text appeared. *Been a while since you took anyone out. You getting back in the game?*

Why is Twitter talking about Rowan?

Jordy's phone rang in response.

"Good morning, sweetheart," Sully bellowed. He was a man who enjoyed annoying people. He also liked fucking with guys who were "too steeped in toxic masculinity, man." Jordy didn't know if he was like this before Adrianna—they'd started dating before Sully got traded here—but Jordy would bet that she helped him build his team-needling vocabulary. She was a graduate in gender studies, after all.

Most days, Jordy didn't know how Sully had convinced someone that smart to fall in love with him.

"Good morning." Jordy refrained from one of his usual nicknames for Sully since Kaira still sat opposite him.

"Shall I take it from your curt tone that Mr. Twitter did not, in fact, put out last night? Does that mean he's not your new beau? Too bad. You could do with some lovin'."

Jordy scowled at the wall. Sully knew full well that he wouldn't be finding out about Jordy dating anyone from Twitter. He was playing dumb on purpose to avoid answering Jordy's question, just to annoy him.

"The charity posted some photos," Sully admitted since he couldn't bear an unfilled silence, "and hockey Twitter immediately had an orgasm over the pictures with you and Mr. Adorable. They're all wild with speculation, what with you never bringing dates to these sorts of things. Well, none that you don't play hockey with. Or that you didn't marry."

Jordy sighed. "Sully."

"Fine. I won't say anything about your pathetically dry dating spell since the birth of your adorable daughter."

That was rude. Jordy had dated… a little.

"All done!" Kaira announced as she pushed her plate away.

"Just a sec." Jordy pulled the phone away from his face and turned to his daughter. "Can you go clean up? You have cream on your nose, peanut."

"Okay!" Kaira skipped off to the bathroom. Jordy called after her to get dressed too, and she shouted back another okay.

Jordy put the phone back to his ear. "Back."

"Anyway, no one knows who he is yet, and it's driving them all nuts."

"He's a librarian."

Silence filled the line. "You're dating a librarian?"

"No," Jordy said exasperatedly. Except—did that sound like it was just sex, because… "Yes. No."

"Wow. That was very clear. I'm going to need more words there, bud."

"I met him when I picked up Kaira. Then I ran into him last night. Since both of us were without dates and trying to avoid awkward conversations…."

"Who were you trying to avoid?"

"Alana Woodruff."

Sully hooted. "Did you pretend to date a cute boy to avoid a socialite?"

"Maybe," Jordy admitted.

Sully laughed harder. "Babe!" he called, his mouth pulled away from the phone. "Babe, you gotta hear this."

Jordy sighed again. Great.

At least Adrianna provided a cooler head. She thought Jordy and Rowan's solution logical, if unorthodox.

"Unorthodox?" Sully cut in. "Babe, it's right out of a Hallmark movie. Jordy, please tell me you're going to keep fake dating until you combust from unresolved sexual tension and pining."

Jordy pinched the bridge of his nose. "I knew Adrianna letting you watch those movies would come back to bite us in the ass."

"I'm flattered that you think I have any sort of control over this lunatic," Adrianna said dryly.

"You should bring him to the team charity fund dinner next month. Please. I've been good. I deserve this."

"Good's debatable," Adrianna grumbled playfully.

"Not what you said this morning," Sully jibed back.

"Can you please not," Jordy begged. He had no desire to know anything about Sully's sex life. It was like knowing about a sibling.

"So," Adrianna cut in, "are you going to see him again? He sounds nice."

"I'm not sure *nice* is the right word. He told Alana her personality was ugly."

"My boy," Sully crowed, at the same time Adrianna said, "Well, now I have to meet him too."

"Besides, it's not like we're *actually* dating. Or that we want to." Rowan hadn't expressed any interest, and even thirty seconds in the man's company made it apparent that he was the sort to say exactly what he wanted. Possibly whether he intended to or not.

Adrianna made a noise. Sully chuckled. "I'm pretty sure that meant 'if the man has eyes and is into dudes, you're his type.'"

Jordy digested that. "Did you just imply that your wife thinks I'm hot?"

"Implied nothing," Sully dismissed. "You're hot and you know it, my wife knows it, the city of Toronto knows it."

"*Anyway*," Jordy said to get off that topic, "I'm pretty sure he's not interested, I'm not looking to date, and besides, he runs story time at the library. That would be awkward."

"Only if you disappoint him," Sully said. Jordy could hear the eyebrow waggle.

Fortunately, Jordy was saved when an elephant came running down the stairs. "My kid is dressed and clean now, which means it's time to say goodbye, Sully."

"Bye, Sully," Sully said, because he loved terrible dad jokes, even if he wouldn't be a dad for a few weeks yet.

"Bye, Jordy," Adrianna added. "Have fun with Kaira. And let us know if you do see Rowan again."

"You know I would," Jordy admitted. Adrianna was just as much of a sibling figure as Sully. "Bye."

He hung up and set his phone on the table, just in time to grab the ball of limbs and mismatched patterns climbing into his lap. He had to be quick; Kaira was bony and a little awkward, and she'd kneed him in the crotch more than once. "What are we going to do next, Daddy?"

"Excellent question. What would you like to do today?"

"Excellent question," Kaira parroted, her expression serious. As she contemplated, Janice wandered in and waved. Even though she had the day off while Kaira and Jordy hung out, she was still dressed and apparently going out today, or so Jordy surmised based on her immaculate wardrobe.

"Good morning." Janice poured herself a cup of coffee.

"Morning!" Kaira hopped out of Jordy's lap and rushed to Janice for a hug.

"How are you today?"

"Good! We made pancakes!"

Janice smiled and brushed a hand over Kaira's head. "Did you, now? Sounds like a great start to the day."

"It was."

"And what are you up to today?"

"I don't know," Kaira admitted with a frown. "I haven't decided yet."

"Well, what are the options?" Janice settled into a seat at the table.

Jordy watched in amusement as Janice and Kaira debated the day's schedule before Kaira settled on her plan—they would go to the science museum. Janice suggested that Kaira go pack a bag and fetch everything Jordy would need to style her hair for the day.

With the child out of the room, they both took a moment to enjoy their coffee in the quiet.

"Thanks for that."

"My pleasure," Janice said with such sincerity that Jordy didn't doubt it.

"Any plans for your day off?"

Janice rubbed a hand over her face and sighed. "I've got to call my mom." Her smile looked weary, which Jordy hadn't expected.

"Everything okay?"

"Yeah. She's been having a rough time of it lately. She still lives in her own home, and the upkeep isn't easy for her. My sister was helping out, but her husband got a two-year posting a year ago, and managing without Sarah has been harder than she thought." She sighed. "My daughter has been doing her best to step in, but she and her husband work full-time."

"I'm sorry," Jordy said. He could understand the pain of living so far from family. "You'll let me know if there is anything I can do to help."

"You're doing it, dear." She smiled. "I just needed a sympathetic ear to brace myself for the phone call."

"Well, if that changes...." He would do almost anything for Janice. "I'm serious. Kaira and I would be lost without you. You are probably the only reason either of us have made it through the past five years."

"That's probably true," Janice joked.

She had arrived like an angel from heaven when Kaira was a week old. She'd taken the screaming newborn from Jordy's sleep-deprived arms and shooed him off to bed. When he'd woken from his nap, he'd found Kaira asleep in her crib, a load of laundry in the washer and another in the dryer, the dishwasher running, and the garbage taken out. Jordy had nearly cried. He had hugged her and told her to never leave. Janice had laughed and asked which room was hers.

"Definitely true. I'm serious, Janice, anything."

"I know, dear. And I won't forget." She stood and patted his shoulder on her way to the coffee machine for a refill. When Kaira barreled back into the kitchen clutching a brush and hair ties, Janice wished them fun and waved goodbye.

"Right," Jordy said, focusing on the task at hand. Judging by the number of ties and clips, Kaira had serious hair plans. "What are we doing?"

"PLEASE TELL me this hellhole has a bottle opener," Gem said, holding up a bottle of pinot noir as she kicked off her shoes.

"Hey, my flat resembles that remark," Rowan said dryly. His place had a few perks, like location and not-horrifying rent, but reliable landlord was not among them. He'd been waiting for his dishwasher to get fixed for about six months now. "Also, what kind of heathen do you take me for? Of course I have a bottle opener—for corks *and* caps." He led the way into the kitchen and pulled the opener from the wine cupboard, passed it to her, and then grabbed two glasses.

"Of course. How could I have doubted you." She opened the bottle.

"You should be ashamed of yourself. So what's brought you to my humble abode with vino tonight?"

"Your accidental date with Jordy Shaw, of course." She followed him to the living room, and they settled on the couch.

"It wasn't a date," Rowan said and tried not to choke on his own bitterness about that.

Gem studied his face, then held up the bottle. "I'm guessing we're not letting this breathe first."

Rowan held the glasses out to her.

Once they both had full glasses and were curled up in opposite corners, Gem motioned for him to continue. "So what happened?"

"You mean aside from the fact that he's a total DILF with an edible ass and an adorable daughter and I want to climb him like a tree but he's not interested in me?"

Gem arched an eyebrow. "There's a lot of unpack there, but sure."

"You were wrong—he doesn't date men. Or women. Or anyone." Rowan pulled deeply from his glass. "As we were leaving the gala, I asked him out. I mean, I thought I asked him out. We went for hot drinks and dessert. He insisted on paying—which in hindsight probably has more to do with our income disparity—but I thought, 'This is going great.'"

"That does sound promising," Gem conceded.

"Then he tells me that he doesn't actually date anyone because who has the time between sporting and parenting."

Gem winced. "The man usually has more tact."

That called for more wine. "Oh, he does. He didn't look the least bit apologetic. He wasn't trying to give me a hint. So not only did I strike out, but I did so with a man who's so uninterested that he didn't even *notice* I made a pass."

"Wow. It sounds like the lack of regular sex has damaged his brain."

Rowan snickered into his cup. He'd defend Jordy, but, well, Rowan wasn't exactly known for his subtlety. "That must be it." Rowan would get over it. The lack of opportunity to sleep with Jordy wouldn't kill him, even if the lack of blood flow to his brain did knock off a few IQ points.

Gem refilled his glass. Rowan had hardly noticed himself emptying it. "My condolences. Just promise me this won't send you running into the arms of the next unwashed underachiever to cross your path."

Rowan pouted. "But how else will I recover my sense of self?"

"Yoga? Therapy?" Gem sipped her wine. "Pole-dancing lessons?"

"Oooh." That did sound like fun. Rowan would have to ask if Taylor wanted to come with, because Gem certainly wouldn't. And who knew—the instructor might be cute. "A pole-dancing teacher wouldn't count as an underachiever, surely?"

"I see you're not too broken up about the rejection."

"I'm crying on the inside," Rowan said with dignity.

"Well, at least you put on a good act for your friend Louis. His happiness on your behalf made him very generous."

"I'd send you my bill, but I think it's been paid, even if sadly no orgasms were involved."

"Hmm." She glanced around and arched one elegant eyebrow. "Perhaps you *should* bill me. Then you can vacate this roach motel."

"I do not have roaches," Rowan said indignantly. Abnormally large spiders, questionable water pressure, and windows that had to be jimmied open with a crowbar, certainly, but no roaches. The garden out back was really cute, though. "And I don't need your money." The trust his grandparents had set up for him had dwindled to a few months' emergency fund, but the library job *did* pay his rent, as long as he didn't expect lavish accommodations, and even let Rowan save a bit so he could buy something nicer one day.

Perhaps it was silly. If he picked a side and sucked up to one of his parents, they'd probably send him money for a down payment. But they'd also take that as a sign that the expense they'd put toward his education had been as wasted as they claimed it would be. Bollocks to that. Maybe Rowan hadn't become a tech-bro billionaire or a venture capitalist, but he had a respectable job that he liked and that let him put down roots in a place he loved.

Or at least it would *eventually* let him do that, if he ever managed to get a permanent position at the library.

"What about a loan, then?" Gem tapped her nails on her wineglass. "I know you're saving up to get your own place. I'll float you the down payment—"

"Gem—"

"—you pay the mortgage, and you can pay me back afterward."

For a moment Rowan was honestly tempted. That was a reasonable offer. It would get him out of his admittedly terrible apartment sooner rather than later.

But it negated half the point of the exercise, which was to prove to the ghost of his parents—okay, to himself—that he didn't need anyone's help. That he could be successful as a *librarian*.

God damn it.

He sighed. "I know you're worried about me, but I'm honestly fine. I might not be living the lifestyle Young Rowan was accustomed to, but there are plenty of people worse off than me, and they get by fine." For varying degrees of *fine*, some of which were, admittedly, not. "If I were that fussed about it, I'd look for somewhere with a roommate. Then I could afford to live aboveground for the same price."

"Yes, why *didn't* you do that? You could probably *save* money, even."

Rowan was too embarrassed to admit that he'd been so excited to leave the UK—and the reminder that even his parents didn't care for his company—that he'd leased the place sight unseen and had simply been too lazy to look for somewhere else to live every time his lease came up for renewal. At least the landlord hadn't raised the rent, which he understood was a rarity. "And have someone mad at me every time I had a boyfriend? A man needs some privacy, Gemma."

"God." Gem set down her wineglass and stretched out in the chair. Rowan might live in a shithole, technically, but he was great at buying quality furniture for cheap. Gem had offered him three times what he paid for that chair, but it was teal velvet and Rowan wasn't giving it up. "If I'd known a roommate was all it would take to keep you from dating anthropomorphized sock lint, I'd have offered to live with you myself. In my apartment, of course."

"At least I only sleep underground because I'm poor."

Gem burst out laughing. She didn't actually sleep in a coffin to avoid sunlight, but Rowan had made enough bloodsucking lawyer jokes that she made the connection anyway. "Fine, I concede this round. And because I'm such a gracious loser, and also I refuse to sit in this chair any longer if you won't let me buy it, I'm taking you out to dinner."

This was probably what she'd been angling for the whole time, but Rowan didn't mind. A man had to eat to keep his strength up. Especially if a man was going to keep drinking wine with Gem all evening. "I accept your terms." He let her pull him to his feet. "But nowhere I have to dress up." Partly because he needed to do laundry. The spin cycle on the washer made the thing rattle so much the landlord had asked him not to use it after nine, and Rowan kept forgetting.

The guy should really get a handyman in.

"Don't even tell me," Gem said, apparently having deduced his objection didn't actually have to do with the clothing. "It'll only depress me."

"Yeah, that's fair," Rowan allowed. "Now—Indian or Italian?"

They ended up sitting at a little café down the block, one Rowan had frequented enough times to be on a first-name flirtation basis with their server, Adrian. He ordered the chicken parm and another glass of red. Gem asked for the same but had her meal boxed up to go because she had a thing about eating in public. She avoided it at her charity events by making the rounds to various tables and ensuring everyone else was enjoying themselves.

Surprisingly, she did indulge in the fresh bread with butter—usually an add-on, but Adrian dropped it off at their table with a wink for Rowan. "On the house."

"You know how to treat a man," Rowan said with gratitude. He needed something to soak up the wine. "What?" he added when Gem gave him the hairy eyeball.

Gem plucked a slice of bread from the basket and slathered it in butter. "Nothing."

Nothing, Rowan's right nut. "Please. I hope you're a better liar than that in court."

She rolled her eyes. She'd pointed out more than once that she wasn't that kind of lawyer. "Getting back on the horse?"

"Horse?" Rowan craned his neck a bit to look after Adrian. "Do you know something I don't?"

"Very funny."

"Anyway," Rowan went on as he snagged his own piece of bread, "I've told you, I'm not going around pining after a man who doesn't date. Not after meeting him twice. No matter how pretty he is. Therefore, no falls from any horses to recover from. Which means I'm in the clear to flirt with Adrian."

One day he'd have to flip the tables on her and ask about why *she* didn't date, but he was having such a nice night. Watching his own intestines spill out onto the sidewalk would ruin it.

And it *was* a nice evening. There was a bit of a breeze, the wine was good, Gem regaled him with redacted tales of idiot clients and Rowan responded with the latest library gossip. If he flirted with Adrian just a little harder than usual to make a point, that was between him and the gods.

Except it must've been more than a little harder than usual, because Adrian dropped off a little something extra with Rowan's chicken parm. "I'm off in twenty," he said under his breath, leaving a slip of paper with a ten-digit number next to Rowan's napkin.

Miraculously, Gem kept her scoff nigh inaudible. It was like she projected it directly into Rowan's brain. But at least Adrian didn't notice.

Adrian might've been off in twenty, but the night was so nice that neither Rowan nor Gem hurried. They finished the wine—and all the bread and butter in the basket—and shot the breeze for another forty minutes before collecting Gem's to-go dinner and settling their tab.

"Walk me around the block," Gem demanded, sliding her arm through his. "Keep all the unsavories away. It's too nice to go inside just yet."

As if she was worried, and if she didn't have a Taser in her purse, Rowan would eat his teal velvet armchair, but he agreed anyway. He could use a little walk to sober up a bit. Red wine gave him a nasty hangover, which he always forgot until he'd drunk too much of it.

They were just making their final lap of the block, coming up on the alley next to the restaurant, when Rowan actually detected the first sign of those unsavories.

"Well," Gem said, in as close to a giggle as she ever got, "at least someone's getting laid tonight."

Rowan narrowed his eyes, suddenly suspicious. "Wait, was this walk a distraction to keep me from calling—"

They passed the mouth of the alley, and an errant streetlight illuminated two figures engaging in something that was certainly illegal in public, even in Toronto.

And then, clear as a bell, they heard on the breeze a distinctly sexual gasp—"*Oh my God, Adrian*—"

Both Gem and Rowan's footsteps faltered. As usual, Gem recovered first. "Looks like he didn't quite get off in twenty," she offered mildly.

Rowan threw his head back and groaned at the sky. "What is *wrong* with me?" he said. "Why am I such a douchebag magnet?"

"It's because your standards are subterranean," Gem offered. For the first time Rowan could remember, she actually stumbled a bit on the sidewalk in her heels. Maybe that was why she really wanted an escort. He caught her without trouble.

"God." Gem was depressingly right. "Okay. I've learned my lesson. I'm going on strike from men."

"I've heard that before. Right before, what was his name? Calen?"

"Owen," Rowan sighed. "No, wait—it was *after* Owen and before—"

"I think you've made my point for me," Gem said dryly.

Unfortunately Rowan suspected she was right. "That's why I mean it this time. I am officially closed for business. No thank you. The Rowan train is leaving the station. Do not pass go, do not collect $200, we don't want no scrubs—"

"I give it a week," Gem interrupted.

"Wretch," Rowan said cheerfully. "Bet."

They leaned on each other all the way back to his apartment.

THE BEST part about the off-season was not just getting to spend so much time with Kaira, but also getting to surprise her with fun trips and activities.

Jordy hadn't been lying about wanting to take Kaira to the cupcake shop, and she lit up when she saw the selection.

After much debate, she finally selected a chocolate cake with a ganache center and chocolate icing. Jordy picked out a vanilla cake with raspberry filling and maple icing and ordered a coffee to go with it.

Five minutes later, Jordy was watching indulgently as Kaira kicked her feet and moaned with delight over her treat.

Jordy sipped his coffee and slowly ate his cake. He had a feeling that he wouldn't get to finish it.

Her mouth was ringed with chocolate, and Jordy sneaked a picture and sent it to Adrianna.

"This is the best cupcake ever," Kaira said with her mouth half full. "We should buy one for Clement when we go to the zoo." Earlier in the week, Jordy had arranged a playdate with their neighbor's kid. His time off during the summer was an advantage for other parents as well.

"Hm, but they don't sell these cupcakes at the zoo," Jordy pointed out.

"Not at the zoo. Before the zoo. Or after. We'll come here after the zoo," Kaira suggested.

"We will, huh?"

"Yes. Because cupcakes are nice, and I wanna give Clement a nice thing. Because I love him. And we're going to have fun at the zoo because zoos are better with best friends. Daddy?"

"Hm?"

"You should bring a friend to the zoo too."

"I should?"

"Yeah. Because the zoo is always better with a friend, and you wouldn't want to be lonely at the zoo, Daddy."

"Of course not. What was I thinking?" The sarcasm was lost on Kaira.

"Wow, I guess you really couldn't wait," a voice said from the right.

Jordy and Kaira both turned to see Rowan a few feet away. "Mr. Rowan! Do you know about the best cupcakes ever too?"

"I do indeed," Rowan said with a grin. He took a step closer and leaned down as if to tell her a secret. "In fact, I was the one who told your daddy about this place. No one should keep cupcakes this good to themselves."

Kaira beamed, delighted. "Are you going to get a cupcake today, Mr. Rowan?"

"I already bought one," he said, waving his hand toward the counter.

"What kind?"

"I love their pineapple one," he said like it was another secret.

"Pineapple?" Kaira said with distrust, because she was Jordy's daughter.

"Yes. Pineapple is delicious."

Kaira wrinkled her nose. "Daddy says pineapple is the devil's fruit."

Rowan jerked back and flung both hands to his heart as if shot. "What? You wound me as you wound my favorite fruit! Daddy, how could you say such things?" He swooned into the extra chair at their table, and Kaira giggled with delight.

Jordy arched an eyebrow and said nothing. Rowan pouted and Kaira giggled harder.

"Rowan!" a server called, and they all turned to see a cup of tea and a cupcake placed on the counter.

"That's me," he said, waving, and Jordy thought for the first time Rowan looked unsure of his next move.

"Mr. Rowan? Can I try your pineapple cake?"

"Uh...."

"Kaira, not everyone likes to share their food. If Rowan doesn't want to share, then you have to accept that," Jordy said firmly. He turned to Rowan. "It's up to you. I don't mind her trying a small bite of pineapple if you don't mind sharing. But Kaira's okay with hearing no."

"Oh, I don't mind sharing." He looked a bit poleaxed, like he wasn't sure how he'd gotten here. When he returned with his food thirty seconds later, Jordy told him again that he really didn't have to share. Rowan waved him off. "It's fine."

He used his clean fork to slice off a semi-generous bite. Not too big, but definitely a piece with more cake than was required to taste-test pineapple.

He placed it on her plate, and Kaira popped it into her mouth. For a beat, she chewed and showed no reaction. Then her face morphed into a look of disgust and she stopped chewing. She looked down at her plate, which still had some chocolate cake, and then up at Jordy, clearly uncertain what to do next.

Holding back a chuckle, Jordy picked up a napkin and held it out for her to spit the cake into. Mouth clear, she grabbed her water and took several long pulls.

"Daddy, pineapple is devil fruit."

"Yes it is, peanut." He couldn't resist looking toward Rowan and giving him a smug smile.

Rowan shook his head sadly. "I feel sorry for you both. You're missing out. It's the fruit of the gods." He took a large bite from his cupcake, unrepentant, and Jordy rolled his eyes. "So, what are you two up to today?"

Jordy loved how his daughter took so much conversational pressure off him. For several minutes Kaira expounded on her plans for the day—getting more books form the library—and then detailed her expectations for their upcoming trip to the zoo.

"We're going to go see armadillos."

"Ah, of course. You can't go to the zoo and not see armadillos." Rowan nodded seriously.

"No, you can't."

"You know, I don't think I've ever been to a zoo that had armadillos, because I've never seen one up close and personal."

Kaira looked horrified. "What?"

"Nope. I've only ever seen them in pictures or on TV."

"But armadillos are the best!"

"I know," Rowan agreed sadly.

"You need to go see them. At the zoo. You should come to the zoo with us!"

"Oh, uh…." Rowan froze.

Jordy took pity on him. Also, he needed to remind someone of basic manners. "Kaira, you can't just order Mr. Rowan to come to the zoo with us. He might be busy or have to work. Remember, not everyone gets the summers off. Lots of adults still work every day, even in July."

Kaira pouted. "But… armadillos."

Jordy did not melt at the sight of those wide eyes or bottom lip. "If you want Rowan to come with us, then you can ask him. But remember, he might have to say no, and that's okay too."

She whirled to Rowan and said in one breath, "Will you come with us to the zoo tomorrow?"

"Um."

"Oh. Do you have to work?" She looked heartbroken at the thought.

"Well, no," Rowan said slowly. Jordy wished he could have told him that lying would have been acceptable.

Kaira brightened. "So you can come with us?"

"Well, I wouldn't want to intrude…." Kaira frowned at the new word. "It sounds like you and your daddy have a nice day planned, and I wouldn't want to get in the way."

"But Daddy doesn't have a friend coming with us. But if you came, then he would have a friend. And I would have a friend, and then everyone would have a friend at the zoo!"

It was hard to argue against such sincere and simple logic. Judging by Rowan's softening expression, he felt the same.

It looked like Jordy was bringing a friend to the zoo after all.

THE LAST thing Rowan expected in his mailbox was a letter from the library board. Now it lay on his kitchen table, taunting him.

"I don't have time for this," Rowan told it.

"For real, Rowan, I have to wrangle eleven six-year-olds in an hour. *I* do not have time for this," Taylor answered through his phone's speaker. "Just open the letter."

"I can't. Jordy is picking me up to *go to the zoo* in twenty minutes. What if it's bad? What if it ruins my mood for the rest of the day?"

There was an ominous pause. "Okay, first of all, can we rewind to the bit where you have a date with the DILF?"

"No," Rowan said reasonably, "because it is not a date. Jordy does not date. And I have sworn off men. I'm going to the zoo with him and Kaira and her friend because she made puppy eyes at me in a café after maligning pineapple upside-down cupcakes. Let's focus on my financial and professional future, please."

Taylor made a derisive noise. "We can do that later. Right now let's focus on how you got parent trapped into looking after children on your day off."

Rowan squawked. "Your claims are accurate and hurtful."

"I know," Taylor said, and then said nothing while she waited for him to break and fill the silence. Why was Rowan surrounded by so many perceptive and confident women?

"There is nothing else to tell! I ran into Jordy and Kaira, and she thinks I should rectify my lack of firsthand knowledge of armadillos posthaste. So now I'm off to the zoo."

"Right. So you're not going just so you can stare at Jordy Shaw's ass."

"That's just a bonus."

"Some bonus. Zoos are full of sticky, screaming children. Why are you agreeing to go on your day off from sticky, screaming children?"

"Excuse me, children do not scream in my library. My shushing skills are unparalleled."

He could hear her roll her eyes. "I'm sorry, sticky, quietly noisy children."

"I'm sensing a lot of hostility toward children right now. Is there something you need to get off your chest?"

"Har har. I am just someone who knows that regular breaks are essential for maintaining composure around children."

Rowan couldn't deny that. And yet he was looking forward to his trip to the zoo, and not just because of Jordy's aforementioned lovely bum. He actually wanted to see Kaira and watch her reaction to the armadillos and hear her lecture about the animals.

"I should hang up," he admitted. "They'll be here in fifteen minutes, and I'm not fully ready." He bit his lip and looked at the envelope once more. He had time to read it....

"You going to open that letter first?" Taylor asked, not unkindly.

"No, I don't think so. No. I can't. Not knowing is definitely the lesser of two evils."

He was tying his shoes when a knock came at his door. He checked the peep hole and then opened it to Jordy's terribly handsome if inscrutable face. Rowan was not going to be ashamed of his shithole flat. He was not.

"Hi! I'm ready to go. Just let me get my keys."

He grabbed them off the shelf, stepped out, and locked the door. His lack of shame didn't mean he wanted to give Jordy a tour.

"Weren't you bringing a couple people with you?"

Jordy motioned over his shoulder, and Rowan could see his point. His large SUV sat a few feet from where they stood. "Kaira wanted to come too, but I figured you probably didn't want two six-year-olds poking around your stuff for the next half hour."

Definitely true. Rowan's place wasn't kid-proofed. Maybe he should consider a locked container for his adult-only toys.

If Rowan thought the drive to the zoo would be awkward, he hadn't accounted for excitable children. Kaira and Clement talked the whole way, wandering between their plans for the day and various other topics of interest. Rowan loved how their little brains jumped from creating a detailed zoo-visiting battle plan to "my favorite show is *Bluey*" to "look at that doggy!" to "Mr. Rowan, have you ever eaten an ice cream cone with chocolate on it?"

At the zoo, Jordy seemed to have a definite plan of his own, and he navigated the parking lot decisively, as though he'd been here enough to have a favorite spot. Once he got both kids out, he slung a backpack over one shoulder, locked the car, and said, "Hands," firmly to both kids. Kaira and Clement interlocked hands. Then Clement took Jordy's left and Kaira took Rowan's right.

At the gate, Jordy led them through the prepaid aisle with tickets on his phone and handed Kaira and Clement one of the free maps. Only once they'd moved well into the park and away from the busy entrance did he pull everyone into a huddle and ask, "Where to first?"

Unsurprisingly, Kaira wanted to see the armadillos first, which made it a done deal. Rowan had only met Clement five seconds ago, but it was clear that Kaira was in charge. She studied the map with an officious manner, grabbed Clement, and then pulled him down the path.

"I guess we just follow, then?" Rowan asked, already moving.

As they fell into step, Jordy smiled. "Pretty much. In case you weren't aware, that is what you signed up for today."

Rowan had to hand it to Kaira and her obsession—without hesitating, she marched them past enclosures designed to mimic the Australian outback and a woodland filled with snoozing wolves.

"She's *really* into armadillos," Rowan observed, with a longing look at the sign for the polar bears. Maybe they'd head that way later.

"She's really into armadillos," Jordy agreed. "Her aunt gave her this book a year ago, *Bilbo the Armadillo*."

"I'm familiar with it," Rowan said. It was a decent picture book with a couple of sequels.

"Of course. Well, it started the obsession."

"Because she's a fan of alliteration and rhyme?" Picture books tended to feature both heavily, but *Bilbo the Armadillo* really leaned into it. Bilbo lived in Amarillo and washed with a Brillo and ate picadillo. "Or because it's from an aunt?" Rowan was nosey about their family dynamics, and the mystery of Kaira's mother intrigued him.

Jordy hummed thoughtfully. "Probably both." Rowan bit his tongue and waited. "Emma sent it for Christmas. She couldn't visit until February. Kaira took the book as a promise, I guess."

Rowan could picture it. Kaira wandering around a large house with a book clasped to her chest and asking for repeated rereads all hours. "Wore out the book in a month, huh?"

Jordy huffed a soft laugh. Rowan was starting to adore Jordy's understated reactions. "Almost wore out my patience." He shot Rowan a look, like he was about to spill a secret. "I had to buy the sequels just to save my sanity."

God, that was adorable.

"So now she loves armadillos. Has Emma apologized yet?"

Jordy snorted. "She sends Kaira something armadillo every chance she gets. Just sent a stuffed toy for her last birthday."

"Ah, an enabler, then. I think I like her."

"You probably would."

"Armadillos!"

The kids stood at a fence, staring into a wooded enclosure with a couple of lumbering gray rocks. One of them seemed to be feasting near a log.

"Look, Mr. Rowan!"

"I'm looking," Rowan said as he stepped closer. Unlike Bilbo, this armadillo appeared to prefer insect salad to picadillo. According to the sign on the fence, her name was Alice, or possibly Arnold. He couldn't tell its gender or, for that matter, distinguish its facial features. "What do you think? Which one is this?"

Kaira squinted at the little plaque with the animals' pictures and names and proclaimed, "That one's Alice. 'Cause she has eight bands, see? And Arnold has nine."

Next to Rowan, Jordy covered a laugh with a cough. Well, Rowan might have expected she'd be better at identifying armadillos than he was. "Not Bilbo?" he teased.

He was surprised when Clement spoke up from his other side. "Mr. Rowan, that's not Bilbo the armadildo—"

Oh Lord. Oh no. The laugh caught in Rowan's throat, so high up he thought he might choke on it. Helplessly, he looked from Clement to Jordy, who was biting his lips, his cheeks an adorable pink.

Help me, Rowan tried to say with his mind. *I don't want to hurt this kid's feelings!*

Jordy's expression said pretty plainly that Rowan was on his own.

"—Bilbo the armadildo lives in Amarillo."

Finally, after several hitching breaths, Rowan managed to speak, squeaking out the words past the laughter he was holding at the top of his lungs. "Ah yes." It felt like laughter was going to start leaking out his eyes. "Silly me! How could I forget?"

Kaira only shook her head at him. "You're funny."

Now the laugh did escape. "*You're* funny," Rowan shot back, poking her in the side, making her giggle too. "Now, where's Arnold, then, hmm? Do you see him?"

Jordy stepped up on Kaira's other side, and they all peered into the enclosure. The sign indicated armadillos were generally solitary unless they were mating or it was wintertime—even armored mammals liked a good cuddle in the cold, apparently—so Rowan concentrated on the farther reaches.

"There?" He pointed.

Jordy leaned closer to follow the line of his arm. "That's a rock."

"How can you tell?"

Jordy gave him an amused look. "There's moss growing on it."

So there was.

Kaira's little face was set in concentration as she scanned for her beloved Arnold, but it was Clement who said, "I see the armadildo! It's in that hole!"

Oh bollocks. Rowan desperately tried to clamp down on the laugh, but when it couldn't escape his mouth, it came out through his nose with a kind of burning sensation. He could feel the fence they were leaning on shaking in time with Jordy's shoulders as he stifled laughter of his own. "Right you are, Clem. That must be Arnold."

By mutual agreement, Rowan and Jordy stepped back from the enclosure then, far enough that they didn't have to hear the kids' conversation and the kids wouldn't hear theirs. Rowan put a hand over his eyes as he hiccupped through a fit of giggles. "Fucking—*armadildos*," he gasped as he finally straightened.

Next to him, Jordy let out a very loud snort. "Shhh, you can't— you can't let them know it's funny," he whispered. "They'll never stop repeating it."

The idea set Rowan off again. "I know," he hissed. "God, how do you do this parenting thing full-time?"

"I've got a nanny," Jordy said dryly.

Rowan wiped a tear from under one eye and finally managed to stand up straight. "Whew, okay. That's not the kind of exotic animal I thought we'd see at the zoo, you know. Next it'll be leather bears."

Jordy looked at him sideways. "Cougars?"

"Anacondas."

A beat. Then Jordy suggested, "Mandrills?"

Rowan hiccupped again. Jordy grinned, almost boyish, pleased with himself for making Rowan laugh. Or… well, okay, Rowan was probably projecting a bit, but he liked that they could have a good time together, even if it was a platonic outing at the zoo with a pair of six-year-old chaperones. Rowan could always use another friend.

They stayed for another ten minutes as a zookeeper brought Alice out closer to show off how good she was at finding food—she navigated quite a few obstacles in her search and then quickly realized when the goodies were gone and waddled back to the meal she'd been eating before.

Apparently the kids took this as a signal, because they turned away from the enclosure like they shared a hive mind. Kaira immediately put her hand in Jordy's, while Clem gave Rowan a somewhat distrustful look before taking his. "So," Rowan said cheerfully, "where to next? I think it's your turn to pick, Clem." He hoped to any god listening the kid didn't say *horny toads*.

"Let's look at the map first," Jordy suggested before Clem could answer.

Right. Because they didn't want to traipse all the way across the zoo between every exhibit.

It took until they finished exploring the Americas Pavilion, where Rowan fell in love with a pair of frisky river otters who seemed as enchanted by their audience as the audience was with them, before the reality of being out in public with a famous person intruded.

They were just heading toward the Canadian Domain when a young couple with a kid in a Shield T-shirt stopped them. "Sorry, I know you're here with your family"—the man gave Rowan and Clem a curious look—"but could we get a selfie?"

Jordy's momentary hesitation made Rowan step forward. "Here, why don't I take it?" That would draw less attention and be a better photo besides. He could see Jordy glancing around, gauging the interest around them.

After he handed the phone back, he slid his arm through Jordy's, keeping hold of Clem in the other hand, and steered them all toward the nearest gift shop. "So I think," he said, "that we need to find you a hat. For sunburn reasons."

Jordy frowned but didn't resist. "I'm wearing a hat."

"Yes. An Under Armour hat. Very under the radar. Let's get you a safari hat. A nice big one with a wide brim."

Once Kaira realized the plan, she was fully on board and insisted they each get one. Luckily for Rowan's plan and Jordy's introversion, the zoo had a family set of safari hats. After some light tomfoolery, Kaira settled them in front of a mirror so she could assess their look. Thanks to the matching hats, Kaira's and Jordy's matching hair, and Clement's darker skin tone landing somewhere between Kaira's and Rowan's, they really did look like a modern nuclear family, ready to grace a progressive advert for the zoo. It was adorable.

Jordy paid for their hats with a black credit card, then stuffed the hats they had arrived with into his backpack. After a brief interlude to hand out water and granola bars, they resumed their tour.

A few animals later, it dawned on Rowan that onlookers' gazes had changed. There was a flavor of indulgence now, as if Rowan wasn't the only one who thought they looked like an adorable family. He tried to see their group from outside eyes. Two men following two children with soft smiles, sharing looks whenever the kids did something especially adorable. Kaira was taller than Clem and bossier, which he supposed outsiders might interpret as an age gap greater than it was—Kaira had keenly explained that she had been six forever but Clem's birthday had been only last week—and see two siblings. Strangers saw a family, a unit.

Rowan didn't hate it.

"Look!" Kaira squealed. "Moose!" She grabbed Rowan's hand and dragged him to the fence. No, Rowan didn't hate this at all.

"Moose," Rowan agreed. The alarmingly large animal, with a head full of antlers big enough to sit in, stood several feet away, slowly munching on vegetation. Rowan had never been so close to one before, and he was starting to question the sanity of anyone who tried to build settlements close to their habitats.

"Did you know that his antlers will *fall off?*" Kaira's tone wavered between disbelief and ghoulish delight.

"What?"

"They do. Daddy says so." Her tone suggested some doubt as to Daddy's honesty.

"So they fall off, huh. That's pretty… a-moose-ing."

Kaira giggled. "A-moose-ing."

Clem and Jordy had caught up by this point, and Kaira turned to them to share Rowan's highly original joke, which was apparently new to Clem as well. He giggled and repeated the word.

"I think it's time for a lunch break," Jordy said softly. "Clem's dragging." He and Jordy had taken longer than expected to catch up.

"What's the plan for lunch?"

"I figured we'd grab something up ahead." He nodded to the sign pointing the direction to a Tim Hortons.

"Wow. They really are everywhere in Canada."

Jordy smiled. "Everywhere is helpful with kids. They like familiar."

They did indeed, if their delighted squealing was any indicator.

"Can I get a chocolate muffin?" Kaira wanted to know.

"I want a sprinkle donut," Clem announced, and after a pause, "Please?"

Smiling, Jordy herded them to the restaurant and bought them each their dessert treat, which he held hostage until they each finished half a sandwich. Rowan tried to buy his own lunch, but acquiesced under Jordy's very flat look.

"My kid dragged you here. I can afford to buy you lunch at Tim's. What do you want, Rowan?"

Rowan wanted tea, a sandwich, and a sour cream donut.

Jordy insisted that they sit to eat, which Rowan was thankful for but which brought its own challenges as the kids grew bored with their meals and wanted to wander. Kaira slumped dejectedly under Jordy's unimpressed, no-nonsense arched eyebrow. Rowan probably shouldn't find that adorable, but he did.

As was the realization that Jordy was equally prepared for this. He tucked the leftover food into some bags he'd brought with him and put it all in his rucksack for later.

The day continued in a similar fashion, with the kids leading the charge and Jordy and Rowan following. Food was just what Clem needed, apparently, because he had no trouble keeping up with Kaira as she led them through the African park.

As the sun climbed higher and the day got hotter, Kaira announced the need for something cool to eat, and they stopped for popsicles. Rowan wasn't sure if he'd angered or pleased the gods, but he must have done one of them, because nothing else explained the low-level torture that was watching Jordy wrap his lips around a round rocket popsicle.

Throat suddenly dry, Rowan tried to focus on his own creamsicle and not on Jordy's reddened lips.

The gods were probably not on his side, Rowan decided, because he was a bad man. He was on a not-date outing with children. He should not be adding fantasies of Jordy to his wank bank.

But he couldn't help but imagine Jordy on his knees with that same look of quiet concentration as he pinned Rowan's hips to the bed and swallowed his cock.

Certain that his cheeks were turning red, Rowan turned away and forced his libido down.

The process became much easier when Kaira put her sticky hand in his and asked if they could go see the monkeys now.

An hour or so later the outing came to an end. Clement was rubbing his eyes, and Kaira had gotten obstinate and argumentative. Her lip quivered when Jordy announced that they only had time to visit one more animal, but her slumped shoulders suggested she was relieved by the decision.

"Probably a wise call," Rowan said in an undertone.

Jordy grimaced. "I should have called it half an hour ago."

"Maybe," Rowan agreed. He reached out and touched Jordy's nose. "If only to save yourself. You're looking a little burnt." Rowan grimaced himself and gave an apologetic shrug. "Sorry for not noticing earlier."

Jordy touched his nose, winced, and sighed. "My fault. Too focused on the kids."

God, this man was endearing. And still unfairly beautiful even with a burnt nose and safari sun hat.

Kaira took them to the tigers and didn't fight Jordy's five-minute warning or his call to go home.

Both kids were dragging their feet by the time they got to the car, and it didn't surprise Rowan to see them both slumped over and sleeping before they reached the highway.

He couldn't blame them. They weren't the only tired ones. Rowan slumped in his seat and let the ride pass in silence except for the low hum of Jordy's music.

When Jordy pulled up to his building, Rowan took his cue.

"Thanks for today," he said, feeling suddenly like he was following a first-date script.

Jordy hummed. "Thanks for indulging my kid and giving me adult conversation." Well, maybe not quite a date stereotype.

"My pleasure." Rowan tipped his safari hat. "See you Sunday at the library."

Jordy nodded and waved goodbye as Rowan got out of the car. He didn't let himself feel warm and fuzzy when he noticed that Jordy didn't drive away until after Rowan got inside.

Sighing, Rowan closed the door and leaned against it. For a brief moment, he allowed himself the fantasy of the day finishing in a different way. Of following Jordy home and getting to know him better. Then he shook himself and stepped away from the door. It was a pointless fantasy, not least because Rowan was taking a break from men and romance.

It was time for food. He scrounged up leftovers and put them in the microwave, and as he stood waiting, he spotted the letter, still unopened, on the kitchen table.

Curiosity got the better of him, and he opened it. When the microwave beeped a minute later, he didn't hear.

... the final date of your contract has been confirmed....

Rowan chewed his thumb and stared at the date stamped on the page. August 27.

Bollocks. He'd been hoping for better news—an update on his application for a more permanent position. He'd been lucky Pamela's maternity leave had started within weeks of Cindy's ending, so he'd gone from one mat leave to another. But he didn't think his luck could hold out for a third, which was why he'd been sending applications for more permanent contracts.

The microwave beeped aggressively, reminding him of his dinner. He tossed the letter onto the table and turned back to his food. As he ate his curry, he contemplated what to do next. The longer it took him to find something stable, the longer he had to stay in this flat. He knew Gem would rescue him if he asked, but that wasn't what he wanted. What he needed. Rowan didn't just need the stability of something long-term, a home to call his own. He also needed to prove to himself that he could do it without relying on others. He wanted to be independent of the bullshit of his parents' lives, and he couldn't do that if he let Gem—or anyone—take their place, financially speaking.

Plate empty, Rowan opened the dishwasher to unload the morning's clean dishes—

And cursed when water gushed out over the floor.

"Fuck!" What in the world? The bottom of the dishwasher held standing water three inches deep. Well, less now that some had flowed out. Rowan groaned. He'd called the landlord weeks ago about how slowly it seemed to drain. The slumlord said he'd take care of it.

Rowan had put that out of his mind, but apparently he should have harped. What a mess. It wasn't only clean water either; there were bits of food in it. Disgusting.

He didn't have the wherewithal to deal with this tonight. It required the services of a professional, and he could take the cost of the repair out of next month's rent. He snapped a bunch of pictures and texted them to his landlord, then whipped out Google to find a plumber.

IT HAPPENED every year, and yet every year it took Jordy by surprise when July gave way to August and he realized his days at home with Kaira were coming to a close.

It had been a good summer. They'd had two weeks in Minnesota right after school let out, another week on a beach in Aruba, and still plenty of time for library group and the zoo with Clem… and now Jordy needed to start training in earnest, because in a few weeks, camp would start, and then the preseason. And Kaira would start first grade.

God, that made him feel old. Old and—something. Wistful? Before he knew it, Kaira would be all grown up, leaving the house to go to college or travel the world with her friends or both. Jordy wanted that for her.

He *didn't* want to think about where that'd leave him in twelve years—in a big house with no Kaira to fill it.

"You've got a frowny face this morning," Janice commented when she popped her head into the kitchen. "Coffee?"

"Time machine?" Jordy countered.

Janice chuckled and slid him a mug. "Bit outside my area of expertise, I'm afraid."

"Doesn't hurt to ask."

She put her hand over his on the counter. "It happens. Kids grow. Believe me, I know." She gently plucked the fridge magnet he'd been staring at out of his fingers. The photograph showed him and Kaira two years ago, on her fourth birthday. She was laughing hysterically, her baby-fat cheeks smeared with chocolate ice cream, as Jordy attempted to put her hair into a ponytail to keep it out of the mess.

He took a sip of coffee. It helped a bit. Janice refused to use a conventional coffee maker or even a French press; she had a little pour-over kit. Jordy was ruined forever.

"So. Speaking of the flow of time."

Oh no.

Janice sat on the stool next to him. "I had a call from my mum yesterday. It's not good news, I'm afraid. She fell and bumped her head, and it was hours before anyone noticed because she lives alone."

That sounded terrifying. "Is she okay?"

"Mostly bruises. A nasty cut on her head that she's lucky didn't kill her." Janice let out a long breath. "She can't live alone anymore, but she refuses to leave the house. You know how parents can be. 'Your father built this house with his own two hands.'"

And now Jordy understood the reason for the conversation. "You're leaving us."

She grimaced. "I wish I didn't have to. Just—there isn't anyone else. She can't afford live-in help, and even if she could, she's too proud to take it from someone who's not family. And—"

"And she's your mom," Jordy finished. He understood. That didn't make his situation any less challenging. "Are you sure she wouldn't accept—"

"Jordy," Janice said gently, "don't you dare offer to pay for it."

His shoulders slumped. *He* could afford it. And if Janice took him up on it, he wouldn't be in a tight spot with Kaira. "I'd be happy to help out, though."

"I know. But I meant it—stubbornness runs in my family. Lucky for me," she added, lightening her tone a little as she jostled his shoulder, "because goodness knows I'd have a time of it with Kaira otherwise."

He smiled wanly. "She gets it from her mother." The old joke felt rote today, the humor of blaming his sister for any undesirable genes falling flat.

Janice smiled. "So you've said."

They lapsed into silence for a moment. Then Jordy braced himself to ask the important question. "When's your flight?"

She sighed. "Monday. I hate that it's so soon, with training camp starting up, but I really can't leave her much longer."

Jordy shook his head. "I understand. And we'll be okay." Plenty of the other guys on the team had kids, whether they had nannies or not, and they were used to doing favors for each other. Kaira could make the rounds with them until he found a... replacement.

It had taken him months to find Janice, and he started well before Kaira was born. It'd take a miracle to find someone he trusted in just a few days. But he wasn't going to make that Janice's problem.

Janice squeezed his hand again. "I know you will."

At least Jordy didn't have to bring it up with Kaira right away. Today was Clem's birthday party, and she had gone over early to "help him get ready." Jordy didn't know what sort of primping six-year-olds did before parties, but as long as Clem's mother didn't mind having Kaira there, Jordy didn't mind having a little extra time to himself.

But he wasn't going to spend it in the house. That would lead to brooding. Instead, he took advantage of what passed for mild weather in August and went for a run.

It was always a risk, running in public. Jordy had a fairly recognizable face, and then there was his size—he outweighed most recreational runners. The upside was that he was an athlete. If he wanted to run, most people weren't going to be able to catch him. He shoved in a pair of earbuds, as much for plausible deniability as actual music, and set out for the park.

The stress of the morning dissipated with each footfall on the warm asphalt. Right now only moving mattered. Controlling his breathing. The sun in the sky. The beat of the song in his ears. The smell of freshly cut grass. The—

The sting of a round disk of plastic hitting the back of his head.

Rubbing at his scalp, Jordy turned to find a Frisbee at his feet and a couple of people in athletic gear running toward him.

"Sorry about that!" called the man in the lead. He chuckled breathlessly as he got closer. "Seriously. Pete's aim is the worst, and it doesn't improve when he's tripping over his own feet." His voice trailed off in a familiar way and his eyes widened. "Oh shit."

"Jordy?" said a familiar voice, and Jordy looked beyond the first man to see the second had a familiar face.

"Rowan."

"Oh my God," the unfamiliar man breathed and turned on Rowan. "That *was* you. I thought it looked like you, but then I thought, no way— he'd have told us if he was hanging out with Shield players."

"Uh." Rowan shot Jordy a look and then shrugged. "I wasn't exactly hanging out with hockey players. I just made a friend at a gala. But that is beside the point. The point is Pete attacked poor Jordy with the Frisbee. Sorry about that."

"I'll live."

"Hey, what's the holdup?" yelled one of the other players from a ways off, and all three of them turned to look.

"Uh-oh," Rowan said. "Is it just me, or is Pete still on the ground?"

"Pete is still on the ground. Looks like we might have to call the game."

"We could always play one man down on both sides."

"Ooooor…," said the stranger, turning to look at Jordy, "we could recruit a new player."

Which was how Jordy found himself pulling off his shirt to join Alex's team in defeating Rowan's.

At first, things went smoothly. Jordy ran, caught the disk, threw it to a teammate. He dodged and distracted his opponents and ran interference using his size—all things he did professionally. Even celebrating a touchdown was familiar, if a little sillier.

"I see how it is," Rowan bemoaned as Jordy high-fived his teammates. "No loyalty among sports."

Jordy rolled his eyes, tossed Rowan the disk. "I play to win. Doesn't mean I like you any less."

"It's like that, is it?" Rowan's eyes gleamed. "Well, I too play to win."

"Oh my God," Alex muttered under their breath. "Are you *flirting* right now?" It always amazed Jordy how people never could tell the difference between friendly and flirty.

"I'll have you know," Rowan said, relaxing out of a game-ready pose and placing his hands on his hips, the Frisbee still clutched in one hand, "that was trash talk, not flirting."

On the next game play, Rowan bumped into Jordy as they were running down the field. "So unfair," he puffed. "You're *my* friend. Stop helping other people win."

Jordy huffed. "Play better, then." He tried to dodge around Rowan, but he was never his smoothest on land.

Rowan spun into his way again, and Jordy cursed and tried to dodge, but Rowan—Rowan cheated. He pushed into Jordy's space, and Jordy, not expecting the sudden full-body contact, fumbled. They crashed to the ground.

"Oof," Rowan wheezed and coughed, his face pressed against Jordy's chest. His breath prickled across his damp skin. He pressed one hand to the ground and the other to Jordy's pec and lifted his head enough to ask, "You okay?"

Rowan's eyelashes were long and thick. They framed his eyes beautifully.

Jordy found his tongue. "Yes. You?"

"Yes." Rowan got up and held out a hand.

"You cheated," Jordy grunted once he was back on his feet.

"What? I would never."

"No-contact sport, hm?"

"Well. It was an accident?" Rowan tried with a little smile.

Jordy might've believed him if that was the end of it, but for the next few plays, Rowan all but stopped trying to get the Frisbee and seemed more intent on getting in Jordy's way, of breaking the no-contact rule to get into his space, to push, to tackle—always with a wheeze of "Oops! Didn't see you there."

Jordy couldn't help but laugh as the cheating grew more blatant. Figuring all was lost, when Rowan next pushed into Jordy's space, he swerved, bent, caught Rowan around the waist, and stood.

Rowan yelped. "Unhand me, you barbarian," he gasped, but laughter threaded through his voice.

Jordy clamped his arm around Rowan's thighs to hold him over his shoulder and asked in the general direction of Rowan's head— which hung somewhere near Jordy's lower back—"I'm sorry. Is this not allowed?"

"Manhandling opponents like a caveman is against the rules," Rowan cried.

"What? Sorry, can't hear you." Jordy cast his gaze around. The situation called for a nice pool or fountain to toss him into.

The best he could come up with was the remnants of a mud puddle, but that might be overkill. Instead he carried Rowan across the goal line and set him down. "How many points do I get for that?"

"That's a red-card offense," Rowan said, flat on his back on the ground, panting and gasping. His brown cheeks were flushed pink. "Match penalty. Total disregard for the rules."

"I didn't see anything," Alex said.

Rowan took a breath, likely to deliver another smartass remark, but was cut off by a cough.

"You okay?" Jordy frowned.

"Ye-yeah—" Rowan wheezed but couldn't get anything else out as he coughed again and again.

Jordy stepped in closer, reaching out. In retrospect, Rowan's panting and gasping during the game felt ominous. He looked to be fighting it, but when he gasped, short of breath, the next set of coughs sounded deep and rattling.

"Rowan." Jordy put a hand on his arm.

"It's fine, just a tickle."

"Do you have asthma?"

"No." Rowan shook his head. "It's nothing." He tried to wave them off, but another cough weakened his efforts.

Jordy scowled. "Have you seen a doctor?"

Rowan shrugged. "I have an appointment."

With both Pete and Rowan out, the game seemed to be finished, and everyone collected their things. Jordy had just about decided Rowan could be trusted to look after himself when he let out another racking cough.

That was it. Jordy grabbed his phone and started dialing.

"Who are you calling?" Rowan eyed the phone suspiciously.

"A doctor."

ROWAN HATED asking his friends for rides, but Pete's wife showed up in her car to take him home anyway, and Jordy accepted her offer to drop them by the office on his behalf before Rowan could protest.

If Gem could see him now, getting steamrolled into accepting help… she'd get all kinds of ideas. She'd be very smug about it.

Truth told, Rowan was worried enough that he didn't have the breath to complain in the car. He'd been wheezing and coughing and sniffling at night for more than a week, but until now it always cleared up in the daytime. He'd never even felt the need to take a day off work. Frankly, he felt better at the library than he did lying around at home.

Gem would probably say he was allergic to his ugly apartment.

In any case, he'd felt fine today. The refreshing air and exercise did him good. And there was nothing like the sight of Jordy shirtless and sweaty to make him feel alive, and also to regret swearing off men. Of *course* Rowan had gotten a little breathless. The way Jordy swung him up over his shoulders like a sack of flour? Like Rowan wasn't taller than most men. Be still his beating heart. And lungs. And dick.

But maybe he'd overdone it with the competition, because now he wanted to go home and crawl into bed and sleep for three days. With the option of sitting in the bathroom first with the shower running as hot as it would go, in an effort to loosen the tightness in his lungs.

He didn't make small talk, leaving Pete and his wife to carry the conversation. He had the vague impression Jordy was probing them for information on how he could pay them back for the kindness, and imagined Jordy showing up at their flat one day with Shield season tickets, or making a surprise visit to their future child's birthday party.

He must've dozed off, because the next thing he knew, someone was shaking his shoulder. "Rowan. Come on." There was a pause and then Jordy added, "Maybe you should come too, Pete. Get that foot looked at."

Pete brushed this off, despite what Rowan was sure was a blistering look from his wife, and Jordy hustled him into a nondescript medical building.

And then, in a surreal sort of parallel universe way, Rowan was sitting shirtless in a posh doctor's office while a woman with thick plastic-rimmed glasses and elaborately braided hair listened to his lungs.

"How long have you had the cough?"

"A week or so? No, maybe longer." He frowned. "A month? But it wasn't this bad before, just like a tickle."

She didn't like that answer, if her frown was any indication. She rolled her chair away from him and indicated he could put his shirt back on. "And any other symptoms? Fever, headaches? Has the cough been productive?"

"Um, like coughing stuff up? Phlegm sometimes."

"No blood?"

Rowan blanched. "I would've gone to an urgent care clinic if there was."

"Good. And the other symptoms?"

He thought about it. "I've been a bit sniffly, I guess. No headaches, no fever."

"And is it worse at night, during the day…?"

"Definitely at night. Today was an anomaly."

"And you had the coughing attack while playing Ultimate Frisbee, right?"

"Right. But I don't have asthma. Or at least I never have before." Sure, he'd been a weedy kid, but he would've known if he'd had asthma.

Dr. Okoye leaned back in her chair and tapped her pen on her clipboard. "What about allergies? Dust, hay fever, pollen?"

He shook his head. "I mean, I'm not about to go sticking my head under the bed to get a deep whiff of dust bunnies or anything, but I'm no more reactive than any other person."

She put down the pen and sat forward. "Well, whatever's ailing you, I don't think it's acute. No sign of infection or pneumonia. Allergies is my best guess—they can develop at any time. I could send you for tests, but you'll be back on the regular wait list, I'm afraid."

Rowan shook his head. "No, that's all right. I know it was a lot to ask to have you see me today. I'm a bit embarrassed Jordy dragged me in here, actually. I'm sorry this is so outside your usual duties."

"That's just Jordy for you." She shook her head. "You should've seen him the first time Kaira had a fever. At least it's not three in the morning this time."

That made Rowan smile. "Good to know he's not always perfect."

She barked a sharp laugh. "I could tell you stories, but it'd violate patient confidentiality. Do keep an eye on that cough, though. And don't cancel your other appointment. Your GP might want to send you for a chest X-ray if this hasn't cleared up by then."

Rowan left her with a promise to follow her advice, and then, after a not insignificant amount of haggling, left Jordy with a promise to take it easy and an acceptance of Jordy paying for his cab home. As though Rowan wasn't perfectly fit to take the subway.

He was grateful for it when he got home, though, because the heat had picked up in the afternoon, and now he was uncomfortably aware of the way his skin felt, caked with dried sweat and dirt and grass. He probably didn't smell great either, but the cab driver didn't comment. Probably Jordy had given him a ridiculous tip.

He let himself into his flat and tossed his keys in the bowl. The shower was sounding better and better every second.

Finally he stood under the hot spray. The steam did help, at first. Breathing came easier. He washed away the grime and then just stood for a moment, leaning with his palms on the tile, letting the water cascade over him.

And then his hand went through the wall.

For a second Rowan just stared at it, wondering what just happened. There was the tile, and there was his arm, on the other side of a hole, the edges of which were soggy and covered in some kind of black… slimy…

Mold.

"Bugger," Rowan said, and then he sneezed.

Gem was going to be so annoying about this.

"BLACK MOLD?" Taylor asked at the library two days later, when Rowan was trying to stretch the kink out of his back—a souvenir from the fashionable torture implement Gem called a couch. "Seriously?"

"Through the whole building," Rowan confirmed glumly. "Everyone has to move out while they fix it. Could be months."

"Jesus."

He rubbed his hands over his face. He'd never been religious, but at this point he was willing to try prayer. It couldn't make anything worse. "So basically, not only do I need to find a new job in a month, I also need to find a new apartment."

Gem had already badgered him about going after the landlord— she was practically salivating to sue on Rowan's behalf.

"Yikes," Taylor said. "What're you going to do?"

Rowan groaned and flopped back into the desk chair. "I don't know, do you know anyone with a storage shed they're not using? I don't need much—"

Taylor coughed.

"—just four walls and a roof without black mold."

"Black mold?" repeated a familiar voice, and oh damn it, if Rowan thought *Gem* was insufferable about it….

He pasted on a smile and turned to face Jordy. "Yes. It's my flat's newest update." He pulled a face, hoping to lighten the mood, but Jordy didn't look appeased.

"Your place has black mold?" He looked alarmed. Kaira, clearly sensing the tension, clung to his hand and watched their conversation without interrupting.

"Yeah. Guess we've discovered the cause of my cough."

Jordy graduated from one-alarm to three. "You have somewhere else to live?"

"My friend put me up for the short term. Still looking for a long-term solution. Sadly I can't stay on her couch for the next couple of months." He pulled an exaggerated face and locked eyes with Kaira. She smiled tentatively. "Mostly because she'd kick me out if I tried to stay that long." This earned a small giggle.

Jordy looked down at his daughter, then back at Rowan. "I also have a problem."

That was a tantalizing opener, if only because Jordy had never struck him as the kind of guy to want to steal anyone's thunder. "Oh?"

He nodded, then said to Kaira, "You had some books you wanted to show Mr. Rowan, right?"

Kaira nodded so hard her pigtails bobbed. "I have lots of book ideas to share."

"Why don't we go find those books?"

"Yes!" Kaira seemed happy to forget about any tension, but Rowan was reeling from the subject change. Kaira let go of Jordy's hand and skipped off to the children's section.

"Join us?" Jordy asked.

"Well, it sounds like I must if Kaira is fetching me books," Rowan agreed as he made his way from behind the desk.

"I didn't want to talk about this in front of Kaira," Jordy said quietly as they walked together. She had almost reached the children's section. "Janice—our nanny—had to leave suddenly."

"Oh. That sounds not good."

"She's been with us Kaira's whole life. It's been an emotional week."

"A week? That is sudden."

"Her mother needs care. It became urgent."

"Ah. So she's not coming back in a week."

Jordy hummed. "Long-term I will need a replacement, but it's not an easy position to fill."

Rowan nodded and tried to keep from thinking about all the positions Jordy could fill him in. He could bet that looking for a nanny who would basically be Kaira's secondary parent wasn't an easy task. Then the words and their implications started to filter in. Was Jordy suggesting what Rowan thought he was?

"I'm not sure I can make any guarantees about the commute, but I can promise black-mold-free accommodations."

Rowan licked his lips. "You're offering to put me up for however long it takes for my flat to be habitable again."

"Yes."

"In exchange for babysitting."

"The season is starting up again soon, which means I frequently have to go out of town for several days at a time."

Rowan stopped walking. "Didn't you just say that finding a nanny you like is hard? You barely know me."

Jordy paused and turned to him. "Maybe. But I trust Gem as a reference, and it's only short term. Are you really trying to talk me out of giving you a place to live?"

"No?" Rowan rubbed his face and ruffled his hair. "Let me think for a second."

"Okay. I'm going to get closer to Kaira." He left Rowan to gather his thoughts.

So. A millionaire just walked into his job and offered him a place to live. What even was his life? Gem was going to laugh her ass off.

Ugh, no, he needed to focus on the problem—think it through logically, the pros and the cons. Pros: A place to live, presumably with a bed and not a couch to sleep on. Roommates he could tolerate and access to the sort of amenities found in a millionaire's house. No rent to pay at a time when his employment was currently about to end. Cons: He'd never lived full-time with a child. How would minding Kaira work with him having a job outside the home? What if Jordy and Rowan got on each other's nerves and hated living together?

Also, Jordy was the most fuckable but off-limits man Rowan had ever met.

He'd see Jordy first thing in the morning. What if he caught him half-naked on the way from the shower? Last weekend the sight of Jordy shirtless in his short-shorts almost put Rowan in cardiac arrest. He would not survive seeing the man dripping and clean. The blue balls from living with Jordy might cause permanent damage.

On the other hand, Gem's couch was *definitely* causing him damage. Not to mention the harm she would do to him if she found out Jordy had offered him a place to stay and he turned it down.

Okay. Rowan needed to ask Jordy some questions.

Jordy stood leaning against a wall, watching Kaira move up and down the aisles in search of books.

"I can't make nanny my full-time job, so how would that work when you're out of town?"

Jordy shrugged. "I have teammates with kids who can help. They've already agreed to it. Once school starts, there's aftercare. You could also bring her here if you needed to."

"Right." Rowan considered the logistics. The whole point of his job was a children's program. There was no reason Kaira couldn't join it. And once he no longer worked at the library, it would be a moot point.

"We can go through a full schedule if you'd like. I can pretty much tell you when I'll be unavailable from now until April, except for some of the promotion and charity stuff. But I could show you what August and September would look like."

"Probably a good idea." Normally Rowan was willing to jump into a new situation feet first, figuring that he'd learn to swim—or at least float—soon enough. But he couldn't take that approach when there was a child involved.

"Janice gave me notice right before I saw you in the park. I've basically been scrambling for short-term solutions—teammates with kids and partners, Clem's parents. I'm going to be in karmic debt forever. I don't want anyone to resent me."

"I'm sure that wouldn't happen. They've gotta know you're in a bind."

Jordy nodded. "Yes, but the point is, having you around to cover the night shift would be a huge help."

Rowan furiously sublimated the mental image he got from words like *night shift* and *huge*.

He must've looked like he wanted convincing, because Jordy went on, "I'm sure Janice would be okay with me giving you her number so she can give you pointers in an emergency. Kaira already likes you, and you've already met her best friend." This was dangerously close to begging. Rowan absolutely did not think about what it might sound like if Jordy begged under other, more naked circumstances.

"Clem's a good kid," Rowan said, forcing his brain back on track.

"The nanny suite is small"—oh God, he was still trying to get Rowan to agree—"but it's got its own sitting room and bathroom, and there's a grade entrance if you, um… had company, on nights I'm home with Kaira."

Okay, now what? "Company?" Rowan asked blankly.

Jordy's ears went pink. "It wouldn't be fair to say you can't have people over. Just… I'd prefer to meet anyone first, before you introduce them to Kaira."

This was hands down the most bizarre conversation Rowan had ever had. Especially because he knew Jordy didn't even introduce his *own* partners to his kid, because he didn't have any. "I've actually sworn off dating for the foreseeable future, so that won't be a problem."

That sounded like he'd agreed to this mad plan, didn't it?

"How come?"

In for a penny. "Weeelllll, you may recall I have the world's most terrible taste in men? Sure, it starts off all right, groping in the club or picnics in the park, and then one day you wake up and he's trying to make meth in the kitchen sink. I'm better off on a no-dick diet." That sounded way worse now that there was a kid in the mix. "Now that I think about it, if I ever date again, 'Would I cut off my arm before introducing this person to Kaira?' is a pretty good litmus test."

"Mr. Rowan! I found some good ones. Can we read one of these next?"

Rowan took Kaira's selections and looked through them. One of them did not feature a single armadillo, which immediately made it his favorite because he kept nearly saying *armadildo* instead. "Oh, I think I can manage that. But next time I'll have to let someone else help me pick out a story, okay? Everyone gets a turn."

He could see the beginning of a pout, so he added, "But you're welcome to check out the others and take them home with you to enjoy."

"Okay," Kaira agreed at last. "Daddy, will you hold my books?" She thrust them into Jordy's hands before he could respond, and returned to her dedicated perusal of the children's section.

When she was out of earshot, Jordy cleared his throat. "So you'll do it?"

Consign himself to several months of sexual frustration in the name of healthy lungs and finances? "Sure," Rowan said. "Why not?"

First Period

IT TOOK a pathetically small amount of time to pack up Rowan's things. Jordy insisted on helping, partly because Rowan shouldn't be spending more time than necessary in his apartment and partly because he was afraid if he left Rowan to his own devices for too long he'd change his mind.

That fear evaporated the second he saw the interior of Rowan's apartment, where walls had been opened up in order to assess the extent of the damage. After that, Jordy was mostly afraid he'd run into Rowan's landlord and "accidentally" put a foot up his ass.

For her part, Kaira was thrilled to have a captive librarian at home. As far as Jordy was concerned, that and her safety were all that mattered.

It should have felt strange to hand over a house key and alarm codes to someone he'd just met, even if he *had* called up Gem and run the idea by her. She said only, "This is an unusually good move on both your parts. I'm impressed." Then he heard clicking; she must be in the office. "Tell me, does Rowan have a preferred china pattern?"

Rowan didn't need china; Jordy had plenty of plates in the kitchen. Maybe she meant for someday when he moved out again. "I don't know," Jordy said. "None of the stuff in his cabinets matched."

He had no idea why Gem found that so funny, but it didn't really matter.

"My bedroom and Kaira's are upstairs. She has her own bathroom," Jordy told Rowan as he led him in the front door. He felt awkward about it after seeing Rowan's apartment, and was silently thankful for the fact that he'd have been ashamed to invite his parents to a house that felt too showy. They'd always been clear about what was important in life. Still, in Toronto his celebrity status sometimes meant gawkers, so he'd compromised and found a home in a gated community that didn't make him cringe. His privacy was one thing; Kaira's safety was another. "The cleaning service comes on Tuesdays."

"Got it."

"But Kaira has to clean her own bedroom." That was important. "So she can learn responsibility."

Rowan broke into a smile. "Good call. Wish my parents had thought of that one. Still learning, me."

"Yes, I saw your apartment," Jordy said wryly.

"Hey! In my defense, someone literally went through with a sledgehammer looking for mold."

"Relax. I was kidding." They left their shoes by the hall closet and stepped forward into the living room. "This is where Kaira and I usually spend our time after dinner. Her taste in TV includes hockey and *Bluey*. She's coming around to football, though. And she loves nature documentaries."

"Especially if they're about armadillos?" Rowan guessed. His eyes flicked up to the tall ceilings, but if the size of Jordy's living room fazed him, Jordy couldn't tell.

"Especially those. Kitchen is right here, obviously." Jordy gestured. The house's open floor plan was self-explanatory, but he still felt like he had to say it. "I usually cook here if I'm home with Kaira."

"Is she a picky eater?"

"Depends on the day. Dino nuggets are always a safe bet. Laundry's through here." He opened the sliding doors that led into the hidden kitchen behind the regular kitchen. "It's sort of, uh…."

"Oh, a butler's kitchen," Rowan said brightly. "Cool."

Jordy blinked at him. "A what?"

"A butler." Rowan gave him a look that said *rich people, am I right?* "You know, the kitchen where you do the actual cooking so that when people come over, you don't have to clean up a mess."

Jordy felt horrified. "*That's* what it's for?"

"What did you think it was for?"

That… was a good question, actually. "I don't know. They put the washer and dryer in there. I thought it was kind of a fancy laundry room." Sometimes Jordy got hungry while folding clothes. He couldn't be the only one that happened to.

"Anyway, laundry." Rowan turned to the machines. "Anything I should know about these?"

"Kaira has sensitive skin, so I wash everything with unscented detergent. It's in here." Damn, they hadn't talked about household chores yet. "Ah, I can do her clothes when I'm home—"

Rowan waved this off. "I know this is hard to believe, but even my clumsy arse doesn't dirty enough clothes in a week to fill that monster. I'm happy to wash our things together if you don't mind. Especially if you're cooking when you're home." He paused and then backtracked. "I mean—not that I'd expect you to cook for me—"

"No point in both of us having to cook."

"Right." Rowan rubbed the back of his head. "Sorry, I'm trying to figure out where the line for roommate-slash-babysitter crosses into something else. Bit difficult as I've never had a roommate."

"I did, when I was a rookie. Lived with the captain for a bit. He didn't just cook for me, he told me how much more I had to eat." Jordy paused. "Maybe that's not a good example of setting normal boundaries."

Rowan smiled. "Guess we'll have to use our words. Don't tell Gem."

"Cross my heart," Jordy said, keeping a straight face.

Rowan snickered and opened his mouth—

"Daddy, is it dinnertime?" Kaira stood in the doorway to the butler, rocking slightly and staring up at him with soulful eyes.

He glanced at his watch. "Uh, you know what, peanut? I think it is."

Jordy led them both into the kitchen and opened the fridge to find the leftovers from last night. "How does curry sound?"

"Delicious!" Kaira bounded forward and looped her arms around his thigh. "The one you made yesterday?"

"Yup." Jordy pulled containers out of the fridge, set them on the counter, and shut the fridge, only to discover his barnacle was semipermanent. Feigning ignorance, he turned toward the microwave and let out an exaggerated groan. Kaira giggled.

"Jordy," Rowan said, "are you okay?"

"I don't know," Jordy gasped. "There's something wrong with my leg." He slowly dragged it, and Kaira, forward, Kaira giggling like a maniac. "It's so heavy," Jordy groaned.

Rowan stepped closer, his face the very picture of concern. "Let me look." He leaned down, then gasped. "Jordy! There's some kind of strange growth clinging to your leg!"

"My leg?" Jordy made a show of looking down and gasping with surprise. "Oh goodness! There's a girl on my leg!"

Kaira snorted and gasped. "No, I'm not a girl!"

"You're not?"

"No. I'm a sloth."

"A sloth? Rowan, did you let a sloth into my house?"

"Who, me? Let in a sloth? No, I don't think so."

Kaira gasped out some pathetic animal noises between giggles. Rowan didn't remember the sloths at the zoo making any sounds, so he couldn't attest to their accuracy. Jordy huffed and puffed, pretending to drag her a few steps before asking Rowan for advice.

"Hm, well, I have heard that the best way to un-cling a sloth is…." He stepped closer, hands out. "Tickling." Kaira shrieked, but Rowan didn't make contact. He was looking at Jordy, eyebrows raised, asking if he could—or should. Jordy nodded—Kaira would be crying *No* if she didn't want to play—and Rowan reached in to gently wriggle his fingers along her ribs.

Kaira squealed in laughter, hugged Jordy's leg tighter, then let go to flop onto the floor. Rowan hesitated to follow, and Kaira caught her breath enough to say, "Tickle me, Tickle Monster!" Rowan obeyed.

Jordy's heart melted.

Kaira pulled Rowan into a game of chase that kept them both occupied while Jordy warmed up three plates of food and set the table. This small blessing was followed by another—Kaira was hungry enough to abandon the game the moment Jordy called, "Dinner!"

Rowan refused a beer but accepted a can of Bubly.

"I thought pineapple was the devil's fruit," Rowan chirped as he popped it open. He took a long drag, then sighed dramatically and smacked his lips. Kaira giggled into her milk.

"It is. That drink is devil's brew." Rowan gave another cheeky smirk, and Jordy sighed. "I guess the pro of having you willingly work through Janice's untouchable stash will be outweighed by you wanting more. And here I thought I'd finally be able to get it out of my house for good."

Rowan smirked. "This is the drink of angels. It tastes of fairy dust and unicorn magic." He winked at Kaira.

"Mr. Rowan, you're weird," Kaira told him. "That sounds gross."

After dinner, Jordy corralled them both for bedtime routine. Rowan hesitated, but Jordy's raised eyebrow and quiet "What, you gonna do this without practice?" made him step into the bathroom.

He tried at first to stay back and observe, but Kaira wasn't having it. By the time she was settled into bed, Rowan had been asked to inspect her teeth, given a tour of her bedroom, introduced to her menagerie of stuffed animals, and roped into reading a bedtime story.

"You can read three to me, and then Daddy can read three," Kaira said magnanimously. She was snuggled in between Bluey and Elmo with Bilbo the Armadillo clasped to her chest.

"Yeah, nice try, kiddo. Two readers does not change the three-book rule. You can have three stories total from both of us."

Kaira let out a gusty sigh, as if she truly suffered under Jordy's outrageous dictatorial rule. "Fine. Two stories from Rowan and one from you."

But after Rowan read the first Bilbo books with such an impressive array of voices, Jordy lost his spot in the lineup. Chuckling, he stepped forward to kiss her head. "Since Rowan's doing such a great job, I'm going to clean up the kitchen while he tucks you in." Rowan looked slightly alarmed, but Jordy just smiled. Rowan totally had this. "Good night, peanut."

"Night, Daddy!" She reached up to give him a strangling hug.

At the door, Jordy glanced back and was gratified to see neither was watching him. They were too engrossed in the story of Bilbo's bus-tour holiday.

Jordy was wiping down the counters, the kitchen tidied, when Rowan arrived, having escaped his charge.

"She manage to con you into any extra books?"

"Are you impugning my honor as a children's librarian, a reader of books to small humans, by suggesting that I would be unable to maintain a book limit?" Rowan asked with mock outrage.

"Yes."

Rowan slumped against the counter. "Okay, so maybe she talked me into rereading the first book. But that was my fault. I forgot about his rocking chair, so clearly I hadn't been paying close enough attention the first go-round."

"Ah, so you're a sucker." Jordy nodded.

"Maybe," Rowan agreed with a hint of a smile.

"You know your life is going to be easier if you stick to the three-books rule, right?"

"Technically we didn't break the three-book rule—" Jordy shot him a look from his place at the sink as he filled two glasses with water. "Okay, okay, I know. But it was the first time, I figured a little rule-breaking couldn't hurt just this once."

"Guess you'll find out soon enough when you're home alone with her and I'm in another city."

"Thanks," Rowan said dryly.

Smirking, Jordy motioned for him to have a seat at the kitchen table and flipped open the folder he'd created after Janice's announcement. He dreaded having to go through all this again, but now that he was faced with it, it didn't feel so horrible.

"So, this is the contract Janice had. I figured we could start there." He handed Rowan a clean copy and a pen. "For changes."

"Changes?"

"Well, we already agreed that you can't be the primary daytime caregiver right now, so let's figure out what will and won't work for you."

Because Jordy's lawyer was thorough—and because Jordy had what Emma called "control-freak tendencies"—the contract was specific about what household chores were and weren't part of the job.

"There's a clause stating that I'm only responsible for curbing the garbage when you're not in the house?"

"What, you want the job full-time?"

"No, no. Just wasn't expecting this level of detail."

Jordy shrugged. "I want you to not hate me and quit in a huff because I asked too much or I'm not clear about what I need."

Rowan hummed and kept reading.

Half an hour later, they had finished making all the changes, including a tense battle over salary. Rowan refused to take the full amount Janice had earned since he didn't have her experience and wouldn't be doing the full job, and Jordy refused to cut the percentage down to his suggested fifty. That was a ridiculous lowball for the time and energy, no matter how much Rowan would save on housing costs. Jordy only won in the end by pointing out that it was a short-term gig and Rowan was saving him a lot of stress and worry over the coming months.

"Great." Jordy snapped pictures and forwarded them to Gem so she could make the changes and send the new contract their way. "She'll probably send it in the morning. I don't have anything scheduled tomorrow except for my workout, and I've already arranged for Kaira to visit with Adrianna—uh, my teammate's wife. So you're off the hook for another twenty-four hours at least. We can figure out the rest of the week after things are signed."

Rowan nodded. "Right."

They sat in growing silence. It struck Jordy then that, for the first time since meeting him, he wasn't sure what to do in Rowan's presence. There'd always been a task to do or a child to mind. For the first time, they had neither. They were also stuck in a limbo state where their relationship was anything but defined.

"Well, since you're technically not my employee, I have absolutely no say in what you do right now. I'm going to grab a drink and find something to watch on TV. You're welcome to join, but I won't be offended if you call it a night or go out for the evening."

Rowan chewed his lip, then shrugged. "I wouldn't say no to another one of those pineapple drinks."

Jordy pulled a face and showed Rowan where to find more of the vile things, and decided not to question why he was so relieved to have the continued company. The week had been long, and tonight was not a night for dental explorations of gift horses.

IT TURNED out that Jordy and Kaira's summertime routine was pretty loose, apart from restrictions on TV time and a formula to keep bedtime going smoothly. Jordy said he mostly tried to go with the flow during the day and get as much fun time with his daughter as he could. But as August was winding down, the schedule became more complicated.

Jordy hadn't been lying when he told Rowan he could lay out his schedule for the next several months. He sent Rowan a digital calendar with all of his NHL-related commitments filled in from now until June.

"Not all of them," Jordy said ruefully. "Some of the charitable stuff isn't firmed up yet. And of course it's not like stuff can't change."

"Like rescheduling a game?" The idea of one's adult life being so regimented was a bit daunting.

"Nah, well, not unless one has to get canceled because of weather or something. More like, if I have to miss a game, or if something happens so they want to book another interview." He shrugged. "But those are pretty minor. The out-of-town stuff isn't likely to change."

Rowan had linked Jordy's calendar to his own so he could figure out how their schedules combined. Then he promptly took over conservatorship of the family calendar in the kitchen.

Using whiteboard markers, Rowan blocked out of all Jordy's work commitments in Shield blue and then used the red to mark in his own work schedule. By some miracle, the conflicts were minimal, and most of them had easy enough Kaira workarounds for the next few weeks. Once the school year started, it would be even easier.

For the first few days, they lucked out. Jordy was mostly around when Rowan was, so Rowan didn't have a lot of one-on-one time with Kaira. But their luck ran out, and soon enough Rowan had a day off and Jordy left the house after breakfast with a kiss goodbye for Kaira and a reminder that he wouldn't be back until after dinner.

Rowan and Kaira eyed each other in the silent entryway. He wondered if she was also questioning all her life choices that had led to this moment.

"Can we watch *Puppy Pals*?"

"Uh, I don't think after breakfast is a good time for TV," Rowan said, mostly confident thanks to Jordy's set routines around TV usage.

"Fine," Kaira sighed, like she couldn't believe she had to deal with such ridiculous limitations on her free time but was willing to go along to get along. "What can we do, then?"

"Uh," Rowan repeated. "Well. What would you like to do?"

"I don't know. That's why I asked you."

Right. Point. This was so much easier at the library, where he had a specific program to deliver, often developed by someone else. "Well, do you want to play something at home? Or do you want to leave the house for an adventure?"

Kaira carefully considered these two options and the rain falling outside. "Stay home."

"Great. Do you wanna make something or play something?"

A few questions—and a lot of hemming and hawing—later, they ended up in the kitchen.

Thanks to contributions from Rowan's former kitchen, they had everything they needed to make nankhatai. The cookies were simple to make, which made them simple and an appropriate task for a six-year-old.

Kaira was clearly used to baking or cooking with someone, because she pulled out a stepstool and set it up at the counter and then pulled two aprons out of a drawer in the butler.

"You can wear this one," she said and handed over a black apron. "It's Daddy's."

Rowan shook it open and nearly choked on his own spit. The plain black apron's center bib was adorned with simple white text that read *Kitchen Daddy*.

"Thank you, Kaira. Where did Daddy get this cool apron?"

Kaira slipped her own apron over her head—it was pink and unicorn themed—and blinked up at him. "Auntie Emma gave it to him after she visited. She says everyone should have an apron so they don't get their clothes dirty."

"I see." He wouldn't laugh. "Are you sure he won't mind me borrowing such a great gift?"

Kaira nodded. "Yes. Daddy says aprons are made to be used and that he wants to use that one so much it gets ruined and has to be replaced."

"I bet he does," Rowan strangled out as he busied himself with putting the apron on and avoiding eye contact with a guileless child.

Once they were both suitably attired, Rowan located bowls and measuring cups and Kaira clambered up onto her step stool to help.

Rowan measured out the sugar and ghee, but gladly gave in to Kaira's demands to help and let her dump them into the bowl. He let her start the mixing process but figured he'd have to finish up to make sure it was smooth.

"What are we making?" she asked as she flailed the spoon around the bowl.

"Nankhatai. Cookies," he tacked on, since he doubted she'd heard of this treat before.

Kaira frowned at the bowl and mumbled, "Nankhatai," as if testing out the word.

"My nani used to make them for me all the time," he told her. "Nani lived in Canada for a long time, but she was born in Pakistan, which is where she learned how to make these."

"Is that far away?"

"Very. It's on the other side of the world. You have to fly for almost a day to get there from here."

Her hand stopped moving and she looked up at him very seriously. "Is it close to India?"

Rowan blinked in surprise. He hadn't expected her to have that good a grasp on world geography. "Right next door. Actually, they were once part of the same country." A vast oversimplification of thousands of years of culture and history, but Rowan didn't think Kaira was old enough for a full geopolitical breakdown of desi politics.

"So it's kinda the same as India?"

Another vast oversimplification, but…. "Kind of, like Canada and the US are similar."

"Oh." Kaira considered the bowl in front of her, then turned to Rowan and said, "Daddy says my birth daddy is Indian."

"Oh." There was a lot to unpack there. Like that Kaira had a birth father or that he might not be white. "Do you, um, get to spend time with your birth dad?" seemed like a safe question to start with.

"No. Daddy says that *he* wanted a baby so bad that Auntie Emma had a miracle baby. Auntie Emma got to give me to Daddy like a present, but she needed my birth daddy to help make me, but he couldn't be a daddy yet. So I don't know him, but my dada and dadi send me birthday presents. And Daddy says I should get to do and see as much Indian stuff as I want, because it's part of my hair-ee-tage."

And Rowan thought the "birth daddy" comment was a lot to process. Apparently she was also in touch with her birth father's parents.

"Well, then, you are in luck. Because nankhatai cookies are made in India too. I bet your dada and dadi know all about them."

"They are?" Kaira stared up at him, wide-eyed.

"Yup, they are. A real desi treat."

Rowan had taken over the mixing of the sugar and butter during the conversation, since Kaira was thoroughly distracted, and it was now ready for the next step.

Kaira was now laser focused as Rowan walked her through adding the flour and semolina and mixing it together with their hands.

It was hard to tell which she liked more—the hand mixing or the shaping of the cookies—but by the time they reached the baking stage, her interest had waned. Considering she'd been occupied for a good half hour, Rowan wasn't surprised.

Rowan placed the cookie sheets in the oven and set a timer for twenty minutes. "So, what are we going to do while we wait for cookies?"

The answer, apparently, was go to Kaira's bedroom to see the lehengas hanging in her closet, all presents from her biological grandparents. "This one is my favorite," she said, petting a pink-and-yellow skirt with a glittering hem.

By the time Jordy got home, Kaira was fed and chill and she and Rowan were cuddled up on the couch watching one of her favorite movies. Apparently she and Jordy had an obsession with Bollywood romances.

"Hey, you two," Jordy said from the den doorway. He was leaning against the frame, arms crossed in an unfairly attractive way. "What are you up to?"

"Showing Rowan the best movie ever! Daddy, did you know that Rowan's grandpa comes from the same place as my birth daddy?" She bounced in her seat, all wide-eyed innocence.

"I did not know that," Jordy said with a raised eyebrow at Rowan.

"Three of my four grandparents are Pakistani," he supplied. "We talked about how that's next to India and a lot the same."

"Ah." Jordy didn't look bothered by the fact that Kaira had told Rowan all about her parentage. In fact, a small smile was tugging at his lips as he headed over to the couch. "So you two have been bonding."

"Yes! Rowan and I made nankhatai—they're Indian cookies—and we ate them with chai."

"Because we're not heathens," Rowan agreed.

"Yeah, we ate them right. And now we're watching *K3G* because Rowan has never seen it!" She snuggled into her dad and got reabsorbed in the movie as a dance number started.

"A true tragedy, I know," Rowan said in an undertone to Jordy. "I could have been enjoying this English-dubbed genius ages ago."

Jordy chuckled. "She's a bit too young for the subtitles, unfortunately, and neither of us speaks Hindi." That would make pronouncing the movie's full title—*Kabhi Khushi Kabhie Gham*—particularly challenging for a six-year-old. No wonder she called it by a nickname.

"Alas, me neither. Which is why I don't watch much Bollywood."

"Ah," Jordy said. He was watching Rowan with that look that said he wanted to ask and wasn't sure if he could. Rowan decided to rescue him.

"I only speak Urdu and English. And also Latin, though admittedly there isn't a lot of listening or speaking called for with that one."

Jordy stared at him. "Latin?"

Rowan shrugged. "I did mention my private-school-and-nanny upbringing, right?"

"So you learned Latin in elementary school in the twenty-first century?"

"What can I say? I was a weird kid."

Jordy chuckled, and damn, that was unfairly hot. "Noted."

Once the film was over, Jordy scooped up Kaira and left to run the bedtime routine, so Rowan got a jump on cleaning up after their day.

He was throwing the last of the toys into the toy box when Jordy reappeared.

"Must have been a good day. She went out like a light," Jordy said as he slouched onto the couch. "Good job tiring her out."

"Ha, thanks. I think it was a mutual tiring, to be honest."

Jordy laughed. "Welcome to life with a six-year-old." He waved the remote at Rowan. "Wanna see what's on TV?"

"Sure. Just maybe no badly dubbed musicals?"

"Well, you've really tied my hands here, Rowan, but if you insist."

Jordy turned on the TV and picked cable. Rowan couldn't remember the last time he'd watched live TV. He wasn't aware anyone under thirty even *had* cable.

"How does *CSI: Toronto* sound?"

"Um, like a cheesy spinoff of a cheesy spinoff of a cheesy show?"

"Right," Jordy drawled, "but do you wanna watch it?"

Rowan shrugged. "I've never seen it, but I'm not against crime procedurals."

"Crime Procedural Spinoff it is, then." Jordy winked and clicked on the show, and as the characters swanned about collecting clues, Rowan realized he couldn't wipe away his smile.

ROWAN DIDN'T know what he expected from life at the Shaw residence, but this wasn't it.

His general experience with people in Jordy's tax bracket was that they handed off as much work as they could to hired help and had cold, sterile homes. In contrast, Jordy was a hands-on dad who didn't expect a perfectly kept house. He liked to let Kaira do things for herself, even if that meant they didn't get done perfectly—too much toothpaste on the toothbrush, missing a few Cheerios when sweeping up spilled breakfast cereal, dressing in an outfit even a rodeo clown wouldn't touch.

But even if Jordy wasn't your typical rich dad, the house did have the trappings—the full nanny suite, for example, and the butler kitchen.

And, most distressingly, the pool.

In theory, the pool was great. In practice….

"*Please* come swimming with us," Kaira begged. She was already decked out in pink-and-yellow polka dots and a lime-green sun hat. "It'll be fun! You have a bathing suit, right? If you don't, you can borrow one of my daddy's!"

"I have a bathing suit," Rowan promised. He absolutely wanted to get into Jordy's pants, but not like that.

"Yes!" Kaira whooped. "Okay, we'll be in the pool. Bye!"

"Not until I get there," Jordy yelled back over his shoulder as her bare feet slapped against the patio tile.

Kaira had already stopped at the edge of the patio, six feet from the pool's edge, and sat down on a chaise longue. "I know, Daddy!"

Jordy turned his body so he could see her. "You don't have to," he told Rowan. "She's got to get used to you saying no to her sometime."

"It's thirty degrees outside and more humid than a bowl of soup," Rowan said. He would love to get out of the house and get some exercise, but he wasn't playing Ultimate in this. "Swimming sounds great."

And it did. Truly. Rowan went down to his bedroom, put on his suit, grabbed a beach towel from the linen closet, and went outside, thinking of nothing more than getting some much-needed exercise in this heat wave.

And then the heat wave attacked him personally.

Rowan was just innocently leaving the house, sliding the patio door closed behind him and shifting from foot to foot to keep the hot pavement from burning his soles. But he was still only two meters from the house when all the breath whooshed out of his lungs.

It wasn't like he'd forgotten Jordy was attractive. Rowan had seen him sleep-rumpled and scruffy before his morning shave, sweaty from his home gym workouts, and dressed to the nines in an actual tuxedo, and somehow he had never had to excuse himself to ice his crotch.

Unfortunately, none of that prepared him for Jordy crouching half-naked in waist-deep water as his daughter scrambled onto his shoulders, only for him to push up suddenly to his full height, tanned muscles glistening as water cascaded down his body, and launch a squealing Kaira several feet through the air. Rowan assumed she splashed down safely in the pool, but she might as well have achieved orbit for all he knew. He couldn't tear his eyes away from Jordy—from the triangular patch of hair between Jordy's collarbones and his nipples, or the smaller diamond-shaped one below his navel, or the definition in his chest, or the extremely generous curve of his ass.

Merciful gods. He might have whimpered.

Then Jordy turned toward him, absolutely *beaming* as Kaira dog-paddled back toward him and clung to his arm. "Rowan! Come on in, the water's great."

Rowan was having an out-of-body experience. At least, he thought hysterically as Kaira's spirited climbing of her father almost resulted in a wardrobe malfunction, he'd had the foresight to carry his towel in front of him.

Clinging to the tattered remains of his composure, he picked his way across the hot cement, dropped his towel on a lounge chair near the diving board, and cannonballed into the water. With any luck, the cool water would keep him from embarrassing himself.

It worked, mostly. Having a six-year-old chaperone-slash-dictator didn't hurt either. Kaira kept them both busy throwing, if not herself (Jordy), then rings onto the bottom of the shallow end for her to retrieve (Rowan). She cajoled them into racing, and Rowan lost spectacularly. She wanted to show off her handstand technique, which was admittedly impressive, though she had the advantage of the water holding up 90 percent of her body weight.

Finally Kaira's energy waned and she dragged a butterfly-shaped floatie into the pool to lounge on. Between the sun and the water and the tremendous energy Rowan was expending restraining himself from licking Jordy all over, he was pretty zonked too and was considering an early afternoon nap.

So of course, before he could make any kind of escape, Jordy turned those beautiful brown eyes on Rowan, smiled, and said, "Can I ask you something?"

Rowan knew he must have heatstroke, because the first thing that popped into his mind was *yes I bottom*, but he managed to say, "I'm an open book" instead, like a semi normal person.

Jordy pillowed his head on his hands on the side of the pool and asked, "Why a librarian?"

It was an innocent question, on the surface. Rowan had heard it enough times from his parents, laced with derision and scorn, so he normally had an instinctive gut-punch reaction. But Rowan felt the weight of Jordy's gaze on him like the heat of the sun, and that light was pure warmth and curiosity.

Oh yeah. Definitely heatstroke.

Rowan skimmed his fingers across the surface of the water. "I usually tell people I'm a nerd who likes learning and organizing."

Jordy hummed and turned himself over, supporting himself with his arms on the sides of the pool and his chest up to catch the sun, as if he were a giant solar panel. "But that's not what you're going to tell me?"

Rowan glanced at Kaira—now wearing her towel like a cape in the pergola and drawing sidewalk-chalk rainbows—and then back to Jordy. "My first friends were books," he said finally, voice lowered. "We had a big house and no close neighbors, and my parents weren't all that interested in spending time with me, so… I guess that's where it started." He paused, feeling a little too bare under Jordy's assessing gaze. "I am actually a nerd who likes learning and organizing, though. I, uh—I guess people don't ask you why you became a professional hockey player?"

"Not when they actually want to know the answer." He shook his head, and a lock of damp blond hair fell artistically over one eye. Rowan bit down on the urge to brush it aside. "Everyone assumes it's the money or the fame. The standard PR answer is that we just love the game, and who wouldn't want to play it forever?"

Rowan licked his lips. "So what's the real answer?"

"I like playing, of course, but one of my favorite parts is being on a team, being part of something. Working with others to create something and being around a team all the time? It's good." He shrugged as if it was no big deal and not terribly adorable that his favorite part of his job was hanging out with his friends. Pink tinged his cheeks, and Rowan didn't think it was from the sun.

"So always the family man, huh?" Rowan joked.

Jordy rubbed his nape and shrugged. "I guess so. I've got three younger sisters, so chaos and people were kind of a fact of my childhood."

"Kinda the opposite of mine. So I guess the single dad thing is maybe not a surprise, then?" he asked tentatively.

"Yeah, maybe not." A helpless smile spread across his face as he watched Kaira coloring.

Rowan cleared his throat, suddenly unable to keep his questions to himself. "So, she mentioned the other day that she's adopted and biologically your sister's. I wasn't prying or anything, but I hope it's okay that—"

"Rowan, I've never wanted or tried to hide where she came from," Jordy said gently. "Sanna and I broke up because we wanted different things. So when my sister got pregnant right around the time we started the divorce process, it felt like more than just a sign. She was also still in high school."

"She's lucky she had such an awesome brother, then."

"I'm the lucky one. Kaira is the best thing that ever happened to me." The sincerity in his voice, the affection on his face, arrested Rowan's tongue. This effortlessly hot-like-burning man had a loving heart that only made him sexier. Rowan needed to get out of this pool before he offered to bend over or drop to his knees.

IN THE week that followed, one thing became clear to Rowan—either he was an idiot or he had a previously unrecognized masochistic streak. Living with Jordy Shaw was just about the dumbest idea he'd ever had, and not because the Shaws made for bad housemates or the job or pay was unlikeable. No, the problem was the opposite. Living with Jordy and Kaira was shockingly *nice*.

Sharing living space just kept being easy. Between the library and Kaira, Rowan wasn't exactly chafing at the quiet, predictable routine of Jordy's household. In fact, the early nights and quiet neighborhood were a blessing. And when it came to chores, Jordy and Rowan had fairly complementary skills and preferences. Rowan enjoyed cooking, more so now that he had a kitchen worth writing home about, and although Jordy was a decent cook, for practical reasons he preferred cleanup. Rowan never minded hoovering, but Jordy hated it as much as Rowan abhorred folding laundry.

But like any life change, this one had a few growing pains. Jordy sometimes forgot Rowan didn't know everything Janice knew, and Rowan found it hard to not feel like a guest. Not to mention that he wasn't used to living with other people—certainly not people who were six years old and under four feet tall.

Setting boundaries was a whole other beast when the other person didn't have an adult's understanding of what they were or the reasons for setting them. Also when you didn't fully want to set boundaries because the munchkin was so cute with their big brown eyes as they begged you to join them for breakfast.

Honestly, Rowan hadn't known he'd enjoy so much domesticity.

Not everything was sunshine and unicorns. All the innocent family time was counterpointed against the absolute torture that was being in close quarters with someone so delicious and so out of reach. Living with Jordy meant seeing him bed-rumpled and grumpy before coffee or sweaty and flushed after a workout. The first time he ran into Jordy as he left his home gym, his skin glistening and his cheeks flushed, Rowan's knees almost buckled with the desire to lick Jordy everywhere.

Jordy blinked obliviously at Rowan, took one AirPod out, and said, "Hey, I didn't hear you come in. Kaira is out with Clement still but should be home for dinner. Meet you in the kitchen in twenty?"

"Uh, yeah." Rowan waited for Jordy to nod and head upstairs, and then he dashed to his apartment. He had twenty minutes to solve the urgent issue in his pants and clean up the evidence.

Living with Jordy was doing wonders for his libido, not so much for getting his daily eight hours. Because another one of Jordy's maddening habits? Inviting Rowan to join him on the couch in the evenings as he watched another documentary… or *CSI: Toronto*. Jordy had a totally endearing love of weird documentaries and seemed to be on a mission to watch every single one posted to Netflix. Rowan couldn't decide what part of the whole situation was more attractive—the way he paid such close attention to everyone, making commentary to Rowan as they watched, or his habit of lounging on the couch in soft-looking sweats, occasionally knocking his knees or feet against Rowan's.

On his sixth night at Jordy's, Rowan lay in a puddle on his stupidly comfortable borrowed bed, his orgasm still buzzing through his limbs, and stared up at the ceiling with fatalistic dismay. It was a toss-up, really, what would break first—his dick, his composure, or his vibrator.

ASKING ROWAN to move in with them was the best impulse move Jordy had ever made. Rowan was amazing with Kaira, and he brought stability into their lives that they wouldn't otherwise have after Janice's abrupt departure.

Which meant that when Jordy left for a day of meetings and practice, he didn't worry about having to leave his phone in his bag for several hours.

"How's Kaira?" Sully asked. They stood side by side on the ice, tucked out of the way against the boards, watching Coach run the offense drill with the second-line D. "She doing okay with the nanny swap?"

Jordy had called Sully in a panic the day Janice gave notice, and Sully had promised he and Adrianna would have Jordy's back. He'd told them he found a temporary replacement, which would ease the burden on him and Adrianna tremendously, but he hadn't given a whole lot of detail.

"She's great. She adores Rowan. Don't tell Janice, but she might like him better." Kaira didn't really, but Rowan was the shiny new toy, and she was clearly enamored.

"Rowan. Rowan," Sully said slowly. "Wait, wasn't that the name of the snack you brought to that charity thing last month?"

Sometimes Jordy regretted having a friend with such a good memory. "Please don't reduce my daughter's new nanny to a quick bite."

Sully hooted, but quietly enough not to attract attention. "It is! Shaw, you cliché. Are you going to woo the nanny? Seduce him after the kid's gone to bed?" He gasped theatrically. "Or have you done it already?"

Jordy rolled his eyes. Sully knew better. "You caught me. Pressuring the guy who now lives at my house—because he became suddenly homeless after finding black mold, mind you—to sleep with me is definitely my style."

"Yes, we all know you're too much of a goody-two-shoes. But come on, your life is a Hallmark movie and I want to watch it." He tucked his stick under his arm so he could bring his mitts together in prayer. "Please, Jordy?"

"I'm not going to live my life to act out your weird romcom fantasy."

"What about for Adrianna? Or Rowan? What if he wants to star in his own Harlequin? Have you asked him? Maybe he wants to play house and make you dinner and get bent over—"

"Sullivan, Shaw, get over here!"

Saved by the bellow.

Jordy skated off, ignoring Sully's disappointed huff.

He managed to put his home life completely out of mind and focus on his job all afternoon, and he didn't think about Rowan and Kaira or how their day was progressing until he was back in the locker room, gathering his stuff.

He blinked down at his phone to see the dozen new messages from Rowan. While they guy liked to talk, he usually didn't inundate Jordy with updates.

The most recent was still popped up in his notifications. *Please tell me you're home soon.* Jordy swallowed back his initial panicked thoughts. Maybe Rowan was passing along an excited message from Kaira, who wanted to share about her day. There was no reason to worry.

He opened his chat with Rowan and scrolled up.

Kaira is mad at me and I don't know what I did wrong.

Okay, now she's really mad. Help?

Jordy grabbed his bag, flung it over his shoulder, and headed out, eyes glued to his phone.

Oh god there are tears. What do I do?

Seriously Jordy

She's lying facedown on the carpet and refusing to move

She won't eat lunch no matter what I make

But is it worth crying over spilled juice?

That text was followed by a picture of dark red juice all over the floor. It resembled a bloodbath scene in a film with comically bad effects.

She's in her room sobbing

Jordy you need to come home

She hates me

Everything is horrible

I don't know what to do

Please tell me you're home soon

Jordy hopped into his car, turned it on, and was about to put it in gear when he thought to text a quick *On my way.*

When he opened the door from the garage, the first thing to greet him was the sound of hysterical sobbing and yells of "I want my daddy!"

"He's on his way, poppet," Rowan wheedled, sounding teary himself.

Well, fuck.

Despite knowing that Kaira was perfectly safe, Jordy couldn't slow his rabbiting heart or hurried strides into the den, even if he wanted to. The sight that greeted him hurt his heart. Kaira stood crying in the middle of the room, clutching her stuffed armadillo and staying out of reach of Rowan, who sat dejected and miserable on the couch, still reaching out for her despite her clear *fuck-off* body language.

"Daddy!" Kaira cried when he stepped through the door, and Jordy crouched down and pulled her into his arms. "Daddy, I missed you!" She burrowed in as if she could actually climb into him for safety and warmth.

"Shh, peanut," he murmured into her hair. "Did you have a rough day?"

Kaira hiccupped and clung tighter.

Jordy shushed her and rubbed her back. When he looked up and caught Rowan's eye, he suddenly felt like he should be giving Rowan the same treatment. He sat with slumped shoulders and tugged at his shirt, thousand-yard-staring at the wall while worrying at his lip.

"Hey," Jordy said softly.

Rowan's eyes snapped to his.

"You need a break. Go have some of that disgusting water of yours, maybe grab something to eat or go listen to music or whatever you need to decompress. I'm going to put this one to bed."

It was a little early for bedtime, but Jordy was pretty sure nothing would salvage this day for Kaira. She needed a hard reset, which would only come from a solid ten hours of sleep.

The bedtime routine took longer than usual since Kaira was extra clingy, but she finally passed out halfway through the second reading of her third book, and Jordy gently extricated himself from her octopus arms, kissed her good night one last time, and crept out of her room.

He found Rowan in the kitchen, slumped over at the breakfast bar with his head in his hands.

Jordy grabbed a water from the fridge, and Rowan's head shot up.

"I'm so sorry," Rowan said, voice rough. "You must hate me. She hates me. This was a horrible idea—"

"Woah." That train of thought needed to hit the emergency brakes. "Kaira doesn't hate you, and this wasn't a terrible idea."

"Jordy, did you not see the texts? They're a pretty good chronicle of why this was a bad idea."

"No, they are a chronicle of a very bad *day*—a thing that children have, just like adults, because they're people."

"Jordy, she hates me."

Jordy blew out a slow breath. Rowan might be used to children, but he wasn't used to living with one. "Why don't you tell me what happened?"

Rowan threw up his hands dramatically. "As you know, she was totally fine this morning until you left, and then everything I did was wrong."

"Okay. Like what?"

"Like I couldn't feed her."

"So you forgot where the kitchen was?" Jordy prodded, because he needed Rowan to get over his drama and start answering the questions.

"She asked for Cheerios, but I poured the milk wrong, so she wouldn't eat them. So I made her toast, but the jam was all wrong." Rowan tugged at his hair.

Jordy raised an eyebrow but didn't point out that Kaira was not picky in the slightest about either of those things. He didn't think hearing that there was no secret milk or jam rule would comfort Rowan right now. "Then what?"

"Then we tried to color, but I kept picking the wrong colors, so we switched to My Little Ponies, but apparently I don't know the correct way of moving around horses. She wanted to watch TV, but I said no because you always say no to morning television, and she stomped off to her room." Rowan huffed and looked up at Jordy with wide, distraught eyes. "Is it bad I was almost grateful for her self-imposed isolation?"

"Definitely not." Jordy would have been equally relieved. "I'm guessing lunch was just like breakfast."

"Yeah. I made her sandwich wrong and cut the carrots wrong and then gave her the wrong juice."

"Is that what ended up on the floor?"

"She threw it," Rowan said bleakly.

Jordy winced. "What did you do?"

"Sent her to her room. Then cried about it."

"No kidding. I probably would have too."

Rowan shook his head. "You probably wouldn't have ended up in this situation to begin with. She loves you and you know what she likes."

"She likes," Jordy said slowly, "raspberry fruit juice. The one she threw on the floor? It's her favorite. Trust me, that wasn't about the juice."

"Okay, maybe not, but everything else."

"Rowan, it was a bad day. They happen to kids too. Only when you're six, your emotions are bigger than your body, and your brain can't regulate them. Sometimes when a kid wakes up on the wrong side of the bed, they stay that way, and there's nothing you can do about it." He shrugged. True, today sounded especially bad—Jordy hadn't seen one like it in a while—but given all the changes in Kaira's life recently, one day of regression wasn't too surprising.

"Okay, fine, so she was grumpy, but you could've done something. You did do something."

"Sure, but if I'd been here all day, I wouldn't have been much of a magical cure. Or maybe we would have sat and cuddled all day. Who knows? But the fact that she wanted her dad doesn't change the fact that she was being an irrational six-year-old who was also kind of a dick all day."

Rowan barked a surprised laugh. "Can you call her that?"

Jordy shrugged. "Who's gonna tell me I can't, her dad?"

That got another short laugh, and Rowan dry-washed his face. "Okay, I concede that maybe I didn't completely fail at looking after her today. But that doesn't mean this isn't a terrible idea. I fell apart in the face of rage-filled child."

Forcing himself to approach this logically, Jordy considered what he knew of the day so far. "Did you yell at her?"

"What?"

"When she threw juice all over the floor and you sent her to her room. Did you yell at her? Strike her?"

"No!" Rowan looked horrified. "Of course not. I'm not a monster. I just told her to go and then had a *quiet* meltdown."

"So my child was a total hellion today, and you were patient enough to make her two breakfasts *and* lunches, you kept trying to play with her despite her constant criticism, and you didn't take the easy road and turn on the TV because you wanted to respect the boundaries I've established." Though honestly, after today, Jordy wouldn't have been upset about it if Rowan had put the TV on. Sometimes you did what you had to. But Kaira probably would've thought Bluey was too blue today anyway. "You kept your cool. You didn't yell or scare her." Jordy cocked his head and said gently, "I'm not sure anyone could have handled it better. From where I'm sitting, it looks like you managed remarkably well for someone who's never lived with a six-year-old before."

"Not yelling at a kid is not a medal-worthy achievement," Rowan protested.

Jordy hooted. He didn't want to be mean, but—"Says the guy who's never lived with a two-year-old. Or a four-year-old. Did you know that stage is called the Fucking Fours?"

Rowan laughed too—another point for Jordy. "No. Seriously?"

"Oh yeah. It's like the Terrible Twos but with more vocabulary and sass. I've never felt more judged in my life, and my job involves regular performance reviews from journalists and all of Twitter."

"Wow." Rowan wiped his face again and sighed. "Okay, so maybe a day spent with an unhappy kid made me a *tad* melodramatic."

"Hmm."

"Oh shut up. She threw her juice on the floor."

"Yeah, I'll give you that one as being especially bad." Jordy winced again, then figured he might as well throw himself under the bus for Rowan's sake. "I should have seen today coming, honestly. Not exactly this, but I should have realized things were going too smoothly and braced us for some bad days or some regression. It's pretty common for kids to react to changes by acting younger or wanting to do 'babyish' things. So being a brat and demanding her dad even though she knows he can't come home? Not exactly out of left field."

Rowan slumped. "So what you're saying is that there will be more days like this."

"Not necessarily. This might be it. Or she might spend a day asking to cuddle or be carried. Last year, after my season ended and I was home more, she carried her armadillo around everywhere for a week and sucked her thumb."

"That just sounds fucking adorable. I'll take that next time."

"If only we got to choose. Chaos and unpredictability are the only constants of parenthood."

"So, get used to it?"

"Well, I wasn't going to say it quite like that…."

"Har har. Those of us who didn't get yelled at all day don't get to be mean."

"What exactly do you *think* happens to me at a practice?"

"Oh, fuck off," Rowan said, but it lacked any heat. In fact, Jordy would say he sounded fond.

Warmth filled Jordy's chest, and he smiled. "Come on. Let's go sit on the couch and watch some of your bad TV, and you can tell me what you like on your pizza."

"Pizza?"

"Yes. I'm ordering because you've done enough meal prep. Unless you'd rather something else? It doesn't have to be pizza." Jordy settled onto the couch and tossed Rowan the remote. "So, what's it going to be?"

By the time the pizza arrived, Rowan had found an episode of *CSI: Toronto* and snuggled under a throw blanket. His muscles were slowly relaxing, and he looked kind of adorable curled up in the corner of the sectional. Especially when his nose wrinkled every time the TV showed anything gross.

It wasn't a bad way to end the day, regardless of the way things started. Jordy could get used to this.

ROWAN STUMBLED out of his room the next morning in search of caffeine. He'd fallen in love with Jordy's stupidly expensive pour-over set and would grieve its loss once he inevitably moved out.

Gem liked to mock of him for his un-English morning routine, but Rowan figured his Canadian genes must be responsible for his coffee taste, because he refused to start the day with anything but a properly brewed cup.

Five minutes later, he sat at the kitchen table, nursing a cup of coffee and noodling around on his phone, when soft feet shuffled into the kitchen.

An adorable sleep-rumpled Kaira wandered in, rubbing her eyes. She paused in the doorway when she caught sight of him, her eyes wide. Rowan held his breath and prayed not everything was ruined after yesterday's disaster. What if she still hated him? What if she threw another fit?

Kaira broke the stalemate when she shuffled enthusiastically in his direction and crawled into his lap. Or attempted to. Rowan did most of the heavy lifting to make that happen, as her limbs were clearly still sleepy. Thankfully, they managed to get her arranged in his lap without any disastrously placed elbows or knees.

Once she'd curled up under his chin, the last of yesterday's tension melted away and relief and affection filled Rowan's chest. He murmured into her hair, "Good morning, poppet."

Kaira hummed and snuggled closer. The sharp contrast to her usual behavior surprised him—he'd never seen her so quiet or so snuggly—but since she didn't look upset, he figured he should take advantage while it lasted.

Fifteen minutes later, he was glad he had. She was wiggling in his lap and chattering away as if she'd absorbed his caffeine through osmosis, clearly having left all of yesterday's grumpiness in the past.

"Why do you sound different from other people?"

"I grew up in England. It's another country."

"Does everyone in England sound like you?"

"Sort of. Some people do." Rowan wasn't sure how to explain regional accents to a six-year-old.

"Do you like pancakes?"

"Yes?"

"Daddy makes the best pancakes. We should ask him to make some."

"Maybe when he gets up."

"He probably went to the gym. He goes really early." She swung her legs, little heels bumping against his shins. "Do you like to make sand castles?"

Rowan blinked. "I'm not sure I've ever built one." His parents hadn't been keen on beach vacations, at least not with their kid in tow.

Kaira stilled and stared at Rowan with eyes wide and mouth open. "*Never?*" Clearly Rowan had committed a faux pas. "Sand castles are the best! We should go to the beach and build one. Daddy can show you how."

"What am I showing now?" Jordy strolled into the room dressed for the gym in an Under Armour T-shirt and shorts that strained around his thighs and biceps. Had Jordy bulked up recently? If clothes could talk, these would probably beg for mercy.

"Sand castles! Rowan never made sand castles at the beach! His daddy didn't show him how, so we should show him. Can we take Rowan to the beach?"

Jordy headed to the fridge to grab a bottle of Gatorade. "It's getting a bit late in the year for a trip to the beach, peanut. Rowan and I will keep an eye on the weather and our schedules, and if we can, we'll go, but Rowan's sand castle education might have to wait until next year."

Kaira squirmed in Rowan's lap. "He could come with us to Curaçao!"

Fortunately Rowan wasn't drinking at that point—he'd run out of coffee, alas—so he didn't choke at the suggestion that Jordy take him on a family vacation.

Jordy was midgulp with his Gatorade and somehow didn't choke. He just pulled the bottle away, wiped his mouth, and tilted his head as if considering Kaira's suggestion. As if it wasn't insane to invite Rowan on a family vacation after a week of cohabitation. "Hm. Maybe. But next summer is a long way off, so it's too soon to make plans. Lots of stuff could happen between now and then."

Kaira looked doubtful. "Like what?"

"Well, Rowan might have another job or make different summer plans, or we might not go to Curaçao again." Kaira's whole body drooped, as if she'd never even considered any of these devastating possibilities. "Or you might decide you hate sand and swimming and castles and you never want to see any of them again."

"Daddy!" Kaira shrieked, animated again and outraged at the sheer ridiculousness of her dad's suggestion. "I would never not wanna swim. Daddy, everyone loves castles and sand." She squirmed out of Rowan's lap to wrap herself around Jordy's leg.

Rowan's attention swung from the total adorableness of the sight and the love and trust between parent and child to how much larger Jordy's thighs looked juxtaposed with a near-toddler.

Maybe before Jordy's work season really started, Rowan should go out and get railed so he could burn off some of the fire Jordy's everything kept stoking.

Jordy did make pancakes.

"Pizza, then pancakes? I'm pretty sure they aren't athlete dietician approved," Rowan said in an undertone.

Jordy waved this off with a shrug and a small smile. "Eh, I'm a defenseman. I'm supposed to be hard to take down."

Once they were settled at the breakfast table and Kaira was deep into her pancakes, Jordy caught Rowan's eye and said, "So, there's a work thing coming up that we should talk about."

That sounded ominous.

"Basically they're sending me to New York for a couple of days for some media stuff. We're invited to bring our families. They'll keep me busy most of the day, but we have our evenings mostly to ourselves."

"Oh?" That sounded intriguing.

"So the question is, can you, and do you want to, come to New York next month? I'm not expecting an answer right now. I know you probably have to look at a calendar, and I know doing *this* job in another city, in another country, is a whole different ask. Technically I think you'd have to come as a friend, even, because you don't have a work visa for the US. Which is fine, I can hire someone while we're there too, or you and Kaira can stay here. But if you *do* want to come, it'll be for three days, and you'd probably have some support in the form of spouses with kids doing the same thing."

That was a lot to take in. Rowan swallowed a bite of pancake. "Uh, wow. You go to this often?"

"Sometimes. I didn't go last year, but our captain is young this year, so I think the team wants me to bring up the average age."

Rowan snorted. "You say that like you're old."

"Only if you're counting hockey years. Just turned thirty-two last spring, and most guys are done before they do."

Rowan's eyes bugged. "Wait, seriously?"

"Average retirement age is twenty-nine."

"Huh. I guess I figured it would be closer to thirty-five. Most footballers last that long."

Jordy shrugged. "There are outliers, obviously, but hockey is fast and hard, and it's only getting faster and harder"—Rowan's libido perked up and wagged its tail, but he swatted it down with a newspaper—"and the players are getting younger."

"I... picked the wrong profession. I will definitely not be retired in five years." He ate some pancake in consolation.

"True, but you'll probably still have the use of your knees and aren't likely to need surgery to hold your body together before you reach fifty."

"Thanks," Rowan said dryly. "Tell me more silver linings. I need some. At this rate, I'll be so old by the time I've got pensionable earnings that I won't be able to retire before ninety."

Jordy frowned. "Doesn't the library have a pension fund?"

"Yeah, and I pay into it in the hopes of one day collecting from it instead of having to buy it all back, but I'm not full-time or even permanent. I've been working mat leaves for the past two years, and my contract is up in a few weeks and I don't have anything new lined up. I lucked out getting two back-to-back, but the odds of getting a third look slim." Rowan had thought his master's in library science would give him job security. After all, modern society still needed systems of organization. But the waiting and hoping and worrying about not having a permanent job was wearing on him.

"I'm sorry to hear it," Jordy said, and he sounded it. "Was the public library where you were hoping to work?"

Rowan shrugged. "Yes? Maybe? I like working with the kids, the outreach to the community. But I don't know. It would be nice to work somewhere I could use my English lit degree."

"Oh, like at a college?"

"Yeah, maybe," Rowan agreed, reluctant to admit that that was what he wanted in case saying it out loud jinxed it.

Fortunately, before Jordy could attempt further inquiry, Kaira put the conversation out of its misery. "Daddy, do you have to go to work today?"

Jordy swooped down to plant a kiss on her nose. "Afraid so, peanut. You and Rowan have lots of fun without me today, okay?"

Kaira returned the kiss, a gesture so sweet Rowan almost died. "We will."

And, amazingly, they did.

AUGUST SPED by in a blur of intense workouts and summer thunderstorms.

When he was younger, Jordy enjoyed his off-season training. It felt good to push himself, to make himself into the best hockey player he could be. He liked the mind-numbing routine of it—lift this, jump over that, sprint this far, work these ropes.

He still enjoyed all of those things. Part of him suspected that a lot of professional athletes were just people who hated making decisions all the time, and having a trainer tell you what to do was a nice break from that. Bonus if you could get paid the big bucks for it.

But these days, training was getting harder. Jordy's body had been through over a decade of professional hockey, and he could no longer deny the wear and tear on his joints. He could push through that—with proper medical supervision, because Jordy's knees were worth millions of dollars a year—but he was missing out on time with his kid. In just a few weeks, he'd be in the grip of the preseason and Kaira would be starting school full-time.

Who let that happen?

But when he texted the question to Sully, the answer he got was less than sympathetic. *Stop bragging. My kid still shits itself and wakes up screaming every 2 hours.*

Which, okay. Jordy remembered those days. But he'd had Janice's help, so when Jordy needed to be in game shape, the night changings and feedings weren't his problem.

Sully's next message bordered on offensive. *How much do you think I would have to offer your manny to get him to work for me instead?*

Jordy sent him a middle-finger emoji. *Get your own!!!* It wasn't like Sully couldn't afford it.

Besides, Jordy was *used* to Rowan being around the house now. Kaira had loved Janice and still Facetimed with her a couple times a week, but Janice had usually made herself scarce when Jordy was home. Jordy got that. It made sense that she wanted to keep a division between her work life and her home life. But it also meant he'd missed out on the experience of living with another actual adult—someone who didn't go to bed at eight and didn't think *Bluey* was the height of entertainment.

"Don't forget I've got an eight-hour at the library tomorrow," Rowan said as he returned from the kitchen with a board of cheese, fruit, and nuts. If he had complaints about this being the go-to snack food, rather than chips or popcorn or junk, he hadn't mentioned it. He leaned forward to set it on the coffee table as Jordy flicked on *CSI: Toronto*. "And Clement's family is on vacation this week. I can take Kaira with me, but uh…."

Jordy shuddered as he imagined it. Much as he appreciated having Rowan around, the schedule didn't always work out perfectly. Until now they'd always been able to wrangle it, either with Clement's parents' help or with Rowan switching to a later shift at the library or Jordy heading to the gym early so he could be home before Rowan had to leave. "It's fine. There's a day care at my gym."

The charcuterie clattered against the tabletop. "There's a *what*?"

The way he was looking at Jordy right now reminded Jordy of Kaira's face when he told her what bacon was made out of. "Uh, a day care?" Jordy ventured. He was sure he'd mentioned this. "It's not, like, ideal. She gets pretty bored if she has to go more than once a week, especially for three hours." Training was starting to ramp up.

He still wasn't sure what the problem was, but maybe he didn't need to know, because after a few seconds, Rowan just shook his head and popped a piece of cheese in his mouth. "You professional athlete types are so spoiled."

Jordy snorted and helped himself to a handful of almonds. "Of the two of us, who's the one who knew what the backup kitchen was called?"

Rowan snatched the remote off the couch and poked Jordy in the stomach with it. "Excuse me, you're the one who has rooms in his house he doesn't even have names for." He cued the episode to play. "Same terms as last time?"

Whoever correctly guessed the perpetrator first got to choose the snack for the next episode and then laze around on the sofa while the other prepped it. Jordy was basking in his first-ever win. "Obviously."

That was another difference he could get used to. Janice didn't cook for him unless she had to feed Kaira anyway, in which case Jordy still needed to heat up an extra meal from a service or gulp down a protein shake or find another way to consume more calories. Since Jordy was either cleaning up after him or paying someone else to do it, Rowan said the least he could do was make food fit Jordy's nutrition requirements, even if that sometimes meant Jordy ate what everyone else ate and then an extra chicken breast.

"Do you think the CN Tower is paying the show for all this free advertising?" Rowan asked idly at another unnecessary panoramic shot of the Toronto skyline.

Jordy wrinkled his nose. "I don't know. I mean, no one goes there, do they? It's kind of just a reminder. 'Don't forget the show is in Toronto.' Which—"

"Is the most Toronto thing ever?" Rowan finished wryly.

Jordy coughed. "Are you allowed to say that? You live here."

"So do you."

"Yes, but I'm *American*. I'm allowed to make fun of Torontonians."

Rowan gasped theatrically. "I'm telling the internet. Wait till your fanbase finds out. I bet they take you off that billboard."

Jordy popped a piece of cheese into his mouth. "They can't do that," he said smugly. "It's in my contract."

Rowan cackled. "Shut up, it is not. You are not vain enough to put that in there."

Even if he was, he wouldn't have. He got enough attention already. But Rowan didn't have to know that. "My agent did it," he lied. "Sells more jerseys. Gotta get her cut."

NHL players didn't get a cut of the sale of jerseys with their names on them. Rowan didn't have to know that either.

Rowan narrowed his eyes, but he didn't call Jordy on the lie. Instead he nudged him in the side again and said, "I guess you have to pay for all this fancy cheese somehow."

Jordy nodded seriously. "Yes. You've figured me out. It's all about the cheese."

"It's good cheese," Rowan agreed, managing to keep a straight face, but his eyes—brown, warm, and framed by ridiculously long lashes—danced.

Jordy grabbed his own bite, wondering why he suddenly couldn't look away. "I always tell my agent, make sure you get those cheese bonuses."

He might have kept looking—and then who knew what would've happened—but the ad break ended, and Jordy needed to pay attention if he wanted to continue his winning streak. He was highly suspicious of the sister-in-law, but he didn't want to call it too early in case a better suspect presented themself.

"It's totally the sister-in-law," Rowan announced. Damn it.

"What makes you say that?"

"She's totally being shady. She even did a classic 'bad guy lying' eye thing just now."

"I think it's the husband," Jordy said, even though he didn't. For obvious reasons, they couldn't pick the same person.

Rowan scoffed. "The husband is a total red herring. Why else would Ersatz Canadian Catherine think badly of him so quickly? Obviously it's because he's a total douchebag, deserving of her contempt but not actually a murderer."

"Oh, obviously," Jordy agreed with a hint of sarcasm. He agreed with Rowan's assessment, but honest support for their theories wasn't any fun.

"Yes, obviously. Just you wait and see. In fact, I bet they're going to figure out his innocence in this scene."

They did. Two minutes later, the husband was cleared and the crime-fighting characters were looking for new suspects. Jordy was totally losing the bet tonight.

Still, somehow, as Rowan crowed in victory and delight, his body animated and his eyes sparkling, Jordy couldn't muster up his usual disappointment over losing a game. Rowan's glee and pride in victory were too uplifting.

Besides, considering the penalty for losing was more snacks and *CSI* with Rowan, Jordy couldn't be mad about it.

LEAVING THE house without Kaira in the morning felt surprisingly weird. Rowan said goodbye to her and Jordy after breakfast and headed off to the library. So far he'd had a string of half days during which he either dropped her off somewhere or left her after lunch.

Work at the library was odd now too, not just because Rowan's last day was approaching but because he wasn't used to having secrets. Sure, he kept some things hidden, but for the most part, he liked to talk with colleagues. But that felt awkward and taboo right now. Sharing details about his life meant talking about a kid who wasn't his and her famous dad. Rowan wasn't naïve—he knew people might want stories about Jordy and Kaira to feel closer to a professional athlete they thought they knew. So while he'd mentioned moving in with a friend of Gem's who had given him a part-time nanny job and a place to live, Rowan was scant on the details, and Taylor didn't know what to make of a Rowan who didn't share stories about his off-day adventures.

Not that they'd have to navigate the changed dynamic much longer. He had a week left here, and though his boss tried, she'd gently but firmly told him she couldn't make money appear for new staffing positions, no matter how much she wanted to keep him.

Sighing, Rowan finally unclipped his seat belt—the car was part perk of the new job, part necessity of the new home address—and got out of the car. Time to stop woolgathering.

He considered his dwindling days as he made bulletin-board signs for the autumn programming he wouldn't be around to run.

One upshot to the change in employment status would be a freer schedule. Trying to work two jobs, one of which was very demanding, left little room for anything else, like job hunting. Rowan had let his research slow to a crawl the past few weeks, but he couldn't keep putting it off, especially once Kaira started school. Rowan's days would soon feel a lot emptier between nine and three if he didn't find gainful employment to fill the hours.

Ugh, that made him sound like a bored housewife. He couldn't decide which part of that was worse—thinking it, or the guilt he felt for thinking it. Rowan might've actually had a nice childhood if either of his parents had stayed at home. And he certainly didn't think the stay-at-home parents he met were doing less than their share of the labor.

No, a quiet part of him said. He knew which part of it was worst. It was the *wife* part. Jordy wasn't accepting applications for that job. And Rowan didn't want to apply, no matter that his libido and his heart seemed to agree that a certain sweet, hot dad would make the perfect partner.

So basically, Rowan needed a new job so he could move out.

He might have slammed the stapler harder than necessary. His thoughts were getting stupid. Spending so much time around Jordy's hotness was damaging his brain. Could lack of regular blood flow to the upper body cause permanent brain cell loss? Clearly, he needed a break from Jordy, which was why he should not go on a free trip to New York City. All the togetherness, the family vacation vibes, the hotel room, would only make Rowan's crush worse. Because at this point, he was past mere attraction. It was a definite crush. Rowan didn't just want Jordy to bang him like a screen door in a hurricane. He wanted to watch dumb TV and documentaries with him. He wanted to hang out with Jordy and Kaira. He wanted not only to drool over Jordy's muscles but bask in his sunny smile as he heaved Kaira into the pool and listened to her shriek with laughter.

Playing happy-families vacation when he should be spending his time looking for a new job didn't seem like the wisest choice.

This was why Rowan only dated losers. They didn't make you want to reorganize your entire life—unless you counted giving up dating.

Of course, the giving-up-dating part of the experience was a double-edged sword. On the one hand, Rowan's life was significantly better without losers in it. On the other hand, at least if he were getting laid, he could stop panting after Jordy like a dog.

Probably.

"Wow, Rowan. What did that stapler ever do to you?"

Taylor's voice was light, but a note of concern rang underneath it. Rowan didn't generally brood. He was like a... duck, maybe. A happy little duck swimming around happily in the pond, unbothered by rain.

Maybe that was a bad metaphor, actually. Didn't ducks get kind of broody? When they were, what was it called, egg-bound? That was a bird thing, right?

He viciously stapled a red maple leaf to the corner of the border. "Asked me why I went and got an MLS instead of becoming a plastic surgeon like my father wanted."

Wincing, Taylor helped herself to a seat on the circulation desk. Rowan could've scowled at her, but the hard wood surface was actually more comfortable than the chair, and there weren't any patrons around to see. "No luck on the job search?"

He huffed out a breath, lips flapping embarrassingly with the force of it, and reached for the poster advertising their fall sewing class, just in time for Halloween costume season. "Who has time to search?"

The sound of her heels clacking against the side of the desk ceased. After a moment of silence during which Rowan debated poster placement, Taylor said, "Is your employer guy taking advantage of you?"

He snorted. "If only."

Then he realized she meant in the sense of *working him too hard*, and—okay, well, Rowan's brain went to the bad place with that too. His whole face felt like it was on fire. "I mean—"

But Taylor was laughing. "No, please, go on. You've been very close-mouthed about the whole thing. And now it turns out there might be juicy details?"

He turned around long enough to glower. "There are no juicy details." Unless you wanted to call Jordy's thighs after a morning workout juicy. Which was a thought. Resolutely, he returned his focus to the bulletin board. "It's just demanding is all."

"I thought Daddy was supposed to be doing all the childcare when he's home?"

"Oh my God, Taylor."

"What?" she asked, her voice a perfect impression of innocence.

"He's a very hands-on father—"

She cackled.

Rowan groaned and gave in to the urge to beat his head against the bulletin board. Maybe he should staple himself to it. Could he get worker's compensation for that? The library couldn't fire him if he couldn't leave.

Finally he got the poster affixed and Taylor got her giggles under control.

"So he's *not* taking advantage of you," she clarified. "In either sense of the term. And he's presumably doing his share of the housework as well as the child-rearing—"

"He's doing all the child-rearing," Rowan broke in. "I'm a babysitter, Tay."

She waved this off as unimportant. "But you don't have time to look for a job because… you're spending all your time jerking off?"

Well, not *all* of it. He spent a great deal of time hanging out with Jordy with or without Kaira—watching TV, making dinner, splashing around in the pool while the warm weather lasted.

But he didn't think telling Taylor as much would make this conversation any less painful. Anything he told her risked her trying to trick him into bringing Jordy around. Rowan put a staple into the bulletin board. It wasn't holding anything else there; it was just punctuating his frustration. "Could you be slightly less perceptive?"

"Yes, but it would be boring." She sobered. "Seriously, though. I know this situation sucks for you. I wish the city would get its head out of its ass and fund some more positions. It's not like we don't need the help."

He raised an eyebrow at her, then looked toward the cart of unshelved returns.

"I'm on my *break*," she pointed out. "Someone reheated fish in the lunchroom microwave yesterday. I'm not staying in there."

Someone really needed to get around to criminalizing that. "It's just—this is dumb. It's not like being a kids' librarian was even my life's ambition." He didn't bother validating the profession—Taylor knew he didn't look down on it, but that wasn't the same as believing it was the perfect fit for him. "But I like serving the community or whatever. I like books. I like talking about programming needs. I like my coworkers *most* of the time. I'm going to miss it here." He paused as he hopped up on the desk beside her. "Well, and also I'm going to miss having a stable income and being able to afford my own place to live."

Taylor leaned her bony shoulder into his. "You'll find something. Once you get around to *looking*, you loser."

"I know, I know. I think part of me's still wallowing. And the other part of me is... distracted."

"With your DILF."

He didn't bother protesting that if Jordy were just a DILF, he wouldn't have a problem. "He invited me to go to New York with him and the kiddo. Some work thing. He says his mom can come if I don't want to, but I feel like I should stick around here and look for jobs."

Taylor hummed. "And also not fall hopelessly in love with your hot single dad boss?"

"I'm not answering that."

"Uh-huh. So let me point something out to you." Taylor paused, because she was all about dramatic effect. It made her *very* popular with the kids. "You said you feel like you should stick around here. But you didn't actually say you want to."

Rowan's shoulders slumped. "You're supposed to be stopping me from making irrational life-ruining choices."

"Maybe I am," she said cheerfully. "Maybe what I'm doing is telling you to stop getting in the way of your own happiness. You want to go to New York? *Go.* But don't spend the trip playing happy family with your boss. Be gay. See a musical. Have an ill-advised hookup in a public bathroom in the Village." She nudged his shoulder again. "Maybe what you really need is a vacation, is what I'm saying. And here's your chance at a paid one, right when you need it. Stop thinking so hard. It doesn't suit you."

He yelped out a laugh. "Wow, thanks. Oh gee, look at the time—I think your break's over—"

She stood from the desk before he could shove her off, but she didn't run away. Instead she gripped him by his shoulders. Her surprisingly strong bony fingers dug into his flesh. "We'll miss you too," she promised, uncharacteristically serious and fierce. "But Rowan? Nobody is dying. Come visit. Bring the sproglet. You know we'll keep you in the loop if there are any openings, and we're all happy to be references and help you look. You live in a big city. There's tons of things a librarian can do here. You'll find something."

If Rowan felt a bit misty-eyed over her support, no one had to know.

They also didn't have to know about Rowan's watery eyes when he discovered the *We'll miss you, Rowan* banner and cupcakes in the breakroom. They were pineapple upside-down, from his favorite bakery.

WITH TAYLOR'S advice in mind, later that night Rowan said yes to the trip, and a week later he found himself boarding a flight to NYC.

"What, no private jet?" Rowan joked as Jordy guided Kaira into the business-class section of the plane.

"I thought about it," Jordy said dryly, "but when I asked to borrow it, the team said it was already booked to take the goalie golfing in Miami this weekend."

"Not Scotland?"

"For one night? Of course not. That would be a ridiculous waste of resources."

Rowan snickered as he settled into his seat across the aisle from Jordy and Kaira. It had been a while since he'd last flown anywhere in such luxury. When he left England for Canada, his parents had already cut the purse strings, so he'd saved his pennies and suffered the cramped seating of economy class.

Kaira was apparently also used to flying in style, because she settled happily into her seat and chattered away to Jordy about what she wanted to watch and eat and do on the plane.

"Remember, this flight isn't as long as the ones we took when we flew to Curaçao," Jordy said gently. "You might not have time to watch a whole movie."

Kaira agreed with him in a way that suggested she didn't believe him but was willing to humor him. Jordy rolled his eyes at Rowan, plugged her into her tablet, and let her pick one of her predownloaded films.

God, they were cute.

Rowan tore his eyes away and looked at the drinks menu tucked next to his seat. He was taking advantage of the free vacation; he was *not* playing happy families. Which was why he should definitely order something alcoholic, because he wasn't on duty.

The flight attendant stopped to check on Jordy and Kaira and promised to bring her juice and Jordy a water straightaway.

"And for your husband?" she asked, turning to Rowan.

Rowan blinked at her. It was an innocent enough mistake, and he didn't want her to feel bad. But he couldn't just claim that role in Jordy and Kaira's lives.

"Rowan, did you want to get a drink?" Jordy tipped his head at the menu still in Rowan's hand.

Right, so they were going to just ignore it, then. "I'll have a white wine?" His uncertainty made his order sound like a question, and he blushed. The attendant didn't notice, apparently, because she smiled, confirmed the order, and hurried away.

As Jordy warned, the flight wasn't long—just under two hours— but it was plenty long enough for the flight attendant to make a half-dozen more comments about Rowan and Jordy's fictitious marriage and their charming child. Not that Rowan could disagree on that point; Kaira definitely was as cute as a button.

When Rowan agreed to the trip and learned that he'd largely be off the clock, he had vague ideas about following Taylor's instructions to find a gay bar or a musical. But somehow, once they got to the hotel room, leaving felt like too much effort.

Kaira said she was too tired to leave and wanted to eat while watching TV, and Jordy, apparently relieved enough to stay in, decided they should order room service and let her break the "no eating in front of the TV" rule.

When he turned to ask what Rowan wanted, Rowan gave up his vague plans for going elsewhere and asked for a burger and fries. He was on vacation. He could do what he wanted.

Somehow, watching *Moana* while having a picnic on their hotel-room floor turned out to be just what he wanted.

BRINGING ROWAN to New York with them was a great idea. Traveling with Rowan was just as smooth as traveling with Janice, if not smoother. Rowan wasn't fazed by the business-class seats or five-star hotel, nor did he question Kaira when she declared that it was time for a picnic and instructed him to put down a blanket for eating. He simply rolled with everything, as if the whole trip was routine.

Jordy could have called his mom to meet them in New York so she could take on Kaira duties in his absence, but as much as he loved his mom, she tended to vacillate between overly strict and too permissive, and Jordy always seemed to be the biggest loser. Kaira wasn't allowed to go in the ball pit that was surely a danger to her, but she could have ice cream for dinner.

But he didn't have to worry when Rowan had her. She would be safe, well-fed, and probably exhausted before dinnertime.

After a couple of audio interviews, Jordy was sent for a photoshoot. He never minded the silly in-uniform photos, but the model-like out-of-uniform poses always felt weird. They slapped makeup on him, styled his hair, and shoved him in front of a plain backdrop. Then he tried to hold still and look where he was told to and not to smile while the photographer moved around him, snapping photos and calling out directions.

Twenty minutes later, Hailey, the PA assigned to keep him on schedule, ushered him to another room for a taped interview and then finally guided him to the dining room for lunch with the players and their families. After a long morning playing dancing monkey, his shoulders loosened as he caught sight of Kaira sitting with Rowan. He barely remembered to thank Hailey before he hurried over to his baby.

Kaira and Rowan were laughing with the rest of the table, so neither of them noticed Jordy's approach. He sat down in the empty chair next to Kaira and waited.

She did a perfect double-take, squealed, "Daddy!" and launched into his arms.

"Hi, peanut. Hey, careful of the table, please." No one would be upset if she sent a few pieces of cutlery toward the floor with an errant elbow, but Jordy preferred not to make extra work for the waitstaff.

Kaira kneed him in the stomach as she turned around. "Sorry, Daddy. Did you have a good day?" She poked her finger into his hair. "You're all crunchy. Did you get to play with makeup?"

"No, but I let someone else try some on me. What do you think?"

Kaira wriggled farther away—the better to judge the effect—and then said seriously, "You look very pretty."

Someone across the table was snickering, but Jordy ignored it. "Thanks, peanut. That means a lot coming from you." He smacked a kiss on her cheek and then deposited her in her own chair. "Did you and

Rowan have a good morning?" He made eye contact with Rowan over her head.

Rowan gave a minute shake of his head. Jordy had already caught the faint whiff of chlorine from Kaira's hair, which meant—

"We went swimming! With Miss Jenna and Gabby and Dan."

Jordy lifted his head and met Jenna Yorkshire's gaze. She waved. Next to her, her husband, Tom, paid Jordy zero attention; he had his head bent in intense conversation with Ryan Wright of the Vancouver Orcas, on his other side, and Dante Baltierra, who was across the table from them. "Of course you did." Why would she want to do something she couldn't do at home? How silly of him. He made an apologetic face at Rowan, but Rowan just shook his head fondly.

"I convinced her to go to the library after lunch."

Oh.

Jordy felt his face freeze and tried to cover for it, but too late. Rowan had noticed, and so had Kaira.

"You should come!" Kaira said enthusiastically.

He shook his head. "Sorry, baby, I can't. I have a meeting after lunch. You and Rowan have fun, though." He'd been looking forward to taking her to the New York Public Library for the first time—she'd been too young to appreciate books much last year—but Rowan was an actual librarian. Jordy wouldn't get in the way of that.

"We can do something else instead so you can come. Ryan mentioned a scavenger hunt thing?" He quirked his lips. "Unless you want in on that as well."

Jordy was pretty sure the scavenger hunt was confined to things that could be found within a two-block radius of the hotel, but his daughter's attention span knew no such boundaries, and he had no desire to rein her in as she tried to drag him all over the city. From the expression on Rowan's face, he knew it too. "Pass. So, library tonight, then? After dinner?"

Or tomorrow morning. Kaira might need a nap this afternoon.

Hell, *Rowan* might need a nap this afternoon if it went the way Jordy suspected. They'd have to keep themselves open to rescheduling. "Sounds like a plan," he agreed, and then the food came out, and there wasn't much time for talking. Jordy only had fifteen minutes to stuff his face before the union reps meeting started.

Mercifully, Nico Kirschbaum kept the meeting to the point in a way Jordy suspected only a German could. Maybe he had somewhere to be, because he kept looking at his watch every three minutes. Kirschbaum had to be the only twentysomething Jordy knew who wore a wristwatch for function and not as a fifty-thousand-dollar statement.

After the meeting ended, Jordy fell into step with him, curious despite himself. "Hey, Kersh, where's the fire?"

Kirschbaum flushed, obviously flustered, and slowed down. "Jordy. Was there something you wanted to talk about?"

It had taken Jordy a minute to get used to that German directness. He used to think Kersh just didn't like him. "Making conversation," he said, bemused. *Something* was going on here, between the whispers at the lunch table and now—

"Nicky!" Ryan came around the corner, waving a sheaf of papers. Dante Baltierra was half a step behind him. "I got 'em! You good to go?"

Kirschbaum looked at Jordy. From his expression, he was trying very hard to be polite.

Jordy shook his head. He really didn't have anything to say. Kersh gave a grateful smile and took off with Ryan at a jog.

"They seem really excited about that scavenger hunt," Jordy commented to Baller.

Baller smiled. "Kids these days, right? So full of energy and zest for life. Brings a tear to your eye."

One of these days, Jordy would stop expecting Baller to say normal things and remember he was kind of a weirdo. "Speaking of kids, where's yours?"

Baller sighed gustily. "Sadly, I'm flying solo this year. Reyna's got an ear infection."

Jordy winced. "Ouch." Definitely not a good time to bring a preschooler on a plane.

"Yeah, I'm gonna owe Gabe so much parent hazard pay when I get back." He gave Jordy a sly sideways look, complete with eyebrow wiggling, as they made their way toward the elevator. "What about you?"

Jordy jabbed the button. "What about me what?"

"You're gonna owe your partner a few favors, right?"

"My what?" Sully was back in Toronto with his own newborn.

"Partner?" Baller prompted. "Or is it boyfriend? The cute guy hanging out with your kid while you're primping for the cameras? I didn't get to talk to him at lunch 'cause I was busy—" He cut himself off as the elevator arrived and he stepped forward into the car. "Anyway. He seems like he fits in. How long have you been together?"

"Uh?" The question threw him enough that the elevator doors started to close before he remembered he needed to get in. Baller was looking at him like *he* was the crazy one. "That's Rowan. He's not my— he's my...."

Baller looked at him expectantly.

Friend? Okay, they were friends, but normal friends didn't fly to New York to help you watch your kid while you had work meetings. *Nanny* seemed reductive. Rowan wasn't Jordy's employee. Okay, he *was* Jordy's employee, but that was a technicality. *Roommate* likewise did not cover it.

"Sugar baby?" Baller suggested eventually.

Jordy facepalmed and slammed his other hand on the button for his floor. "He's a friend I'm paying to help look after my kid because my nanny quit suddenly at the same time he found out his apartment was infested with black mold."

Three floors ticked away in silence.

Baller said, "So you're not sleeping with him?"

"Of course not."

"Why not?"

Jordy shot him a look. Did he have to explain ethics? For all that Baller was a weirdo, he'd always been a good man. Jordy hadn't ever come out so much as he just didn't bother to hide things. It helped that, by the time Jordy and Sanna split, Baller and Gabe were already public, so Jordy's quiet, romance-free lifestyle—queer or not—didn't draw attention. Still, Baller, the self-proclaimed fairy godmother of the NHL, extended membership into the queer group chat he'd started. Not that Jordy spent much time in the Rainbow Hockey chat—a name he could only guess at since Baller had named it with emojis. After about a week of Ryan, Max Lockhart, Liam Belanger, and Baller inundating the chat with a combination of animal and queer memes and photos of their pets and children, Jordy muted the chat without guilt.

Baller waved a hand. "Okay, yes, obviously you're not putting moves on the nanny. But you just said he's a friend, so...."

"Exactly. A friend."

The doors opened on their floor—curse Jordy's luck that he couldn't escape this conversation by means of closing elevator doors—and they stepped out.

"A very hot and gay friend who likes spending time with your child," Baller agreed.

Jordy shot him a look. That wasn't enough to build a relationship on.

They arrived at Jordy's door first, and he stopped with his keycard in hand and waited. Rowan and Kaira might be on the other side, and Jordy did not want them to overhear Baller's ridiculous ponderings. People who found the loves of their lives when barely out of puberty should be officially banned from meddling into the love lives of others, since the experience clearly warped their brains.

Baller shook his head. "Fine, I'll stop questioning your life choices and leave you to your adorable modern family so that I can go call mine." He gave a cheery wave and all but skipped down the hallway.

Shaking his head, Jordy unlocked the door and found Kaira and Rowan in the hotel room. As expected, Kaira was asleep, facedown and starfished across his bed, looking as if she'd crashed into it and lost consciousness. Jordy glanced over at the other bed, but Rowan wasn't curled up in it, taking advantage of the downtime. Instead, he was tucked into the corner farthest from Kaira and whispering into his phone.

"—only two days?" He chewed on his thumb as he listened to the answer on the other end of the line. "No, I have my laptop. I just need to find a minute."

Jordy wondered if he should step back out into the hallway. Before he could decide, Rowan looked up, caught his eye, and waved him in.

"Yeah, no. Thanks, Gem. I owe you one. … Yes, another one." He rolled his eyes at Jordy, who smiled. He could picture her tart response to the idea of being owed favors. "Cheers," Rowan said and disconnected the call.

Since he was no longer interrupting, Jordy settled in the other chair to keep things quiet. Not that he could let Kaira sleep much longer, since he did want her to go to bed before midnight.

"Everything okay?" Nervous energy during phone calls with lawyers, even ones who were friends, didn't seem like a good thing.

"Yeah," Rowan said distractedly as he stared at his blank cell phone for a long moment. Then a smile broke across his face. "Everything's fine. It's great. Well, no, it's good, but it might be great soon."

That illuminated nothing. Jordy arched an eyebrow.

"That was Gem—okay, yes, obviously. She called because she heard about a job." Rowan still looked a bit dazed.

"A good one, I'm guessing."

"Jordy, it's perfect." Suddenly, Rowan's body was alive with restrained energy. His leg bounced and his hands waved in the air as he enthusiastically, if quietly, explained. "The English lit reference librarian at U of T had to leave suddenly—I don't know why—but that means there is a full-time indefinite position opened up, and they want to staff it before the start of term."

Jordy blinked. "Isn't that, like, two weeks away?"

"Yeah," Rowan breathed. "So they're looking for applicants ASAP. Gem says they're calling qualified applicants for interviews before the application deadline. Which means I need to apply immediately if I want any hope of getting a call."

"What do you need?"

"Time to read over my CV and package up an application?" Rowan looked a bit overwhelmed at the prospect, and Jordy couldn't blame him. Not that Jordy knew what it was like to apply for a job the normal way, but he could remember the dread and nerves involved in interviewing with NHL teams prior to his draft.

"How about we leave the library for tomorrow and I take that one downstairs for dinner. That would give you a few of hours of peace and quiet in the room."

"Really?" Rowan looked so surprised and grateful that Jordy kind of wanted to hug him or pat his head. "I know I'm supposed to be working—"

"No, you're not," Jordy reminded him. Rowan didn't have a US work visa, and Jordy truly didn't expect him to work. He just needed a heads-up to arrange alternative care. "You're on vacation and you're occasionally watching my kid as a favor." Jordy knew they were blurring the lines between employer/employee and friendship, but he thought Rowan understood those lines anyway.

"I know," Rowan reassured him. "Still, you must be exhausted. At least if there's two of us we might make up one semirested adult."

Jordy snorted. "Maybe, but this sounds important."

Rowan let out a long breath and nodded. "It's kind of my dream job," he admitted almost shyly, like he couldn't believe he was saying it out loud.

"Well, then, Kaira and I better get out of your hair so you can do what needs doing." Jordy slapped his thighs and stood, filled suddenly with restless energy. Rowan would get this job, Jordy was sure. And Jordy would be left nannyless again. Hopefully Jordy could at least convince Rowan to continue living with them in the short term so there was someone to pull the dusk-to-dawn shift every day, even during road trips.

Pushing away thoughts of nannies and job searches and interviews—ugh—Jordy gently shook Kaira awake and failed utterly at not finding her grumpy pouty face to be completely adorable. The NHL had booked one of the event spaces downstairs for the evening, so Jordy packed up his kid, wished Rowan luck, and left him hunched over his laptop.

As PROMISED, they made the library their first priority after breakfast, and it did not disappoint. Kaira clung tightly to Jordy on one side and Rowan on the other as they walked up the steps. Jordy would never forget the look on her face when she looked around the Rose Main Reading Room or the awe in her voice when she whispered, "Daddy, it's *even better* than Belle's library in the castle!"

Yeah, he was glad he hadn't missed this. "It's pretty special," Jordy agreed in the same hushed tone.

"Feeling a little bit like chopped liver here," Rowan muttered on her other side, and Jordy looked up at him with a grin.

They had opted out of a full guided tour, both because Jordy had obligations later and because a six-year-old's attention span could only stretch so far. Instead, they hit the highlights. After the reading room, they went straight down to the Children's Center to see the Winnie-the-Pooh exhibit, where Rowan made sad noises about his country's cultural heritage being stolen by the New York Public Library.

Jordy raised a pointed eyebrow and Rowan, without missing a beat, said, "Well, what goes around comes around. Colonize the colonizers."

Kaira didn't get the joke, but she laughed at his tone anyway and then begged for a trip to the gift shop.

As *if* they were skipping that. What was the point of making his salary if he couldn't spend an absurd amount of money in a library gift shop?

Of course, he didn't want his kid to get spoiled, so *some* of the things he was going to buy would have to be for later. Maybe a happy-first-day-of-school gift for next month?

"You can have *one* stuffed animal," Jordy said firmly. He would not be swayed by Kaira's puppy-dog eyes or the way she looked back and forth between Piglet and Eeyore.

Finally she sighed and put Eeyore back, "Because Piglet looks kind of like an armadildo, Daddy."

That was Clem's fault. She'd never had any trouble pronouncing it before.

A woman browsing the stuffies next to them valiantly choked back a laugh.

"Good choice," Jordy said seriously. "You can pick out two books, okay? Do you want to go look at those next?"

When she nodded, Jordy looked over at Rowan. "Can you take her?" He glanced at Eeyore, knowing Rowan would understand the assignment.

Rowan saluted. "Meet you at the kids' books."

Jordy only meant to buy Eeyore, which he easily could've hidden away somewhere—the stuffed animal wasn't that big. But somehow by the time he reached the checkout he'd also picked up a Winnie-the-Pooh tote bag for future library trips. Then, when he was about to pay, his eye caught on the display of Hundred-Acre Wood throw blankets behind the counter, and he thought about Rowan's penchant for curling up on the couch while they watched *CSI: Toronto*.

Sooner or later Rowan would move out. Did he have a throw blanket of his own? Jordy didn't know how bad the black mold situation in his apartment had gotten. Maybe he'd had to throw some things away.

A good friend would get him a housewarming gift, right? Jordy would hate for Rowan to get cold in the evenings with no one's leg to stick his feet under.

Jordy added the blanket to his purchase, paid, and was wondering how to be subtle about it when Rowan appeared at his elbow with Kaira on his other side. "I've got this if you can cover me for five minutes after?"

Jordy didn't ask questions, just handed him the bag. Rowan didn't have to know the blanket was for him.

Last stop was the café, where they grabbed a snack for Kaira and caffeine for the adults and Jordy sneaked a peek in Rowan's bag. Gift editions of *Alice in Wonderland* and *Through the Looking Glass*—beautiful, but maybe not enough pictures for a six-year-old. Jordy wondered if he collected them for himself.

He was clearing away their tray when he almost ran into the woman from the armadildo incident. "Sorry," he said automatically as he sidestepped so she could go first.

He thought she'd ignore him—that happened in New York, where sometimes ignoring people in your space was the politest thing you could do—but instead she smiled. "You're fine. It's good to see a young family out enjoying the library. Looks like you're having a great time."

"We are." He laughed at himself a little. "Although the two of them more than me, I think. Kaira didn't get her love of books from me." Not that she got it from Rowan either, but—well, it didn't matter. He wasn't going to get into his complicated family dynamic with a stranger.

"Mm-hmm," she said. "I saw you at the checkout. I think you like indulging them."

So someone else had caught him. "I think I'll plead the Fifth," he said as sweetly as he could and grinned when she laughed. "You have a good day."

Encumbered by so many bags, they opted for a cab back to the hotel, which Jordy was grateful for when, three minutes into the ride, Kaira declared she had to use the bathroom, even though he'd asked if she had to go before they left the library.

Then there was another group lunch, this time with smaller round tables instead of busy long ones that made it impossible to navigate the room. Unfortunately that meant it was more of a challenge to find three seats together and impossible to turn down an invitation from Brady Silver, the Shield's baby-faced captain.

It wasn't that Jordy didn't like him. Everybody liked Brady. But he was twenty-three and married with a baby on the way, and he made Jordy feel *so old*.

He offered Kaira a fist-bump as she climbed into the seat beside him. "My favorite Shaw."

"Hi, Cap!"

"And you brought a new friend." Brady smiled his golden-retriever smile at Rowan and stood up to shake his hand. "Hey, I'm Brady. Everybody calls me Cap."

Rowan raised his eyebrows at Jordy over Brady's shoulder as if to say *is this guy for real?* But he shook his hand anyway. "Uh, Rowan."

"Oh, Rowan. You must be the new Janice."

Jordy's brain screeched to a halt halfway through pulling out a chair.

Kaira, though, didn't miss a beat. "Don't be silly, Cap." She settled into her chair and reached for her napkin, which had been folded into a swan shape. "He's Rowan."

Fortunately Rowan seemed to think nothing of it, so Jordy had a moment to stow his discomfort. What was wrong with him anyway? Technically, from Brady's point of view, he hadn't said anything weird.

Jordy pushed away the feeling of disquiet and focused on getting lunch for Kaira.

Any hopes Jordy might have had for a quiet evening were dashed by Ryan Wright. They ran into him, Nico, and Dante in the lobby as the other three were headed out of the hotel, but Ryan, having caught sight of them, lit up. "Hey, you have to join us at the bar tonight. We're having our traditional Gays Night."

"*Is* it a tradition?" Nico asked behind him.

Ryan gasped in offense. "Yes. Look, we gotta have drinks anytime more than three of us are gathered in one place. Jordy—" Ryan paused, turned to Rowan, and continued. "—Rowan, I'll text you details."

He did, unfortunately, text details, including the detail that the Yorkshires had offered to look after Kaira while Jordy and Rowan went out. With no excuse—and feeling like he owed it to Rowan to give him a night out—Jordy sucked it up and put on his going-out pants.

The bar Ryan had chosen wasn't a gay bar, but it was within walking distance of the hotel and had a small private room. Rowan and Jordy found the other three already settled into it with drinks in front of them.

"You're here!" Ryan looked like he'd already finished off a couple of shots, but he perked up out of his slouch against Nico to greet them.

"Welcome, boys." Dante handed Rowan and Jordy each a shot. Jordy sniffed his. This didn't smell like the vile brew of vodka, tequila, and Schlager he'd once naively downed, but you could never be too careful.

"It's just vodka," Dante explained. "I wanted tequila, or at least a blowjob, but Nico overruled me."

"But I like blowjobs," Rowan said mournfully.

"Vodka is good," Nico insisted unapologetically and lifted his shot.

"So good," Ryan cooed, holding up his drink.

Good grief. Jordy didn't think they'd taken that long to get here, but the evidence was staring him in the face. "Wright, are you drunk already?"

"Maybe," Ryan admitted. He shot a coy, under-the-eyelashes look at Jordy, then Nico. "But I'm celebrating." Nico turned positively pink and gooey-eyed under Ryan's gaze. Despite himself, Jordy's curiosity was piqued.

"What are you celebrating?" Rowan asked.

"Mawwige!" Ryan crowed. "It's what bwings us togevvah!" He smacked a kiss to Nico's cheek.

Jordy blinked. "What?"

Something must have made sense to Rowan, because his eyes widened. "Seriously?"

Dante laughed. "Seriously. We drove up to the small town of Tuckahoe—" Rowan and Jordy both choked, and Ryan giggled. "Tuckahoe, I shit you not, it's just north of Mount Vernon. Anyway, I can't officiate a wedding in New York City without a two-to-six-week waiting period. Fortunately that doesn't apply to any small town that's willing to accept my credentials and the court filing fees."

Jordy stared at Dante, then Ryan and Nico, then back at Dante. There was so much to unpack there.

Rowan recouped faster. "Wait, wait, wait. So you're telling me that sometime after bitching about wedding planning yesterday morning, you two got a license and then drove out of the city so you could get married?"

"Yes," Ryan said. He kissed Nico's cheek again. "As much as I was enjoying fucking with people with all my dumb wedding ideas, all the planning made Nico a nervous wreck. So we decided to skip it."

"Wow," Rowan said. "That's... actually adorably romantic."

"It was *so* romantic." Ryan enthused. He sat up and fished his phone from his pocket. "Wanna see pictures?"

"Of course." Rowan leaned across the table to get a better view, his beer forgotten.

Jordy wasn't against seeing wedding photos, even ones taken during a batshit elopement, but he had to ask. "You're ordained?"

Dante shrugged. "I did one of those online courses a couple of years back."

Jordy waited for further explanation. None came. "Why?"

"Short answer? I was bored, stuck at home on IR." Jordy let out a bark of laughter. "Long answer? Yorkie and Jenna ran into some issues trying to fast-track things, and I always thought it would be cool to perform a wedding."

"So," Jordy summed up, "you were high on pain meds and got ordained to perform marriages on the off chance it would someday be useful."

"Totally worth it." Dante grinned and tipped his head at the others. "I swear Kersh is finally back to looking his age today, and Ryan's walking on air." He wiped away a fake tear. "Young love. So beautiful."

Jordy had to admit that Nico did look looser and happier this evening. Since he didn't know the kid, Jordy hadn't noticed how tense he was on that first day.

"To young love," Jordy agreed. "Though this has to be the weirdest wedding reception I've ever attended."

"And also the drunkest?" Baller guessed. He lowered his voice. "Yeah. I think Ryan's drinking to drown the anxiety of what Nico's mom's going to do to him for eloping with her baby."

"Ah." Jordy winced. He could imagine his own mother's reaction, and he wasn't even the youngest. She'd barely forgiven Sanna for divorcing him, and that had been mutual. "If he doesn't slow down, they're not going to have much of a wedding night."

Rowan elbowed him. "Aw, let them get drunk together. They have the rest of their lives to fuck each other stupid." He looked over Jordy's shoulder; Jordy followed his gaze. "But maybe we should switch to something softer. Shouldn't we be drinking champagne anyway?"

"And there should definitely be food," Jordy added, partly because however grateful he was that Yorkie had taken Kaira tonight, tomorrow held no such guarantees. Besides, it was a travel day. That was a big no on the hangover.

"Smart." Baller nodded. "You order bubbly, I'll order pizza."

Rowan looked back and forth between them and nodded. "Teamwork," he said. "I get it."

The rest of the evening was conspicuously more chill. The champagne smoothed some of Ryan's rougher edges, or maybe it just soothed his nerves. By the time the pizza arrived, Nico was more or less sitting in his lap and Jordy started to feel… unnecessary.

"They know they can start the honeymoon anytime, right?" Rowan asked in a murmur, right in Jordy's ear. Jordy shivered involuntarily at what had to be the accidental brush of lips against his skin. "Um. Unless there's some weird hockey exhibition initiation thing I'm not privy to."

"No," Jordy said automatically. Then he realized there might be and turned wide eyes on Baller. "There's not, right?"

"I knew you had the group chat muted." Baller shook his head in disappointment.

"That's not an answer."

Off to the side, Ryan and Nico seemed to have forgotten their presence entirely. They were holding their ringed hands together; Ryan wore his on the left, but Nico's was on the right, so the bands lined up. They had their heads leaned against each other too, and they practically glowed with contentment.

Jordy looked away, rubbing his chest.

Baller followed his eyeline for a moment and then shook himself. "And on that note, I need to excuse myself to call my husband and gush about how much I love him. Sorry. I think it's contagious." He paused. "If they start taking each other's clothes off, just pour them in a taxi."

Don't leave us alone with them! Jordy wanted to shout, but it was too late. Could you be a third wheel when there was also a fourth wheel? Because that was what this felt like.

The door had barely closed behind Baller when Rowan thankfully budged over just a bit, tapped his fingers on the base of his champagne glass, and said, "We could probably make a run for it. I don't think they even know we're here."

"I think they might be too stupid to leave unsupervised." Could you get arrested for that in New York?

Rowan smiled, not wry at all, just uncomplicated and happy. "It's good, though, right? I mean that they get to stay together. I didn't know sports worked like that."

With one final glance to make sure Ryan and Nico were well and truly occupied staring deeply into each other's eyes, Jordy said, "It doesn't."

Rowan blinked. "What?"

"It *doesn't* work like that. Nico has a no-movement clause, I think, but that mostly means he gets to pick where they'd trade him. Ryan can be dealt at any time if Orcas management feels like it." Jordy tore his gaze away from the happy couple. "They just… got married anyway." They chose each other, even though they knew they might be separated.

"Shit." Rowan looked from Jordy to the newlyweds and back again. "Wait, so does that mean you…?"

"I have a limited no-movement clause," Jordy confirmed. "But it's pretty broad." Fortunately Kaira was still young enough that changing schools wouldn't disrupt her life too much, and he only had a couple more years in him anyway.

"What? But how do you…?" Rowan seemed totally thrown. "How do they expect you to just pick up your whole life? I mean, you have a house, people have families…."

"Yeah, well, that's why they pay us the big bucks." Jordy couldn't put his finger on why smiling was so difficult right now. He'd made his peace with his life. "It's okay, really. I'm not losing sleep over it."

"I couldn't do it," Rowan said. "I mean… maybe it's just a me thing? I spent my childhood in dormitories. I barely saw my parents. Now I finally have a place that feels like home, you know? Even if it's Toronto and not a specific apartment. And living your whole life knowing you might have to give it up any day?"

Suddenly the pizza Jordy had eaten wasn't sitting so well, but he couldn't think about why just now. He needed air. Space. Possibly some sobriety.

At that moment Baller rejoined them, took a look in the corner where Ryan and Nico were trading chaste kisses every twenty seconds like they couldn't believe they got to do it, and then said, "You guys want to share a cab? I think the newlyweds should have their own."

"Maybe one with plastic seat covers," Rowan agreed just loud enough for Jordy to hear.

Baller settled the tab—Jordy would Venmo him their share later—and they stepped out into the warm August night.

They probably could've walked back to the hotel, but with Ryan and Nico barely able to keep their eyes off each other, never mind their hands, Jordy didn't like the odds of them staying out of traffic. Wrangling them to safety would take forever. They took a pair of cabs instead, the newlyweds in the first one and Rowan and Jordy sharing the second with Baller.

In the car, Baller was uncharacteristically quiet. It was *weird*. Jordy suspected him of plotting something until he caught the reflected glow of Baller's cell phone screen—he was in the front passenger seat with Jordy behind him—and realized he was… was he texting someone? Or looking through photos…? No, that was a flight app.

Baller took a left in the hotel lobby and headed toward the reception desk, leaving Jordy and Rowan behind with a wave.

"Where's he going?" Rowan asked as they waited for the elevator.

"Checking out, I think."

"At midnight?"

"I think he's homesick. He probably got an earlier flight."

They stepped into the car, and Rowan selected their floor. "Thanks for letting me come along tonight. It was… interesting."

He still didn't get it, did he? "You were invited," Jordy said pointedly. "I told you, I didn't bring you along so you could watch Kaira."

He brought him along because—because Jordy enjoyed his company and thought he might enjoy the trip. They were friends. Jordy just wanted him around.

That wasn't weird, Jordy told himself.

Rowan opened their hotel room door. "Yeah, yeah, I get it." He put the key on the table and toed his shoes off, but when he attempted to nudge them under the table in the dark, he ended up cursing and staggering.

Jordy caught him by the elbow, picked up the key card with his other hand, and slid it into the holder on the wall, which turned the lights on. "You okay?"

"Apart from the clumsiness?" Rowan's cheeks reddened. "I'm okay. Just tripping on my own shopping, apparently."

It took him looking pointedly at his arm for Jordy to remember he could let go. His fingers didn't want to cooperate, and complained about him forcing them by tingling afterward. Then Rowan ducked under the table and pulled out his purchase from the library to check in on it. "No harm done," he announced.

Which reminded Jordy—"What did you buy, anyway?" Of course he knew *what*, but he wanted to know *why*.

"Oh." The flush renewed as Rowan reached into the bag and withdrew the books. "They're just... well, they're so lovely, and they were some of my favorites growing up. Classics, you know? I thought Kaira might like them. I know she's too young now, but—"

Jordy's heart beat furiously against his rib cage, like it had something to say.

"They should last forever," Rowan went on. "Really nice bindings. They reminded me of the sets my grandparents bought me when I was a kid."

Now Jordy's lungs had joined in and struggled to pull in enough air. His brain was completely silent, as though to avoid splitting attention from the other two.

"It's okay, right? I'm not overstepping?"

Jesus. "It's perfect," Jordy said, then immediately felt the urge to clear his throat. Why did his voice sound like that, hoarse and broken? "She's going to love them."

He could've added that Rowan didn't have to do that. But Rowan *knew*. He did it because he wanted to.

He did it because he loved Jordy's kid and she loved him.

And so, said Jordy's stupid heart, doing its best to crawl out his mouth, did Jordy.

Rowan set the books back into their hiding spot and wandered into the bathroom, listing slightly to one side.

Jordy watched him go, his heart still hammering, beating out a love-song tattoo even as his stomach sank with the knowledge that Rowan, though perfect in so many ways, was no one's hockey spouse.

Well, fuck.

Second Period

NEW YORK City had been just as terrible an idea as Rowan predicted. He'd done all the things he said he wouldn't do and none of the things Taylor suggested. Rowan had not gotten over his infatuation, and to make matters worse, he'd spent an evening all but cuddled up with Jordy and a pair of newlyweds. As if Rowan needed a reminder of what he wanted and, for so many reasons, couldn't have.

Not that Rowan wasn't happy for Nico and Ryan. They were adorable together and surprisingly good company for a couple of sports bros—when they weren't drunkenly staring into each other's eyes. It was hard not to like Ryan, who'd shown up in a rainbow T-shirt with the caption "Rainbros" and then immediately gushed over Rowan's, with its library cart and "They see me rollin'" slogan.

Still, as a means of getting over Jordy, New York City was a total failure from start to finish.

Fortunately Rowan had no time to dwell on that when they got back home. Between looking after Kaira full-time now that Jordy's training schedule was filling up, and applying, waiting, and stressing out about his application to U of T, Rowan didn't have the energy to worry about romance.

Jordy's Monday started with morning practice and Rowan and Kaira planning their week. It was the last full week of summer vacation before Kaira started first grade, and Rowan suggested they make a list of everything Kaira wanted to do. Only a six-year-old could make a to-do list that rated *eat ice cream* and *one more trip to the Science Centre* of equal importance.

Rowan had been banned from including, or even telling, Kaira about the most exciting item on the to-do, which was a visit from her aunt. Emma was due to arrive on Friday and wanted to spend a night with Kaira in a hotel to kick off her visit, but given the patience of six-year-olds, Jordy wanted to keep it a secret until the day before Emma's arrival.

So on Tuesday, Kaira and Rowan were at a playground to swing on the swings—item number five—when Rowan's phone rang and *University of Toronto* popped up on caller ID.

"I got an interview!" he blurted out the instant Jordy got home. Jordy froze in the entryway, the door half open and his hands stretched toward the hook to hang his keys. "Sorry," Rowan babbled, "I didn't mean to ambush you, but I was here and I have an interview tomorrow morning at the university."

Jordy stepped into the house, closed the door, hung up his keys, dropped his bag, then finally turned to Rowan. He wore a bright smile, and he sounded sincere when he said, "Congratulations."

"It's just an interview." Rowan didn't want to get his hopes up. "They're probably interviewing loads of people who are more qualified than me."

Jordy stepped closer and forced Rowan to meet his eyes—*Has Jordy been avoiding eye contact for the past few days?* Rowan wondered distractedly, which was a dumb thought to have right at this moment—and said, "They'd be crazy not to hire you. Getting an interview is an achievement. Don't sell yourself short."

Rowan felt almost light-headed. "Right. It does mean that I'm suddenly busy tomorrow morning at ten." Because Rowan shouldn't lose sight of the important details.

Jordy shrugged. "No problem. I'll text Adrianna. She should be able to watch her for the morning, and I can carpool with Sully."

Then he moved toward the living room, away from Rowan. Which was a silly thought to have. He wasn't moving away from Rowan, he was moving toward his daughter. Something he was definitely allowed to do and totally not out of character. And he wasn't avoiding eye contact with Rowan either. Why would he be?

Rowan agonized over his clothes for a full hour before he got himself out the door to arrive at the university library at half nine. The front desk sent him up to the second floor for his interview, and Rowan took his time getting there. The less time he spent waiting in one place, the better.

The university had obviously spent money keeping the library up to date. There were so many places to sit and work—comfortable chairs and couches in the open for reading, desks and workspaces tucked in corners or behind doors for quieter study or research. Rowan could imagine booking one of the rooms to review with friends or complete a group project.

He wanted this so bad he ached with it.

At ten he met the chief librarian, Andreu Iulian, and his deputy chief, Marina Chifundo.

Marina, as the faculty liaison coordinator, would be his supervisor if Rowan got the job, and Rowan had no bloody clue if she liked him. He suspected she was nearing retirement age, not that you could tell based on her attitude toward the job, and had a no-nonsense air that suggested she'd seen and heard it all. Considering she was a Black woman in a position of authority at a university, Rowan suspected all of that was well earned.

Andreu might have been the one in charge, but it was clear he trusted Marina's judgment and let her run the interview.

Half an hour later, Rowan stumbled out of the chief librarian's office and found his way back into the sunshine. Marina had grilled him not only about his experience and expertise, but his hobbies and favorite films, all presumably to get a better sense of Rowan as a person, but the breadth and unpredictability of the topics left him feeling like he'd just left a police interrogation rather than a job interview.

Unbalanced, he decided to get some lunch before he picked up Kaira. Maybe the calories would settle his emotions before he had to worry about anyone else's.

Fortunately, Kaira kept him busy for the rest of the day and all of Wednesday working through her list. Then on Thursday, after his morning workout, Jordy came home for lunch and told Kaira the news.

"Auntie Emma is coming?" she shrieked.

"Yup. Her flight gets in tomorrow morning. She's going to come here for lunch, and then she wants to take you on an adventure."

"An adventure?" Kaira squirmed in her seat and cocked her head.

"Yup. Auntie Emma has booked a room at a hotel for the two of you to stay in on Friday night. She says you'll do lots of fun girly things."

"We will?"

"Uh-huh. She wouldn't tell me what." Jordy mock pouted. Rowan wanted to nibble his bottom lip. "Because I'm not a girl." Kaira giggled. "But she did tell me that the hotel has a pool with a very cool waterslide."

By eight that evening, Kaira had asked Jordy a million and one questions when he was available and turned them on Rowan when he wasn't. Unfortunately, Rowan knew even less than Jordy, a fact Kaira needed frequent reminders of.

By the time she passed out forty-five minutes after her usual bedtime, Rowan was all but ready for his own bed. He groaned and flopped onto the couch, primed for mindless entertainment.

Jordy chuckled as he settled into an armchair. "Told you it was better to wait."

Rowan lifted his head off the couch and stared at Jordy, so far away. Guilt churned in his stomach for having taken up so much space that he chased Jordy out of his usual spot. "Sorry," he grumbled as he sat up to give Jordy more room. But Jordy didn't move over.

"I forgive you for doubting my wisdom," he said magnanimously and turned on the TV.

Rowan was definitely not going to think or obsess about Jordy's seating choice tonight. Definitely not.

JORDY HAD mixed feelings about Emma's arrival.

On the one hand, Kaira loved her aunt. Some people had complicated relationships when it came to intrafamily adoption. That had never been an issue with Emma. If she felt the least bit maternal, or jealous of Jordy's relationship with his kid, or regretted giving her up, she had never given the slightest indication. She played the part of fun aunt perfectly, from the colorful outfit and outrageous heart-shaped sunglasses she wore on her arrival to the way she pretended not to recognize Kaira: "Now, where's my niece? Have you seen her? She's about this tall"—she held her hand out at knee height—"with brown hair and brown eyes.... She looks a little bit like you, actually, but you're *way* too tall—"

Kaira shrieked with laughter. "Aunt Emma, it's *me*."

Emma clutched her chest in mock surprise. "Oh my goodness! My little Kaira!" She knelt down for a hug. "What is your dad feeding you to make you get so big, huh?"

Jordy raised his hands on cue. "I promise I haven't given her HGH." Even if he did know where to get it.

With one last smacking kiss to Kaira's cheek, Emma stood and planted one on Jordy too. "Hey, big brother." She patted his stomach. "Off-season's going well, I see."

Kaira giggled again, although she almost certainly didn't understand Jordy was being teased for putting on the necessary muscle, and the layer of fat that came with it. "Good to see you too, Em. Congratulations on the new job."

She beamed. "Thanks."

The teasing didn't bother him either. That was just standard sibling stuff, the same banter Jordy exchanged with his teammates every day. And it would've been a pretty sad situation if a little jab about his belly bothered him when he'd developed it on purpose.

No, the problem came Friday afternoon, when Emma packed Kaira into her rental car and waved goodbye to Jordy and Rowan, leaving Jordy without a convenient waist-high buffer between himself and the object of his affections.

Why couldn't Emma have gotten time off for her visit *before* the New York trip? Back when Jordy was cheerfully living in ignorant bliss of the fact that he'd somehow asked a handsome, kind, funny guy to move in with him and then fallen unwittingly in love?

Jordy had never felt more like the dumb jock stereotype.

He should have seen this coming. Hadn't he even thought, months ago, when Rowan rescued him from that awful dinner, that there might be something between them? A fact he'd conveniently forgotten because he needed Rowan for something else.

He didn't regret that. Kaira and Rowan's mutual adoration society was something out of a wholesome children's book. He just wished he'd opened his eyes a little sooner so that he could have protected himself.

Of course, he probably wouldn't have done anything differently. He just would've been prepared for his own complicated feelings.

Sully was going to laugh his ass off. Baller's I-told-you-so would probably come in a singing card full of explosive glitter.

Meanwhile, Jordy had to contend with Rowan pacing the house, glancing at his phone every twelve seconds to see if he'd missed a call from U of T. At one point he started chewing a fingernail, which objectively should have been gross, but apparently putting fatherhood first meant Jordy had repressed his sexual desires so far that now he couldn't stop staring at the damp corner of Rowan's mouth.

"Maybe we should do something," Jordy said when he couldn't take it anymore.

It was a dumb thing to say. He should've made his excuses and gone to the gym. Rowan would never know it wasn't a scheduled day. He didn't even have to *go* to the gym; he could've just said that and walked into a Tim Hortons and crushed a ten-pack of Timbits about it. But sooner or later Rowan would get a new job—if not this one, then another—and his landlord would fix the mold in his apartment, and he'd move out, and then Jordy would never see him again. So he might as well get his fill now.

But the pacing had to stop. "You're going to wear a hole in the floor."

Rowan looked down at the floor, or perhaps more pointedly at his *bare feet* on Jordy's obscenely expensive hardwood.

It had really been too long since Jordy had a proper date if he was looking at another man's ankles like this.

But after a second, Rowan conceded with a sigh and flopped onto the couch. "I'm sorry. I know I'm being—a lot. It's just kind of a dream job."

As if Jordy needed the reminder. He wasn't about to forget Rowan's words from Ryan and Nico's wedding reception. *I couldn't do it.* He couldn't live with the specter of a possible cross-continental move hanging over his head when he'd worked so hard to put down roots.

Which was just one more reason, if Jordy needed one, that he should keep his distance. It would be foolish and cruel to pursue something with Rowan knowing he could be traded at any time. Jordy felt bad enough that part of him hoped Rowan *didn't* get this job so he'd stick around longer.

If he found one more thing to feel guilty about, he'd have to convert to Catholicism.

He was just about to suggest they do something to distract themselves—get out of the house, find somewhere to have dinner, fuck each other stupid on the couch in the den—when an earsplitting noise made them both jump.

Rowan dropped his cell phone, swore profusely, and then scrambled to pick it up.

Jordy held his breath.

"Hello?"

He could tell from the tense way Rowan held his body that this was the call he'd been waiting for.

"This is he."

From his vantage point, Jordy couldn't see Rowan's face, and while the volume on his ringer might have been cranked up to *wake the dead*, the same could not be said for his phone speaker. Jordy hunched forward on tenterhooks.

"Absolutely. Yes, I understand. No, I think I have everything I need ready…. Monday morning? Of course. I'm looking forward to it."

Fuck. Wait. Yay? He wasn't *upset*. He was happy for Rowan. Just—

Rowan hung up the phone and turned around, and Jordy scrambled to school his features. "Well?"

"I got it," Rowan said softly, almost disbelievingly. Then a wide, brilliant smile stretched across his face. God, he was gorgeous. "I got it! I got the job!" He looked ready to start hopping in place. Jordy wanted to kiss him. In the face of Rowan's enthusiasm, he couldn't be sad, really, even if he could feel his heart start to crack.

"I knew you would." Jordy honestly couldn't imagine anyone not loving Rowan.

"Liar," Rowan said with a giddy laugh.

Jordy would need to hire a new nanny. Rowan got his dream job, and he would be leaving them soon.

Suddenly any barrier Jordy had erected to protect his heart seemed stupid and wasteful. He closed the distance between them and wrapped Rowan in a tight hug. He was warm and solid under Jordy's hands and the scent of him made Jordy dizzy. His lips brushed Rowan's ear as he murmured, "Never. I always had faith." Rowan shivered and didn't disentangle himself from Jordy's arms.

The hug went on too long, but Jordy found it difficult to let go once Rowan was in his arms. He wanted to breathe him in—his scent, the warmth of his body. But he couldn't hold on forever. Reluctantly, he loosened his grip and pulled back.

When there was enough space between them that Jordy could see Rowan's face, he couldn't help but look down at Rowan's mouth. It was so close and tempting—

Rowan surged forward and pressed his mouth to Jordy's in a brief, ecstatic kiss. Jordy's head swam. Rowan's lips were soft and warm, and Jordy wanted to stay there forever.

Abruptly, Rowan lurched back, his eyes wide and horrified. "Oh God," he gasped. Jordy's heart started to sink. "That was way too forward. I never should have—I'm so sorry!"

Wait, Rowan was apologizing for not asking? Not for the kiss?

It was Jordy's turn to push forward. He closed the gap and placed a short, soft kiss on Rowan's half-open mouth to stop the flow of words. Then he pulled back just enough to catch his eye—just to make sure it was okay—

Rowan leaned into Jordy's weight and parted his lips in invitation. Jordy didn't need to be asked twice.

The third kiss was longer. Jordy raised a hand from Rowan's waist to cup his face and tilted him just so to deepen the kiss. He pressed in closer, swiped in with his tongue. He wanted to devour Rowan. If this was Jordy's only chance to have even a little piece of Rowan while he could, he was going to take it. He was going to imprint every square inch of Rowan onto his memory and claim him in turn—cover him in love bites to leave an impression behind, to claim rights to Rowan, if even for a moment.

Would it make the heartbreak worse when Rowan inevitably left? Maybe. But for once, Jordy was going to take something just for himself, even if it led to heartbreak and misery later. At least his heart could go down in a blaze of glory.

No MATTER how many fantasies he'd had about Jordy, Rowan hadn't planned on acting on any of them. Jordy had made his position clear at the charity gala. But then Rowan got the job, and Jordy hugged him, and his gaze lingered on Rowan's mouth, and Rowan lost his head.

Not that Jordy was complaining. He was much too busy mapping out Rowan's mouth, nibbling on his bottom lip. Jordy slipped his hand into the small of Rowan's back and pulled him forward, pressing his thigh between Rowan's legs and Rowan's hardening dick into his hip.

A moan bubbled out of Rowan, and he twined his arms around Jordy's neck to pull him closer. Jordy growled and the kiss got hungrier. Rowan must have been a very good boy if he deserved this. He smoothed his hands over Jordy's shoulders, back, chest, touching everywhere he could, feeling up all that very nice muscle under its round layer of fat. Jordy needed to put that body to use right now.

They broke the kiss, gasping for air.

"Do you—"

"We should—"

They snickered awkwardly. Then Jordy asked, "This okay?"

"Yes." Rowan maybe said that embarrassingly fast. Whatever. He wasn't about to hold back now. "Very okay. Like 'how about we go to my room because it's closer and more comfortable' okay."

"Good," Jordy said gruffly, and then he turned them in that direction, his grip still firm on Rowan's back, and practically waltzed them across the room and down the hall.

I need to get this man back on the dance floor. Giddy bubbles filled Rowan's chest, and he pulled Jordy into another kiss.

Somehow Jordy maneuvered them to Rowan's bedroom without running them into anything until Rowan's legs hit his mattress. Then Jordy lifted him with a little growl and all but threw him onto the bed.

"Oh my God." Rowan stared at the ceiling, then at Jordy climbing after him. "Rail me."

Jordy groaned and dove in for another kiss.

"Does that mean—" Rowan moaned as Jordy dragged his hot mouth from Rowan's lips down to his neck. "—it's a yes to the railing? Uhh!" He gasped under the press of teeth. Apparently Jordy was into biting, and so was Rowan. His hips bucked. "Please say it's a yes."

"Later I'm going to touch every inch of you, get my tongue on you," Jordy promised. He scraped his teeth down Rowan's neck. "I'm going to suck your cock and eat your ass. And I'm going to open you up on my fingers until you're begging me before I fuck you through the goddamn mattress."

"Yes." Rowan writhed under the filthy promises and grabbed at whichever parts of Jordy he could reach. Part of him was dimly aware that he could be doing more, bringing Jordy pleasure, touching him in all the right ways, but most of his brain was caught on a loop of *God, finally* and *fuck me.*

"But it'll have to wait," Jordy groaned, one hand fisted in Rowan's hair, the other clutching at Rowan's hip, "because I want to take my time. Do it right."

"Yes, do me right," Rowan agreed. "Fuck, do me. Rail me."

Jordy *pulled away.* He knelt up and pulled off his shirt in one move. Then he turned his focus back on Rowan. "Get naked."

"Yes, sir," Rowan quipped, only his chest was heaving and his breath coming in short, and it sounded more sincere than sarcastic.

Jordy's eyes darkened, and Jesus, Rowan must have been very good, not just in this lifetime, but past ones too.

Like, godly levels of good, he added hysterically after he untangled himself from his polo and got his first look at Jordy naked.

He was layers of muscle under fat basically everywhere. If this was what playing shape looked like, then clearly the gods were doing Rowan a solid.

Jordy slipped out of briefs last, and Rowan's mouth watered.

"I need that perfect cock inside me yesterday," he said, out loud apparently.

Jordy prowled up the bed. "Maybe later, if you're good. But first, you have to get. Naked."

Rowan had never taken off his clothes so fast, and he once had an allergic reaction to cheap washing soda. The way Jordy looked at him, dark eyes hot with lust as he ran his gaze down Rowan's body, made him feel like a three-course meal about to be devoured. Cannibalism had never held so much appeal. If Jordy wanted to eat him alive, Rowan would get him a spoon.

He was opening his mouth to beg some more—his dignity had vacated the premises about the time he threw himself at Jordy—when Jordy straddled him and pinned his wrists to the mattress, effectively removing words from the equation.

A vowelless sound escaped Rowan's lungs.

Tragically, Jordy made no move to fuck him. Rowan didn't complain about it because Jordy slotted his thigh between Rowan's, and honestly? Rowan's ass could get in line; his dick was getting the attention now.

Jordy's thighs lived up to every filthy thought Rowan had about them, broad and thick and powerful, perfect for rubbing off against. Except Jordy wasn't letting Rowan move—he pinned Rowan's wrists to the mattress above his head with one big hand, and Rowan had neither the leverage nor the lower body strength to do anything but lie there and take whatever Jordy gave him.

Right now that meant dirty, slow grinds of his hips, every movement rubbing Rowan's hard cock between Jordy's leg and his own belly. He'd leaked enough to make a puddle, and every time Jordy thrust against him, the puddle grew and Rowan's dick slid a little more and a more embarrassing noise wisped out of his throat.

Jordy was dripping too, his erection a hot, heavy weight against Rowan's hip. Rowan wanted to touch it, wrap his hand or mouth around it, but he had to settle for feeling it move against him and *wanting*.

And that was going to be enough.

Jordy had been watching him with those dark, assessing eyes, but when Rowan finally managed to reboot his nervous system and arch up against him, Jordy let out a groan and pressed his face into Rowan's neck. Rowan's brain disintegrated under the onslaught of hot breath, lips, teeth, the burn of Jordy's stubble. God, he was going to come like this— with Jordy's thigh pressed just, *just* behind his balls, a promise or a tease or both.

"Jordy," he finally managed to gasp, and something must've gotten through.

Jordy didn't let him up. He sucked a bruising kiss into the side of Rowan's neck and slipped his free hand between them to wrap tight around Rowan's cock, stroking roughly.

Then he pushed his leg up harder, higher, until his knee slid between Rowan's asscheeks like he might try to fuck him like that, and Rowan's orgasm punched out of him along with all the breath in his lungs. It went on forever, filling the bedroom with slick sounds and the scent of come and sweat, until finally Rowan couldn't take it anymore and flinched away.

All at once, Jordy released him. He sat back on his haunches, giving Rowan a perfect view of him in all his glory. The muscles in his forearm bunched as he took himself in hand. Rowan watched the head of his dick disappear and reappear in his fist, then dragged his eyes up from between those tree-trunk thighs to the solid slab of Jordy's stomach and the wall of his chest. A drop of sweat ran down between his pecs.

Rowan licked his lips. "Jordy," he said again. He raised his hands as far as Jordy's thighs, squeezed the meat of them under his fingers. The power coiled there…. God, Jordy would destroy him if he ever fucked Rowan *properly*.

"Yeah," Jordy agreed, and he looked down at Rowan's perfectly normal-size hands on his own godlike thighs, pressed his free hand to Rowan's chest, and came all over him.

Rowan's brain went to static.

Above him, Jordy heaved, his whole huge body moving with every breath. He looked like Rowan felt, fucked-out and brainless.

Suddenly Rowan understood the appeal of all kinds of sports.

"Wow."

Oops. He didn't mean to say that out loud.

Jordy made a sound kind of like the one Rowan had made a minute earlier. Rowan was pretty sure that was agreement. Then he grabbed a handful of Kleenex from the bedside table to clean up.

And this was the part where it got awkward, right? Rowan knew the drill. Time for Jordy to disentangle himself from Rowan's bedsheets and make his excuses.

Jordy tossed the Kleenex box down onto the bed beside Rowan and then keeled over.

Rowan mentally reevaluated the amount of time until Awkward. While he did that, he wiped the evidence from his stomach. Well, he tried. Jordy had been… enthusiastic. Rowan would need a shower.

He was still trying to make his brain make words when Jordy leaned his head against his shoulder.

So if it wasn't like *that*, Rowan thought, then it was like *this*. "Probably shouldn't have done that, but I kinda want to do it again."

Slowly, Jordy raised his head until Rowan could meet his eyes. He cleared his throat. "Only kinda?"

"Well…," Rowan hedged. "I mean, I have notes."

The lust faded from Jordy's eyes. He narrowed them. "*Notes*?" he repeated, half incredulity, half amusement.

"I didn't even get to touch your dick," Rowan pointed out. "*And you ignored my repeated requests to rail me into the mattress—*"

Jordy propped himself up on his elbows. Rowan was impressed. He didn't even have circulation back above the neck yet. "I was saving them for later. Good things come to those who wait."

"So we *are* doing this again."

"Only kinda," Jordy deadpanned. "I have notes."

Rowan laughed, still breathless. "Oh my God, let me go get a pen. I want to write this down—"

He rolled to try to get out of bed, but Jordy caught him with an arm around the waist and dragged him back toward Jordy's body. "First note," he said. "No books in bed. So rude."

As if Rowan wanted to leave his embrace in the first place. He turned back around to face the music, suddenly serious, and met Jordy's eyes. "If this were something other than… what it is… I'd be negotiating for that." His heart thudded painfully in his chest, but it would be worse to hold this in than to say it out loud. "But I think we're pretty clear, yeah? I can't commit"—somehow he managed the word without throwing up—"to someone who could move away at any moment."

Jordy reached for Rowan's hand and laced their fingers together. It made Rowan think of Ryan and Nico in the back room at that bar, matching rings and matching grins. "And I can't promise to stay."

Right. So that was clear. Rowan made himself take a deep, steady breath instead of the short, sharp one he wanted. "Still," he said, desperate to lighten the mood, "I think you'll find there's plenty of wiggle room." He glanced pointedly between them and then added, "Well... I'm confident we can *make* room, anyway."

Jordy shoved a pillow over Rowan's face.

THEY LEFT Rowan's bed for a shower and food. Jordy needed calories and a rest if he was going to pound Rowan through the mattress.

"No matter what my libido says," he murmured after a filthy kiss, "my body actually needs a break before round two."

Rowan groaned in exaggerated disappointment but let Jordy pull him into the shower, then the kitchen.

They ate leftovers on the couch while watching *CSI*, and if their usual smack talk got a bit flirtier and they inched closer after the plates were set aside, no one else had to know.

As the episode finished and Jordy crowed his murder-guessing victory—he only won because Rowan was distracted—he turned hot eyes and smirking mouth in Rowan's direction and all but melted him into the couch cushions. Rowan would not admit out loud how hot the smugness made him. Especially since sex apparently dialed it up to eleven for Jordy. He'd never looked so much like a douchey frat boy after winning their game before. Fuck. Why was Rowan into it?

Minutes later, when he was pinned to the couch under Jordy's weight, Rowan decided he didn't care.

Jordy had just slipped a large hot hand under Rowan's T-shirt when his phone rang.

"Who even calls? Who has their ringer on?" Rowan whined after Jordy hoisted himself off the couch. The climate-controlled room felt freezing without his hockey-player blanket.

"Parents have their ringer on," Jordy mumbled, though he didn't look any happier about the interruption. But his sulky expression turned to a frown when he saw his screen, and he answered quickly. "Hello?" His expression softened, and Rowan didn't have to wonder who was on the other end of the line. "Hi, peanut. What's wrong? … You did? Oh no." He shot Rowan a longing look. "Hmm. Yes, I can do that. See you soon."

He hung up and let out a deep sigh. Then he looked at Rowan, who was still laid out on the couch, though he'd propped himself up on his elbows, and gave him another hungry look—one that normally would have Rowan dropping to his knees, or parting them, but he couldn't think about that now.

"What's up?"

"Kaira forgot her stuffed Piglet." Jordy rubbed a hand over his face. "Which is of course her very favorite, and she can't possibly sleep without it."

"And she's six and having an exciting but maybe a little bit scary sleepover with her aunt, so you can't tell her to not worry about it," Rowan finished. Disappointing, but, well—if he were honest, he wouldn't like Jordy half as much if he weren't the kind of man who'd drop everything for his daughter.

Jordy sighed and looked at the clock. "It'll take me at least an hour, probably closer to two, to do the drive and make sure she's settled. Which means even if things go smoothly and she doesn't permanently kill the mood for the night, I don't think we'll have time for that promised railing."

He was right. Rowan had an appointment to fill out paperwork at the university first thing in the morning. As much as he wanted to stay up all night fucking, showing up looking like he'd been ridden hard and put away wet would not make a good impression on a new job.

Rowan allowed himself a dramatic flop back into the cushions.

"Sorry," Jordy started, but Rowan wasn't having that.

"No. Don't apologize for putting your kid before sex. I will survive. I will get by the same way I've been for the past few weeks—I'll go to sleep after I give my hand, or maybe my vibrator, a workout." Rowan wasn't sure he would, honestly. The idea of a teary, distraught Kaira was better than a cold shower. But telling Jordy that felt weird. Also, maybe he wanted to tease the big tease a little.

Suddenly Jordy was looming over Rowan and kissing him hungrily, filthily. "I… am going to go rescue my kid. But soon. Soon I'm going to plow you like you've been begging."

"Yes please," Rowan said maybe a bit too sincerely, then pushed him away with a gentle shove to his chest. "Go. See your kid. Play hero. And I'll see you tomorrow." Jordy pulled away with gratifying reluctance. "Need help finding Piglet?"

"No," Jordy grumbled from the hallway. "I can see him by the front door." Because of course.

In the silence left behind, Rowan finally rose from the couch, cleaned up their dinner mess, tidied their snogging disarray, and got ready for bed.

He didn't jerk off, but he did have some rather lovely, inspiring dreams.

JORDY HAD hoped Rowan might return home before Kaira and Emma did, so that they could take advantage of the last hour or so of an empty house, but it was not to be. Three or four hours ticked away, and Emma and Kaira burst in with wet hair and demands to be fed. Jordy swept Kaira up in the air, tossed her little body, caught her again, and blew a kiss on her cheek. "So demanding. How do you feel about lasagna?"

Emma answered for both of them. "Feed us, Jordy."

There would always be tonight and tomorrow. Kaira went to bed early. Jordy and Rowan would have time.

When Rowan returned, Kaira and Emma—well, mostly Kaira, with Emma occasionally chiming in—were regaling Jordy with stories of their adventures.

"Rowan! Rowan! Guess what?" Kaira launched herself at him when he entered the kitchen.

"Um," Rowan pondered as he scooped her up. "You bought a pet elephant?"

Jordy's heart thudded. Rowan loved to indulge her, and it did terrible, painful things in Jordy's chest.

"No!" she shrieked.

"You went to the moon?"

"No!"

"You… ate broccoli for breakfast?"

"No! Rowan! We went swimming!"

"Swimming?" Her hair was still damp. Rowan could not have missed it. "I never would have guessed."

"We did! There was a waterslide, and Aunt Emma said I couldn't go on the big one alone, but I got to go on the little one by myself, but then Auntie Emma took me to the big one and we went down it so fast!"

"That sounds amazing. You had a good time with Auntie Emma, then?"

"Yes. Rowan, why do you say her name funny?"

"What? Auntie Emma's?"

"Yes, you say it funny." Kaira giggled.

"No, *you* say it funny," Rowan countered.

"No!"

"Yes. Where I grew up, everyone says *awnt*. No one says *ant* unless they're talking about bugs."

"But why?"

That was one nice thing about having another adult around, Jordy decided. He didn't always have to answer the difficult questions. But he felt like he had to intervene or he'd just sit here all day watching them go back and forth and Emma would take one look at him and see he was completely besotted. "Because Rowan grew up in another country, peanut. I know we talked about this already. Saying *awnt*"—Jordy's accent was adorably atrocious—"is just like how he says *boot* instead of *trunk*, or *bin* instead of *trash*."

Kaira considered this, then shrugged, apparently satisfied.

"We're just finishing up lunch," Jordy told Rowan. "Plenty more on the counter if you want some."

"Ooh, yes, please. I'm famished." He found the pan of lasagna and plated up a healthy portion.

"How was the visit to campus?"

"Good. It turned into a tour and tech visit, though, so it lasted longer than anticipated. But at least I won't get lost first thing Monday morning."

"Campus?" Emma asked.

Damn. Jordy had thought maybe their little domestic play could go unnoticed or at least unremarked upon, but judging by her smile, it was a futile hope.

Jordy cleared his throat. "Yeah. Rowan's starting work at U of T on Monday."

Emma cast him a sideways glance. Jordy carefully avoided her gaze. He'd consciously told his family very little about the situation with Rowan, which in retrospect was kind of a giveaway. He'd been happy to regale them with details of Kaira's adventures with Janice, but with Rowan, Jordy often partook in the same adventures. He thought that might give them the wrong impression.

If he'd been more forthcoming, they could've teased him about his crush and he could've started sleeping with Rowan weeks ago. But that would probably make things worse when they ultimately broke up.

"Wow," Emma said with her mouth, to Rowan. "You're a little young for faculty, aren't you?"

I have many embarrassing follow-up questions and I'm going to laugh at you, Emma said with her eyes, to Jordy.

Rowan snorted, apparently oblivious to Emma asking obliquely if Jordy was robbing the cradle. "God, uh, thank you, I think? But no, I'm a librarian. I—" He'd made a move to grab cutlery, but he didn't get very far, because Kaira had pulled her limpet routine.

Worse and worse. She'd never done *that* to Janice. Jordy had never seen her do it to Rowan either.

"Excuse me," Rowan interrupted himself. "I think I stepped in something. Let me just—*oh*! It's Kaira!"

Jordy didn't even want to know what his face was doing. Maybe he could suggest they get takeout and then hide in a menu? Except who even had paper takeout menus anymore, and also they'd already eaten and Rowan was heating up the leftovers right now.

Kaira giggled wildly as Rowan dragged her around the kitchen. "Anyway, I was saying—that's where I met this little legwarmer. But it was only covering for a mat leave, so… here I am."

"Here you are," Emma agreed. "Well, it's great to meet you. Obviously my niece is, aha, *very* attached."

"Oh, the feeling is mutual. And—I guess the attachment is mutual too, although I'm not sure how Kaira would get around if I glued myself to *her* leg—" He gave a little shake and Kaira made a show of letting go, rolling across the floor as though Rowan had kicked her, laughing manically all the while.

Freed from his shackle, Rowan shook Emma's hand. "Anyway. Hi. Sorry, I'm absolutely famished."

"And probably thirsty too," Emma said, all innocence. "It's sticky out there." She batted her eyelashes at Jordy. "My brother should get you a drink."

Oh my God. Jordy was going to crawl into a hole. Right after he got Rowan the promised drink, which would at least let him turn his back on Emma long enough to stop blushing.

He realized the mistake as soon as he was putting the can in front of him. The label clearly read *pineapple*. And as Jordy had not revised his totally correct opinion about pineapples, now Emma knew he kept those on hand just for Rowan.

Or—or maybe he could convince her Rowan had bought them. It didn't have to mean anything, right?

Jordy probably should've realized his feelings when he kept buying pineapple-flavored things, he thought. Overall he'd been very willfully blind and now he was paying for it.

"Um," Rowan said into the sudden silence. He had to be aware of the way Emma was watching Jordy right now. The *thirst* comment wouldn't have slipped by him either. "Thanks."

Jordy cleared his throat. "You're welcome. Anyway, part of the reason Emma is here—" He paused to give her a dirty side-eye of his own. "—is because we have to take this little peanut back-to-school shopping."

Rowan raised his eyebrows. "Left that kind of to the last minute, no?" School started on Tuesday.

"It's first grade," Jordy pointed out. "It's not like she needs binders and textbooks. She needs clothes and a lunch bag."

"I want one with armadillos!" Kaira enthused.

Emma cracked an enormous grin. Rowan raised his eyebrows higher.

"Okay, that might have to come from Amazon," Jordy conceded. "But the point remains."

Emma leaned on the counter next to him and offered up a smile. "You're welcome to join us. Technically you're *also* going back to school, right?"

Rowan's face couldn't entirely drain of color, but all expression went out of it, and he paused midchew with his eyes bulging. Finally he swallowed. "Oh sh—shoot, uh, yeah, I probably should actually get some grown-up work clothes. The public library was pretty casual."

Jordy wasn't fooled—Emma definitely just wanted the opportunity to discover more ammunition to ruin Jordy's life—but it didn't matter. Having another adult on hand to wrangle Kaira when she got tired of trying on clothes after ten minutes could only make the situation less awful.

And it turned out he was right. Being able to trade off Kaira duty—by which Jordy meant alternately sending her to the bookstore with Rowan and the Lego store with Emma—made dividing and conquering the mall decidedly tame, if domestic. But it turned out Jordy was good with domestic.

A fact Emma wasted no time pointing out that night, once Kaira was in bed and Rowan had excused himself, allegedly to organize his closet but more likely to give Jordy and Emma private time together.

"So." She sipped her wine, which was weird. Jordy knew his baby sister was old enough to have given birth to his kid, but somehow being old enough to enjoy a glass of wine was a totally different mindfuck. "Playing house?"

Jordy huffed through his nose. "Who's playing?"

Her eyebrows went up. Her wineglass went down. She set it on the table next to her. "So it's serious, then? I kind of thought we'd have heard about him if that's the case. Plus there's the whole, you know, separate bedrooms thing."

"It's complicated."

She threw her head back and laughed. "Big brother, do you have any other *kind* of relationship?"

"Hey!" Jordy didn't think that was fair. "Sanna wasn't complicated."

"Yeah, well, maybe if she had been, you wouldn't have gotten divorced. Love's supposed to be messy."

It was embarrassing to get love-life advice from his younger sister. The wisdom of her statement only made it worse. "He just got a job in Toronto," Jordy said meaningfully.

Emma played dumb. Apparently she wanted Jordy to say it. "So?"

"He's a good friend, and maybe if my job couldn't send me to live in California or Florida or BC tomorrow, or maybe if he had a job he could take with him, then sure, maybe I'd ask. But his life is here and mine is…." He shrugged.

"For how long, though?"

"What?"

"Come on, Jordan, how much longer are you going to play? Will you be subject to bouncing around the continent? I mean, you're not planning on pulling a Jagr, are you? I'm sure you could figure out how to manage long distance or whatever for two, three, five years tops."

"Gee, thanks for putting an end date on my career," he grumbled to avoid answering the rest of her question. That was a lot of uncertainty to put a relationship through, even if he didn't plan to play into his fifties.

She poked him in the ribs. "Fine. We don't have to talk reasonably tonight." She sighed and then, with a twinkle in her eye, added, "But do tell me more about this fake date at a gala."

Jordy groaned theatrically but gave in and told her about his run-in with Rowan at the charity ball and their mutual agreement to use each other as cover. It was a good story, so he spared no detail and had her laughing into the cushions.

Later, when she left to find her bed, she kissed the top of his head and murmured, "Just remember, you deserve to be happy too. That's all I want for you."

Which was a ridiculous thing to say. Jordy *was* happy. He had a great career and a great kid, and he couldn't imagine anything better.

Except maybe someone to share it all with, but Jordy couldn't just will such a person into being.

Maybe because he'd just seen Baller the other day, but he thought about how Gabe Martin was now following Baller around the continent. Baller had played in three different cities in the past four years, and Jordy didn't doubt that Gabe was the one managing their home life, organizing moves, building their new homes, dealing with their daughter when she threw temper tantrums over having to leave their lives behind.

And their situation was so different. Gabe was retired; he'd had his career, and he had more than enough money to be a stay-at-home dad. Plus, with an Olympic gold and a Stanley Cup, he had pretty high career satisfaction. Then there was the fact that Gabe was Reyna's parent—they had adopted her together, after being married for years.

All of which meant that Gabe wasn't new. He wasn't a twentysomething at the beginning of his career contemplating a new relationship. He was a retired married man who had probably made the decision to support his husband's career this way even before he stopped playing hockey.

Sighing, Jordy tidied the living room and the kitchen and then headed to bed. If he paused for a moment near the closed door of Rowan's suite… well, no one was around to witness.

BUT BY the next afternoon, Jordy was half-convinced he and Rowan were cursed.

Emma was safely dropped off at the airport, and judging from Kaira's current behavior, the day was already successfully tiring her out and preparing her for an early bedtime. Everything had been progressing perfectly. Jordy had perhaps zoned out once or twice thinking about all the ways in which he could ruin Rowan tonight. Sure, Rowan had begged to be fucked, but there were so many paths and positions to achieve that goal.

And now those plans were going up in flames thanks to the updates in the team chat.

To help us all cope with the tragic loss of our favorite most-Canadian and wisest veteran—sorry Sully and Jordy—we are taking advantage of this preseason trade to raise a glass with our A one last time.

Jesus Brady. He's been traded, not assassinated.

laying it on thicc brah!

Drinks drink drinks!

As I was saying! You're all invited to Overpressure on Bloor at 7pm for drinks, snacks, and thorough roasting of Hiller.

Well, fuck. Jordy had always liked Justin Hill. He was pushing thirty-five, so it wasn't exactly surprising that the GM had sold him to another team for a younger prospect. Still, he was the kind of guy everyone always called "good in the room"—he kept the rookies on an even keel and was unflappable in the face of all sorts of bullshit goonery.

Even if Jordy felt like he could skip out on such a team event, he wouldn't want to. Usually trades happened midseason and fast. Players often had to be in their new city the next day for a practice or a game. Sometimes they flew out in the morning to hit the ice that night. Or they happened in the off-season when players were scattered around the world, on vacation, or visiting home. Teams couldn't often gather for a farewell party after the news hit.

Sighing, Jordy gave a thumbs-up to the group to show he'd be there and headed off to break the bad news to Rowan.

KAIRA AND Rowan had one last day to themselves on Labour Day. Jordy, however, had no such luck.

"Bye, Daddy!" Kaira said that morning as he left for training camp. She wrapped her arms around his knees. "I love you! Skate hard!"

Jordy leaned down so she could kiss his cheek.

"Bye, Jordy," Rowan echoed dutifully. He felt like he should add something else, but he didn't know enough about hockey.

Fortunately Kaira came to his rescue. "Rowan, you gotta tell him you love him and give him a kiss for luck."

Jordy looked up, startled, met Rowan's eyes, and then quickly looked away. After a beat he cleared his throat. "Peanut, it's just training camp. We should save the luck for when I'm playing games."

Rowan was impressed he could hear anything over the pounding of his heart in his throat.

Kaira made an exasperated noise. "Daddy, kiss luck doesn't *run out*."

"Maybe Rowan's does," Jordy said, voice admirably even. Why did Rowan feel like there was a whole second conversation going on here? "We wouldn't want to use it all up before the season starts."

Before Rowan could formulate an answer or even decide if he could kiss Jordy on the cheek in front of his kid, Jordy went on. "Besides, I don't make you hug anyone you don't want to, right? So we can't make Rowan do it either."

Rowan couldn't believe he was going to be alone with Kaira the whole day with no time to himself to have a breakdown. "What about if I blow him a kiss instead?" he suggested.

Or I could just blow him, but not with you standing there.

Kaira accepted the compromise, and Jordy pretended to catch the kiss and put it in his shorts pocket.

He was such a dork. Rowan was going to die.

"Home in time for dinner," he promised Kaira with a kiss to the top of her head. Then he winked at Rowan and blew him a kiss back, picked up his gear bag one-handed, and slung it easily over his shoulder. "See you guys later."

You do not have time for this crisis, Rowan reminded himself. He and Kaira still hadn't had breakfast, and a special one would provide a welcome distraction. He turned to his charge and asked seriously, "How do we feel about waffles this morning?"

Kaira felt great about waffles. Her enthusiasm extended to a walk to the park and a picnic lunch in the backyard with Clem.

Then he left, and when she fell asleep on the floor in the living room, the panic Rowan had successfully kept at bay by cramming his brain with responsibility rushed in to fill the sudden void.

What the hell was wrong with him? Why did he think sleeping with his friend/roommate/boss was any kind of good idea? Especially when he knew he was destined to catch feelings? Rowan had taken one look at a hot sweet dad and his heart had screeched DANGER, WILL ROBINSON. But then he'd not only moved into Jordy's house, he'd done the equivalent of shoving a block of kryptonite into his mouth like an alien squirrel.

He lay on the floor next to Kaira, who was sound asleep with her mouth open and drooling on the carpet, and breathed.

Okay, Chadha. Walk back the panic. This is actually fine. You can handle this.

If you thought about it, he was doing pretty well, considering. Tomorrow he'd start a new job—a *career*—with good pay and benefits that would let him start putting down the roots he'd longed for and start building a *home*. He'd find a nice apartment—an above-ground one, even!—and get a houseplant he couldn't kill, and….

And he'd get over Jordy eventually.

He was just drifting off when his phone vibrated on his stomach.

Gem: *Dinner tonight. My treat. 8pm at La Trat.*

Rowan had two options. One, decline the invitation on the chance that he and Jordy could find some time together after Kaira went to bed, and then deal with Gem's intrusive questions tomorrow when she inevitably showed up at his workplace.

Two… he once more pushed back having his brains fucked out in favor of an emergency crisis intervention.

Rowan: *Yes please you benevolent goddess. I love you.*

He let himself have five more minutes to stare at the ceiling. Then he woke Kaira—because if she spent the afternoon napping, she wouldn't go to bed at a reasonable hour—and suggested they bake cookies to take in tomorrow's lunches.

GEM DID not drive in Toronto. This was for the safety of others, not because she was a poor driver but because other people were and Gem did not suffer fools.

Although she might have to change her mind tonight if Rowan came clean about everything.

Even knowing he wouldn't be around to eat, Rowan had made dinner for Kaira and Jordy. Accepting Gem's invite felt a bit like running off with his tail between his legs, and he didn't want Jordy to get the impression that Rowan had regrets. He *did*, but he wasn't changing his mind about anything, and Jordy might if he realized Rowan was in his head about it.

So he made himself sit with them while they ate and Kaira grilled Jordy about all the hockey he'd done today, most of which made no sense to Rowan, and then he read Kaira a story so that he could be waiting out front at seven forty-five when the car Gem ordered for him pulled up.

Rowan was so used to meeting her at the restaurant when she did things like this that he slid into the back seat without looking and almost jumped out of his skin when Gem said, "Oh good, you're sleeping with him."

Rowan yelped and let go of his seat belt to clutch at his pounding heart. "Good grief, woman! Do you need a bell?"

Tutting, Gem reached over and fastened him in so he couldn't get away. "Don't be ridiculous." She smoothed the strap over the lapel of his coat. Awkward creases simply would not do. "And don't change the subject."

Rowan eyed her as the car glided smoothly into motion. "I'm neither confirming nor denying." *Technically* there had been no sleeping involved.

"Translation—you jumped him the moment you had another job lined up. As predicted."

He gaped soundlessly for a moment before he managed, with the desecrated remains of his dignity, "This is why people don't like lawyers, you know." He wouldn't put it past her to have arranged that job falling into his lap simply to be able to hold an I-told-you-so over his head.

She patted his knee. "A spring wedding is always nice, you know. Just as the trees are flowering and leafing out. Although I suppose that would require the Shield to flop out of the playoffs early again. Not *unlikely*, but a bit unromantic to plan on it."

"We're not getting married," Rowan protested, having finally found his tongue underneath an enormous pile of Gem's audacity.

She smiled, sharklike. "But you *are* together." When he didn't answer right away, the smile disappeared and exasperated dread took its place. "Rowan. You're together, *right*? You haven't fallen into bed with a lovely man who was handcrafted by the gods to turn your insides to jelly without *defining your relationship*, right?"

The back seat of Gem's hired car was very plush, but unfortunately not plush enough to swallow Rowan and protect him from Gem's judgment. "It's complicated?" he offered meekly. The alternative was to admit that Jordy had not yet had the opportunity to liquefy his insides, which seemed like too much information even for Gem.

Gem muttered a curse, either on Rowan or the aforementioned hockey-thigh-crafting gods, and closed her eyes. "I swear to Christ you're going to give me ulcers."

"Do we have to talk about this?"

For a moment the only sound was the muted rumble of tires on asphalt. Finally Gem sighed, opened her eyes, and pasted on a brittle smile. "No. I'm sorry. Not if you don't want to. Tonight is supposed to be celebrating your professional achievements." She paused for dramatic effect. "Not your personal flaws."

He blinked. "Wait, seriously?"

Gem exhaled a gusty breath through her nose. "Darling, if you're not ready to stop sabotaging your own happiness, there's nothing I can do to force you. Trying would only spoil my appetite. And you know how I feel about La Trat's wine list."

Okay, then. "I feel like I've got away with something," Rowan admitted.

The car pulled up to the curb outside the restaurant, and Gem gave him a pointed look. "Oh, we'll revisit this when it blows up in your face," she promised. "Which it will. But for now—celebrations and wine."

Rowan didn't know what he appreciated more—the reprieve, the night away from Jordy to try to get his head on straight, or the friendship he hardly deserved—but either way, he wasn't going to take it for granted. "Well, in that case—" He popped open the car door and climbed out, then offered his hand. "—I think our table awaits."

JORDY DIDN'T want to admit that he was dragging his feet with the whole replacement nanny thing. He wasn't *not* looking, but it was possible he'd been overly critical of the profiles the agency had sent his way and hadn't agreed to interview anyone.

Unfortunately, Rowan was starting a new job, and even though school had started and Kaira was registered in the aftercare program on the days Jordy couldn't pick her up at three, it wasn't fair to ask Rowan to keep working two jobs.

But Jordy didn't actually want anything to change. He didn't want to hire a new nanny who would need the suite for their own use, which would push Rowan out of it. And though he had guest rooms aplenty for Rowan to use, Jordy didn't think he could talk Rowan into staying in one of them when his new job would give him enough funds to find his own place.

It was selfish, but just because Jordy couldn't give Rowan long-term didn't mean he couldn't keep him just a little while longer.

Training camp had finished and now the preseason was only a few days away, so Jordy *should* be putting all his energy and concentration into hockey. But even at practice, whenever he stopped to hydrate or rotated out of a drill, his thoughts went to Rowan.

Somehow they still hadn't managed to make good on Jordy's promise to rail him into the mattress. They hadn't had much time together at all this week, and any time they were together, either Kaira was wide-awake or one of them had somewhere else to be. Rowan had gone out Tuesday evening and then gone to bed early on Wednesday and Thursday, derailing any possibility of intimate encounters. Thinking about it now, it seemed odd, considering how eager Rowan had been last Friday.

Jordy dropped his forehead onto his gloved hands, which he'd rested on the butt of his stick. The last thing he needed this practice was to give himself more Rowan-related turmoil. Rowan was not being weird; he wasn't avoiding Jordy. It was perfectly legitimate to not want to have sex. Jordy should know. He'd spent most of the last decade not having sex with other people.

In their stalls after, as they were taking off their on-ice gear, Sully grinned and pulled off his chest protector. "So, are you excited for today's riveting session about off-ice behavior?"

Jordy figured his eye roll said enough. Plenty of the younger guys needed lessons on a variety of topics, but the annual refresher courses grew wearisome, especially since teams tended to forget all about them after the preseason.

After the Don't Be a Douchebag in Public, and Yes, That Includes Social Media seminar and before the special teams strategy meeting, Jordy checked his phone. There were no new texts from Rowan. Jordy hadn't realized how much Rowan, and by extension Kaira, had been texting him until Kaira started school and Rowan started his job, and now no one sent him updates.

Sully handed Jordy one of the Clif Bars he had swiped on his way back from the restroom. "So, thoughts on the Don't be a Douchebag session this year?" He crunched into an apple like a college student debriefing after a lecture.

Jordy slid his phone back into his pocket. "Same as always."

"My favorite part was the bit about not hitting on employees," Sully said before taking another big bite.

The instructor had been talking about team, NHL, and arena employees, of course, and not one's personal nanny, but Jordy flushed under Sully's teasing gaze. "I hate you."

"Aw, love you too, boo."

Jordy sulkily ate his Clif Bar.

"All joking aside," Sully said in an undertone, "you really should make a move on someone who makes you smile like that at your phone. Or pout at it. Don't think I didn't see your face just now."

"I thought I wasn't allowed to hit on him," Jordy bitched.

"That's why we gotta solve your nanny problem. That and so you don't have to use my wife as free childcare anymore."

"Adrianna loves me," Jordy said, because if he didn't hold firm to that belief, he'd drown in guilt for how often he'd put her out this summer.

"Adrianna loves your kid." Sully gave him a no-nonsense look. "And I love her, and that means no more babysitting, Jordy. Seriously."

Jordy sighed. "School started this week. She has after-school care now. And Rowan only works until five most days."

"Work?" Sully raised his brows. "So Pinocchio is a real boy again? Does that mean—"

Fuck it. Jordy should've kept his mouth shut. He knew better than to give Sully a scrap of material. "It means that it's none of your business."

They had enough problems. Aging defense, inexperienced forwards. Somehow they were too old and too young at the same time. The new guy would help—Lord knew they needed all the twenty-five-year-old skaters they could get—but unless the trainers were going to start handing out robotic knees and HGH, Jordy had his doubts about a winning season. And that meant the media was going to be brutal. They already were—calls for trades, for their coach to be fired, for their GM to be fired, for Brady to be replaced....

"Oh, so you're already fucking him, then," Sully said.

While they were replacing people, they could replace Sully.

"We're not talking about this," Jordy said firmly, slinging his duffel bag over his shoulder. Apparently not talking about it at all was the only way to avoid Sully knowing all of his business. Sully didn't get to figure out Jordy's business before Jordy did. That was rude.

"I'll call you later!" Sully shouted at his back as Jordy headed for the door.

Jordy gave him the finger over his shoulder.

JORDY DID not want to talk about it, which sucked because he could think of about a dozen things, off the top of his head, that he really should talk about. For example, he needed to hire a new nanny, but he didn't want to because it might push Rowan into moving out. If he talked to Rowan about it, he could forestall that by offering him one of the upstairs guest rooms instead, but then it would sound like Jordy wouldn't rather have Rowan in *his* bed, and they'd have to talk about *that*. That would lead Rowan to the realization that Jordy had big feelings, when Rowan had already been clear that he could not commit to Jordy because Jordy was inevitably going to leave Toronto, whether that be next month or next year, and Rowan would try to spare Jordy's feelings by, again, moving out.

Then there was the whole thing where Jordy already felt like Rowan was avoiding him, but he couldn't come out and say that because Rowan had started a new job this week so of course he was tired. Jordy didn't want to make that about him. Obviously not talking about it was the way to go. Either Rowan would become more available this weekend and next week and Jordy could relax, or he wouldn't and Jordy would....

Jordy would....

Jordy would figure it out when that happened.

Today, camp had finished early enough for Jordy to pick Kaira up on his way home, so he focused on that.

Kaira had been in daycare before, and obviously Jordy had chosen a nice one. But day care pickup and first-grade pickup were in totally different leagues as far as how much of a pain in the ass they were. When Jordy was Kaira's age, he took a school bus and liked it. But these days parents all wanted to pick their kids up from school in person because they were—understandably—paranoid, which meant traffic nightmares even in cities that were not Toronto, which meant Jordy sat in his car for fifteen minutes while fifty other parents also sat in their cars, all waiting for their turn to be allowed to collect the correct child.

Jordy loved that he had the money to send his kid to the best school in the city. He loved having the freedom to pick her up some days. He just wished that didn't mean *this*.

Sully texted him three times while he was waiting. Jordy shot his dashboard the finger and muted their chat.

Finally it was his turn, and whatever child-herder they had on duty released Kaira into his custody. He scooped her up for a hug, planted a big, silly kiss on her cheek, and got her settled into her car seat. "Hi, peanut. Did you have a good day today?"

"So good, Daddy!" She spent five minutes breathlessly telling him about it while he waited in the agonizing line to leave the school parking lot—surely someone somewhere could solve this traffic issue? Surely the school's parents would pool their money to hire someone to figure that out? Should Jordy join the PTA?—and then said, "Daddy, we should go out for dinner."

The abrupt shift in direction threw him so much he almost missed an opening to turn left, which would result in seven hundred parents all laying on their horns behind him. But he made the turn fine. "We should, huh? Why do you say that?"

He knew his kid was spoiled, but dinners out were one place he had actually managed to create what he thought was a pretty good home life balance. She didn't expect things like that.

"Because," Kaira said as though Jordy had asked a question with a very obvious answer, "you and Rowan had your first week of work and I had my first week of school and we should celebrate."

Jordy rewound Kaira's rundown of her day and identified key phrases like *weekend plans*, which sounded like a thing a six-year-old shouldn't care about but at least explained the sudden request.

He couldn't fault the logic, though. And with Kaira providing such a convenient excuse, maybe he could get Rowan to come and relax. They could go for an early meal, walk along the lake, tire out the kid—

"I think that sounds like a great idea," Jordy agreed. "You and I can choose a restaurant when we get home, okay?" One that was not McDonald's or Tim Hortons.

"And we have to invite Rowan."

"And we have to invite Rowan," Jordy agreed. "We'll make sure it's someplace he likes too."

"Can I get dino nuggets?"

"If the restaurant has them," Jordy tempered, not wanting to make binding promises while also hoping he could talk his daughter out of the sort of restaurant that served dino nuggets.

It wasn't until Jordy was searching the fridge for an afternoon snack and caught sight of leftovers that he got the idea.

As a bonus, it didn't take much to get Kaira on board.

"Rowan, Rowan! Daddy says we can go out for dinner tonight!" Kaira said the moment Rowan was in the front door.

"Oh? Did he now?" Rowan lifted one eyebrow and smiled.

"Yes. He said we can go to get *us* food!" She collided with Rowan, wrapped her arms around his leg, and looked up at him.

"Us food?"

"Yes, like how you make," Kaira explained.

"Ah, of course. Us food." He shot Jordy a look, curious, maybe, about Jordy's choice.

Jordy waited until Kaira hurried off to get her shoes and then said in an undertone, "I figured it was the only way to talk her into a restaurant that didn't serve dino nuggets."

Rowan snorted. "Right. So where are we headed?"

"I have some recommendations from the internet, but if you have a place in mind…."

"I know the perfect place."

The restaurant was a tiny hole-in-the-wall, decorated with minimalist Indo-Asian flair. Kaira loved it. She stared at everything and asked questions, and when their server arrived, she almost fell out of her chair trying to touch the soft fabric of her embroidered tunic.

"Are you from India?" Kaira wanted to know.

Fortunately the server smiled, unoffended, and said, "Sorta. My parents were born there."

"Oh! Like Dada and Dadi! They send me pretty dresses, but not one like yours."

"Well, maybe Papa can put in a good word for you," she said with a wink in Rowan's direction.

Jordy sent up a thankful prayer that Kaira seemed oblivious to the insinuation. "Can you ask them, Daddy?"

"We'll look into it, peanut," Jordy said. "But right now we need to order food."

"Oh!" Kaira squirmed in delight at the prospect, dresses forgotten.

An hour later, they were walking down the sidewalk, Kaira between them, holding their hands and calling out "One, two, three, swing!" before lifting her to dangle her feet.

It struck Jordy, as Kaira shrieked with joy, that he'd never been able to give her this before—a stupid, common, everyday thing that kids liked to do and that Jordy and Kaira never had done because Jordy didn't have a coparent.

The tender feeling swelling Jordy's heart might have been why he asked, "Shall we get ice cream?"

At least the extra excitement knocked her out. She was dead asleep by the time Jordy pulled into his garage.

Jordy waved Rowan off as he headed down the hall with his limp baby. After swapping her dress for a nightie, he kissed her forehead and left her to her sweet dreams.

He shut her door and stared at it for a long moment. Rowan was downstairs. He might have gone to his room or sat on the couch for some TV, or maybe he was waiting for Jordy so they could take advantage of their evening off. The possibility of that—and all the other possibilities it could lead to—warmed his blood. But once he was downstairs, he'd have an answer. No more Schrödinger's sex.

But if Rowan was waiting, it was unkind of Jordy to linger. He swallowed, stepped away from the door, and went in search of Rowan.

He found him in the hallway, apparently as uncertain as Jordy as to what would happen next.

"So did you want—"

"We could—" they said at the same time. They both paused and stared. Then they spoke together again.

"Yes."

"Please."

The *please* was a gut-punch that pushed Jordy into movement. He closed the gap between them, cupped Rowan's face, and kissed him with all the hunger of a week of waiting.

Rowan moaned and opened his mouth to Jordy's tongue. The memory of how Rowan had acted and responded the last time flooded Jordy's senses. He slipped his hands from Rowan's face, grabbed his hips, and pulled until their groins collided. Rowan hissed and wrapped his arms around Jordy's shoulders. "Fuck, I could get used to the manhandling."

"Good." Jordy grabbed Rowan's thighs and lifted.

"Oh *fuck*." Rowan clamped his legs around Jordy's hips and huffed a laugh into the space between their mouths. "That was hot."

"Good," Jordy said again and made for Rowan's bedroom.

Someday, Jordy wanted to strip Rowan, take off each item slowly and make a meal of him. But he didn't have the patience today. He set Rowan down and tore at his clothes as they fell onto the bed, then draped himself over Rowan and reveled in the way he squirmed and pressed up against Jordy's weight. "What do you want?" he asked between kisses.

Rowan shivered under him, but the voice he answered with was full of *are you kidding?* "*Fuck* me," he demanded.

Jordy just wanted to hear him say it again. "I don't think that's exactly what you want. What was it you said last time?" He bit down on Rowan's jaw. "Rail me?"

"Yes, that."

Jordy pulled back so he could get a good look at Rowan's face. He wanted to do this right, to be good. "*How* is the question. What do you like?"

"What part of 'rail me' is unclear?" Rowan groaned. "Hard, fast, and deep."

Jordy pinched his thigh. "Brat." Rowan shivered again, and his cock twitched. Jordy's responded in kind. He was discovering lots of things about himself while in bed with Rowan. He added that to the list of things to explore later. "On your knees? Your back? Up against the wall?"

"Oh God, you probably could." Rowan stroked Jordy's pecs as if considering the strength of the muscles. "Hold me up against it, just fuck me right into it."

Jordy let his own hand wander, stroking up Rowan's inner thigh, teasing higher and higher, brushing the crease of Rowan's ass but not pushing in.

"But that's not what you want tonight." He pulled back, changed direction, and headed for Rowan's dick.

"Hands and knees," Rowan gasped. "Wanna… wanna feel you in my throat—fuck!"

Jordy stroked once, twice, swiped his thumb over the head—a reward for good behavior.

"And before that?"

"Before?"

"How do you like being opened up? Can I do it? Do you want my fingers?" Rowan shuddered and grabbed Jordy's head to pull him in for a kiss. Jordy let him, opened up for Rowan's tongue and let himself be kissed, hungry and deep.

"Or," he said, "maybe you'll let me use my tongue first."

"Use whatever body part you want, just get me wet and *fuck me.*"

Jordy grinned. "As you wish."

He flipped Rowan over and dived down.

Rowan howled when Jordy made contact and spread his legs in invitation. Jordy gripped Rowan's asscheeks and held them open so he could press his tongue in.

Rowan sobbed into the pillows and pushed back, impaling himself on Jordy's tongue—or trying. Jordy pressed him into the mattress, keeping his mouth attached where he wanted it. The wet noises he made sounded obscene, but they barely registered over Rowan's continued refrain. "Oh fuck, please, fuck me, Jordy, *fuck!*"

Jordy would fuck him as soon as he was ready. Right now Rowan was getting him hot just talking about it. He made a rough negative sound against Rowan's ass and slid his thumbs inward to tease the edges of his hole.

"Oh fuck, never mind," Rowan hiccupped into the pillow. "Keep— keep doing that, just—"

Jordy should have bought more expensive lube. This one tasted like plastic. But he didn't care when Rowan was spread out in front of him, body hitching back and forth automatically, with Jordy's thumbs hooked into either side of his hole to make room for his tongue.

This was supposed to be foreplay. The way Rowan was moaning and sobbing, Jordy didn't know if he'd ever let him stop. If Jordy would ever *want* to. He pressed in deep, curling his tongue, then pulled back to flick over the edges of the muscle, teasing. Traced the rim lightly with just the tip, stretching him wider with his thumbs.

Still not *wet* enough, Jordy thought. He wanted Rowan sloppy and dripping so that when Jordy finished his task he could slide right in. But he *wasn't* finished.

He wasn't thinking when he pulled back and spat on Rowan's open hole.

Rowan's elbows collapsed and his shoulders pressed flat to the bed. "Oh fuck," he gasped, chest heaving against the mattress. "Oh fuck, Jordy, please."

Jordy hummed an affirmative against his rim and flicked his tongue over the open, waiting hole.

Beneath his hands, Rowan started to tremble. His breath quickened. "If you don't—*uh*, Jordy if you don't stop, I'm going to come."

Suddenly Jordy was the one shuddering. Rowan would come from this? From Jordy's tongue on him, inside him, nothing on his dick?

Jordy pulled one hand away from Rowan's ass to wrap around his own cock and squeezed the base. "Can I still fuck you after?"

A tiny, ruined sound escaped Rowan's lungs. "Yeah, God—"

Jordy put his mouth back on Rowan's hole. He was ravenous for it—for every stifled cry of pleasure and tremor of Rowan's thighs, for the way his toes curled into the sheets. He pulled Rowan open wide and devoured him, filling the room with slick wet sounds and breathless pleas until every line of Rowan's body went taut.

"Jordy, Jordy—*fuck*—"

Anything else was lost in the sob that escaped him as his hole spasmed under Jordy's lips, trying to close around his fingers. Jordy didn't let it, fucking his thumbs in and out along with his tongue as Rowan's cock spilled between his legs, untouched, making a puddle on the sheets.

Jordy had never been so turned on in his life.

"Rowan, I have to—can I—"

"*Yes.*"

It took him three tries to get the condom on. He almost dropped the lube drizzling it down Rowan's crack because the sight of his hole spasming made his fingers numb.

"Come *on*," Rowan urged, shoving backward like he could take Jordy's cock faster that way. Like he was still desperate even though he was lying in a puddle of his own come.

Jordy lined his cock up and pushed inside.

Rowan's body was tight and slick, and Jordy could feel the last of his orgasm trembling through him as he thrust, both hands on Rowan's hips, yanking him back every time Jordy pushed forward.

"Oh fuck. Your thighs," Rowan gasped. He was white-knuckling the sheets, his hair slick with sweat. And then just "Oh—fuck me, fuck me, *fuck me.*"

Jordy fucked him. He rammed in again and again, until Rowan's body stopped fighting the intrusion and the pressure around Jordy's cock relaxed. His blood pounded in his ears. When he looked down, the skin around Rowan's hole was red and raw from Jordy's stubble. He ran his thumb across the thin skin and pressed down, feeling it against his cock.

"Fuck—Jordy, come on, I can take it. *Please*—"

Did he mean Jordy's thumb? Did he just want Jordy to fuck him that much harder? Jordy didn't know. He didn't ask. Rowan could have both. He coated his thumb in the lube he'd spread down Rowan's crack and worked that inside him too.

The pressure had built so high now that Jordy couldn't last. His body was tight with anticipation, straining toward orgasm. The clench of Rowan's hole was intense. Jordy could barely see, barely breathe. Beneath him Rowan had gone almost silent.

No—Rowan hadn't gone silent. The whole world had, whiting out in a thick haze of pleasure as Jordy's orgasm caught him. Release thundered through him, his balls jerking against Rowan's ass. Only the clutch of Rowan's body remained, the endorphins singing in Jordy's blood.

Jesus Christ.

When it ended, Jordy pulled out, brainless with pleasure, and rolled Rowan onto his back. His cock was hard, shiny with come, his eyes glassy.

Jordy pushed two fingers back inside him and wrapped his other hand around Rowan's cock.

Sound returned to the world as Rowan howled, his feet braced on the bed. "Jordy, oh my God—"

Jordy rubbed his thumb in a circle under the head and Rowan came apart in his hand and around his fingers, shaking as his orgasm wrung out of him.

Finally Rowan whimpered at the overstimulation and nudged Jordy's hands away.

Jordy knew the feeling. He figured his brain and Rowan's body felt about the same right now.

"Yeah," Jordy agreed. He glanced at his hand, at the condom hanging off his dick like a sad flag, and then at the ruin they'd made of the sheets. Fuck it. He'd just buy new ones. Rowan could sleep in his bed tonight. They could set an alarm.

He wiped his hand and then pulled off the condom.

Rowan made a noise of protest so weak it barely counted.

"You wrecked them first." Jordy lifted a thigh to prove it. His leg hairs were clumped together. He'd maneuvered himself right into the wet spot.

"Fair."

"I'll buy new ones tomorrow."

"Do you not have a washing machine?"

"I don't have a sewing machine." Jordy gestured toward Rowan's head, where three small tears had rent the fabric.

Rowan turned. Looked. Turned back. Blinked. "Oops."

Jordy bit down on a grin.

Rowan, on the other hand, didn't bother trying not to laugh. "God, how smug are you right now?"

"I made you rip the sheets!" Jordy's teammates would have a bad time next week. His ego had just tripled in size. Not that he'd tell them why. Not unless Sully pissed him off, at least. Then Jordy could traumatize him like he deserved.

"Is that a first for you?" He eyed Jordy's thighs as though doubting this were possible.

Jordy felt like any answer he could give would incriminate him. "Is it a first for you?" he countered.

"You could say that." He winced. "Okay, I need a shower or you're going to have to throw me out along with the sheets."

A shower sounded fabulous.

KAIRA WAS talking a mile a minute as Rowan followed the automated voice to "Turn right."

"I want a hot dog and a soda!"

"Sure," Rowan agreed, because Jordy had suggested Rowan buy her food at the arena and said not to worry about spoiling her dinner.

He hung another right, stopped at a gate, and rolled down his window to show security the parking pass Jordy had given him.

Attending Jordy's final preseason game in Toronto was a tradition for Kaira, Jordy had explained, and Janice had previously been her chaperone. Of course, Jordy had offered to find someone else, but Kaira was ecstatic to bring Rowan to his first ever hockey game. Because "field hockey doesn't count, Rowan!"

Kaira took his hand and skipped up to the private entrance, continuing her narration of everything she wanted to do today. "We need to go to our seats so that we can see Daddy do warmup. We can't miss it."

Not that Rowan wanted to deny her anything, but he didn't know how to get there from here.

"Hello! Are you Kaira Shaw?" A young employee dressed in a team-branded blue polo with a bright lanyard around her neck stood nearby, smiling and waving.

"Yes. Who are you?"

"I'm Jessica. Your dad asked me to check in to make sure you found your seats okay."

"Oh! Do you know where they are? We have to go now so we don't miss warmups."

Jessica smiled brightly, clearly charmed, and guided the way. "I hear it's your first game," she said to Rowan. "Is there anything else I can help you with while I'm here?"

"Uh, I'm guessing it should be straightforward to find food and bathrooms from our seats."

Jessica laughed. "It should be. You're right at the glass, regular fan seats, so everything is clearly marked." She led them into the stands and pointed down the steps. "All the way down and to the right."

"Thank you, Jessica," Rowan said as Kaira tugged on his hand. "Kaira, don't forget to say thank you."

"Thank you, Miss Jessica. Come on, Rowan!"

Jessica waved them away, and Rowan followed Kaira to their seats.

Naturally, Kaira did not sit down. She stood at the boards she was just tall enough to see over with her nose pressed to the glass in eager anticipation, even though there was nothing to see. The ice was empty.

Rowan figured these must be good seats, since they sat on a longer edge of the ice, halfway between the middle and one of the nets. From here, he had a pretty good view of the home bench and could see most of the ice.

He leaned back and watched Kaira vibrate with excitement. She'd dressed for the occasion in rainbow leggings and bright yellow shoes, her hair tied into two pigtails with Shield-branded scrunchies. The look was completed, of course, with an official Shield jersey.

Rowan couldn't claim any fondness for the uniform. According to Jordy, the eye-searing blue and yellow came from the city crest. Kaira's jersey had a yellow torso with blue shoulders and stripes around the cuffs and hems. The team logo, a stylized blue T on a yellow shield, didn't exactly help tone things down. He'd gotten the better end of the jersey deal at least; the one Jordy had lent him was blue with yellow highlights. It was somewhat boring in that it simply had Jordy's name—Shaw— and number—7—on the back. But Kaira clearly wore a special order, because above the number 7 on her back read DADDY.

She'd pulled it out of her closet and showed it off with pride earlier in the day, and Rowan had melted at the label and manfully tried not to picture Jordy holding an even tinier Kaira in her special jersey.

Of course, Kaira had then declared that Rowan also needed a jersey and run to find her dad to solve the problem. Jordy had rubbed his jaw, looked Rowan up and down—while Rowan thought very boring, pure thoughts—and said, "Guess he'll have to borrow one of mine."

Rowan had never understood the clothes-sharing kink before, maybe because he was tall and broad enough that he rarely had a boyfriend who outsized him. Or maybe because he had never been all that attached to any of his previous partners. But when Jordy pulled the jersey out of his closet and explained that they needed them for off-ice events, and Rowan had to pull it on under Jordy's watchful eyes? Well.

Rowan flushed hot and desperately wished they didn't have a six-year-old chaperone.

Now, at the rink, he tried not to think about Jordy's name and number branded across his back. He could think about it later. Judging by Jordy's hot gaze, he had also been into it.

"Rowan!" Kaira cried. "Look!" She pointed across the ice toward players trickling in from whatever you called backstage when it was a sport.

Even if Rowan hadn't been able to recognize Jordy by his jersey or stance or familiar face, he couldn't have missed his arrival. Kaira squealed and pressed her palms against the glass. Rowan scootched forward in his chair. She didn't need him, but suddenly he felt like he should be closer.

Jordy said something to the guy on his right, who was just as big as Jordy if not bigger, laughed, and then smoothly glided in their direction. He stopped opposite Kaira and tapped the glass with one gloved hand. Kaira grinned and put her hand on the same spot. For a moment, they made faces at each other and stared adoringly.

God, Rowan was going to die from the cuteness.

Then the guy from before arrived at Jordy's side and bent over to pull a face for Kaira, who cried, "Uncle Sully!"

A few other fans were scattered about, and some of the adults murmured, their attention caught by Kaira's outburst. Some of the kids who were lined up around the boards trying to get a closer view drifted nearer, clearly wanting to join the fun.

But Jordy and Sully had jobs to do, so after pulling a few more silly faces, they both waved goodbye and skated off to do…

Something that looked like it should involve a partner. Rowan's ears burned as he watched Jordy stretch low to the ice, his thighs spread wide, and tilt his hips. Rowan was pretty familiar with that position.

He didn't know how he felt about Jordy doing *that* in front of strangers.

Fortunately, it only lasted a few minutes before the stretching gave way to something less pornographic.

"Rowan," Kaira called, and he gave in to the temptation to join her at the glass. She rested her head against him and kept her eyes on the ice. After a few minutes, she asked to be picked up, so Rowan settled her on a hip and they watched together, Kaira chattering about what was happening on the ice—who she saw and what they were doing.

He was so busy watching her face as she explained about goalies that he didn't see Jordy's approach until Kaira cried out and the glass was suddenly sprayed with snow. Rowan jumped and Kaira shrieked with laughter. On the other side of the glass, Jordy laughed. Apparently hard stops could shave up ice and throw it high enough to spray a grown man in the face—at least if one didn't have the protection of the plexiglass. Rowan narrowed his eyes at Jordy and pouted. "Not funny," he said, enunciating slowly so Jordy could read his lips.

Jordy kept grinning. "Very funny," he said back. Then he blew Kaira a kiss and skated backward several meters.

Kaira blew a kiss back and waved. "Bye, Daddy!"

There went any hope of staying incognito. Not that they were trying, Rowan reflected as he thought about Kaira's jersey. Jordy waved once more, turned, and slipped off the ice.

"So, poppet, what next?"

What next was three hours of—well. Not *torture*. Kaira's not-so-secret identity was definitely out, though, which meant people were looking at Rowan and wondering where they knew his face from, and Rowan was remembering that approximately a hundred lifetimes ago he'd been Jordy's fake date at a fancy party and the internet had found out about it.

Maybe he'd escape without anyone putting two and two together. After all, how many people cared about hockey games that didn't even count for anything?

He did his best to put it out of his mind and concentrate on the game and on keeping Kaira from falling off her chair, which she kept trying to stand on to get a better view. Rowan couldn't help but think that while their seats were perfect for warmups, he might have liked the relative safety of box seats for the game itself.

And in the box seats, no one would wonder who Rowan was to Jordy or what he was doing here with Jordy's kid.

No one except Rowan, anyway.

Meanwhile, Rowan was experiencing the lure of hockey for the first time.

If anyone had asked, he would have said he was a pacifist. The closest he'd ever come to committing physical violence was accidentally clotheslining someone in ultimate Frisbee. He *should* be appalled at the entire concept of checking.

Unfortunately, watching Jordy crush people into the boards and take the little rubber thingy away woke the caveman that slept in every human person's brain, dosed him with Ecstasy, and set him loose on Rowan's imagination with an industrial-size bottle of lube.

Thank God he and Jordy were already sleeping together or he might've had a stroke.

The players left the ice after an hour or so, and Rowan might've thought the game was over, except the Jumbotron indicated that they had only finished the first of three periods, and now there was an intermission. Anyone who'd spent more than five minutes with kids knew what that meant.

"Bathroom break?" He could certainly navigate his way to a restroom, but... then what? Gods, would he be forced to wait outside the ladies' room for her? He could handle that in a mall, but there were, what, ten thousand people here? How did Jordy do this?

Of course, if Jordy took her to the arena, he could probably find her a private bathroom so he never had to let her out of his sight.

Rowan was debating his next move when Jessica appeared as if by magic. "Let me show you the VIP restrooms," she said. "And then we'll get you some dinner."

Thank you, Jordy, Rowan thought. Maybe next time they did this, he'd think to ask about the logistics first.

But then his thought train screeched to a halt. Because what did he mean, *next time*? Jordy was already looking for a new nanny. Rowan had seen the printed-out résumés, annotated in Jordy's haphazard professional athlete handwriting, on the end of the kitchen counter yesterday. Not a moment too soon either—with the regular season starting in just over a week, Jordy would be gone half the time. And Rowan had to work too, at his real job that he actually liked that had benefits and a pension and everything.

Even if he did miss getting to spend almost every day with Kaira. And he'd miss it more in the future, when Jordy hired a real nanny.

When Rowan moved out of the house.

"Rowan! Look, they have *space ice cream*."

Rowan dutifully followed Kaira's tiny, slightly grubby finger toward a vendor selling Dippin' Dots, then pulled a Wet Wipe out of his pocket to clean off the ketchup before she got any on her jersey. "Is it time for dessert?"

"Pleeeeease," Kaira said sweetly, hanging on his arm.

Jessica caught his eye over Kaira's head and hid a smile.

Sighing, Rowan kissed her crown and steered her toward the counter. "Come on, then. Let's make good use of Daddy's credit card."

@No1Sh13ldF4n

So I'm at the Shield game and don't look now but this guy looks really familiar? And then I realized THAT'S JORDY SHAW'S DATE FROM THE THING THIS SUMMER. He's here with Jordy's kid!

@punchritudinous

Pics or it didn't happen

@No1Sh13ldF4n

I'm not posting a pic of his kid, that's creepy

@No1Sh13ldF4n

Besides you can check out the official team photos on Instagram, you can see him in the background in the one of Jordy and his daughter pressing their hands against the glass

@punchritudinous

OH MY GOD THAT'S TOTALLY HIM!!! AWWWWWH THEY'RE STILL TOGETHER.

"YOU'RE FAMOUS again," Sully told Jordy when he got out of the shower after the game.

Jordy reached for his shirt. "Did I stop being famous?"

Sully rolled his eyes right into a smirk. "Sorry, I should clarify—your nanny is famous again."

Oh God, Jordy was afraid to ask. "Why?"

"Looks like he and Kaira were the stars of the team's Instagram posts tonight."

Of course they were. Normally the team's PR department at least pretended to get Jordy's signoff if they wanted to use a picture of his kid on official social media channels, but it was preseason. Just as the team had a bunch of fresh-faced kids skating with them—none ready for their call-up; they'd be getting sent to the minors tomorrow—the PR department had a green crop of interns.

It wasn't like Kaira's face had never been on the internet. Or Rowan's, for that matter, after the gala pictures.

Jordy pulled on a pair of boxers and crossed the locker room—around the team logo on the floor—to put his towel in the laundry. "Why are you telling me this?"

"Because fans love gossip and you never give them any."

Jordy arched his eyebrows as he returned to his locker and his clothes. Sometimes the best way to get Sully to the point was to wait him out. Asking questions would delight him and keep him in teasing mode.

Of course, Jordy wasn't the only guy in the locker room—or the only one who was curious.

"What's the tea?" Brady asked, completely sincere and without any malice or even, unfortunately, irony. He wasn't looking for dirt to tease Jordy with. He just wanted to know.

"Aside from the fact that Jordy and his daughter are too cute for words?"

Brady nodded. "Yeah. I mean, they say that every time, so it's not exactly gossip."

Sully laughed. "Too right. What they don't talk about every time is the boy." Shit. "Your fans remembered him, boo. They're convinced it must be true love since you trust him with your kid."

Jordy shook his head but said nothing, in part because he couldn't say anything that Sully wouldn't mock him for and in part because anything he said, even a denial or joke, would be confirmation for Sully. The man knew him too well.

Brady, on the other hand, had no such issues. "Isn't Rowan the nanny?"

Sully shook his head. "Oh, sweet summer child," he sighed, because apparently he was an aging meme, "Rowan isn't just the nanny. He was Jordy's accidental date to a charity gala this summer."

Brady's eyebrow rose. "Really?"

"Yup. And the internet obsessed about it because Jordy is a man of mystery when it comes to romance and his fans are starved for information."

"Rowan was a friend and we were helping each other get through a difficult evening," Jordy said dryly, because Brady looked like he'd stumbled into the middle of a Hallmark movie.

Sully nodded. "Yes. Just bros helping each other out. Which is why Rowan is the new nanny. He and Jordy had compatible problems. But he's not a permanent replacement."

Jordy groaned theatrically. "Don't remind me."

That caught Sully's attention. "Nanny hunt going well, then?"

Jordy pulled a face. He wasn't sure if nanny hunts were always this difficult and he'd simply forgotten the pain of the first search, or if he had simply lucked out with Janice. Either way, the hunt had proven frustrating.

"Hiring someone to parent your kid isn't easy," he admitted.

That garnered sympathetic nods from Sully and Brady, not that either of them had been through the nanny search themselves.

"Guess it would be hard to find someone that you gel with," Brady said thoughtfully.

Jordy wished that was all it was, that he couldn't find someone he felt any sort of connection with. But every applicant he'd reviewed had felt wrong. Too young, too old. Too into hockey, too into fringe child-rearing ideas. He'd barely found any that he wanted to interview, and the few people he'd talked to on the phone had left a bad taste in his mouth.

Of course, he wasn't exactly motivated to find someone new. What he really wanted was for nothing to change—or at the very least for a new nanny not to chase Rowan out of Jordy's house.

"Well, I'm sure you'll find someone," Brady said positively.

Sully slapped Jordy's shoulder. "Yup. And let us know if you need any help—that's not babysitting. Happy to help with the search, though."

"Thanks," Jordy said dryly. "You're a mensch."

The issue, Jordy reflected as he got into his car, wasn't the nanny. The problem was that he didn't know where he stood with Rowan. The problem was that Jordy was in love and desperate to hold on and there were so many question marks about the future and Rowan and their relationship.

Shaking his head, Jordy started his SUV and made a decision. He needed to talk to Rowan. Maybe Rowan would say no, but maybe…. Either way, Jordy needed answers.

Besides, if he was headed for heartbreak, maybe sooner was better than later.

At home, Kaira was fed and cuddling with Rowan on the couch, watching another Bollywood film, though Jordy didn't recognize this one.

"She wanted to watch a Pakistani one, for my sake," Rowan explained. Ah, so not Bollywood, then.

"Any good?" he asked as he settled on the couch on Kaira's other side. She shifted to lean into him but didn't otherwise move away from Rowan.

"It's great," she told him, and then stayed quiet, watching the movie. High praise.

"What did you think of your first game?" Jordy murmured over Kaira's head.

Rowan shot Jordy a look full of heat and promise. "I think I'll save my review for later."

Jordy blinked. Wow. Okay. "Uh. Right. Sure?"

Rowan dropped the sex eyes and chuckled. "Kaira and I had a lot of fun, didn't we, poppet?"

"Yup." But she didn't take her eyes off the screen, to Rowan's clear amusement.

"We watched, we laughed, we ate lots of junk food," Rowan explained. "Thanks, by the way, for sending someone to help us."

Jordy shrugged. "Least I could do. I know the box would have been more ideal but… she likes the glass."

"Fair enough. Still. Thanks."

Getting someone who was paid to chaperone VIPs around the arena to chaperone Rowan, who was only there for his kid, didn't feel like something he should be thanked for, but Jordy could accept it with grace. "You're welcome." He thought about what Sully had said. He didn't want to bring up something that might upset Rowan, but saying nothing could be worse. "So, uh, I don't know if you know this, but after the gala some fans online were talking about you?"

Rowan arched an eyebrow. "I'm aware."

"Well, it seems that they remembered and they spotted you tonight."

"Oh, I know." He waved at his phone, which lay dark on the armrest. "I heard from Taylor, my former coworker at the library. She's a Shield fan, and she wanted to know why I never mentioned that my friend-slash-roomie was a familiar face."

Jordy winced. "Is she mad?"

"Nah, she gets why I didn't say anything. Though she teased me about turning down her offer to go to a game. I told her I was just waiting for the right date." He stroked a hand over Kaira's head and tugged one of her pigtails. Kaira swatted him away with a disgruntled "Rowan."

Jordy would have to get the name of this movie. Clearly they'd be watching it again. "That's good."

"Yeah. The new coworkers are a different story. They don't know about the nanny gig, so they all want to know how long we've been dating."

"Oh." Jordy's heart thumped. "What, uh, what did you tell them?"

"That a bunch of researchers and librarians should know better than to believe everything they read on the internet." He flashed a cheeky grin, and Jordy wanted to kiss it for being so adorable, even as his stomach lurched with mixed emotions.

In a perfect world, Rowan would tell anyone he asked that he and Jordy were in love and Kaira was their daughter and never think twice about it, except maybe to bask in some smugness. Actually, yes, Jordy wanted that. He wanted Rowan to be *insufferable* about him. He wanted him telling the world how smart Kaira was. He wanted him wearing Jordy's name across his back because he was showing off—letting everyone who saw him know he belonged to Jordy.

Maybe tomorrow Jordy could take a step toward making that wish come true.

Tonight he'd enjoy what he had.

"Good advice," Jordy said.

"Shhh!" Kaira hissed at them.

Rowan met Jordy's gaze, eyes dancing, and mimed zipping his lips.

It was too late for Jordy to get invested in the movie—it was already almost done—and he was probably going to have to watch it seven hundred times in the next year, so he'd have plenty of opportunities to pick up the plot. He planted his ass in an armchair and pulled up a game of Angry Birds.

He needed something to focus on or he'd spill his guts everywhere.

Twenty minutes later the movie ended, and Jordy swept Kaira off the couch and threw her over his shoulder. "Tooth-brushing time!"

"Daddy!"

Jordy shot Rowan a look, hoping to convey his plan. As if he needed to—Rowan was already looking back, eyes lidded.

Kaira did not get a double bedtime story, and thankfully didn't seem to need one. After the excitement of the day, her eyelids were drooping by the time Jordy got halfway through. He closed the book and kissed her forehead. "Good night, peanut."

Kaira didn't answer, already asleep.

Quietly, Jordy flicked off the light and pulled her door closed.

From the sound of things, Rowan was in the kitchen, probably loading the dishwasher and cleaning up the remains of their snack. Jordy allowed himself a short detour to brush his teeth and then padded back down the hallway.

Rowan hadn't turned on the kitchen lights, so the only illumination came from the living room lamps. It lent the scene a daring kind of intimacy. *This could be yours*, Jordy's subconscious shouted. All he had to do was admit out loud that he wanted it.

He opened his mouth do to just that, and Rowan stepped into a pool of light.

He was still wearing Jordy's jersey.

Rationality got a game misconduct penalty and left the ice.

Jordy took three strides forward and backed Rowan into the refrigerator.

Before Jordy could kiss him, Rowan looked up, eyes sparkling, mouth set in a smirk. "Well, hello, stranger," he said, all innocence, like he didn't know exactly what he was doing.

Jordy pinned his hips to the fridge and kissed him.

It wasn't a gentle kiss. It was a kiss that crushed the air out of Rowan's lungs and made him curl his fingers into Jordy's chest. It elicited a sharp, needy sound from Rowan's mouth. Jordy licked that out of him and swallowed it, scraped his teeth over Rowan's lower lip, and smoothed his thumbs over the jut of his hipbones.

By the time Jordy moved his mouth to Rowan's neck, Rowan was breathing hard, his cock a thick, solid line against Jordy's thigh. Jordy ground forward and Rowan gasped as he arched into the pleasure. "So the jersey. You like it?"

Jordy used his teeth on Rowan's earlobe. Rowan's knees buckled, but he had nowhere to go; the pressure of Jordy's body held him up. "I want to fuck you in it," Jordy growled. "Against the wall." His cock throbbed in approval, and he thrust forward again to let Rowan feel the power of it.

Rowan squeaked. "*This* wall?"

Yes, said Jordy's lizard brain.

No, said the part of Jordy that was a responsible dad. It added, *This is a fridge.*

But there was no way they were going to make it all the way downstairs to Rowan's room. Jordy didn't even want to try. Instead—

"Put your arms around my neck."

Rowan obeyed, even as he began to ask, "What—"

He cut off with a quiet yelp as Jordy fitted his palms under Rowan's thighs and lifted.

"Oh my God." Automatically, he wrapped his legs around Jordy's waist. "So many bucket-list items tonight—"

Jordy cut him off with a kiss, but that was short-lived too as he carried Rowan down the hallway toward his bedroom and dumped him on the bed.

He looked so good there. Jordy's lizard brain approved. But Jordy had promised something specific, and he was going to deliver.

"Top drawer," he told Rowan, who scrambled backward to open it and grab the lube. Meanwhile Jordy straddled his thighs and yanked his jeans open, freeing his cock.

Rowan swore when Jordy pushed his legs apart and pushed two slick fingers inside him—not *too* loud, but loud enough.

Fuck, Jordy didn't want to stop. He spread his fingers, stretching. "Can you be quiet?"

Rowan let out a soundless laugh. "Is that a trick question?"

Not intentionally. Jordy pushed in a third finger and reveled in the groan that produced, the pearl of precome beading at the head of Rowan's cock. "Take that as a no."

"Fuck off, stop being so—*ah*—smug and take your pants off. You promised me wall sex."

Jordy pulled his fingers out and slapped Rowan's hip. "Get up, then."

He scrambled to his feet, half tripping in his haste to get his pants off all the way. Jordy pulled his shirt over his head one-handed, undid his belt, and stepped out of his own clothing.

Rowan reached for the hem of the jersey.

"No." Jordy put a hand on his wrist. "Leave it on, remember?"

Rowan licked his lips as Jordy crowded against him once more. This time he'd picked an actual wall—an exterior one. No point in borrowing trouble. This should keep the noise to a minimum. "Do you, ah—" He swallowed. "—want me to turn it around so you can see the name, or…?"

Jordy inhaled a sharp breath. Rowan took the opportunity to snake his hand between their bodies and wrap lube-slick fingers around Jordy's erection. "Tempting." But no. He would fuck Rowan against the wall like he'd been asking for, until he clenched down on Jordy's dick and spilled between them.

And then Jordy would throw him on all fours on the bed and take what he wanted.

"But I want to do what you've been asking for." Then he grabbed Rowan by the backs of his thighs and hoisted him up.

"Fuck." Rowan wrapped arms and legs around Jordy's shoulders and hips to hold on.

Jordy pressed him into the wall, trusting Rowan to hold his weight so Jordy could position his dick at Rowan's entrance.

Then he pushed.

"Ahhh-ah!" Rowan gasped into Jordy's ear and tugged a fistful of his hair. "Oh God," he slurred, "s'good as I imagined."

"Haven't—haven't done anything yet." Jordy grunted and tested his grip—good—and started to move.

Rowan tugged Jordy's hair again in retaliation. "So fuck me and make it better."

Jordy would give him whatever he wanted. With his grip still firm on Rowan's thighs, he gave his first grinding thrust.

Rowan's mouth dropped open. "Oh fuck—yes, that."

Through half-focused, hazy eyes, Jordy registered the pleasure on Rowan's face. He looked so good like that, slack-jawed with lust in Jordy's jersey. Jordy pressed their mouths together for a sloppy openmouthed kiss and ground forward in short, sharp thrusts.

Pressed together like this, sharing breath, Rowan's cock trapped between them, Jordy was all too aware of the fact that they hadn't fucked like this before—face-to-face. For the past few weeks, Jordy hadn't been brave enough to be inside Rowan while looking him in the eye. He didn't think he could keep everything inside in such a moment of intimacy.

But the sight of Rowan in his name made his blood burn. Damn the consequences—right now Jordy didn't want Rowan any other way.

He pulled back from the kiss to press his face into Rowan's neck and sucked a mark into his skin.

"Jordy—"

Jordy pulled back and after a hard grind asked, "Think you can help me out, sweetheart?"

Rowan dug his nails into the skin of Jordy's upper back. The pain sparked along Jordy's nerve endings and made his nipples stiffen. "Wha-at?"

"Brace yourself against my shoulders and push back into the wall. If you can hold yourself up, I can fuck you harder."

Rowan moaned and did what Jordy told him—and now Jordy could move his hips, pulling back far enough to get momentum and slamming back in hard, using gravity to get in deep—

"*Fuck*! There, there, there!"

—and nail Rowan's prostate just right.

Rowan had always been what locker-room talk called a screamer, but never so loud.

Jordy slammed in again, then held still, a wicked tease that let him regroup.

"I can't believe—that you can actually—" Even his babbling had risen in pitch and volume.

As much as Jordy loved it, as much as it stroked his ego, as much as he wanted to make Rowan fucking *sing*—Jordy was a dad, and his house wasn't that big.

With his next hard thrust forward, he shoved his jersey into Rowan's open, gasping, moaning mouth. Rowan's legs spasmed around Jordy's hips, his eyes widened, and he clamped his teeth around the fabric as he let out another wail, this one muffled.

"I wanna hear your pretty noises," Jordy promised, staring Rowan in the eye as he gave it to him, "but those noises are for me, not anyone else. God, you, fuck, you sing on my cock, and I want every goddamn note."

Rowan's nails dug into Jordy's shoulders hard enough to draw blood, and Jordy felt wild with it. Rowan was so turned on he was almost screaming, clawing Jordy's skin, and his dick was leaking so much Jordy's jersey was soaked with it. Jordy did that. Jordy made Rowan feel this good, made his sex fantasies come to life, made him incoherent with lust. That had to mean something. It did mean something.

So Jordy braced himself and put his back in to it, to give Rowan the railing he asked for.

Rowan was mouthing wetly at the jersey now, ruining it for any use other than as lingerie for Rowan. Jordy pulled it up enough to uncover his dripping cock and fisted it, swiping his thumb over the head on the upstroke and squeezing the way Rowan liked.

Rowan clutched at Jordy's shoulders and screwed his eyes shut, and for the first time, Jordy saw his whole beautiful face as he came wailing on Jordy's dick.

The sight of it was a punch to the gut. Jordy's own orgasm caught him off guard. Instinct took hold, and he thrust his hips in hard, burying himself as deep as he could as he held Rowan to him, his face buried in Rowan's neck.

They clutched each other as they rode out the aftershocks, muscles spasming and breaths gasping as they came down.

When he recovered, Jordy pulled back just enough to press their foreheads together. Sure his limbs could hold them both well enough, Jordy reached up to pull his jersey from between Rowan's lips. Definitely ruined.

"Was it ev-everything you dreamed of?" Jordy gasped out.

Rowan huffed. His color was high. "And more." Then he pulled Jordy in to a sloppy postorgasm kiss. "So," he said, several filthy second later, "how do I dismount?"

Jordy barked a laugh. "Good question." He reached down to grasp the condom and pull out. Then, with a glance over his shoulder, he spun and tumbled them onto the bed. Thank God for hockey training, because Jordy didn't crush Rowan into the mattress but caught his weight long enough to untangle their limbs and roll to the side.

Then they were lying side by side and Rowan was laughing breathlessly. "Oh my God, I can't believe we—I—we just did that. Also, I think I ruined your jersey."

"Mmm, definitely." Jordy rolled over and smushed a kiss to Rowan's still rosy cheek. "You should keep it. Wear it again some time." Then, because he was still kind of a coward, he rolled back and out of bed before Rowan could react.

Rowan joined him in the en suite before Jordy could return with a washcloth, which was probably for the best. The jersey might have taken the brunt of Rowan's come, but he was still a glistening mess that no cloth could truly solve.

Once clean, they fell back into bed. Jordy didn't ask and Rowan didn't offer, it just sort of happened. Rowan detailed other sexual fantasies he'd previously thought unattainable and asked Jordy if he thought they could do this or that.

Jordy fell asleep with an arm thrown over Rowan's ribs as he listened to Rowan lazily break down his favorite parts of "the ice hockey sport," most of which involved Jordy's muscles and alternative uses thereof.

In the morning, Jordy woke to too much sun streaming through his open blinds, Rowan's warm body still tucked into his own, and a text from his agent saying the Sheild's GM wanted his no-trade list.

Third Period

ROWAN WOKE up to an unfamiliar ceiling and had a brief, half-panicked moment of wondering where he was.

Then he registered the muscle aches in his thighs, back, and shoulders, as well as the accompanying tenderness in his backside, and the night before flooded back to him.

So *that* happened. And it should happen again as soon as possible, or at least as soon as possible once Rowan had recovered enough that he could stand up without wincing.

The part that maybe should not have happened was when Rowan fell asleep in Jordy's bed afterward. From the sunlight filtering past the curtains, it was still early enough that Kaira probably wasn't awake, so he had time to get up and sneak out of Jordy's room. Not that she would know any different, really; if he stole one of Jordy's T-shirts and started walking around the house, there'd be no reason for her to suspect where he'd slept, and even if she did, it wasn't like—

He stopped that train of thought. No sense borrowing more trouble than he already had.

So. Last night Jordy had fucked him into incoherence. In his bedroom. While Rowan wore his jersey. While Rowan used his jersey *as a gag*.

That felt... possessive, in a pleasant way Rowan didn't want to interrogate but probably should.

It might not mean anything beyond the obvious—that Jordy liked pretending, in the heat of the moment, that the people he fucked belonged to him. Rowan could hardly fault him for that. He'd enjoyed the fantasy too. The evidence of that was all over Jordy's jersey.

But last night had felt different from their previous encounters in other ways too. For one, it was the first time Jordy had kissed him while they fucked. It was the first time they'd done this in Jordy's room and not in Rowan's temporary quarters downstairs, and the first time they'd actually spent the night together. So... maybe it did mean something.

Hadn't they agreed weeks ago that a physical relationship was all they could have, and a temporary one at that? Rowan was putting down roots in Toronto. Every day he looked forward to his job. His bank balance informed him that he could begin looking for his own place very soon. Not a nasty basement apartment either but a proper one-bedroom, maybe even one with a balcony. A place of his own that he could *make* his own—choose his furniture, paint his walls. Do his bathroom in a Parisian theme if he wanted.

And Jordy might get traded at any minute. Rowan understood that. That was a risk. But all relationships had risks. The person you loved could get hit by a bus, or turn out to be a serial killer. Or just an asshole. Rowan had dated enough of those.

And he was pretty sure Jordy wasn't an asshole, and a serial killer wouldn't have invited Rowan to live in his house and catch him.

Okay, now Rowan was going around his head in meaningless tangents to avoid coming to the conclusion that he had feelings for Jordy and maybe he should just… take the risk. Jordy might get traded—but he might not.

Did Rowan want to give up this life on a maybe?

He sat up and rubbed his eyes. First order of business was hauling himself out of bed.

He took his time stealing a T-shirt. Anything team-branded might inspire a repeat of last night, which normally he'd be in favor of, but if he wanted to have a serious conversation, neutral was better. He picked a plain black shirt and pulled on his jeans from the night before.

Jordy was in the kitchen, sitting at the breakfast bar, hunched over a pad of paper. He had a coffee cup at his elbow, and he didn't look up when Rowan entered. Lost in thought, apparently. Rowan allowed himself a moment to fantasize that Jordy was making a list of all the reasons they should throw caution to the wind and make their relationship something more than physical.

He stopped on his way to the pour-over set to press a kiss to Jordy's cheek. "Morning. Kaira still in bed?"

"Mm. It's a miracle."

Rowan took down his favorite mug—God, he was an idiot; he had a favorite mug in Jordy's house and he'd been telling himself he could avoid entanglement—and spent a moment going through the routine of filling it with life-giving caffeine. "Breakfast plans?" he asked. He wanted to get a feel for the morning schedule—Kaira was still in bed *now*, but that could change anytime. When was the best window for this conversation?

"No, I'm just—" A sigh.

Rowan turned around.

Jordy still had his head down to stare at his piece of paper, but after a moment he looked up. "Distracted."

Rowan was a light sleeper. He knew for a fact Jordy hadn't spent last night tossing and turning, because he'd have woken up. So the dark circles under his eyes were not from lack of sleep.

So something else was bothering him. Rowan knocked back half his mug—it looked like he'd need it—and braced himself. "What's going on?"

"My agent called this morning."

At ass o'clock on a Sunday? Rowan put down the mug and placed his hands on the counter for support. The bottom dropped out of his stomach. "That sounds ominous."

"Yeah. It's—it could end up being nothing. But…."

"But," Rowan repeated.

Jordy dropped the pen. He flexed his fingers a few times and then stretched out his arm toward Rowan, almost like he wanted to take his hand. He pulled it back before he could. "The team asked for my list."

"Your list." Rowan sounded like a stunned parrot. He forced his mouth to shape meaningful words this time. "I'm assuming this isn't a list of groceries or top-ten Toronto nightclubs."

Jordy didn't laugh. "It's a list of teams they can't trade me to."

Did that mean what it sounded like? Rowan shouldn't jump to conclusions. Jordy's serious, pinched mouth suggested otherwise. "I'm guessing this isn't a routine thing."

"It is when you're looking to trade someone." He rubbed his brow. "They might be looking at options, and they might be shopping around me and other defensemen hoping to sell one of us for more forwards. So it could all come to nothing. But the rumors aren't wrong. It makes sense to trade me over most other guys."

"Do—" Rowan cleared his throat. He just had something caught in it, was all. And not emotions. "Do you think you'll get traded?"

Jordy sighed. "Honestly? They don't need me as much as they need kids who can get the puck in the net."

"But they sent you to New York," Rowan argued, floundering. How could a team spend so much on a player when they wanted him gone?

"They also sent Brady. And they could have had a million reasons to send me that weren't about me being a billboard face or a good defenseman."

"Like?"

"Like proving my capital to other teams."

Which was an especially mercenary view of things, but also probably not the worst thing sports management had ever done in the name of bettering their team.

"How long?"

That got another unhappy sigh. "Who knows? It could be tomorrow or it could be never. Just because Toronto wants to offload me doesn't mean other teams will want me."

Before Rowan could open his mouth and say something totally sincere and epically stupid, like "Who wouldn't want you?" Kaira walked into the kitchen and saved Rowan from himself.

Jordy flipped over his notepad, shot Rowan a pleading look that managed to convey *Please don't say anything to my child*, and brightly asked what she wanted for breakfast.

Rowan stood frozen while Jordy put on a brave face and found food for his daughter, because the idea of the trade wasn't some unknown specter now but a full-on apparition sitting at the breakfast table, waiting to ruin their cute little domestic scene. Rowan couldn't confess anything now, couldn't ask for anything when Jordy might be in Florida by the end of the week. What was the point of asking for more when the shelf life was so brief?

Sure, they could do long distance, but long distance when Jordy was a single parent with a demanding job that had him on the road half the year? Jordy didn't have time for long distance. In the past couple of weeks, Rowan had gotten a glimpse of what a relationship with a player would be like during the season. Between practices and games, there would be stretches where Rowan and Jordy would only be able to eke out stolen moments here and there. Just yesterday, before they went to bed together, they'd barely seen each other all day beyond quick meetings in the kitchen. If they lived apart, they wouldn't have those moments, and Jordy probably wouldn't even have time to chat with Rowan. He'd be too busy being a dad.

No, the ticking time bomb that was Jordy's trade was a firm reminder that anything more was just a pipe dream.

Shield on the Move? Shaw Trade Rumors Abound
By Krista Eckhart
October 27

Trade whispers are echoing in the hallway outside the Toronto Shield front office.

Nothing is officially confirmed yet, but rumors persist that the Shield are entertaining—or even soliciting—trade offers, and one name keeps coming up: Jordan Shaw. A source within the Shield confirmed that Shaw, who has a limited no-move clause in his contract, was asked to provide his list of teams he cannot be traded to.

Despite being a fan favorite, a Norris Trophy winner, and an Olympian, Shaw is a good candidate for a trade. Shaw is a talented defenseman and a veteran with plenty of experience. He's also thirty-two years old with steady numbers and two years remaining on his contract—years the Shield, with their 3–4–3 record so far this season, are unlikely to be Cup contenders.

No one wants to give up an All-Star talent, but the Shield aren't in a position to put him to good use unless it's a trade for a piece that will be ready when the Shield's forward core hit the peaks of their careers. And plenty of teams are willing to pay for experienced defensemen, especially when it comes in the form of Jordan Shaw, who is well-known for his amiability and boring off-ice life. Expect several front offices to review Shaw's résumé and check their AHL stables for anyone who could sweeten the pot for the Shield.

Read More

WHEN THE season started, Jordy's busy schedule only got busier.

Thankfully, Rowan's and Kaira's work/school routines were already established and getting more practiced, which meant that despite Jordy's chaos, their day-to-day felt almost uninterrupted.

Almost.

Because of course Kaira had big feelings about the season starting and her dad being back at hockey. Rowan did his best to hear her and help her process those emotions, but even as he helped her find balance, he couldn't help but feel guilty for not being Janice and for knowingly keeping a secret about even bigger changes to come.

Because no matter what, Daddy getting traded and moving them to another city—maybe even another country—and the finding of a new nanny? Well, that would probably inspire feelings that needed more than just a couple of heart-to-hearts.

Not that Jordy was getting any closer to hiring that new nanny, or if he was, he hadn't told Rowan about it.

When he asked, back at the beginning of September, Jordy had admitted to having trouble finding applicants he wanted to interview. But when Rowan sorted through a stack of candidates and picked out a handful he thought were promising, Jordy had rejected them all.

"Okay, clearly I missed something. Tell me what's wrong with these two so I can help better."

"Which two?"

"Uh, let's start with Allison."

"She was a volunteer canvasser for Pierre Asshat," Jordy said and shuddered.

"What?" Rowan flipped through her CV and wow, okay, yeah. She'd listed canvassing for a right-wing extremist. "How did I miss that?" He shook his head, then asked, "Don't tell me Christine had the same problem."

"No," Jordy admitted slowly. "But her first-aid certificate is out of date."

Rowan flipped through the paperwork. It had expired at the end of July. She probably just hadn't updated her résumé. But it wasn't as if he could just ask, *That's it?* when this was Kaira's life that might be at stake, so he accepted the feedback and kept wading through the CVs.

In his weaker moments, Rowan thought maybe Jordy just didn't want to replace him because he was that amazing and Jordy wanted to keep him around. Of course, in his more realistic moments, he reasoned

Jordy was a paranoid single dad who'd been just as ridiculous the first time around. After all, these were nannies through an agency. They'd already been vetted by someone else. It wasn't like they were going to serve Kaira candy for dinner and let her drive the SUV. Jordy might not like them all, but surely some of them qualified for a conversation.

Whatever. It wasn't Rowan's problem. If Jordy wanted to drag his feet, let him. It was his kid. It wasn't like this was affecting *Rowan*'s life at all.

Rowan thought this last bit to himself rather sarcastically as he pulled up to the school's aftercare program to pick up Kaira. Jordy had left yesterday morning on the first of many road trips. It just so happened that today also happened to be Rowan's monthly staff meeting, which some arsehole had scheduled for half six on a Wednesday night.

"Hi, Rowan!" Kaira cheerfully kicked her feet as he buckled her into her car seat. "Can we have dino nuggets for dinner?"

Rowan tweaked her nose and reminded himself he was annoyed with Jordy, not her. "Sorry, poppet. We won't be home for dinner tonight. How do McDonald's nuggets sound instead?"

Jordy might not like it, but Jordy wasn't here and Jordy hadn't hired someone to help out, so Jordy could suck a lemon.

"With *french fries*?"

"Of course with french fries."

"Yay!"

Rowan maybe felt a little spiteful giving the McDonald's drive-thru attendant Jordy's credit card.

"Where are we going?" Kaira asked between bites of nugget. "Are we going to the hockey game?"

She hadn't quite grasped the fact that not all of Jordy's games happened on home ice. Rowan couldn't blame her; from what he'd seen on TV, the rinks did all kind of look the same.

"Not tonight. I have to go back to work." Which Jordy knew about, because Rowan had told him three days ago, when Jordy was stubbornly refusing to interview someone because she didn't have a passport, as though having a passport would qualify her to work in the States anyway. "But I'll put the game on my phone and you can watch in the office, okay?" He could rustle up a pair of earbuds so she wouldn't disturb the rest of the staff.

"Okay."

They stopped briefly in the family restroom at the library so Rowan could help her wash grease from her face and hands. By that time he was almost late, so he scooped her up and booked it toward the conference room.

It was 6:29 when Marina spotted him in the hallway. "Mr. Chadha." She raised her eyebrows in surprise to see Kaira. "I didn't realize you were bringing an assistant to this meeting."

He couldn't tell from her tone if she was annoyed or just curious. "Sorry," he said automatically. "This month's schedule is a bit chaotic. She won't be any trouble." *I hope.*

"The books here are *so big*," Kaira put in seriously.

Rowan could've sworn the corner of Marina's mouth twitched like she wanted to smile. "That they are, young lady. My name is Marina Chifundo. And you are…?"

"Kaira Shaw."

Marina's eyebrows ascended to another plane of existence. "Nice to meet you, Miss Shaw. Why don't you go inside and ask Mr. Iulian—he's the tall man with the bow tie—where he keeps the coloring books."

Kaira squirmed out of Rowan's arms. "Okay."

Someone should probably teach this kid about stranger danger. Rowan thought sourly it ought to be Jordy, but he wasn't here.

"Trouble in paradise?" Marina asked mildly as they closed the conference room door behind them. Rowan thought he had to field a lot of questions after those preseason game pictures. Now that he'd brought Kaira to a work meeting, he could only expect the third degree.

"Jordy is dragging his feet hiring a real nanny." Rowan immediately hated himself for how bitter that sounded. "It's not like I mind spending time with Kaira, of course," he added. "She's great. It's just…."

"He's gone and has no appreciation for the amount of work he's put on you?"

Rowan felt his ears heat. Jordy certainly appreciated *some* things about Rowan. It wasn't as though he wasn't being well compensated, what with a roof over his head and a car to drive and food to eat on top of a salary. And Jordy, er, *appreciated* him plenty when they were alone together as well.

Although that appreciation felt different since that night in Jordy's room. They hadn't had sex there again. Now that a trade was on the horizon, it was like Jordy had changed his mind about what he wanted from Rowan. Which mostly consisted of childcare.

Probably Rowan should stop bottling up this resentment. "Something like that," he agreed.

Marina clapped him on the shoulder and nudged him toward a seat. Andreu had procured a beanbag chair and an enormous box of crayons from somewhere and had set Kaira up in a corner.

Rowan prayed that would keep her occupied. He had no idea how long this meeting might go.

"All right," Marina said, clapping her hands. She motioned toward Ravi, who nodded and opened his laptop. "Everyone's here, so let's call this meeting to order."

For the first twenty minutes, everything went smoothly. Rowan almost couldn't believe his luck.

It obviously couldn't last.

At five to seven, Kaira had to use the bathroom. Marina kindly suggested they all take a five-minute recess, even though no adult needed a break. Then Kaira wanted to watch the hockey game. Rowan put it on his phone with the volume muted, but she wanted to sit on his lap to watch.

By the time the meeting wrapped up at quarter to eight, Kaira was cranky and listless and had kneed him in the kidney seventeen times. Rowan didn't know how she managed to do that; weren't the kidneys supposed to be in the back?

"Can we get ice cream?" Kaira asked as Rowan settled her back in her car seat.

"Not tonight." She needed a bath and then bed. She was going to be late for bedtime as it was.

Kaira pouted. "But I want—"

"No," Rowan said firmly. He'd been at work since just before nine that morning. They were not making any stops on the way home. "You had a treat for dinner. It's time to go home and get ready for bed."

That cued a pout, but no tears, at least.

She did kick the back of the passenger seat all the way home, but at least she wasn't behind Rowan.

Bathtime was the usual fight. Kaira splashed water all over the bathroom, and Rowan wasn't cleaning it up. Let Jordy pay someone to clean the mold off. Then Kaira wanted to stay up to watch the end of the hockey game. She wanted to stay up to talk to her dad once he got off the ice. She wanted a third bedtime story.

Rowan wanted a drink and twelve hours by himself where he didn't have to talk to anyone.

Finally Kaira fell asleep and Rowan retreated to the den downstairs, just for that extra level of insulation between himself and the nearest human being.

So of course, after only one episode of his favorite library documentary, his phone rang.

JORDY PULLED off his tie and rubbed his temples.

The Shield hadn't played badly, but they'd lost 3–1 in a lackluster fashion, and he felt vaguely embarrassed that the team hadn't been able to match Florida's energy.

Jordy took off his jacket and sat on the edge of his hotel bed. He wished he could tiptoe into his daughter's room and watch her sleep, maybe kiss her downy head. The older he got, the more he hated road trips. In the beginning, he'd enjoyed the travel and excitement of new cities. Now that he was in his thirties and with a six-year-old at home, each anonymous hotel room blurred into the next, and every missed day with his kid felt like another moment or memory he couldn't recover. Somehow his baby had grown up into a school-age child, and Jordy didn't know when that had happened, but he worried it was while he was sitting in hotel rooms across the continent.

And maybe he was being maudlin.

He rubbed his face again and sighed.

The past week had been long and stressful, partly because of the impending trade talk and partly because his plans to bring up the possibility of a relationship with Rowan got derailed. As much as he wanted a future with him, it wouldn't be fair to put his feelings on Rowan—to ask him to make a choice between long distance or giving up his job. That was, of course, if Rowan was even interested in long-term. Telling Rowan about his feelings when he couldn't offer him stability and when Rowan was still living in his home felt selfish.

Besides, Jordy was a defenseman. He couldn't leave his own heart unprotected. He knew how much it would hurt to hear Rowan say no after Jordy laid his heart on the line.

All week he'd done his best not to think about it, not to overstep. And if that meant no more scorchingly hot, possessive sex in his bedroom? Well. Pinning Rowan facedown to his own bed and grinding into him so slowly that Rowan was sobbing by the time he came wasn't terrible. At least he was living up to their no-strings bargain.

Jordy pulled his phone out of his pocket. He had new texts from his parents and sisters, wishing him luck and condolences on the game, but nothing from Rowan.

He glanced at the time—just after ten. Rowan would probably be awake. Jordy could call him, hear his voice, get stories about Kaira's day. By the time he hung up, he'd be in a much better mood. Besides, he doubted he'd be able to sleep without hearing Rowan's voice or hearing his baby was safe and sound.

The phone rang three times before Rowan picked up.

"Jordy." There was something in Rowan's voice Jordy couldn't decode, but he felt better hearing it anyway.

"Hey, Rowan."

"What's up?" Rowan asked, voice clipped.

Jordy hesitated, not sure what to make of it. "Just checking in, wondering how my peanut is doing."

A long beat of silence stretched down the line before Rowan said, "She's fine."

"Okay. What'd she get to up to today?"

"You want a full recap? You know you'll be able to get that from in her in the morning."

Jordy paused, breathed. It might not be heinously late, but clearly it was late enough that Rowan didn't want to play telephone between father and daughter. That was understandable. "You're right. I'm just missing her today."

Rowan hummed.

Jordy thought about his lonely hotel bed with its generic everything that would smell like laundry soap and the bad sleep ahead of him, and missed his kid so much he ached. "Send me a picture of her?"

"You must have a million of those on your phone," Rowan pointed out.

Which, yes, obviously Jordy did, but none of them were current. "No, I mean—I just really need to see her." It wouldn't be a kiss good night, but it would do.

"You want me to sneak into your kid's room in the middle of the night to take a picture of her sleeping?" When put like that, it did sound a little silly. "Bugger that. I'm not risking her waking up."

There was an edge to his tone that suggested.... "Hard night?" Jordy tried to say it lightly, inject some sympathetic humor, because he knew those nights.

"Fuck you, Shaw."

Jordy gaped. What?

"Hard—my whole evening was a humiliating shitshow. I told you I had a staff meeting tonight days ago. But instead of finding alternative care, you left me to deal with it. Showing up with someone else's kid to a staff meeting isn't exactly a move that impresses the boss."

Guilt gnawed at Jordy's gut. He knew he needed to find someone else, but the threat of a looming trade put another kink the plan. If he was traded south, Jordy would have to do the whole nanny hunt all over again—unless he managed to find someone licensed to work in Canada and the US and willing to move at a moment's notice. Hell, he would probably have to find someone new even if he got traded to Ottawa, their closest rival. Most nannies weren't looking to relocate.

"I know I need to find a nanny," he conceded. "It's complicated—"

"That and a million dollars will get me an apartment on Yonge," Rowan snapped, "but it's not exactly a consolation when I've got a cranky kid whining for ice cream and another story because she's up past nine because you can't get your head out of your ass."

Jordy inhaled sharply. "Fuck you too." He could understand Rowan being tired or stressed, but that wasn't fair. "Do you think I like having to deal with this? Having to find a nanny on such short notice? Trusting a stranger with your kid isn't easy. And I might have to start the search all over again—"

"All the more reason to get someone now. Jesus, Jordy, if you might get traded tomorrow and need to start the search over, then someone good enough for the after-school shift shouldn't be hard to find." A direct hit with merit, so naturally it stung worse than a baseless accusation. "And don't think I haven't noticed your bullshit excuses. You're dragging your feet on purpose and refusing to hire someone."

Okay, maybe Jordy was being a little overly critical now that he had Janice and Rowan for the gold standards of nanny care, but—"What do you want me to do? Kaira is the most important person in my life. I'm not going to trust her with just anybody!"

"Are you fucking kidding me? You basically picked me up off the street and gave *me* the job."

Jordy reeled. He hadn't—he'd already known Kaira was safe with Rowan, Kaira had already *known* Rowan. It wasn't—

He hadn't given Rowan the job because *he* wanted to keep Rowan around—

"And now that I'm reminding you of our original deal, you're trying to change the terms."

Finally Jordy found his tongue. "I'm sorry it's so difficult for you living in my house, eating my food, driving my car, having everything taken care of—"

"Everything except *your kid*, you mean?"

All the air left Jordy's lungs in a rush, as if Rowan had boarded him.

His whole life, he'd only wanted to be good at two things: hockey and being a father. And now it seemed like he couldn't get either one right. Didn't Rowan understand? Kaira was happier with him than she'd be with a nanny. Leaving her with Rowan was the right thing for her. And that made it the right thing for Jordy.

But maybe it wasn't the right thing for Rowan. Jordy didn't feel great about that either. He'd failed at being a friend too.

And if Rowan thought Kaira was a burden....

That idea cut in a whole new unexpected way.

Jordy thought he might throw up. "I didn't realize you hated her so much. I'll send someone from the agency over first thing in the morning."

He ended the call and then, because he could not deal with any more of this tonight, put his phone on Do Not Disturb. If Rowan texted or called back or... whatever, Jordy didn't want to hear from him.

But he did need to talk to somebody tonight, because this situation obviously couldn't continue.

"Gem! Hi, yeah, no, I know it's late. It's urgent. I need you to hire a temporary nanny."

ROWAN HAD thought he'd dreaded Jordy leaving for a weeklong road trip. Now he was dreading his return.

The day after their explosive phone call, Rowan woke at six thirty to his phone buzzing—someone was at the front door. He hauled himself upright to answer it and found a thirtysomething woman in a business suit, carrying a briefcase.

Rowan had not slept much the previous night. He'd tossed and turned, frustrated with Jordy and annoyed with himself for not growing a backbone sooner. If he'd bothered putting his foot down in September, when he should have, this whole thing wouldn't have blown up in their faces.

But he hadn't, and it had, and now, having made his bed, Rowan found it very uncomfortable.

So he wasn't exactly functioning at peak capacity when the woman handed him a business card. "Hello. My name is Emily Gionet. I'm here from Greater Toronto Emergency Nannies. I was told you'd be expecting me."

I'll send someone from the agency over first thing in the morning.
Well. Jordy had certainly followed that promise to the letter.

"Uh," Rowan said. He didn't want to be rude, but he didn't want to let someone in without confirming they were who they said they were either. "Can you just—one moment."

He took the card and, as calmly as he could, closed the door in her face.

Was he getting evicted? Was that what this was?

What the fuck.

Blearily, he unlocked his phone in search of answers.

He didn't have any texts or emails from Jordy, and he was too tired to decide if that surprised him. He did have a text from Gem, timestamped just after midnight. It contained an attachment of a CV complete with headshot. *Emily will arrive first thing tomorrow and remain on duty until seven. An amended contract regarding your duties concerning Kaira is attached. Please sign it and return to me.*

So... not getting evicted. Or not yet. That was—Rowan didn't know what that was. He needed coffee.

Gem's second message read, *As your very good and concerned friend, I will withhold my I told you so for now, but please do not make this professionally awkward for me. You owe me a drink.*

Rowan exhaled shakily and opened the door again. Emily hadn't moved; she looked nonplussed by his rudeness. "Hi," he said. "Come in. I'll make coffee."

That was three days ago. In those three days, Rowan had never had to do more than drop Kaira off at school, help her brush her teeth, and read her a story. The Nannies—they were an emergency service, so he got the feeling the agency simply sent whoever had a day off they might prefer to spend working—handled picking Kaira up from school, making her dinner, and keeping her occupied until seven o'clock every day.

On the one hand, he really needed the help. Knowing he could let the agency know if he needed later coverage because of a staff meeting or other commitment took a huge weight off his shoulders. The first day with Emily, he'd come home from work and faceplanted straight into bed for an hour.

But then it was the weekend. And…. Rowan knew Kaira was not his kid. Being able to join his ultimate Frisbee game for the first time in weeks should have put a great big smile on his face.

It just might have been nice, was all, if Jordy had taken Kaira to the park at the same time, and then they all went to a late lunch afterward. Toronto had some beautiful restaurant patios. The trees were a riot of reds and oranges, and the sky was that crystalline sapphire you only seemed to get in the fall.

"Well, well, well," Pete chuckled when Rowan rolled up. "Look who's not too good to hang out with the little guy after all."

Rowan accepted a high-five bro hug, knowing she meant nothing by it, and then moved on to Alex.

"What happened?" they teased. "Your sugar daddy cut you loose?"

Rowan tried not to wince. "Why, you want me to put in a good word for you?" he asked instead. "Come on, are we going to play or what?"

So Saturday was a mixed bag. Rowan *did* enjoy spending time with his friends. They even invited him out to lunch with them afterward—on a patio like he'd wanted.

It was just that, as they shot the breeze and debated which appetizer to order, Rowan kept thinking about the time he and Jordy and Kaira went out for Indian food and ordered a little bit of everything.

Well, Rowan still didn't have to pay rent. Not for another few weeks, though he'd made a note to talk to a real estate agent tomorrow.

He asked the server to bring one of each appetizer and put it on his tab, and when Pete gave him a weird look about it, he said, "What's the point of being a sugar baby, really?" all cheek, feeling like he was going to be sick at any moment.

Sunday Jordy was coming home.

Some of Rowan's anger had burned out, but the heart of the issue remained unresolved. Rowan had been stretched thin for weeks working two full-time jobs because Jordy had—had—well, Rowan didn't really know what Jordy's actual deal was, but this middle-ground shit where Jordy was treating Rowan both like the hired help and like a coparent couldn't continue.

Even if Rowan did feel guilty for swearing at him and implying he was a bad father. Rowan knew about bad fathers. Jordy didn't qualify.

That didn't mean he was ready to forgive and forget when Jordy hadn't said two words to him.

Their whole fuzzy-boundaries friends with benefits hadn't been a problem for Rowan until suddenly it was. Jordy had been way too careful for that. But in the wake of the past weeks and their argument, something about the arrangement had started to feel cheap.

Rowan needed an explanation before he made any decisions that landed him and Jordy back in bed. Unfortunately an explanation probably required a face-to-face meeting, which Rowan very much did not want to have, since he didn't know what to say.

Very manfully, Rowan opted to run away. Not to Gem, because she would ask questions. He called up Taylor and they went out for brunch. And then he ran an errand or ten and took his sweet time getting home.

Naturally, when he snuck in the front door several hours after Jordy's return, Kaira immediately caught sight of him, squealed, and tackled him.

"Rowan, you have to come watch a movie with us!" Her chin dug into his abdomen as she turned imploring eyes up to him. "I haven't seen you in forever."

Now Rowan felt like a complete heel for spending no time with her this weekend—or all week, beyond breakfast and bedtime. Just because Jordy should have found a way for Rowan to back out of her daily life weeks ago didn't mean Kaira understood that. As far as she knew, Rowan was with her every day, and then suddenly he wasn't and a series of someones had taken his place.

Rowan resigned himself to one more viewing of Kaira's favorite Bollywood film and let her pull him into the TV room. Jordy was already there, setting popcorn on the table and looking awkward as fuck.

"Hey," he said, sounding stilted and looking like a man unsure of his welcome in his own home.

Rowan felt a twinge of guilt. "Hi." He tried to settle into one of the armchairs while Jordy turned on the TV, but Kaira let him know exactly what she thought of that.

"You have to sit here," she declared and pointed to the seat on her right.

Since arguing with six-year-olds was dicey even when you had logic on your side, Rowan conceded. She wouldn't take a "because," and "your daddy and I had a fight and now our casual sexual relationship and friendship is somewhat in flux" was not an excuse Rowan wanted to give to a child of any age.

He sat on the goddamn couch.

When Jordy also tried to sit in an armchair, he was likewise reprimanded. "Daddy, you're doing it wrong!"

So there they were, in their usual spots on the couch, a foot of space, an adorable child, and a whole lot of unspoken awkwardness between them. And they only had one ninety-minute film and a child-friendly dinner to get through.

For the first time, Rowan thought about all the ways in which he and Jordy had made a tangled emotional mess of things. No matter what happened in the next few months, he was going to miss Kaira and she was going to miss him. The nearest teams were several hours' drive away. Kaira and Rowan wouldn't have an easy commute if they wanted to spend time together. There would be no chance encounters or fun outings to ease the pain of separation.

Rowan was an idiot.

Kaira twisted and snuggled closer, and Rowan leaned over to press a kiss to her messy pigtailed hair. When he straightened up, his gaze locked with Jordy's. They stared at each other for a long, painful beat before Jordy turned back to the TV.

Kaira insisted on family dinner, and then on three books that they alternated reading and a cup of water and one last kiss before Jordy put on his stern dad face and told her, "No more stalling," kissed her good night, and turned out the lights.

As much as Rowan wanted to run away again, he owed it to himself, to Jordy, but most of all to Kaira to stay and talk things out.

By unspoken agreement, they ended up in the kitchen. At least the cleanup gave them something to do.

"I'm sorry," Jordy said to the plate he loaded into the dishwasher. "I know you don't hate Kaira."

"I know," Rowan said, though it was still nice to hear.

"You were right. I should have found a nanny or a temporary one ages ago."

Why didn't you? Rowan wanted to ask. But he had something more important to say first. "Yes, but I should have said something sooner." He pulled a face. "It was kind of a dick move to wait until I had such an exhausting, stressful day that I started cursing you out over the phone."

Jordy lifted a shoulder. He still wasn't meeting Rowan's gaze. "I deserved it."

Yeah, he'd definitely deserved the cursing, but…. "Not the part where I called you a shitty dad."

Jordy let out a loud breath and his shoulders drooped. "Thanks."

Rowan knew that would weigh on him.

"There's still another problem, though."

Finally, *finally* Jordy met his eyes.

Rowan swallowed against the snakes squirming in his stomach and forced himself to open his mouth. "We can't do this anymore. You know that, right?" He gestured between them.

Jordy pressed his lips together. "This being…."

Rowan shouldn't be mad at Jordy for making him say it. Clearer communication would have prevented this mess in the first place. He couldn't blame Jordy for wanting clarity now. "This—sleeping together, playing house, all of it. It's too… much." Rowan *wanted* too much, and he wouldn't be able to have it. He needed to start weaning himself off the placebo. "I need to take a step back from—us. It's not fair to you, or me, or *Kaira*, for that matter, if I'm…."

Fuck, the whole point was clear communication, and he couldn't even finish a sentence. "If you were staying, it could maybe be different. But you're not, and acting like we can just keep doing this indefinitely without anyone getting hurt isn't doing us any favors. I don't want to confuse Kaira… or you."

A pathetic, desperate part of him wanted Jordy to argue. He wanted Jordy to convince him they could have it all. He wanted to matter enough for Jordy to fight for him, to tell him they could make it work against whatever odds. That they could have something real.

Jordy only nodded, head bowed. "No, yeah… I get it. I'm sorry."

Rowan swallowed his disappointment. "Me too. Uh." He took another deep breath for fortification. "I'm going to start looking for apartments, like, seriously. You're going to need to pick a permanent nanny before that, or, I don't know, you're going to need the temps overnight or something."

"I'll take care of it," Jordy promised.

"Okay." And now Rowan needed to get the hell out of here. "Uh, I'm just gonna… I have to go pack my work bag for tomorrow."

He made his escape.

His eyes were stinging by the time the bedroom door closed behind him, but Rowan kept a stiff upper lip. This was always going to end. He knew what he signed up for, and he didn't have anyone but himself to blame.

It still sucked.

He let himself wallow for a few minutes and then wandered into his en suite. If he only had a few more weeks left with the oversize tub in his bathroom, he was going to make the most of them.

JORDY HAD been traded before. This was different.

He hadn't had a kid the last time, for one thing. For another, he hadn't seen it coming; one minute he played in Nashville and the next he was putting on a blue-and-yellow jersey. He hadn't had time to say goodbye to the team, but he hadn't had to deal with drawn-out uncertainty either.

He decided he liked the first trade better.

But if he squinted, he could find the barest hints of a silver lining— at least Sully thought Jordy was being a sad sack about getting traded and not about the way things had fallen apart with Rowan.

"This is depressing," Sully told him as they lined up for the anthem. "It's not like you were Mr. Sunshine before, but now it's like someone kicked your puppy."

"I don't have a puppy," Jordy reminded him.

"Took candy from your daughter, then."

Jordy's lips twitched. At least he could still count on Sully's ridiculousness to cheer him up. "I'm the only one brave enough to take candy from my daughter." Which reminded him he needed to hide the Halloween candy, or the nannies might actually have to *try* to take candy away from Kaira, and that would end in headaches for everyone.

"Maybe put some of that bravery into being less of a sad sack," Sully advised.

Then the organ drowned him out.

Jordy put his feelings into checking instead. He racked up a new personal best for hits during the game and notched two takeaways. Let management stew on that. If they didn't keep him, they'd have to play against him.

To punctuate his point, he put a blistering slap shot in the back of the net in the dying minutes of the third to put the Shield up 3–1.

"I take it back," Sully said, slapping Jordy's helmet in congratulations. "Grumpy Jordy can stay as long as he's going to play like this."

Jordy face-washed him.

After the game, he did his cool-down workout, gave his obligatory "defenseman scores a goal" interview, and showered off three hours' worth of grime as he debated his next move.

A win at home with no game tomorrow meant the team would go out for drinks. Jordy often bowed out under the guise of seeing his kid, but Kaira would be in bed anyway. The only one who might be awake at home was Rowan, and Jordy was avoiding Rowan.

Or not avoiding, exactly. He was doing the right thing and giving Rowan the space he'd asked for. He told himself a little emotional distance would help him too. It only made sense; eventually he would have to leave Rowan behind.

But he didn't want space. He wanted the inverse. He wanted to pull Rowan close to him and never let go. Rowan had fit so perfectly into their lives that Jordy had convinced himself he'd never want to leave.

But he'd been thinking about himself and Kaira and what they wanted, not what Rowan wanted.

"Drinks," Sully said seriously when he caught Jordy deliberating which shirt to put on. When they went out, they wore their pregame suits, but if he was just going to go to the players' lot and then home, he usually wore athletic clothes. "Don't argue with me."

"Didn't know Brady died and made you captain," Jordy grumbled.

He put the shirt on. One beer wouldn't kill him, and Sully could keep him entertained with sleep-training horror stories. Laughing at Sully always put him in a good mood.

A few drinks later, Jordy was slumped into his seat, staring moodily at his beer.

Sully had wandered off to the bathroom, and in his absence, Jordy's broken heart took the reins. Alcohol was probably a bad call when he was still regretting all the life choices that had led him to this moment. Because he couldn't pinpoint which of his many decisions had been the disastrous one—making friends with Rowan, inviting him into their home, treating him like a partner or roommate instead of a nanny, sleeping with him, not hiring a new nanny?

In hindsight, the whole thing felt like a slow and inevitable decline.

He finished the last of his beer and wondered if shots would be as stupid an idea as he suspected.

"Jesus," Sully said as he sat back in his spot. "The very sight of you is depressing."

"Your face is depressing."

"Guys who played like you did tonight and scored a goal don't get to mope in the corner." Sully jostled their shoulders together. "Especially if you might not get to do many more of these."

Jordy instantly felt like an asshole. This situation sucked for Sully too. "You're right. I'm boring. Tell me something fun."

Sully laughed and started in on a story about Adrianna and the new baby. Adrianna and Sully were good parents, but every parent had hiccups, and Sully was able to package one of those mini disaster moments into a fun three-minute bit.

Jordy was giggling when his phone chimed Rowan's tone—which Jordy had set weeks ago to ignore Do Not Disturb since he was a single father and Rowan might need him in an emergency.

It wasn't an emergency.

Rowan had sent an adorable picture of Jordy's daughter snuggled into her pillow, clutching her armadillo and… was she wearing one of her jerseys?

Refused to take off her jersey. Said it was good luck and you'd lose without it. Can't get her changed now without disturbing her.

Jordy's heart melted.

And broke all over again because Rowan had just taken the creeper picture Jordy had asked him for last week.

"What is your face doing?" Sully demanded.

Jordy showed him the picture and caption.

Predictably, Sully cooed. "Still doesn't explain the face, though."

Jordy sipped his water. More alcohol at this point was a terrible idea. What could he say? That he'd fallen in love with someone who didn't want him back? Even if Jordy was willing to say that to Sully in theory, he wasn't willing to say it in a bar full of their teammates.

Instead, Jordy said, "There's only two things in life I ever wanted: the NHL and parenting."

Sully hummed. "Your jobs are hockey and dad, it's true."

Jordy pointed at him. "And I'm good at them. Maybe not the best ever, but I'm good at hockey and dad."

"Yes, you are."

"So why does it feel…" *Sad. Lonely. Unsatisfying. Incomplete.* "…off lately?"

Sully gave Jordy a long look over his beer. "Can I ask you something?"

Jordy shrugged. "Sure." If it was too personal to answer in a bar with their teammates, Jordy just wouldn't.

"Have you ever wanted and worked towards anything else in life?"

The question hit Jordy right in the solar plexus. He didn't think it showed, though. He hoped it didn't—hoped he kept his cool and that his confused head tilt and inquiring, "What do you mean?" didn't sound as breathless as he felt.

"Like, look, I know I met you postdivorce, so it's been a minute since you were married, but surely at one point you wanted to marry her and be a good husband."

And sure, Jordy had wanted that. He had loved Sanna and married her because he wanted to be with her, but Jordy hadn't ever… worked for her. They'd been high school sweethearts, and their love story had had a sense of inevitability. They were a perfect match. Of course they would get together, of course they'd marry. Hell, Jordy had missed most of his senior year, and their peers had still voted them most likely to get married in the next five years.

Jordy didn't have to work for their relationship. It just happened.

And maybe now, weeks later, Jordy understood what Emma had said about his relationship with Sanna not being messy enough.

Not sure how to even begin to say any of that out loud, Jordy shrugged.

Because Sully was a good guy, he just patted Jordy on the shoulder and asked if he was ready to call a cab.

A WEEK after Jordy's return, he left on another overnight trip. This time it was only twenty-four hours out of town, but it gave Rowan a reprieve from the tension for one night.

Since they weren't having sex or watching bad crime dramas, their interactions were limited to Kaira handoffs and togetherness enforced by Kaira herself, who, despite their best efforts to not be awkward, was unimpressed by their unwillingness to spend time together. Whenever both Rowan and Jordy were home, she insisted on activities that involved all three of them.

With Jordy playing games three times a week and Rowan throwing himself into all the non-Jordy relationships in his life, Kaira's opportunities were limited. But Rowan couldn't and wouldn't avoid the house completely when doing so would have resulted in Kaira's devastated big brown eyes.

But God, enforced family time with Kaira as a buffer was a knife to the ribs—a tantalizing view of everything that Rowan couldn't have and hadn't known he wanted until he was in the middle of it. Who knew that domesticity was so goddamn nice?

Except—Rowan had always suspected, hadn't he? That was the whole point behind wanting to put down roots and make a home for himself. After a childhood of a cold home and impersonal dormitories, of being left behind and ignored, he wanted something that felt worn-in. Cozy.

Like those stupid bad-TV nights with Jordy, snuggled up under the blanket on the couch and wagering chores against who could identify the murderer.

But today was Sunday, and with Jordy gone and no nanny available, Rowan and Kaira could have some cute domestic time together. At least he'd get a partial fix.

"Hey, poppet." He pressed a kiss to the top of her head, then sat across from her at the kitchen table to eat lunch. "What do you think about a trip to the library this afternoon? We could see if they have anything new on armadillos." The weather had turned chilly, but the day offered a bright blue sky and plenty of sunshine, and Rowan had spent enough time in Toronto to know one did not take a gorgeous fall day for granted.

Kaira picked at her sandwich and shrugged.

Maybe he could drum up some enthusiasm if he sweetened the pot. "And then I thought on the way home we could stop for a cupcake. We haven't been to that cute little café since the summer."

"No!"

Surprised by the vehemence, Rowan pulled his sandwich away from his mouth. "No you don't want to go to the library, or no you don't want a cupcake?"

Kaira shoved her plate away so forcefully it shattered on the floor. "No!" she shouted, sounding more like a toddler than a six-year-old. "No, no, no!"

Before Rowan could say another word, she stomped off to her room and slammed the door.

Okay, then.

Rowan finished his sandwich. Then he carefully picked his way across the floor to the hallway, slipped on a pair of Jordy's slides, and grabbed the broom and dustpan. If this was going to be one of those days, the last thing they needed was one of them cutting their feet on top of everything else.

Cleaning he could manage. Now he had to switch to the child-minding brain.

Clearly Kaira was upset about something. Unfortunately there were too many possibilities to narrow it down. Wrong sandwich. Missing her father. Angry there was no nanny today. Woke up on the wrong side of the bed. Stubbed her toe two hours ago (Rowan had witnessed that breakdown too). Sun too shiny. Mercury in retrograde. She probably couldn't even articulate which of these, or more likely which combination of these, had caused the outburst, and Rowan couldn't fix any of it.

Giving in to a tantrum wouldn't set a good precedent either. And she definitely needed to eat some lunch or he was going to be dealing with this all afternoon, when all he really wanted was fun, drama-free times followed by a nice cuddle.

Of course, real parents probably preferred that to this also.

Sighing, he made another sandwich, cut the crusts off, placed it on a plastic plate—lesson learned—and knocked on Kaira's door.

"Go away!" she said, but she sounded sulky and miserable rather than angry, so Rowan ignored her and opened the door.

Kaira was sitting on the floor with her Piglet stuffie, red-faced and snotty. Her lower lip trembled.

"You need to eat some lunch," Rowan said firmly. He set the plate beside her on the floor. Normally she didn't have the privilege of eating in her room, but Rowan was picking his battles today, and he didn't have the troops to spare for that one. "Finish your sandwich, please. We are going to leave the house in twenty minutes."

Kaira made a face like she was fighting back tears, but she picked up half of her sandwich and took a bite.

The day progressed in a similar fashion. Kaira was docile and sweet for an hour and then bratty and recalcitrant. For once Rowan was glad the first meltdown occurred at the library rather than at the sweet shop, as at least it was a book and not a cupcake that got thrown on the floor. He felt a bit bad for thinking that—he was a librarian; he should protect the books—but the book had survived the encounter with library carpet. The cupcake would have been lost forever.

She finally settled down after dinner (dino nuggets—Rowan was taking no chances), and they watched two episodes of *Bluey* cuddled on the couch with a blanket.

Then Kaira said, "Can I watch the hockey game with you?"

Absolutely not. She'd been a bear most of the day, and if she didn't go to bed at a reasonable hour, she'd disgrace herself at school tomorrow. Rowan didn't know if Canadian private schools gave first-graders detention, but he didn't want to be the one to find out and have to tell Jordy.

But the game had an early start, and he didn't want to give up the closeness. He only had so many more days like this. He'd already looked at three apartments, and one of them was just about perfect. He was going to see it again this week. He had the application all filled out.

"Tell you what," he bargained. "If you put on your pajamas and brush your teeth and agree there will be no story time tonight, you can watch the first period with me. And then first thing tomorrow morning I will tell you the score, and we can watch clips if your dad did anything cool."

Kaira had a very serious Thinking Face—she screwed up her forehead and pursed her lips and squinted her eyes. Jordy made that face sometimes when he was exaggeratedly deliberating whether they should eat food they had at home or order pizza. She made it now, and Rowan's heart gave a painful, loud beat, because he loved her, and he was going to lose her.

And Jordy too.

"Okay," she said finally, nodding once. Then she climbed out from under the blanket and ran to the bathroom.

Rowan took a deep breath and flicked from Disney Plus over to cable to find the game.

When Kaira returned, smelling of mint and wearing her favorite Pooh pajamas—Rowan noted with alarm that they were suddenly an inch short—she climbed up onto the couch next to him.

They took a selfie together and sent it to Jordy "for luck," Kaira said, after she insisted on kissing his cheek during it.

Then she fussed with the blanket and squirmed until she could use his leg as a pillow. "I'm not going to fall asleep," she assured him.

"I won't let you," Rowan lied.

By the time the game hit the first commercial break, Kaira was breathing deep and even, keeping Rowan warm even if he couldn't feel anything below his knee on the left side.

He debated for a second but then took another picture. It didn't show much, just the back of her head and his legs under the blanket, the television in the background. Objectively it wasn't very good.

Rowan saved it anyway, then put away his phone. He could pick Kaira up and put her in bed after the first period was over.

THE SHIELD won their next away game, but Jordy didn't exactly feel like the returning hero.

Rowan wasn't home, and Kaira was with one of the temp nannies in the living room. The nanny was sitting on the couch with a book, keeping an eye on Kaira while she played. Which Jordy might have been miffed by if Kaira hadn't placed herself as far from the nanny as she could with her back turned. Jordy kind of doubted this tense parallel play situation was the nanny's idea.

"Hi, peanut," Jordy greeted softly.

Kaira counterpointed by squealing, running into Jordy's arms, and demanding to be held. He scooped her up, enjoying her little kid smells and her soft hair as she pressed her face into his neck and clung to him.

Jordy rubbed her back and murmured softly that he'd missed her. She clutched his neck harder and made the ridiculous whining noises she used to make after he returned from away games two years ago.

Jordy's heart broke.

Kaira wouldn't let go of him while he spoke with the nanny and sent her off for the day. She didn't look familiar, but "Hi, I'm Liz" seemed kind and competent. She was certainly able to give an informative recap of Kaira's day so far in a way that was sensitive to her presence while still giving Jordy a clear picture of how difficult she had been.

Jordy thanked her profusely and made a mental note to make sure she was paid for the whole day. Given that Kaira was wearing her pajamas at two o'clock, had refused to leave the house, and had made repeated requests for Rowan or Jordy to come home, the woman didn't deserve to get shortchanged.

Especially when the whole situation was Jordy's fault. Asking Rowan to play temporary nanny had probably been a mistake. He should have accepted the temporary nannies back in the summer and found a more permanent replacement sooner. Bringing in a stable temporary had clearly made everything worse for Kaira, and she was pushing back against losing a second stabilizing presence so quickly.

Looking back, Jordy wondered if his dick and heart had always been calling the shots with Rowan, even if he hadn't known it.

Kaira didn't want to do anything but cling like the cutest koala bear, and Jordy didn't have the heart or energy to say no. So they watched too much TV, ate too many snacks, and had a quiet day together.

Not that all of that togetherness helped much at bedtime. Kaira stayed clingy and kept asking for more stories, and Jordy finally turned out the lights and said no to story time but promised not to leave until she was asleep. He rubbed her back and drowned in parental guilt until her breathing evened out.

Back in the living room, the house felt empty, so Jordy turned his sudden energy to tidying the den and the mess Kaira had made with her toys.

Rowan still wasn't home, and Jordy aggressively didn't care why. He didn't wonder who Rowan was with or why he was still out at eight on Sunday. And he wasn't unreasonably mad at Rowan for letting down his daughter, who had whined about wanting to say good night to her Rowan before bed. Being mad at Rowan for being a bad parent would be dumb and selfish, and Jordy wasn't allowed to do that. Rowan had made his feelings clear. He didn't want what Jordy had to offer, and Jordy had to respect those boundaries.

Of course, that didn't mean that Jordy wasn't allowed to give up halfway through tidying to sit on his couch, clutching a stuffed toy.

Days after his night out with Sully, Jordy had finally admitted to himself that he *did* want love and romance and to be a good husband. In fact, he wanted that desperately, with an ache that filled his whole body. He just wanted it with someone who didn't want it back.

His phone rang, and Jordy fumbled to grab it so he could see the caller ID. What if it was Rowan? What if there was a reason he wasn't home yet?

Emma Shaw

The idea of rejecting his baby sister's call so he could mope more was too depressing to contemplate. Jordy hit Accept.

"So, what miracle do I owe for you actually calling over texting?"

"I saw a clip from a recent postgame interview. You okay?"

Apparently Jordy had become such a sad sack that his sister could tell when watching clips of him at work. "Why do you ask?"

"Because you have bags under your eyes and you look kinda... resigned," she settled on.

Well, the bags were easily explained at least. "Haven't been sleeping so great. Last couple of weeks had been hard on Kaira, and the nanny woes continue."

"Oh. Kaira is okay?"

"She's fine, just... change is hard."

"Right." Jordy didn't need to see her face to know she was hesitating to say the next thought. "The trade rumors probably aren't helping."

He swallowed. "No. It's... probably going to happen, and soon. Not that I, uh, told you that."

"Right, confidential, I know. Shit, Jordy. That sucks."

"Tell me about it."

They sat in silence for a moment.

"So, can I ask, what's happening with Rowan?"

That shouldn't have blindsided him. "Rowan?"

"Yes, Rowan. You know, the guy who's been living with you."

"I know who—what are you asking, Emma?"

"Well, is he going with you?"

"Am I bringing my friend-slash-roommate with me on a possibly international move?"

She sighed. "Can we not play this game where we pretend he's not important?"

And that broke him. "I'm not pretending he's not important. But he doesn't want me."

"I don't believe that either. I was there, Jordy. I saw you two together. You weren't the only one looking all settled and domestic, you know."

"Just because he—he likes me and having sex with me"—he ignored Emma's indrawn breath and the mortification of having snapped *that* at his sister and barreled on—"doesn't mean that he wants to give up his life here and follow me around."

"Wow. Okay, lots to unpack there, and because you sound so sad, I will graciously ignore the whole sex-having part of that statement, even though I'm dying of curiosity about your situationship. Instead, let's focus on the whole 'doesn't want a life with you' thing. And because I know boys, I gotta ask, Jordy, have you asked him?"

"What?"

"Have you straight-up asked him to come with you? Let him know you want him to? Has he specifically and directly said no to an offer of domestic bliss?"

Jordy opened his mouth to say yes, of course he had. But now that he thought about it, maybe he hadn't. Maybe they had just talked around it. "Well… he said he thought it was a bad idea to start something not permanent."

"Right. But you didn't actually offer anything permanent."

"He meant stationary. Not subject to transcontinental moves at a moment's notice."

"Okay. But Jordy, sometimes people need to know they can have something before they're willing to ask for it."

Jordy wished that didn't make sense. "When did you get so smart?"

"I've always been smart," she sassed back. She really was his sister. "But outside perspective always helps. Why do you think I always run to you for advice?" He'd been her first call after the third panicked pregnancy test came back positive. "Also, I'm highly motivated to find a solution here."

"Oh?" He wiped his cheek of the tear that had escaped.

"Yeah. When I visited, you looked... so happy. Happier than I can ever remember you being. Obviously I want to help you keep that and anyone who makes you smile like that."

And after an emotional conversation where Emma landed careful, unpulled punches, that one landed a direct hit. Jordy was laid flat. KO.

He knew what he needed to do next, even if it blew up in his face. Jordy wanted—and for once he was going to try for—something that wasn't hockey or fatherhood.

ON HIS lunch break on Tuesday, Rowan signed his lease paperwork.

That one-bedroom, one-bath apartment with a balcony—overlooking an alley, sure, but still a balcony—would be all his come mid-December. Which meant Rowan should start saving money now for all the furniture he'd need, never mind stocking his pantry. Which meant he should stop asking coworkers to go out for dinner or picking up takeout to eat in the car just because Jordy was home.

So after work, Rowan went straight home.

Today, there was no extra car in the driveway—no nanny. Jordy must've picked Kaira up from school himself. Rowan hit the garage door opener and was confronted with the fact that yes, Jordy and Kaira were home.

He parked the car, grabbed his bag, and girded his loins.

He forgot all about his loins when his nose registered what was going on in the kitchen.

"Hello?"

"Rowan!" There was the sound of bare feet slapping on tile. Kaira had outgrown her unicorn slippers, and the new pair hadn't arrived yet. She latched on to his leg at the knee. "You gotta come help Daddy! He's being *so silly*!"

Rowan widened his eyes comically. "Your dad? *Silly*?" He scooped her up and tossed her in the air. "I don't believe it."

"Yes. He's slicing pizza cheese with a *knife*, Rowan. Everyone knows you have to shred pizza cheese."

So the scent in Rowan's nostrils was rising yeast and a homemade tomato sauce, soon to be followed by homemade pizza. "We'd better go save him, I guess," Rowan agreed. He set her down and followed her into the kitchen.

The kitchen where Jordy was wearing the world's tightest T-shirt under the Kitchen Daddy apron.

"It's perfectly normal to slice fresh mozzarella for pizza," Jordy protested. "Ask anyone Italian. They'll tell you. Or just go to a fancy pizzeria."

Rowan could not, just now, speak to Jordy or even look at him without causing an incident, so he turned to Kaira. "Are you telling me your daddy has never taken you out for fancy pizza?"

Maybe it was the novelty, but Kaira was at her most angelic when Jordy was home. She might make demands for family time or *Bluey* or bedtime stories, but all kids did that, and there were fewer tantrums with Jordy around. They spent a relatively tension-free thirty minutes in the kitchen, arguing good-naturedly about pizza toppings. Rowan made steady eye contact with Jordy while putting pineapple on his, just to be funny, and felt far too pleased about it when Jordy laughed.

Dinner was delicious. There were even leftovers for Rowan's lunch, and because he was clever and put pineapple on his, no one else would eat it. He packed those up in a reusable container, feeling smug, and let Kaira pleadingly invite him to watch an episode of *Scooby-Doo*. He even sat on the couch on purpose, knowing Kaira would climb up onto the middle cushion and put her feet in his lap. He tucked what had become his lap blanket around her bare toes, let it fall to the floor to warm his own, and smiled when she sighed happily with her head on her father's lap.

Five minutes into the episode, Jordy cleared his throat. "The hotel owner did it."

Rowan squawked. "No fair. You've seen this one."

But Jordy wouldn't admit it, and Rowan thought if making a snack could bring back some of the camaraderie they had before they added sex to their friendship, it was a small price to pay. He could put together a charcuterie board tomorrow night, or whatever.

After the show, Jordy packed Kaira up for a bath and bedtime while Rowan put the kitchen to rights. It seemed only fair since Jordy had gone to such trouble making dinner and the cleaning service didn't come until the weekend. He couldn't leave a mess for the nanny, assuming one was coming tomorrow.

He'd just put away the saucepan when Jordy returned from Kaira's room and cleared his throat. "So, uh… I was hoping I could talk to you for a few minutes, if it's…. Can we do that?"

Without storming off or ending up in bed? Historically…? Well, there was that time before they started sleeping together. Rowan cleared his throat and leaned on the counter so he wouldn't fidget. "Sure."

"I just—I want—" Jordy ran a hand through his hair.

Stop, Rowan wanted to tell him. He could handle confident Jordy, working Jordy, Jordy the self-assured dad. But Jordy struggling for words and touching his hair made Rowan's stomach flip-flop.

"I want to explain, I guess," Jordy said finally, "about what happened between us, and why I, uh, why I've been such a jackass."

For once in his life, Rowan could not come up with a snappy response. What a time for his wits to desert him. "Um. Okay."

"So you know I was married before Kaira came along. And that kind of… I don't want to say it ended badly or that me wanting to adopt Kaira ended my marriage, because if I'm honest I knew it was over already. But I've never been a dad and a partner at the same time."

Rowan stared at him. He didn't have the slightest clue what Jordy was getting at, but he didn't want to admit that out loud in case Jordy thought he was stupid. "Okay?" he said again.

Jordy was looking right into his eyes, his gaze intense, like he was willing Rowan to understand through the power of eye contact. "I think that's why I didn't notice, you know? I was—I mean, we were friends, but then you moved in to help me look after Kaira, and that was kind of…. It was domestic. It was never—I never treated you like a nanny. I never saw you that way, I guess."

Nope, Rowan still didn't get it. "Uh… that's okay," he said. "I know I'm—we're still going to be friends." Though long-distance ones, probably, once Jordy got traded. The kind who lost touch after a few months and then maybe only sent Christmas cards for a year or two, but never deleted each other's contact information.

When Rowan offered nothing more, Jordy ran a hand through his hair again and went on. "But then we started sleeping together, and that's where it all fell apart for me. I started treating you like a partner, not—not a friend or a nanny. And I couldn't see that I had put those expectations on you without, uh, talking to you about any of it. Because it was nice for me to have that."

Rowan's poor, stupid heart cracked.

It was nice for me to have that.

That was what Rowan was. A nice thing for Jordy to have, without thinking about.

Jordy made a move like he wanted to step closer, but he stopped when Rowan released his grip on the counter and leaned back.

"For the past six years, it's just been me and Kaira. I thought focusing on her was the right thing to do. And it was, or it wasn't the wrong thing. I wasn't ready for anything else. And then there you were, and there, uh, *we were*"—Rowan had a visceral, ill-timed flashback to the wall episode—"and you were just there, all the time. Not just for Kaira but for me too. And I took advantage of that without thinking about it."

Jordy paused for breath, his cheeks flushed, and ran a hand through his hair. He was talking quickly, like he needed to get this conversation over with. Like he was ripping off a Band-Aid.

Rowan's stomach flipped and his lungs cramped. His mouth wouldn't open.

"And it was *easy*. I didn't even know I had almost everything I could want until I lost what I had with you."

Almost everything.

"And that's what made it so hard to pick a nanny," Jordy pushed on, like he didn't know he was stomping on Rowan's dreams right in front of his eyes. "It wasn't really a nanny I wanted anymore, because I'm finally ready for a *partner*. Someone who's there for both of us. Someone I can share the burden with, not that—I mean, Kaira isn't a burden, but—choosing what's for dinner and what color to paint the guest bathroom and where to go on vacation. *That's* what I want, but I didn't know it. Um, until now."

If that wasn't a kick in the chest—to realize he'd been the pale imitation that made Jordy realize he wanted the real thing.

Rowan's heart seized, because he knew the feeling. Jordy was everything Rowan had never known he'd wanted, everything he'd never had, and Rowan was so goddamn in love with him that he wasn't sure he'd ever get over it.

Rowan loved him—had done for months—and now was a hell of a time to throw off all his denial and finally admit to it. Rowan was in love with a man who saw him as a stand-in. Rowan was imitation cheese.

This was Devon Jones all over again, the "straight" boy Rowan had kissed and been thoroughly rejected by for being so very wrong about Devon's sexuality... six months before Devon started publicly dating another boy.

Only this time it was so much worse. Rowan hadn't loved Devon.

Belatedly Rowan realized Jordy was standing there waiting, like there was an expected, scripted reply Rowan was supposed to give and he couldn't relax until he did.

Rowan had no idea what that might be. *You're welcome* seemed a bit... off. "Right. Well, I'm glad you've had your epiphany." He hoped he sounded normal and not like a man who'd had his own gut-wrenching epiphany not thirty seconds prior.

"I—" Jordy was still going for eye contact, but Rowan couldn't meet his gaze. He needed to get out of here. "You—you deserved to know why I—"

"Yes." Rowan nodded, then nodded again like an idiot. He couldn't stop nodding. He took a step toward the door. "Anyway, I have stuff to get done. Paperwork to fill out. Things to do. Early rise tomorrow. Night."

Then he fled.

Once in his suite with the door locked behind him, Rowan crumpled. God, he was such an idiot. How long had he spent deep in denial about his own feelings in a deluded attempt to protect himself? Naturally this only set him up for worse heartbreak. Because there was nothing hypothetical about Jordy and their relationship now. Rowan knew exactly who and what he was losing—what he'd be missing for the rest of his life. No one could blame him for going to bed about it.

Overtime

JORDY STARED at the dripping dishes on the drying rack and tried to breathe.

Judging by Rowan's panicked flight from the room, an actual relationship with Jordy was the last thing he wanted. He literally ran away from the idea.

Rowan had always said that he and Jordy couldn't be more than casual. Jordy had hoped that was just about logistics, but looking back, he had to wonder if that line had been anything more than an easy out—advance warning he was letting Jordy down easy.

Jordy felt like a fool.

It was barely after eight, but he turned out all the lights and retired to his bedroom, ready to call an end to this disastrous day and hope for a better tomorrow.

Naturally he slept like shit, and the next day wasn't any better. If he thought Rowan was avoiding him before....

He stayed in his rooms until Jordy left with Kaira for school drop-off. He was gone by the time Jordy got home, but Jordy hadn't expected otherwise since he'd gone straight from the school to morning practice. Then Rowan didn't come home for dinner. In fact, he got home so late that Jordy was already brushing his teeth and staring manically at his phone, wondering if it would be creepy and overbearing if he texted Rowan to ask him if he was still alive.

Just as he was about to give in and text a short *you okay?* he heard the front door open. Jordy dashed for his bedroom door—then took a deep breath and forced himself to slow down, play it cool.

He opened the doorway a foot so he could look out and spotted Rowan sneaking down the hall. There was no other word for it. He wasn't on tiptoes, but he was moving quickly and quietly in sock feet.

Rowan paused at the door leading to the lower level, as if he knew Jordy was watching. For a long, agonizing few seconds, they stood there in the quiet darkness of the house, holding their breaths, waiting.

Then Rowan took the steps down.

So. Jordy had fallen in love with his friend, and then he made such a mess of things that he had probably ruined any hope he had of retaining that friendship.

Maybe there was a good reason why Jordy had been single since his divorce.

After another morning of invisible Rowan, which did not make for a pleasant breakfast with Kaira, who didn't understand why her favorite person had missed two breakfasts in a row, Jordy decided to look on the bright side. At least it couldn't get any worse.

So of course that was when his agent called and let him know he'd been traded to Vancouver.

Two thousand miles away from his baby.

Because Kaira would have to stay in Toronto, at least for a little while.

The only good thing about the trade was that Vancouver had played last night and had a rare three days off, and Orcas management had been kind enough to give Jordy a full twenty-four hours to organize his life before he hopped a plane.

Instead of napping for his upcoming game, Jordy called Gem and started to put things in order. Thank God he had finally settled on a nanny a few days prior, so he had someone to stay with Kaira for the next few weeks. With just over a month left before the winter break, and since Jordy would be busy trying to learn a new team and wouldn't have time to find and set up a new home, pulling Kaira out of school and dragging her to Vancouver tomorrow didn't make sense. As much as it killed him to leave her—the longest they'd ever been separated was any of his weeklong road trips—he knew it would be better for her and less disruptive than spending those weeks out of school and hanging around a hotel room with Jordy's mother.

Jordy had never felt his lack of partner more. There was so much that needed doing, and even if he was delegating through Gem and a series of professionals, just making the decisions was exhausting. Pack up and sell the house in January or wait for the summer? Move everything to Vancouver or put some in storage and wait until he signed his next contract? Public or private school in Vancouver? And their new home—buy or rent? Condo or house? He just wanted to be able to turn to someone—to Rowan—and say, "What do you think?"

He almost forgot to pick up Kaira, but Gem called back around three with another question and signed off with, "I should let you go, since you probably have to go get your kid."

Kaira was too young to hear about breaking news from her peers on the schoolyard, so she hadn't heard about the Shield's roster changes and was in a bright and sunny mood as she chattered away in the back seat.

While Jordy was glad he didn't have to deal with fallout from the insensitive way children could deliver news, he hated that he'd have to be the one to shake up her whole world.

Thirty minutes later, Kaira was yelling that she hated hockey and the NHL and Vancouver and the Shield and she didn't want to go anywhere. Jordy tried not to cry in sympathy and wished Rowan was here to make everything better.

And then, because the universe was laughing at him and probably hated him for some horrible shit he'd done in a past life, Rowan came home.

Something hard thumped against the wall in Kaira's room. Jordy winced and accidentally met Rowan's eyes.

"Uh," Rowan said. From his expression, he already knew Jordy's news. Well, that made sense; at least one of his coworkers was bound to be a Shield fan. "I take it she's not excited about Vancouver."

"You could say that." Jordy didn't even try to smile. "Just—one second." He backed down the hall to Kaira's room and pushed open the door. "Kaira, I know you're upset, but that doesn't make it okay to throw things."

His red-faced, tearful daughter turned toward him. "GO AWAY! I HATE YOU!"

Somehow Jordy sucked in a breath through his teeth and managed to close the door before Kaira saw him cry.

He'd barely taken his hand off the handle when Rowan touched his arm.

"She doesn't mean it," he said gently. "You know that, right? You're her favorite person. She adores you."

Jordy made himself squeeze back tears instead of burying his head in Rowan's shoulder. He had to have some self-respect around here somewhere. After another breath, he trusted himself to answer, even if he couldn't meet Rowan's eyes. "I know. She just doesn't like me very much right now. And I can't blame her for that." He rubbed the skin under one eye with his forefinger. He should wash his face. It felt gritty.

"Hey." Rowan waited until Jordy raised his head. "Do you... do you want me to talk to her?"

Jordy swallowed. He'd asked for far too much from Rowan already. "You don't have to do that."

"Jordy. I don't mind. It's not...." He sighed. "It's not easy for me to know she's suffering either. If I can help, I want to. All right? Maybe you can figure out dinner?"

Jordy's reaction must've looked as pathetic as the suggestion he make another decision made him feel, because Rowan amended, "Order takeout from that Vietnamese place. Kaira will eat the chicken bánh mi. Spicy lemongrass pork for me, and you want to split the large spring rolls?"

Jordy did not. "I'll get two orders of spring rolls."

Rowan gave a wry smile. "Good idea."

Then he disappeared into Kaira's bedroom and Jordy went to go make a phone call and sulk some more.

It took a few minutes to get through to the Vietnamese place. By the time Jordy had ordered and agreed to pay a ridiculous sum for delivery, Kaira's room was quiet.

A moment after he hung up, Rowan emerged. There was a wet patch on the front of his blazer where Kaira had obviously buried her head to have a cry.

Jordy hated himself a little for his jealousy, but mostly he was grateful Rowan had been able to calm her down. "Is she okay?"

Rowan shook his head, evidently feeling as helpless as Jordy did, even if he'd managed to soothe Kaira when Jordy hadn't. "What's okay, really, when you're six years old and you're not only leaving your whole life in a few months, your dad's leaving now?"

Miserably, Jordy buried his face in his hands and then ran his fingers back through his hair and scratched at his scalp as if that could focus him. "She's going to hate me forever."

"Jordy. She's going to forget about all of this the first time she sees a whale."

That—did actually seem likely. Jordy let himself laugh pathetically. "Sorry. I'm just—yeah. I haven't even had time to be upset for me yet, you know?"

"No." Rowan sat next to him at the kitchen island. At least he was no longer avoiding Jordy. Of course, after today, he wouldn't have to. They wouldn't even be in the same time zone unless Jordy was in Toronto for a game. "But I can extrapolate."

"There's just so much to do. I want to be there for Kaira, but I'm going to have to leave, and she can't—I can't take her with me yet. Not until I've got a place to live and someone to look after her. I'm not going to ask a nanny to relocate when she's just started working for me." Especially to Vancouver, where housing was expensive even for Jordy.

Saying it out loud didn't change it, so Jordy couldn't understand why he felt calmer now that he had. Giving Gem his to-do list hadn't taken any of the stress of his shoulders.

He should probably shut up, because Rowan hadn't signed up for this, but now that he'd started, he couldn't seem to stop. "And it's shit, because it's just been change after change for her over the past few months, with Janice leaving and then you moving in and then me going back to work and then *you* going back to work. And now the temporary nannies are at least going to settle down into one permanent nanny, but I'm going to be gone and so are you—"

"Hey. Hey!" Rowan put his hand on Jordy's wrist. "Take a breath."

Jordy swallowed, then followed the direction. Unconsciously, he found himself mimicking Rowan's breathing—long, steady inhales and exhales.

Then Rowan cleared his throat, patted his hand, and stood up. "Look, this is—call it extenuating circumstances. I know things with us have been, um, different. But I'm not going to leave Kaira in the lurch, okay? I can stick around a couple extra weeks until she can join you in Vancouver. You're planning to bring her out at winter holidays, yeah?"

Thank God for this man. But Jordy had taken advantage of him enough. "I can't ask you to do that."

"Good thing I'm offering, then," Rowan said firmly. Then his cheeks pinkened a bit. "Besides, I already promised Kaira. Don't make me a liar."

Incredibly, Jordy laughed—just a short one, but he'd felt like he might never find anything funny again. "All right," he said. "All right, but I'm going to keep paying you until then. You've got rent now."

"Deal. I promise I'll buy myself something really posh with the extra."

"Espresso maker?" Jordy suggested.

"Oooh. I was thinking massage chair, but an espresso maker…. Where would I put it, though. It's not like my new place has a butler." He nudged Jordy with his elbow. "You going to be okay?"

Jordy managed another smile, bittersweet though it was. "Yeah. I just have… a lot of decisions to make on top of learning a whole new hockey system and abandoning my child. It's a lot."

"Hmm." Rowan contemplated him. "I'm going to pretend 'learning a hockey system' is a phrase that has no meaning. We've dealt with the abandonment as much as we can. So what's the rest of it?"

"The housing situation—here and in Vancouver. The nanny situation. Figuring out where to send Kaira to school. Somehow having the time to find a place to live while learning said new hockey system"— Rowan rolled his eyes theatrically—"and being gone half the time." Another thing occurred to him. "Getting Kaira settled in Vancouver and not having her hate me at Christmas."

Rowan winced. "That last one."

Jordy huffed. "Yeah."

Tapping his fingers on the countertop, Rowan said, "Let me ask you something. Best-case scenario, what does the solution look like? Don't think about logistics, don't think about how. Dream scenario—go."

"Okay. Well, selling the house is quick and painless." The extra liquidity would give him a lot more options. "I find a place I like in Vancouver and it's close to the arena and a good school for Kaira." He closed his eyes and envisioned it. Maybe they could even be close enough he could walk her to school in the mornings sometimes. They could take trips to the park on the weekends and look out over the water trying to spot orcas. "I find some way to make it up to her about the move, and the perfect nanny…." Someone who'd pick Kaira up from school and drop her off, dress her up in a banana-yellow rain coat and galoshes when the weather was bad and hold a bright pink umbrella over their heads while Kaira stomped in every puddle.

But Jordy didn't want a big house this time. He would feel closer to her in a cozy house. Three bedrooms, maybe. One for Kaira, one for guests, and one for Jordy and—

"Come with me," he blurted.

He opened his eyes just in time to see Rowan recoil, clearly dumbfounded. "What?"

"Come with me," he repeated, feeling dumb and desperate. He knew Rowan didn't want him, knew it was stupid to ask after everything, but Jordy couldn't *not*. He couldn't move across the country wishing Rowan was with him for every awful moment of it and not try one last time to get Rowan to want him—to want this life with him—back. If nothing else, he needed to hear a definitive no. "I know it's not—you don't want—but I have, have to...." He had to ask because he was stupidly in love and just as stupidly hopeful. "You make things... easy." Which was a pathetically simple way of saying that all of Jordy's life felt more manageable when Rowan was around.

"No."

Jordy flinched.

"That's—no. You don't get to do this. To fucking change the game—" Rowan took a deep breath. "We already talked about this."

Right. Asked and answered.

Jordy was saved from having to say anything else by the sound of the doorbell.

"I'll get the food," Rowan said and left Jordy alone. He didn't have time to patch together his broken heart, but he could at least pull himself together enough to get through the night.

JORDY LEFT the following afternoon amidst a flood of tears and tantrums. Kaira had spent the day alternating between clinging to Jordy and yelling at him, which Rowan found painful to watch. He loved Kaira and couldn't stand to see her in such turmoil, especially since he could do so little to stop it. Not to mention that whenever Jordy didn't look like he wanted to break down and cry with her, he had clearly decided the best way to deal with all his emotions was not to feel them.

During the time it took for Rowan to collect their dinner and gather his own emotional fortitude, Jordy had apparently gathered up all his anxious overwhelmed feelings and stuffed them into a box. Rowan returned to find Jordy setting the table for three people, all of the nervous, untamed energy of earlier gone. And he stayed deliberate and bland when dealing with the practicalities of the move with Rowan, and only unbent for Kaira.

Who screamed and cried at Jordy before he left, and then at Rowan for pretty much the rest of the day, until she passed out a good hour before her usual bedtime.

Rowan forewent her entire nighttime routine, including changing her into pajamas, since she'd refused to get dressed that day.

All of which meant that it was more than twenty-four hours after Jordy's shitty selfish invitation before Rowan could think about it.

And be hurt and mad and frustrated about the whole thing.

Because he needed something to do other than sit and brood, Rowan tidied the mess left by two emotional Shaws. He started in the den, picking up toys and rounding up dirty dishes, and then he tackled the kitchen.

And if he threw any of Kaira's soft toys a little too hard at the toy box... well, she didn't have to know. Her stupid, selfish dad certainly wouldn't.

God, he couldn't believe that after everything, after Rowan had clearly laid a boundary of friends or partner, not both, that Jordy would ask him to keep being the fucking nanny. To give up his career for one he never even wanted just to make Jordy feel better.

Rowan stared at the helpless stuffed rabbit clutched in his hands, then tossed it in the toy box before he did it serious harm.

He hadn't thought Jordy could be that selfish.

Okay, that was a bit harsh. Jordy had clearly been emotional, and he'd told Rowan recently how much he felt the lack of an actual partner and coparent. Of course he wanted to hold on to the closest thing he'd ever had to that during a very emotional time. Rowan could understand that.

He also knew that he'd never told Jordy how much this limbo hurt. It wasn't like he told Jordy that he was breaking Rowan's heart; Jordy didn't know that if Rowan said yes it would be the emotional equivalent of exfoliating with a cheese grater.

But that didn't make it hurt any less to hear Jordy ask, like he wanted to give Rowan everything Rowan wanted, and have him not mean it the way Rowan wanted him to mean it.

Rowan took a deep breath and stared at the dishes piled next to the sink. He needed to stop chasing his own thoughts in circles. It wouldn't fix anything. But he could fix this mess.

At least, he thought later as he scrubbed the counter, the house would be immaculate in Jordy's absence, even if Rowan's thoughts weren't.

Or maybe the house would become a wreck and ruin of its former self, he reconsidered the next morning after Kaira dropped her oatmeal on the floor and then took her revenge against gravity by dumping her orange juice on top and bursting into tears.

Biting back a sigh, Rowan ignored the slowly spreading mess to scoop Kaira up into his arms. He carried her away from the scene of the crime and into the den, where they could settle on one of the comfortable chairs and just be together.

Several minutes later, once she'd calmed down, Rowan asked, "Are you having a rough morning?"

"Yes," she shuddered out on a sigh.

Rowan blinked back tears and kissed her head. "Wanna tell me about it? Sometimes talking about our big feelings makes them easier to handle." He definitely did not think about how he'd all but said the same thing to Jordy two days prior.

"I miss Daddy. I don't wanna leave Tronno. I wanna go be with Daddy. Why can't I go live with him in 'Couver now?"

Rowan did not comment on the contradictory nature of her woes. Instead he squeezed her and pressed kisses to her hair and walked her through Jordy's reasons once again. He had a feeling he'd be rehashing this conversation over and over again before she was boarding a plane for Vancouver.

Finally he couldn't justify sitting still any longer. Besides, moving would be good for Kaira. He pressed one last kiss to the top of her head and set her down on her feet. "Come on, poppet. I need your help this morning."

She wiped her eyes with a chubby hand and made her Thinking Face. "With what?"

"Well, Miss Anna is going to be staying with us for a while, and she needs her own space. So your dad said I should move my things into his room." This suggestion had been accompanied by the admission that the guest bedroom mattress was an orthopedic special he'd ordered for his parents and that it doubled as a torture device for anyone else. After having lain on said mattress for twenty seconds, Rowan could only agree. "I need your help to carry my clothes."

"I am really strong," Kaira said seriously.

"Are you? Well, I'm really lucky, then." He nudged her toward the stairs. "Come on. Do you know if your daddy has any empty boxes?"

Moving into Jordy's room should have made the injured animal of Rowan's heart want to kick and bite and scream. It was a sick parody of the life he wanted. In deference—and self-defense—Rowan let Kaira tell him where everything should go. Underpants in the bottom drawer? Sociopathic, but why not. Jumpers hanging up in the closet? The shoulders would stretch out, but he could move them later. Right now letting her be in charge made this less painful for both of them.

They finished just before lunch. Anna wouldn't arrive until tomorrow, and Rowan didn't think hanging around in the house would do either of them much good, so he made them sandwiches and posed the question.

"All right, poppet, I have one more big job for you. Do you think you can handle it?"

Moving all of Rowan's things—and throwing her breakfast on the floor—had clearly helped her work up an appetite, because she nodded without stopping to speak, too focused on her baby carrots and dip.

"I need to pick out some Christmas presents for my friends. Would you come with me to help me choose?"

Mercifully, the distraction worked. Kaira's patience with Christmas shopping far exceeded her patience for back-to-school shopping, likely because Eaton Centre was decked out in lights and garlands with children's displays everywhere. She certainly spent more time composing her own Christmas wish list than helping Rowan cross people off his. But a peppermint hot chocolate at the end of the trip and a promised dinner of her favorite pasta kept her happy.

At six o'clock, the timer on Rowan's phone went off, reminding him of their other appointment. He directed Kaira to the bathroom to wash her hands and get the pasta sauce off her face while he pulled out her iPad and set up the call with Jordy.

He didn't mean to hit the Call button, but his fingers slipped when he was setting the iPad on its stand. The familiar ring of FaceTime echoed through the kitchen for less than a second before Jordy answered.

"You look like shite," Rowan said before his brain could catch up with his mouth.

"Thanks," said Jordy dryly. "I missed you too."

On the plus side, at least Rowan hadn't sworn in front of the poppet. He pushed down on the hopelessly lovelorn part of himself that wanted to read into Jordy's confession. "Um. Long few days, I suppose."

"You could say that. We had morning skate today and I was up three hours before that because my body's still on Toronto time." He sneezed, scrunching up his face and making the dark circles under his eyes all the more pronounced. "And I think I caught a bug on the plane."

"And you have to play tonight?" Rowan asked, aghast.

Jordy gave him a rueful look. "You would too, if they paid you tens of thousands of dollars for it."

For ten thousand dollars, Rowan would bathe in Vick's VapoRub and stuff his nose with cotton balls to play a game, so he didn't argue. But that meant he didn't have anything to say, suddenly, to keep his mouth from saying all the other things that wanted to spill out.

I love you and *Why did you invite me here?* and *Why don't you love me back? How could you give me a taste of this life and take it away?*

Why am I such a stupid git?

His mouth opened. "Listen—"

Jordy must've had the same idea. "I'm sorry—"

Before things could devolve, Kaira returned, mostly sauce-free. "Daddy!"

Rowan had meant to quietly exit stage left and allow the two of them to talk one-on-one. But Kaira had other ideas. She climbed up onto his lap and held him hostage while Jordy gave her a tour of his hotel room, including the view of the water out the window.

"I'll send Rowan the picture I took this morning," Jordy said. "I saw a whale!"

Kaira gasped theatrically. "*I* want to see a whale!"

"You will," Jordy promised.

After that, Rowan did his best to tune out the conversation, as Kaira and Jordy made plans for after the school year—plans that didn't involve him. Plans that could've involved him, if he'd been willing to throw away everything he'd worked for and put his heart in a meat grinder, besides.

Sunday, Anna arrived, and though Rowan found her pleasant, energetic, and kind, Kaira didn't have much interest in warming up to her. Since she'd be Kaira's nanny for little over a month, Rowan supposed that didn't matter.

"She's fond of you," Anna said Sunday night when Rowan returned from putting Kaira to bed. She was sitting on the couch reading something she'd plucked off Jordy's bookshelf.

"I'm still a poor substitute, I'm afraid. You should see her with her father."

"I will, when I bring Kaira out to Vancouver at Christmastime." She put the book down. "It sucks to have my contract cut short, but I'm getting a month's severance and a free vacation in Vancouver, so it could be worse."

"And in the meantime there's that soaker tub," Rowan pointed out.

"God, *yes*," she said, practically jumping to her feet. She picked the book up again. "I'm just going to… well. Read in the bath."

"Good night," Rowan told her.

The house suddenly felt too empty. Rowan turned on the television just for the noise and accidentally fell asleep.

DESPITE THE fact that he rounded out his first game as an Orca by chugging a bottle of Nyquil and passing out for twelve hours, Jordy was pretty sure it was a success.

The Shield might have touted him as one of their superstars, but while he was the most decorated defenseman in the lineup, they hadn't lacked in talent. The Shield had a string of solid d-men of various ages. They would be fine without him.

The Orcas would have been fine without him too. It wasn't like they'd been losing every game. But…. Jordy wouldn't say this out loud at the risk of sounding up his own ass, but it felt like the Orcas needed him. There'd been a Jordy-shaped gap in their lineup, and playing with them was easy. And sure, they hadn't yet decided who would be his go-to linemate and none of these guys clicked the way Sully did, but the rest of the team, the system, the game play, all felt made for him.

Jordy hadn't felt so energized playing a home game against one of the worst teams in the league since his rookie year. Career-wise, this trade might be one of the better things to happen to him.

And wasn't that a kick in the teeth to realize.

Especially when he woke up from his medicated coma to find a voicemail message from Rowan and Kaira.

"Hi Daddy! Me and Rowan watched the game highlights this morning and you skated so good. Rowan says the internet says you played a really good game and we should be proud of you for it, 'specially 'cause you didn't feel your bestest yesterday."

"... goodbye...."

"Okay, Rowan. Rowan says I have to say goodbye now because I gotta go to school. Bye-bye, Daddy, I love you!"

"Good job, poppet. Go put on your shoes.... Hey, Jordy, she really wanted to talk to you this morning, and time zones are a hard concept. I hope this didn't disturb your sleep.... Bye."

Jordy slumped back in his hotel bed. If he hadn't been traded, maybe he and Rowan would have had time to grow into something solid and real so that when his contract was up, they could have talked about moving like adults.

Or maybe it would have given Jordy two years in the same city as his ex, the love of his life, suffering through awkward visits to the park for Kaira's sake.

Jordy needed to get over himself and worry about practical shit, like finding a nanny and someplace to live.

He was scrolling through local real estate listings, aghast—they wanted *how much* for a two-bedroom condo?—when someone knocked on his hotel-room door.

Frowning, Jordy looked through the peep hole and caught a view of a distorted, grinning Ryan Wright, and Ryan's moody husband over his shoulder.

Okay, so Nico probably wasn't as moody as he looked. The more Jordy got to know the guy, the more he realized that he was just a prime example of resting bitch face.

Jordy opened the door and gave Ryan a look. "Aren't young people supposed to abhor showing up without texting first?"

Ryan laughed. "One, I'm barely younger than you. Two, we totally did text, but you didn't answer and I got tired of waiting."

"That's true," Nico muttered. Jordy had a sudden vision of Ryan pacing and bouncing around their home, begging his phone to buzz.

"Three, you can totally tell us to fuck off and get out of your hair— we were in the neighborhood."

"That is *not* true," Nico said. "Well, the neighborhood part. You can definitely tell him to fuck off."

Jordy snorted. "Good to know." He eyed Ryan and his barely restrained energy and decided *fuck it*. He didn't really want to sit alone in his room all day worrying about which adulting tasks he should do first. "You know what? I'm feeling generous. I'm willing to hear you out before I tell you to fuck off."

"You're a good man, Charlie Brown."

Nico shook his head at Jordy, encouraging him not to ask, and Jordy shrugged and let them in.

Three hours later, Jordy was dressed and fed, had contacts in his phone for the nanny search, and was on his way to meet Ryan and Nico's real estate agent, who was waiting for them at a house with an in-law suite that was listed on the market for 2.5 million. Sure, Jordy would be able to afford the mortgage once he'd sold his place in Toronto, but the bump in price came with a decrease in square footage that alarmed him.

Kim, the agent, was pretty great. She walked Jordy through the house, asking what he liked and didn't, then pumped him for more information about his home in Toronto and whether he'd sold it.

"I think I have the perfect rental for you," she declared. "Because you really should rent until your place in Toronto is sold. Taxes, you know? And I think this place in Burnaby might meet your short-term needs."

Sure enough, Jordy found himself signing a lease for a four-bedroom house that might not have a nanny suite but at least had two full baths so he could have live-in help without things getting awkward.

Afterward, Ryan insisted on taking Jordy out for more food and dragged him to one of his favorite restaurants.

"So now that we got all the boring adult stuff out of the way, let's catch up! How are you? How's the kid?" His expression turned sly. "How's the nanny?"

"I'm fine. 'The kid' is mad at me for moving to Vancouver, though I think the promise of whales is going a long way to fix that." The team even had a whale mascot, which should also help.

Jordy pointedly ignored the final question.

Ryan propped his chin on his hands and ignored Jordy's sidestep. "And the nanny?"

Jordy wanted to stab a sushi roll, but he knew that was rude. "You mean Anna?"

"Not unless the nanny you brought to New York and had sexual tension at during *our* wedding reception has changed his name, no." He rolled his eyes. "Obviously."

Jordy took back every nice thing he'd thought about this team. "We did not—"

He expected the flat, unimpressed stare from Ryan. He didn't expect how much more effective the expression was on Nico.

Ryan took a long sip of bubble tea to wait Jordy out.

Nico didn't blink.

"We didn't work out," Jordy finally said.

Ryan kept drinking and Nico continued not to blink. After a moment Jordy had to break eye contact and appeal to his husband. "Is he just going to stare at me like that?"

Without looking, Ryan reached his hand to the left and snapped his fingers in front of Nico's face.

Scowling, Nico blinked and pushed his hand away.

"German interrogation technique," Ryan said. "Very effective. It's the eyebrow. Ow!"

"How did you fuck it up?" Nico asked.

Jordy hunched his shoulders. "How do you know it wasn't him who fucked it up?"

"If it was, you'd be talking about why he sucks."

Ryan chewed a tapioca ball—he'd ordered pineapple bubble tea; the whole thing turned Jordy's stomach—and then swallowed. "My husband has a point. You have a guilty conscience. Tell Uncle Ryan all about it."

Jordy debated telling Uncle Ryan something else, but he couldn't bring himself to be so rude after Ryan and Nico had saved him from not only a miserable afternoon, but a miserable and stressful home search. At least now he knew that he'd have room for Kaira when she arrived. He could even send her pictures, through Rowan, and ask what color he should have her room painted.

Besides, it was probably like excising a sliver. You couldn't start to heal until you pulled it out.

"Same old story, I guess." He stuffed a California roll in his mouth to give himself time to formulate the words. "We were attracted to each other, we acted on it, and I started thinking of him as more of a partner than an employee-slash-friend with benefits. I didn't realize I was treating him that way, we never talked about it. Rowan got reasonably pissed off with me for dragging my feet on the nanny search, we fought, and I realized I fucked up, but it was too late." He knocked back his cup of jasmine tea, which had gone cold. "I apologized, but he doesn't want what I'm offering, so."

Ryan and Nico exchanged looks. Nico pushed the last spicy tuna roll across the table toward Jordy, as if offering comfort.

That one was his favorite. Jordy ate it.

But apparently the tuna roll was just to lull him into a false sense of security. There were *follow-up* questions.

Or, more accurately, a follow-up inquisition.

"What you're *offering*?" Ryan repeated, raising his eyebrows. "Dude. I hope you phrased it better when you were talking to him."

Nico picked up a piece of tempura. "It sounds like you asked him to be your mistress."

"I didn't ask him that," Jordy protested. He wasn't an *idiot*. "Anyway, it's—whatever. When I asked him to come to Vancouver, I knew he'd say no. He just got his dream job. He made that pretty clear. But I had to ask anyway, right? Even my kid loves him."

Another look. Nico snorted.

As though responding to a comment only he had heard, Ryan nudged him. "Hey, come on. I was not that bad."

Whatever Nico was saying with his eyebrows, Jordy couldn't translate.

"Okay, I was that bad," Ryan capitulated.

Nico leaned forward. "Please tell me you didn't ask him to come to Vancouver *for your child*."

"Of course not," Jordy protested. Although—

He'd been clear about why he wanted Rowan to come, hadn't he?

"Please tell me," Nico continued, "that you did not ask him to abandon his 'dream job' and move to Vancouver without telling him, in these exact words, that you love him."

Jordy licked his lips. "Look, it's—he isn't interested, okay? I wasn't going to just… humiliate myself."

Ryan finished his bubble tea. "You, my friend, have not seen enough eighties romcoms."

"Why would I watch eighties romcoms?"

Nico patted Ryan's shoulder consolingly. "Never mind," he said to Jordy. "He means you should humiliate yourself for love."

"Love is humiliating." Ryan shrugged. "At least if you're doing it right."

At first Jordy wanted to argue. That sounded wrong. Then he thought about how he felt right now, the gutted sting of rejection, feeling like he'd spilled his guts and bared his heart and been found wanting—it wasn't like it would feel worse if he'd added *please, I am in love with you.*

And on the off chance that that somehow convinced Rowan to give a real relationship a shot, Jordy could not have given less of a shit about the groveling.

Ugh.

"Well," Ryan said when Jordy didn't say anything else, "all is not lost. We play in Toronto in January, so you can humiliate yourself then."

"At some point the self-humiliation becomes stalking and not taking no for an answer," Jordy pointed out.

Ryan wrinkled his nose. "Yeah, maybe. Do we need to switch to sake?"

Jordy sighed. "No. I need to chug a bottle of Nyquil again tonight."

"Just dessert, then," Ryan decided, and flagged down a server.

LATE NOVEMBER turned gray and grisly, as if Toronto missed having Jordy in it and was determined to make everyone who lived there miserable too. Rowan got an interesting new project at work when a local philanthropist passed away and left the university library her collection of first-edition classic British literature. He threw himself into cataloguing and preserving and resisting the urge to slap English professors' grubby fingers with a ruler.

Kaira continued to tolerate Anna's presence when Rowan wasn't home, but as soon as he walked in the door from work, she clung to his legs and begged him for a story or to make her a snack or to watch *Bluey.*

It turned out living with a six-year-old with situational depression was exhausting and the depression was contagious. Kaira alternated between clinginess and angry outbursts with bouts of tears.

The situation only got worse the closer they got to Christmas and Kaira's departure date, because Kaira now realized that the flight west would mark not only her reunification with her beloved father but Rowan's departure from her daily life.

Rowan did his best to distract her—and himself—from missing Jordy. He kept their weekends busy with trips to museums and parks so they didn't give in to the temptation to spend two days lazing on the couch.

The last week of November, the sky opened up early on a Saturday morning and dumped twenty centimeters of snow. The charm of snow—which had been rare during Rowan's childhood—had somewhat worn away after a couple of winters in Toronto, where snowfalls quickly turned to dirty slush on downtown streets. But watching Kaira greet the morning with wide-eyed awe and press her face to the patio doors brought his own sense of wonder back.

He managed to wrangle Kaira away from the window and into the kitchen long enough to get them both fed, and then it was up to her room to put on clothes.

Kaira ran through the yard without a clear direction, yelling and jumping. Rowan recorded her mad dash through the yard and screams of "Look, Rowan, snow!" and "You can see my footprints!" But he pocketed his phone when she waved him over and declared that they had to build a snowman.

Luck was on their side, and the snow was perfect for snowball making. There wasn't enough for anything ambitious, but they made a respectable Olaf-sized creation. They found some stones to make a face and sacrificed Kaira's scarf with the understanding that they had to go inside soon anyway. Then Rowan took several pictures to "send to Daddy."

Afterward, they drank hot cocoa and watched Christmas movies and snuggled on the couch. Rowan took more pictures to share with Jordy. He might still be heartbroken, but he couldn't deny the man pictures of the kid he missed so badly.

Days later he wondered if it wouldn't be the last good day together.

Kaira all but refused to do anything with Anna when Rowan was home, and bedtime and morning routines were getting longer. Two days after the snow, Kaira wet the bed. She woke up hysterical the next morning.

It wasn't the last time.

The second time it happened, Rowan woke in the middle of the night to find Kaira at his bedside, teary-eyed and sucking her thumb.

"Poppet?" Rowan groaned. "What—? Poppet, what's wrong?"

"I'm wet."

Fuck. "Okay. It's okay, poppet. Let's get you cleaned up." He scooped her up, heedless of her wet nightie, and carried her into the bathroom. Once she was clean and dry, he brought her back to her bedroom and got her into clean clothes and stripped her bed. Before he could remake it, she asked, "Rowan? Can I sleep with you in Daddy's bed?"

He didn't hesitate, just picked her back up and carried her to his— Jordy's—bed and tucked her in. After changing his own shirt, he crawled in next to her. She scootched in close, curled toward him, thumb in her mouth and stuffed armadillo clutched to her chest.

"Night, Rowan," she muttered around her thumb.

Rowan pressed a kiss to her hair and wondered what the hell he was going to do. Hopefully she wouldn't have another accident. "Night, poppet."

A few mornings later, Rowan was starting to seriously reconsider Kaira's travel plans. Sending her on a cross-country flight with a woman she treated as a stranger at best and an interloper at worst... honestly, Rowan could think of too many nightmare scenarios to name. Just yesterday, Kaira cried because Anna had to drive her to school. Would she behave on a five-hour flight? Rowan imagined her screaming and news reports of a kidnapped child grounding the plane.

He was gearing himself up for an awkward call with Jordy, and maybe dragging his feet in denial, when he had to stay late for another staff meeting.

Marina raised her eyebrow and smiled when he walked in solo. "No kid this time?"

Rowan gave an anemic smile. "Fortunately we got the nanny situation sorted out."

Not that another late-night meeting was doing Rowan any favors regardless. Kaira was not happy that he'd be missing bedtime, and Rowan anticipated some form of payback when he got home. Finding her still awake but calm or crawled into his bed were two of the milder scenarios he was imagining.

He definitely hadn't expected a phone call an hour into the meeting from a frantic Jordy.

"Rowan," Jordy gasped. "She's gone!"

"What?" Rowan had ignored the first call, but when the second came in immediately on its heels, he had apologized and stepped away from the others.

"The alarm at the house is going off, and I looked—Rowan, she left the house!"

"Who did?" Rowan asked as patiently as he could over his racing heart.

"Kaira! The camera shows her leaving with boots and a backpack five minutes ago." He sounded on the verge of a panic attack.

"Shite." Rowan strode back to the table, grabbed his stuff, and headed for the door, apologizing and claiming a family emergency as he did so.

"Why aren't you with her?" Jordy asked.

"I was at work. Did you call Anna?"

"What? No, I—"

"Hang up and call her. Then call me back. I should be in my car by then."

He barely felt the bite of the wind as he jogged to the SUV. He was getting into the driver's seat when he realized he'd left his coat in the library.

He jammed the button to start the engine and made himself take two slow, deep breaths. Then he set the nav system to give him the directions home. He didn't have any spare brain cells to worry about Toronto traffic. Let Google figure out that part.

Just let her be okay, he prayed as he tapped his fingers on the steering wheel at a red light that seemed to be on an agonizingly slow timer. At least she'd left the house of her own accord. No one had taken her.

She was a six-year-old alone outside in the dark in the winter. No one had taken her *yet*.

Rowan was going to throw up.

Ring, he silently begged the phone. *Please.*

The GPS indicated thirteen minutes until he made it home.

The QEW was clear, at least as far as the QEW was ever clear.

Eleven minutes.

How long had Kaira been outside before Jordy called? Had she dressed warmly enough? Was she—

The ring of the phone sent Rowan stabbing for the Answer button. "Hello!"

"She's got her," Jordy said thickly, all in a rush. "She's—she's in Clem's treehouse. Anna just had to follow the footprints—"

"Thank fuck it snowed," Rowan blurted. Without thinking about it, he eased off the accelerator. Thank fuck they hadn't used all of the snow on that snowman. Thank fuck it hadn't all melted into a slushy mess already.

"—but Rowan," Jordy said, still urgent, "Anna can't get her to come inside."

"Okay." Rowan took a deep breath. "Okay, it's fine. I'll be home in, like, ten minutes, I'll get her to come inside. Anna's not going to let her freeze to death."

"I know. I *know*." Rowan was pretty sure Jordy was repeating it to make himself feel better. "Just—fuck, I can't—I have to play a game in an hour. *What if I hadn't looked at my phone?*"

Rowan's hands shook. "Jordy, uh, I can't—I'm driving right now. Okay? So you need to not, uh. Not freak out on me." He exhaled. That shook too. "Not freak me out. I'll call you when I'm with Kaira."

"Yeah, okay—sorry. Fuck. Sorry."

"I'll call you soon," Rowan promised, and he hung up.

He didn't bother parking in the garage. He left the SUV crooked in the driveway, blocking Anna's vehicle.

He didn't bother grabbing a coat from inside either, or changing out of his dress shoes. Not three steps into the yard, his feet had turned to pre-popsicles. "Kaira!"

The neighbors' yard had a gate. Enough snow had drifted up against it to stop it from opening more than a foot or so. Rowan squeezed through. "Kaira!"

"Here," came Anna's voice. As Rowan's eyes adjusted to the dark, he made out her form at the base of the playhouse. She wore a long coat pulled on over pajamas and boots with the laces untied. She looked especially small and pale in the moonlight reflected off the snow. "She won't talk to me—I can't get her to come in—"

Rowan caught her by the elbows. "Go back to the house and put the kettle on, okay? And run a bath for Kaira."

She nodded, obviously grateful to have someone to defer to. "Okay. I'll—okay."

Rowan heaved out a breath and climbed the ladder to the treehouse.

Kaira sat curled up in the corner, hugging her legs for warmth. In the dim light cast by her tiny Cars flashlight, her cheeks were red with cold, her eyes swollen and puffy.

Rowan's heart twisted, but something else came out ahead of the sympathy. "Poppet, what were you thinking? You scared me half to death."

Kaira's lower lip trembled.

Unfortunately that didn't stop the next words from popping out. "Your dad is beside himself, you could have been *hurt*—"

Kaira let out a sob and curled up farther into the corner.

Oh hell. Rowan wiped a hand over his face. "Oh, poppet. Come here, please. I'm sorry, I was just so worried about you. Will you come inside, please? It's freezing out here."

She sniffed. "I wet the bed again. Like a baby!" The words came out in a wail. "I'm not a baby! I don't need a babysitter! I don't need a nanny! I want my dad!"

Oh *hell*. Rowan swallowed and held out his arms. "Right now you need to come inside before you get sick, poppet. Aren't you cold? I know I am."

She wiped her nose. "How come you're not wearing a coat?"

"I forgot it," he admitted. "I was so worried about you I couldn't think. My feet are icicles. Please come inside?"

Finally she capitulated and let Rowan lead her back to the house.

He set Kaira up in the kitchen for the call to Jordy. While they talked, Rowan made Earl Grey for himself and a weak blueberry tea with honey for her. When she'd finished, he told Jordy he'd call him back, popped her in a quick bath to warm her up, and set her up in Jordy's bed. Anna had put Kaira's sheets in the wash, although at least there was less mess this time, as Rowan had purchased a package of "nighttime underpants" a few days ago.

He'd been surprised Kaira let him maintain the polite fiction that they weren't diapers, but too relieved to let the surprise show.

"She's getting worse," Anna said when Rowan pulled the bedroom door closed behind himself.

He heaved a sigh. "I know."

"It's not—I don't mean to be unsympathetic." She tugged at the end of her ponytail. "She's been through a lot. And I can see she's a good kid. She *wants* to be a good kid. But she's...."

"Struggling," Rowan supplied.

"To say the least." Anna settled in the armchair next to the fireplace and crossed her legs on the seat, cradling a mug of cocoa. "I think she might need to see a doctor, just in case."

Oh fuck, Rowan had never considered that Kaira might have a medical issue. "I'll bring it up with Jordy, but I'm sure he'll agree."

She exhaled gustily as though she'd been afraid he might not. "Okay, great. Uh. Can you…? I'm going to go to bed and cry a little."

"Go," Rowan told her. "You've earned the night off." Besides, he had other things to do.

When Jordy picked up, he didn't mince words. "I have ten minutes."

"Kaira is asleep," Rowan told him. "She's—she was upset because she wet herself again, and I wasn't here. I don't think she wanted to go to Anna with it. She feels like a baby."

"Fuck." There was a hollow plastic sound. The thump of a helmet, maybe? "This is my fault. Poor kid."

"It is not. You're doing your best. Anna thinks we should take her to a doctor, just in case, though. To make sure she doesn't have an infection or something."

"God, yeah, okay. That's a good idea. Can you take her to the clinic? Maybe tomorrow? I know it's not convenient—"

"Jordy. I think work will understand that this is important."

"Fuck." In the pause that followed, Rowan could picture Jordy rubbing a hand over his face. "I hate that I can't do anything from here. I feel useless."

Rowan sighed. "I don't think there is much to do except love her a lot while we wait it out. Things will start to get easier once you're in the same city again."

"I know." Jordy sounded so bleak that Rowan wanted to hug him. "Doesn't do much to make things easier in the meantime."

Rowan cleared his throat. *Here goes nothing.* "I've been thinking about that. There's no way Anna can take her on a flight. Like, literally. I'm pretty sure they'd kick Kaira off the plane."

Jordy groaned. "Maybe my mom—"

"Jordy, I can do it."

"What?"

"I can take her. I'll be on holidays anyway, so I'll have the time. I can take her to Vancouver." Rowan let out a breath. "And I think knowing that might actually make things easier for her until Christmas."

"Are you sure?" Jordy sounded small.

"Of course I'm sure," Rowan all but snapped. Did Jordy think Rowan was heartless? Of course Rowan could take a couple of days to get Kaira across country.

"I don't want to ask you—"

"You're not asking, I'm offering. I mean, you're paying, but I'm offering. I'll take her as soon as school is out and stick around a few days to help her get settled."

"Thank you," Jordy breathed. "Rowan, thank you. I can't—what? Fuck. I have to go. I'll text later about the tickets."

"Great. I'll text tomorrow once I've got details about a doctor's appointment."

"Thanks. Again. Seriously. Thank you." Before Rowan could tell him to stop thanking him, Jordy said a hasty goodbye and hung up.

DECEMBER BEGAN in a blur of back-to-back games and rushed road trips that left Jordy feeling his age and the loneliness of his very empty rental house. Vancouver was wet and cold and miserable, though Jordy was probably biased, as he was counting down the days to Kaira's arrival.

The day after talking with Rowan, Jordy purchased two tickets to get Rowan and Kaira to Vancouver the Friday before Christmas, and waiting that long felt like remarkable restraint. Before Rowan had offered to bring her—which was definitely the right choice for Kaira's happiness—Jordy had been on the verge of declaring "Fuck it" and begging and bribing Anna to bring her to him sooner and staying with them on the West Coast for a month until Jordy's new nanny could start in January.

But thankfully, Rowan was bringing Jordy's baby to him, and he breathed easier for the last few weeks apart. By the time Jordy buckled into his rental car and headed for the airport, the rental house didn't look half bad and even had some Christmas décor to welcome the Christmas enthusiast and connoisseur that was his six-year-old.

Jordy had deliberately booked the tickets on an off day so he could be the one to greet Kaira and Rowan at Arrivals, even if it meant Kaira missed the last day of school.

Whatever, she would survive.

At the airport, Jordy shifted from foot to foot as he waited. Rowan texted once they were off the plane and again at the baggage carrousel. Jordy alternated between desperate looks at his phone and the door for more news.

There.

Rowan, taller than average, was easy to spot coming through the doors. For a second Jordy couldn't breathe because he was completely blindsided by how good Rowan looked in person. He was one of those people whose beauty never fully translated to camera, and seeing him live and without a lens for the first time in weeks was a punch to the gut.

"DADDY!"

The crowd shifted, and Jordy's focus was consumed by one thing.

He crouched down and caught Kaira as she surged past the barrier, and crushed her to him.

"Daddy, Daddy." Kaira buried her weepy face in his collar. Emotions too big and numerous to process swamped Jordy. Guilt, relief, pain, joy. He cradled his baby close and cooed soft reassuring nothings in her ear.

"I'm here. I have you. Daddy's here, peanut. I've got you."

Someone touched his shoulder, and Jordy looked up to see Rowan at his side. "We should get out of here," he said in an undertone with a pointed glance around.

Right. It might not be Toronto, but it was still Canada. Judging by some of the expressions on the onlookers' faces, not everyone watching was simply moved by the emotion of the situation. Rumors of Kaira's—and probably Rowan's—arrival in Vancouver were sure to hit the internet soon.

Jordy stood without letting go of his baby and asked quietly, "You have the bags?"

Rowan motioned to the luggage cart at his side and waved off Jordy's halfhearted attempt to help. "You've got her, I've got the bags."

Thank God for Rowan's long legs, because he matched Jordy's anxious pace. Kaira was still clinging to Jordy. The sooner they could get out of view, the better.

Once they got to the car, Kaira calmed enough to talk, and she and Jordy rebonded with stories of her trip here while Rowan loaded the bags into the trunk and returned the trolley.

Now that Kaira had calmed down from the initial rush of seeing her daddy again, she was entranced by the adventure of seeing her new house. "Daddy, what color is my new bedroom? Can it be rainbow? Can I have an armadillo bed?"

Jordy buckled her into her seat and did his best to answer her questions, then stepped back to find that Rowan hadn't yet climbed into the car but was apparently hovering in case he was needed.

One more thoughtful, Kaira-oriented decision that choked Jordy up. He gave in to the impulse and pulled Rowan into a bone-crushing hug.

The feel of Rowan once again in his arms settled something in Jordy he hadn't even known needed soothing. He felt real and grounded for the first time since he arrived in Vancouver.

"Thank you."

"Jordy," Rowan protested.

"Shut up and let me thank you. You looked after and then brought me my baby."

"Jordy," Rowan repeated, but this time it sounded almost fond. He squeezed back for several heart-pounding seconds.

"Daddy, I'm hungry. Can we get 'Donalds?"

Jordy pulled back and offered Rowan a less-than-impressed look.

Rowan's cheeks pinkened a bit. "Look, it was six very long weeks followed by a *very* long flight. We did the best we could, but promises had to be made."

Fuck it. Jordy pulled him into another hug, briefer this time. He let go before Rowan could respond. "Just shut up and tell me your order."

They ate in the car. It was rented on the Orcas' dime anyway; what did Jordy care if the company charged them a cleaning fee? He even got everyone a McFlurry for dessert. Ice cream seemed called for. Jordy was celebrating having his family together again, even if only temporarily. Rowan might not love Jordy the way Jordy loved him, but he loved Kaira. That was enough.

It would have to be enough.

By the time Jordy pulled into the garage, his McFlurry was half melted, Kaira had talked his ear halfway off, and his heart felt full.

He put the car in Park, not missing Rowan's raised eyebrow.

"No butler in this place," he said apologetically.

"I like it," Rowan said. "More house, less fortress."

They brought the bags in while Kaira ran inside, too excited to wait for them. "Take your shoes off!" Rowan reminded her before Jordy could get the words out.

When Jordy turned to look at him, he hunched his shoulders sheepishly. "Sorry, I should let you—"

Jordy shook his head and nudged open the door with a suitcase. "You should quit worrying about it. You've basically been her parent for half a year. More than I have." It hurt to say, but not more than it hurt that it was true in the first place. "I'm not going to get upset about it."

Rowan set Kaira's bag down in the entryway. "Well, that's good to—" He cut off as he looked around. "Wow."

Jordy didn't realize what he meant until he put down the bag he was carrying and lifted his head to look around.

"Uh." Jordy remembered buying Christmas decorations. He remembered putting up the tree and hanging the stockings.

He did not remember hiring half a dozen psychotic reindeer to deck his halls with brightly lit evergreen boughs, ribbons, and candy canes.

"You really went all out," Rowan said.

"I really didn't," Jordy said. After another moment of looking around, he found a red-and-green sticky note on the back of the front door.

Merry Christmas, ya filthy animal!—RW & Co.

Rowan read it over his shoulder. "Friends of yours?"

"My captain." Smiling, Jordy stuck the note in his pocket. Ryan didn't even celebrate Christmas. He did love *Home Alone*, though. Which was weird because that movie was older than he was.

Jordy was just thinking he'd have to send Ryan something nice, not as a Christmas present but maybe for New Year's, when Rowan looked up.

Jordy followed his gaze.

Someone had hung a sprig of mistletoe from the chandelier. Ryan definitely hadn't done that himself; the foyer ceiling was twelve feet high.

Rowan cleared his throat and took a step back. Jordy let the moment break. What he had was enough, he reminded himself.

"Daddy! Rowan!" Kaira careened back toward them, beaming. "Look! It's so beautiful!"

Jordy swept her up in his arms and planted a half-dozen kisses all over her face. "It's just for you, peanut."

"Can we see my room?"

Jordy gave them both the tour, starting with Kaira's room, which Ryan and whoever "& Co." was had also decked out in fairy lights. Jordy had ordered a complete set of the Winnie-the-Pooh plushies for her bedroom, because a parent with a guilty conscience shouldn't have access to the internet and a major credit card. He wasn't supposed to paint the walls in the rental, but he'd picked up some colorful decals and applied those—Disney and storybook characters and a giraffe that doubled as a growth chart.

And on the bedspread—

Kaira gasped. "Daddy, it's an armadillo!" She flung herself onto the bed and starfished against the giant cartoon animal, hugging it.

She was too young to notice or care that this room was half the size of the one she'd had in Toronto.

"I didn't realize you had such a flair for interior design," Rowan teased.

"I have layers," Jordy informed him loftily.

They continued with the tour, which mostly consisted of the guest bathroom and kitchen. The basement was finished with a family room perfect for movie nights, but that could wait for another time. Kaira and Rowan had to be tired from their long day; their body clocks were set three hours ahead now.

"And this is your—um." Jordy took a deep breath through his nose. "I mean, the guest room."

Not that his slip mattered, when he opened the door. The room's furnishings might appear generic and neutral, but he'd chosen accent colors Rowan favored—a lovely plum for the throw pillows and a pale sage for the armchair next to the window. There was a low bookshelf beside it with a lamp on top, a cozy little reading nook.

And a replica of the throw blanket Jordy had purchased at the New York Public Library, artfully draped across the arm of said chair, because Vancouver might be warmer than Toronto, but Jordy doubted Rowan's circulation would improve.

For a long, painful second Rowan said nothing.

Jordy opened his mouth. "If you don't like it—"

Rowan made a noise in the back of his throat and put a hand on Jordy's arm. "No, it's—it's perfect. Thank you. You didn't have to... I'm only here for a few days."

In person, maybe. But Jordy didn't think he'd get Rowan out of his heart anytime soon.

"It's the least I could do." He cleared his throat and finished wheeling Rowan's suitcase into the room, then turned around to usher everyone back toward the communal living spaces. It was easier to keep his hands off Rowan when Kaira was so convenient and his arms had been bereft of his daughter for so long. He scooped her into a fireman's carry—God, she'd gotten so much taller in just a few weeks—and carried her back toward the living room, speaking over her giggles. "So, I was thinking maybe *Frosty* and hot chocolate?" He set Kaira down less than gently on the couch, knowing she'd get a kick out of being thrown around like a sack of potatoes. "And then bathtime and bed for the weary travelers."

Rowan and Kaira both made it to the end of the special and through their bedtime routines, but barely. Kaira was practically sleepwalking by the time Jordy led her to bed and tucked her in. When he returned to the living room, looking forward to some alone time with Rowan, he found him nodding into his chest.

Chuckling, Jordy shook him awake. "Sorry, Rowan, but I figured leaving you here was the worst of all options. Do you want to push through and stay awake? Or go to bed at... eight."

Rowan groaned. "Bed. Someone woke me up at six."

Jordy smiled. "You've had a long day. Come on, off to bed, sweetheart." He nearly bit his tongue off when the term slipped out, but Rowan didn't react to it, just grumbled as he tried to heave himself off the couch.

Now Jordy couldn't hide his grin. He offered his hand and hauled Rowan to his feet, then made sure that Rowan safely stumbled to the guest room, wished him good night, and left him to his own devices.

ROWAN EXPECTED to wake up early. Instead, by the time he rolled out of bed in search of caffeine and sustenance, he found everyone else already awake... and discussing a surprise announcement for the day's plan.

"The Orcas are hosting a family skate today."

"Skate?" Kaira gasped, forgetting about her breakfast.

"Yup. Skate." Jordy booped her nose.

"But Daddy, I didn't bring my skates."

Rowan strongly suspected last year's skates wouldn't fit her anymore, so it didn't surprise him when Jordy said, "I got you new ones, peanut."

"Oh. Are they pink? Did you buy skates for Rowan too? He didn't bring any either."

"I'm sure we can find Rowan skates if he needs some." Jordy looked up and met Rowan's eyes over the breakfast table, as though trying to apologize if this came across as an implicit promise.

"Yay!"

Meanwhile, Rowan was still several exchanges behind, his heart thudding as though it could salvage the situation if it could just distribute the caffeine more efficiently. "Family skate?"

Jordy broke their gaze. "It's a family-friendly holiday party. Anyone who skates has fun on the ice. There's tons of food and usually some off-ice activities. It's fun."

Family. Family. Family. But not Rowan's family. Not for much longer, at least. "Oh."

Jordy went on with a casual air that felt forced, "Anyway, Kaira and I will be going today, and I was hoping we could talk you in to coming too. There's no pressure to skate, and you can say no, but you totally deserve to have some fun and eat free food on the Orcas' dime."

"Rowan has to come! He has to skate with us!" Kaira declared.

"Rowan doesn't have to do anything he doesn't want to," Jordy told her gently. "He's welcome to, but he might have other plans."

"But—" Kaira started to protest, but Rowan cut her off with a blurted, "I don't skate."

Kaira turned on him. "What? *Never?*"

"No?"

"Rowan, you have to skate."

At least, Rowan reflected ruefully, if he wasn't going to be Kaira's caregiver anymore, it didn't matter so much that he was so terrible at saying no.

For the most part, the Orcas were a laid-back group. No one so much as batted an eye when Jordy introduced Rowan as his "friend who saved him and Kaira from tears by bringing her to Vancouver."

Everyone encouraged Rowan to eat and drink whatever he liked and offered to help him tie his skates or hide from the ice, whichever he preferred.

More interesting for Jordy's teammates—and Rowan couldn't blame them—was Kaira. Rowan had gleaned through his limited interactions with hockey players that they tended to be baby-crazy if they liked kids at all.

Kaira took their attention as her due, which made the guy Rowan thought was the Orcas' goalie crack she must be Jordy's polar opposite.

Rowan had to look away and rub his chest when someone else chimed in that she clearly took after her other dad. Fortunately no one but Rowan seemed to have heard.

Soon enough Kaira ordered them into their skates. Jordy, of course, could stay on the ice all day and never tire of it, but Rowan eyed the slick surface with deep distrust.

"I won't let you fall," Jordy promised. "You'll be fine."

They were alone by the gate, if only for a moment, since Kaira had sprinted out onto the ice, momentarily forgetting her adults in her joy.

Rowan shot him a look of deep betrayal. "I'm going to be terrible at this."

Jordy didn't laugh or mock, even though Rowan knew his pout had to rival one of Kaira's from the past six weeks. He took Rowan's hand and solemnly vowed, "I won't let go first."

If only he meant that the way Rowan wanted him to. Rowan took a shuddering breath and nodded. "Okay."

"Now get on the ice before Kaira comes back and pushes you."

Rowan barked a laugh and stepped forward.

Immediately his feet tried to go out from under him. *Obviously* they tried to go out from under him; that was what feet *did* on the ice. He fumbled to try to catch his balance, except the fumbling only made it worse. "Oh *fuck*—"

Jordy never let go of his hand. With his other, he grabbed Rowan's elbow, firm but gentle, until suddenly Rowan was standing up straight. "Easy."

"Easy?" Rowan repeated incredulously. Except now he was looking right into Jordy's kind, soft brown eyes while Jordy smiled at him, and he could only look away if he wanted to fall on his face. Or his ass.

Skating might have been a mistake.

"If Kaira can do it, you can too."

That didn't seem fair—Kaira had obviously been skating since she could walk. Right now she was looping around the ice backward, somehow managing to avoid running into any of the other kids.

"Something tells me learning as a child is not the same thing."

"Come on," Jordy coaxed. "It's easier when you're moving." And then he was gliding backward without even seeming to move his feet, tugging Rowan along with him.

"Are you *barking*?" Rowan asked, but—okay, it wasn't *so* bad. Movement was definitely preferable. Especially forward movement, as opposed to downward.

"When you're starting out, you're going to be strongest on your inside edges," Jordy said, towing Rowan along like he weighed nothing. Rowan made the mistake of looking down for a moment and got utterly distracted by the way Jordy's thighs strained the seams of his jeans. Those had to have some kind of elastic in them. Ordinary material could not contain that.

They went over a small imperfection in the ice, and Rowan stumbled. Jordy caught him before he could even start to panic.

Rowan looked up again, clearing his throat. "Inside edges?"

"Your skates. They've got two sharp edges each, inside and outside. You'll feel more stable if you're bending your ankles inward like, uh— what's the opposite of bow-legged?"

"Are you telling me to *close my legs*?" Rowan asked incredulously before he could help himself, and Jordy threw back his head and laughed.

"Come on. Move your feet. Just push out to the side. There, see? You can do it."

It turned out Rowan *could* do it, if not particularly well. Jordy skated him around the ice three times—Jordy moving backward while Rowan went forward, never letting go of his hand—before he pronounced Rowan ready to try it one-handed.

"You're a little late for tryouts," Ryan commented as he went by, tugging an entire chain of children with Kaira at the rear. "But maybe next year."

Rowan didn't waste any energy flipping him off. He *did* watch in fascination as Ryan sped up, the kiddie train behind him along for the ride, and then stopped and used their momentum to fling them across the ice. "Oh my God, he's a maniac."

At the end of the chain, Kaira was laughing gleefully, even as the grip she had on the next child broke and she rocketed off toward the boards.

"Crack the whip," Jordy explained. "It's fun."

"I'm not doing it," Rowan said firmly.

He might not be brave enough to look over—he needed to keep his eyes on his feet—but he could hear Jordy's smile. "Maybe next time."

Two laps later, Kaira wanted a turn with her dad, so Rowan gratefully begged off and wobbled off the ice. Even after such a short time, the insides of his thighs ached. No wonder Jordy had legs like he did.

And no wonder he ate like he did too—Rowan had worked up an appetite. He pried himself out of his skates and slipped back into his regular shoes, which suddenly felt too big and too cold the way his hands felt too empty without Jordy's in them. To compensate, he grabbed a mug of hot chocolate and a donut from one of the tables and made small talk with a few of the other nonskaters, one of whom was an expectant mom.

Everyone accepted his presence without question, which meant they definitely all thought he and Jordy were dating, but that was fine. It was better than them wondering what Rowan was doing there.

Finally his bladder demanded his attention and he begged off to find a restroom.

But when he pushed open the door, he forgot about his need to relieve himself and found himself standing stock-still without quite knowing why.

"—stay out of it," came a familiar voice. "It's none of our business."

"Okay, but Jordy's my friend," and that was Ryan. "And he's been heartbroken, and not just because of his kid, you know? But did you see how Rowan was looking at him? There's no way that's unrequited—"

"You're so cute when you try to save other people from your own mistakes."

"Excuse you, I'm *always* cute."

At this point Rowan realized he was standing in the door eavesdropping and about to get caught. It startled him into action, and he accidentally opened the door the rest of the way until it banged into the wall.

Smooth.

Ryan Wright looked up at him from his place by the sink, where he was drying his hands on a paper towel. "Woah there, killer. What did the door ever do to you?"

Beside him, Nico rolled his eyes fondly and shoved Ryan toward the door. "Come on. Don't you have kids your own size to pick on?"

They exited the restroom, leaving Rowan alone with a full bladder and an even fuller brain.

There's no way that's unrequited.

Okay, first things first. He focused on the task at hand. Then he wandered back out and found a spot where he could watch Kaira chase Jordy around the ice.

There's no way that's unrequited.

Ryan had been talking about Jordy's feelings for Rowan, but that couldn't be right. Jordy had said being with Rowan made him realize he wanted a partner. Why would he have phrased it that way if he meant he wanted *Rowan to be his partner*?

Well, that was a stupid question. It wasn't like either one of them had a stellar communication track record.

On the ice, Jordy scooped Kaira into his arms and plonked her onto his shoulders, apparently unconcerned about her tiny skates cutting into him. Or about dropping her. Of course he wouldn't drop her; he could skate her around safely with his eyes closed. Both of them were beaming.

Rowan's heart thumped.

That man—that generous, kind, dedicated, flawed, gorgeous man—loved him. That man *loved him back*.

And he thought Rowan didn't.

But that wasn't true. Rowan did love Jordy. Rowan had basically already given Jordy his heart on a plate. He'd all but asked, *Would you prefer that with soup or salad?* Only somehow Jordy didn't know.

That wasn't fair. Jordy deserved to know how Rowan felt, even if it didn't change anything. Even if Rowan was going to go back to Toronto in a week and live in his beautiful untouched apartment and work his perfect job, Jordy deserved to know it wasn't because Rowan didn't love him.

Rowan resolved to tell him that night, when Kaira went to bed. They could talk, maybe cry a little. Polish off a bottle of wine, if Jordy didn't have a game tomorrow. They could lay everything on the table.

And then maybe they could start to get over it.

ROWAN HAD to wait until Kaira was asleep before they could talk, but at least bedtime was early thanks to the jet lag and the busy day. Jordy was barely gone ten minutes before he returned from her room.

"Didn't even make it through the second book." He had a look of such fond amusement on his face that Rowan felt overcome by his beauty and overtaken by affection. God, he loved this man so much.

Rowan blamed his big feelings for what happened next.

"Are you in love with me?"

Jordy froze in the middle of tidying throw pillows—they always ended up everywhere after Kaira had been through—and stared at Rowan, caught. "Uh."

"Shit. Sorry." Rowan hadn't meant to start the conversation like this.

Jordy looked even more baffled. "You're... sorry?"

"Yes, for just... blurting that out. I meant to be more, you know, delicate. Smooth."

"Oh." Still clutching the pillow, Jordy sat on the couch. "Since... since you're asking, I'm guessing that you didn't already know that."

Rowan stared. "How would I know that when you never said?"

Jordy frowned at his pillow. "I guess I figured it was pretty obvious and that's why you kept running away from me every time I tried to talk about it."

Well, that was totally not fair. Rowan opened his mouth to argue, then paused and thought about it. He could see how his desperate escapes from emotional conversations might have seemed like a rejection of the feelings behind them. "Oh. That, uh, wasn't what was happening. That was me running away for fear of hearing the opposite."

"What part of begging you to move across the country...?" Jordy legitimately looked lost, so Rowan threw him a bone.

"You mean right after you told me how worried you were about finding a nanny?"

Jordy's eyes widened. Apparently he didn't remember that part. Rowan wanted to kiss his dumb face.

"Look, I know this doesn't actually change anything about our whole situation, but—" Rowan took a deep breath. "—you deserve to know that I wasn't saying no because I didn't want it, or you, or Kaira." Jordy stared at him, something that looked a lot like hope shining in his eyes. Hope Rowan was going to have to crush. "Even if it doesn't solve anything or fix it or make Vancouver and Toronto one city, you should know I do love you."

"Yeah?"

"Yeah, Jordy, of course I do."

"Oh." He licked his lips. "But you still don't want to stay with me." He wasn't asking.

"It's not about wanting." Sometimes romances didn't have happy endings. Sometimes you were Whitney Houston and Kevin Costner and you had to break up because your lives weren't compatible. Sometimes love wasn't enough.

Jordy looked back down at his pillow. "Okay." Then his jaw firmed up and he looked Rowan in the eye. "But you're here until the New Year."

"Yes...."

"And if we're in the same city and we want to be together, then... why not just be together until then?"

Because it would break Rowan's heart. Because he might never recover. Because getting back on the plane would be ten times harder. Because... because....

"A holiday romance?" he joked.

"Exactly." Though his lips twitched, Jordy's eyes were too intense to be anything but achingly sincere.

Fuck it. Rowan's heart was going to be broken and bleeding come New Year's anyway. What was another knife or two jabbed into it?

The answer must've shown on his face, because Jordy dove across the couch into Rowan's opening arms, his throw pillow aptly tossed to the floor, and brought their mouths together. Rowan pressed into it, parted his lips and twined his arms around Jordy's neck. He'd missed Jordy so much—his touch, his closeness. Rowan's whole body lit up from the knowledge of Jordy alone.

Jordy devoured Rowan's mouth like he was starving, his hands hard, hot brands where he pressed Rowan into the couch cushions. Rowan hadn't exactly forgotten how demanding and possessive Jordy got, but maybe he'd repressed it, too afraid to look at the memories when he thought it didn't mean anything.

One of Jordy's hands slid into the small of Rowan's back and pulled them closer. Then his fingers slipped under his waistband. Rowan was very much on board with that, but also—

"We should—ngh!—get off, off the couch—fuck!"

Jordy hummed around the mouthful of Rowan's neck he was sucking and nibbling.

"Bedroom," Rowan gasped as he arched up into the touch.

Apparently Jordy liked the sound of that, because suddenly Rowan was airborne and Jordy was striding down the hallway.

Rowan groaned into Jordy's mouth. "Manhandling still hot," he groaned out, then tasted the sound of Jordy's laughter.

"Good to know."

In the bedroom, Jordy placed Rowan on his feet so they could scramble out of their clothes, which took forever because they couldn't stop touching each other. Then they dove onto the bed together.

Jordy shoved the duvet to the side, and then they were tangled up together on the bed, touching each other everywhere, pressing as close as possible but still not close enough.

"Lube," Rowan gasped with a beg, and Jordy scrambled in the nightstand. "Fuuuck," he moaned as Jordy pressed a finger into him. He'd missed this, missed Jordy. He pulled him back in for another kiss, trying to show Jordy how much he wanted this—not just the sex but the closeness.

When Jordy was three fingers in and Rowan was ready, he gasped out, "Enough. Condom," and Jordy froze.

"Fuck."

"What?"

Three fingers deep in Rowan's ass, Jordy blushed and asked awkwardly, "I don't suppose you have any?"

"Why would I take condoms on a flight when traveling with a kid to see a man I was determined not to sleep with?" Honestly.

"Well, why would I have condoms when living alone and brokenhearted?" Jordy bitched back.

Oh.

Bugger.

"So we don't have any...."

"No." Jordy kissed his hip. "Guess a change in plans is in order." He twisted his fingers and Rowan went cross-eyed.

Maybe it was the pleasure coursing through him, or maybe it was the desperate, caution-to-the-wind attitude of the moment, but suddenly Rowan wanted to make only one change to their itinerary.

He took Jordy's face in his hands and looked him in the eye. "I haven't been with anyone since before I met you. If… if it's the same for you and you've been tested recently…."

"Rowan."

"I really want you inside me right now."

Jordy lurched forward, kissing Rowan hot and messy. Then he slid his fingers out, and then—

It was probably Rowan's imagination that it felt drastically different, but he was sure that the press of Jordy's cock was hotter and wetter, skin to skin. Rowan gasped and squirmed and swallowed Jordy's stunned groans.

Then Jordy was all the way inside him, bare, as close as they could get. Their limbs tangled together, their chests pressed tight, and Jordy pulled back from their kisses to lean their foreheads together. "I love you."

Rowan sobbed.

He had known, but Jordy hadn't actually said it yet.

Apparently Jordy realized the same thing, because he leaned forward and kissed Rowan sweetly and then slowly dragged his cock out and pressed back in. As their hips reconnected, he said in the hot, wet space between them, "I love you."

Rowan dug his heels into the backs of Jordy's thighs and pulled him in deeper, sharper, harder. He could hear it now, the truth Jordy'd hidden from him when he was nailing Rowan against the wall in his bedroom. He could feel it. The best thing he'd ever heard, the best thing he'd ever felt. "Jordy," he gasped into Jordy's mouth. "I love—I love you, oh *God*—"

Jordy made a hot, sweet sound and straightened his back so he could look into Rowan's eyes. Rowan would've complained—he wanted Jordy's mouth back—but then Jordy got both hands on Rowan's hips and started pulling him down onto Jordy's cock with every thrust, and he kept *looking* at Rowan while he did it, like Rowan was the best thing he'd ever seen, the only thing he ever wanted to look at, like Rowan was *his*.

Rowan became one raw, exposed, sensitive nerve, like his soul had a sunburn. He was on the edge before he realized it. It took just one stroke of his hand, one moment with Jordy watching him, red-faced and sheened in sweat and looking like Rowan had just solved the answer to all life's riddles, and then he was coming, pinned under Jordy's gaze and Jordy's hands and Jordy's cock.

Jordy kept fucking him until Rowan was delirious, overstimulated but loving it, and then suddenly he bent into another kiss and everything seemed a lot wetter and Rowan was trembling into Jordy's mouth.

Then, "Okay, ow, ow, charley horse," he admitted, and Jordy made a noise of empathy, pulled out of him, and helped Rowan stretch his hamstring.

Unfortunately, this had a predictable effect on the integrity of the bedsheets.

They stayed tangled up in each other for several long minutes anyway, trading slow, sweet kisses as they caught their breath. Jordy touched Rowan's face, and Rowan leaned into it, leaned into him. He might only get to have this for a few days, but—

"Hey," Jordy said.

Rowan took a shaky breath.

"Stay here." Off Rowan's blink—surely they couldn't be having this conversation again already—he amended, "In the present, I mean. Not…. Let's just enjoy now."

Rowan swallowed. "Right." He could do that. "I'm glad you meant the present and not, you know. This bed. Because I don't know if you know this, but there is one hell of a wet spot. Also, related, you might have to carry me to the bathroom unless you want to wash your floors."

Jordy poked him in the side, right where Rowan was ticklish. Then his eyes took on a playful light and he started to inch his way downward. He scored his teeth over the jut of Rowan's hip. "Okay," he said, "but let's live in the moment a little more first."

JORDY HAD thought it would be difficult, having Rowan like he wanted, for real, knowing it was going to end. But somehow he put the inevitability of the New Year out of his mind and made good on his promise to live in the moment.

The second full day of Rowan's visit, Jordy had a game, the last one before the Christmas break. With the jet lag, Rowan and Kaira woke up at the same time he did, and they all ate breakfast together before Jordy went off to do his morning workout. The game was a matinee, so the team wouldn't have a morning skate.

He thought Kaira might be extra clingy, with Jordy leaving her for the first time since their reunion, but she just kissed him on the cheek and hugged him around the waist like she always did—*almost* like she always did; her arms reached a lot higher all of a sudden—and then wandered back over to Rowan and asked him seriously what they were going to have for lunch.

Jet lag did a real number on the stomach. Jordy knew all about that.

He returned home an hour and change later to find Rowan and Kaira, pink-cheeked and giggling, making a popcorn garland. God only knew where they got the materials; Rowan must have brought them. Well, of course he had.

"Daddy!" Kaira got up so suddenly she almost upset the bowl, but Rowan caught it before it could tip.

Jordy swung her into a hug and then set her down with a kiss to the top of her head. "Hi, peanut. Are you and Rowan having a good time?"

"We're making decorations!" She narrowed her eyes and tried to peer behind him. "Daddy, what's in that bag?"

"What bag?" Jordy asked innocently, switching hands and moving it to the front.

"Daddy!"

"Oh, this bag?" He lifted the bag from the team store.

Rowan met his eyes and mouthed *spoiled*. Jordy ignored him.

"Welllll," Jordy hedged. "Christmas is coming, but there's a game this afternoon, and I thought you and Rowan might want to come. But what would you wear?"

Kaira made a face. "I don't have an Orcas jersey yet."

"Right," Jordy said seriously. "You don't have an Orcas jersey yet. So I thought… maybe you could open this present a little bit early?"

"I could. I could do that." Kaira looked up at him with wide, pleading eyes. "Daddy, I've been *so good* this year—"

You literally ran away from your nanny, Jordy thought, but he managed not to laugh. That was his fault anyway.

"—haven't I been good, Rowan?"

Rowan raised his hands. "I plead the Fifth."

"The Fifth Amendment is about *self*-incrimination," Jordy said dryly. "And we're in Canada."

"Rowan!"

Rowan sighed dramatically. "Well, she did help me make our prelunch snack today. That was very helpful. And she went to bed on time last night with no complaining."

"See!"

As if Jordy would've denied her, or himself, the pleasure of having her in his new jersey for the game today. "Okay," he capitulated and handed over the bag. He hadn't had time to wrap it; the shop had only finished the custom order this morning. He hadn't wanted to order it until he knew how much she'd grown.

But Kaira wasn't the only one he'd shopped for today. He cleared his throat and passed Rowan the bag as Kaira wriggled into her new Orcas home jersey. "Didn't want you to feel left out."

He hadn't had time to get Rowan's jersey customized, or he might have been tempted—maybe Rowan's last name with Jordy's number, or maybe the year with Jordy's name. But this would have to do for now.

For once, Rowan did not protest that Jordy shouldn't have. He just smiled and ran his fingers over the stitching, then pulled it on.

They made lunch as a family, Jordy assembling cheese sandwiches, Rowan grilling them, Kaira parceling out fruit and vegetables onto each plate. And then they had a pregame nap as a family too, cuddled on Jordy's king-size bed, because Rowan had washed the sheets.

They traveled to the arena together, since Rowan didn't have a car or know the city, which meant Jordy got to bring them in and introduce them to the staff who would look after them. After getting Rowan's input, Jordy had arranged for the box seats he promised back in September and for Kaira to be rinkside during warmups, since that was her favorite part of the game.

Jordy wasn't able to bring them up to the box, but Rowan had him covered. Jordy was half-dressed for warmups when Rowan sent a video of Kaira rushing around the room, trying to take in everything at once.

Not what I was expecting when you said box, Rowan added. Then, *Is that a private bar with bartender?? I feel like I should be looking for the champagne and caviar… don't tell me if there is thanks.*

Laughing, Jordy typed back, *K. I won't tell you about the oysters or truffles either.*

Ryan, who was nosier than anyone's grandma, leaned over to get a view of Jordy around his new D-partner and not-so-subtly asked what was so funny.

Because Jordy was in a very good mood, he showed him the video of Kaira. Predictably, Ryan cooed over Kaira—also more than anyone's grandma—and peppered Jordy with questions about her attendance.

As promised, Rowan and Kaira found their way down to the ice for warmups, so Jordy and Kaira were able to do their usual routine at the glass. Rowan, because he was a dork, held his own fist up for a bump, much to Kaira's delight.

Back in the dressing room, Jordy checked his phone one last time before the game, just to make sure they'd made it back to the box okay. Rowan sent a new picture with the caption *Forget the truffles and caviar, only the finest dino nuggets for this kid.* Kaira had ketchup on her nose.

Jordy heart-reacted the image, then put his phone away. Time to focus on his job.

Twenty minutes later, Jordy found the back of the net for the first time as an Orca. He yelled in triumph and his teammates surrounded him in celebration. Ryan whooped next to his ear and yelled, "Now that's what I'm talkin' about!"

Back at the bench, Nico, who was kind of a bitch, patted Jordy's helmet and said, "Nice dad and/or boyfriend goal."

Before Jordy could protest, Ryan returned to the bench and flipped Jordy the puck. "Gotta keep your first one as an Orca," he said cheerily. "Or, you know, give it to the kid or the beau."

Nico snickered all the way to center ice.

At the end of the game—a 4–2 win—Jordy was kept busy with his cool-down and media, but Rowan replied to Jordy's apology text with pictures of Kaira finding plenty of entertainment in the box. Eventually he escaped and found his two favorite people snuggled on a couch looking at something on an iPad, a cute and cozy scene that was immediately ruined when Kaira caught sight of Jordy and rushed into his arms.

The puck he'd slipped into his pants pocket felt heavy against his thigh, but he didn't pull it out.

Kaira had some of Jordy's game pucks already, including the one from the first goal he scored after her birth and adoption. She didn't need this one.

So Jordy held on to the puck until after she'd gone to bed and he and Rowan collapsed onto the couch together.

"So, what did you think of your second NHL game?"

"Being in the box was different," Rowan said. "Also, I still have no idea what's going on most of the time and Kaira is still terrible at explaining things. At least this time some of the neighbors were helpful."

"Oh?"

"Yeah, a couple of wives took pity on me and gave me some pointers." Then he shrugged and smiled. "Thankfully I got the most important details down. Puck in net good."

"Wow. With insight like that, they'll be asking you to do game commentary soon."

"I try."

"Well, to mark your new insights, you should have this." Jordy handed him the puck.

"A rubber disk, what I've always wanted," Rowan snarked, but his grin took the sting out of the words.

"Not just any rubber disk. That's an 'in net good' one."

"Oh?"

"Yeah, it's tradition for players to keep pucks after important or milestone goals. Like your hundredth or first in a league or on a team."

"Wait, this is your first Orca goal puck? Jordy, that's yours."

"Yes, and I'm giving it to you."

"But—"

"I want you to have it. After all, you get some of the credit for it," he said, trying to sound nonchalant.

"Yeah?"

"Yeah. Not sure that goal happens tonight if not for last night." It was cliché but true. Jordy had been riding high all day, and Rowan had inspired that invincible feeling. Jordy might not get to keep Rowan, but knowing that Rowan thought him worthy of love? An ego boost of the first order.

"Well. Since you won the game today and I helped, we should probably go celebrate," Rowan suggested coyly, sending a bolt of heat rocking through Jordy.

"Yeah. Let's go do that."

CHRISTMAS EVE was a whirlwind of hyperactive child and last-minute jobs. Rowan had never done Christmas with a small child before—not since he was one himself—so he was unprepared for how the day seemed to alternate between hurry-up-and-wait and a mad scramble to get everything done.

Kaira was ecstatic that Santa would definitely be able to find her new house, cross their hearts. Rowan was just relieved Jordy had taken care of all the gift wrapping before their arrival.

And that Jordy had barred the rest of his family from joining him over the holidays, given that more chaos of any sort would make things more difficult for Kaira. Not to mention that spending the holidays with the rest of the Shaws would be an awkward in-law-esque time for Rowan.

Especially since anyone who didn't sleep like the dead might have heard the howling Rowan had licked out of Jordy in celebration of his goal. Rowan had figured he should reward that perfect hockey ass for doing its job so nicely by eating it.

By some miracle, they got Kaira into bed at a normal time, set up the presents under the tree, and then fell back into Jordy's bed for dirty, if rushed, blowjobs before sleep.

All in all, a great day.

So naturally, Kaira woke them at 5:08 a.m. by vomiting on Jordy's bed.

Rowan was sprawled facedown into a pillow and in the middle of a REM cycle when it happened, so he went from a soothing dream about winning an award for creating the perfect organization system to replace Dewey to wondering why his leg was wet.

The room was dark except for the light cast by one of the motion-sensor night lights Jordy had scattered around the various outlets, ostensibly for Kaira but probably also so that any adult wandering around an unfamiliar house at night had a 90 percent chance of getting where they were going without stubbing their toe.

"Zzzt?" he said, blinking, and started to roll over.

A heavy hand landed on his shoulder. "Uh, Rowan, just—don't move for a minute."

Then Rowan registered the smell, and his brain helpfully filled him in on the sounds that had filtered into his sleeping brain just before he woke up.

"Kaira?" he asked hoarsely.

"Daddy, did I growl?" came Kaira's voice.

The mattress shifted as Jordy got up. "No, peanut, you threw up. Let me just—" A soft exhale. "Okay, you've got a bit of a fever. Just give me one second here."

The blankets at the foot of the bed grew heavier around Rowan's legs as Jordy folded them around the pile of sick.

"You can get up now," Jordy said. "Uh. If you want. Without the risk of getting more puke everywhere."

Rowan sat up. "Well, I am definitely awake." He wiped his hand over his eyes. "You take the bath, I'll take the laundry?"

Jordy looked at the bedsheet and grimaced. At least they'd thrown off the coverlet last night. "I think these sheets are telling us something. Trash them, I have another set. And then maybe coffee?"

"Coffee," Rowan agreed.

But he didn't get up until Jordy carried Kaira out of the room toward the bath, because unlike Jordy, Rowan had been too lazy to put underwear back on before they went to sleep the night before.

Now *there* was a mistake he wouldn't make again.

By the time Jordy emerged from the bathroom with Kaira in a fresh pair of puke-free pajamas, Rowan had the coffee ready and breakfast going—plain oatmeal and pancakes with no chocolate chips. He didn't know whether Kaira would have much of an appetite, but he and Jordy needed to eat, and they could add fruit to bland food.

And protein, in Jordy's case, but Rowan had not had enough time to caffeinate to be thinking about protein.

"Here." He nudged the bottle of Gatorade he'd unearthed from the pantry toward Jordy. Jordy only drank it cold, but there was only so much room in the fridge, and room temperature would be better on an upset stomach. "I couldn't find a straw."

"That's what the sports caps are for." Jordy broke the seal and passed the bottle to Kaira, who was curled up on the couch under a lurid red-and-green throw blanket that Rowan suspected had been bestowed on them by Jordy's captain. "Drink some of that while I try to find a thermometer, okay, sweetheart?"

Oh boy. "Try to find?" Rowan echoed.

Jordy grimaced. "I didn't think the first thing she was going to do when she got here was projectile vomit."

And now here it was, Christmas Day, and Jordy without the necessary supplies.

"At least one pharmacy will be open," Rowan pointed out. "You just have to figure out which one." He pulled a notepad and pen off the fridge. "Thermometer, Pedialyte, Children's Tylenol…?"

"Replacement Christmas?" Jordy said, wry but also defeated.

"No one's immune to plane crud." Rowan flipped a couple pancakes onto a plate. "Eat these, drink some coffee, and go play hunter-gathering hero. Kaira and I can be pathetic sad sacks without you. We have lots of practice."

"I can't believe I actually find that reassuring." Jordy sighed and kissed Rowan's cheek. "Love you." He repeated his departure with Kaira, reassured her he'd be back as soon as he could, and then it was just Rowan and Kaira and a whole lot of germs.

It looked like Kaira had fallen asleep on the couch, so Rowan closed the Gatorade bottle and set it beside her, then spent ten minutes googling how to make a sick child comfortable. By the time Jordy returned, Kaira was still asleep and Rowan had raided the cupboards and decanted an entire array of sick-kid necessities—a big steel bowl for vomit, her favorite books, Piglet, a sleeve of plain crackers, and a handful of the sweet "fruit" flavored granny candies Jordy thought Rowan didn't know he favored. The television remotes were all at hand, and he'd turned on the Christmas tree as well and set a pot of orange slices and cinnamon sticks simmering on the stove in case Kaira *did* throw up again.

It should still smell like Christmas, at the very least.

Jordy opened his mouth as if to say something, but Rowan jerked his head at the couch, where Kaira had turned onto her side and was sleeping soundly, or as soundly as one could when one was a sick child.

"This is not how I wanted today to go," Jordy sighed in a whisper as Rowan wrapped him in a hug.

"I expected her to wake us up early to open presents, not the contents of her stomach," Rowan agreed. Jordy snorted in his ear. "It's fine, hey? We'll improvise. Turkey soup instead of a roast." Though if he was going to make stock, he'd better get to roasting.

"There's just three of us," Jordy said. "I bought a chicken."

"Even better."

While Jordy went to check Kaira's fever, Rowan spatched the chicken and put it in the oven to roast. He might as well; chicken soup was a cure-all whether it was ten in the morning or seven at night.

He would've liked to curl up on the couch next to Jordy, but with Kaira sleeping on it, there wasn't room, so he made himself comfortable on a pillow on the floor and leaned back against Jordy's legs to read a book while Jordy scrolled on his phone.

"Emma says Merry Christmas," Jordy murmured sometime later.

Marking the page with his finger, Rowan looked up from his book and smiled. "Tell her I say it back."

"She also sends her condolences for the demised cheer," he added as he tapped out Rowan's answer.

Rowan snorted. "Kind of her. But I don't know, could be worse."

Jordy groaned softly. "Why would you say that? Don't tempt fate."

"It's not tempting fate. I just think some people are having a worse holiday than us. There's bound to be someone, right?"

Jordy shook his head and regarded Rowan with a bemused smile. Then he leaned forward and kissed Rowan's nose. "I'm glad you're here."

"Me too." Because Rowan wouldn't rather be anywhere else this Christmas, vomit and all. Though he'd really been looking forward to the magic of secondhand delight and watching Kaira tear into her presents.

When he voiced this sentiment aloud, Jordy snorted. "She'll still do that. We'll know she's feeling better when she starts ripping wrapping paper."

They were watching *It's a Wonderful Life* on very low volume—thank goodness for closed captioning—when Kaira woke up a second time. They were able to get some Tylenol, Pedialyte, and a banana into her easily enough, since her stomach seemed more settled. She snuggled between them and watched the last half hour of the movie, by which point her fever had subsided enough that she almost perked up.

"Should we see what Santa left in your stocking?" Jordy asked, and she perked up even more, though not enough to get off the couch.

Jordy fetched the stockings from the fireside and brought all three over. Rowan wasn't surprised to find his just as stuffed as Kaira's, since no six-year-old would understand Santa forgetting one of her adults. Still, he hadn't expected this lapful of gifts.

Kaira's eyes nearly popped out as she took in her overflowing stocking. "That's all for me?"

"Yup, all for you, poppet." Rowan snuck a kiss to her head because he could.

Jordy was apparently a traditionalist when it came to stockings, as it was full of small necessities as well as toys—Disney toothbrush and toothpaste, animal-shaped Lip Smackers, armadillo socks (which Rowan was amazed existed), unicorn underpants (which didn't surprise him), rainbow barrettes, crayons and a coloring book, stickers, and some candy. Kaira marveled over every new find, but the best part was undoubtably the brand-new Bilbo the Armadillo book—*Bilbo the Armadillo Hosts Christmas*. Naturally, both Rowan and Jordy had to read it to her immediately.

After one read-through each, Kaira noticed their untouched stockings and demanded to see what was in them, so Rowan let her pull out each item and inspect it. If Jordy wanted to give him something not child-appropriate, he wouldn't have given Rowan the stocking in front of Kaira. She pulled out pairs of fun socks, lip balm, some nice pens, a travel notebook, toothbrush and toothpaste, and an array of packaged snacks and candies not usually for sale this side of the pond. Rowan was delighted by the Hobnobs, but he'd found those here before.

"Where did you find Twirls and Flakes?" he demanded. "Or the Branstons?" He waved the jar of pickle at Jordy, who shrugged like it was no big deal.

"I found a local shop that stocks British food."

"I," Rowan said magnanimously, "am not going to think about how much this stupid jar was marked up, and instead I'm going to eat every delicious bite before I fly out of town."

Jordy's smile twitched and dimmed a fraction, but only for a moment. He rallied with a laugh. "I'll remind you of that next week, if and when you fail."

"I won't!"

"What is it?" Kaira asked, curious.

"Pickled vegetables. It's a type of relish."

"Gross," Kaira said with feeling, pulling a face.

"Yeah, you probably wouldn't like it. Me, on the other hand? I'm going to eat so many cheese-and-pickle sandwiches."

And then he decided he'd better stop talking before Kaira's queasy face became Kaira's upchucked banana, and reminded her she had one more stocking to oversee the emptying of.

Jordy wasn't expecting any surprises, of course, since he'd been the one in charge of gifts, but Rowan had found a few small items to slip into the stocking when Jordy's back was turned.

Seeing Jordy's baffled face when Kaira pulled the matching novelty socks and tie out was priceless. They were kind of terrible—navy blue with neon pink and covered in cartoon dinosaurs. Kaira loved them.

"Daddy, Santa gave you a tie for work!"

"Yes, yes he did," Jordy said dryly and shot Rowan a look. Jordy would have worn them anyway, Rowan was sure, but getting Kaira in on it ensured he would probably wear them to his next game.

The next item Kaira unearthed was the large flat magnet Rowan had found for the fridge—a comprehensive chart that converted kitchen measurements from Imperial to metric, and in some cases between volume and weight. Jordy's struggle to conceptualize metric was a constant delight to Rowan, who enjoyed Jordy's consternated expression every time Canadian packaging betrayed him and failed to include both sets of measurements. Not that it happened as often as it would elsewhere. Canadians couldn't make up their minds about anything. Weather was measured in Celsius but ovens in Fahrenheit?

Jordy shot Rowan the bitchiest of bitchfaces, clearly salty about Rowan's dig, but how could he resist? The one time Kaira asked him to use one of Rowan's cookie recipes while Rowan was at work, he'd sent a string of grumpy, petty texts about incomprehensible measuring systems.

"Ooh, magnet. What's it for?"

"It's to help Daddy bake." Kaira nodded like this made perfect sense and pulled the next item out.

As each was revealed, Rowan was glad that he'd contributed, since Jordy seemed incapable of getting himself anything that wasn't purely functional. His stocking looked like he'd emptied his bathroom cabinet into it.

Well, other than the boring sports socks and granny candies, of course.

By that point Kaira had worn herself out and was ready for another snuggle, so they cleared away their presents and put on *The Muppet Christmas Carol*, the only one worth watching, and passed the rest of the morning like that.

By lunchtime, the chicken had cooled and was ready to be turned into soup, so after their meals of eggs and toast for Kaira and leftovers for the adults, Rowan set the pot to simmering. It might not be a traditional Christmas feast, but the smell of chicken soup permeated the house and had them all ready for dinner that night.

After the sun had set and Jordy had transferred a snoozing Kaira back to bed, he and Rowan cuddled up on the couch, looking at the tree.

"So it might not be morning anymore, but you still have a present under the tree to open," Jordy murmured.

"Mm." Rowan was curled into Jordy's side, his head resting on his shoulder, and he didn't want to move. Any other night and he would have suggested they make use of Kaira's shockingly early bedtime in an adults-only fashion. But tonight it felt good just to be close. Not to mention that a five o'clock wakeup and a day with a sick kid weren't exactly great for one's libido.

"Rowan, I'm asking if you wanna open your present."

"Present?"

"Yes, present. Someone was a very good boy"—Rowan shivered; maybe his libido had gotten enough rest after all—"and has presents under the tree."

"But Kaira…."

"She won't notice. She's a bit young to care too much about presents from other people to other people."

So Rowan let Jordy extricate himself enough to grab their gifts for each other. The large bag he placed on Rowan's lap wasn't exactly heavy, but it had weight enough and was stuffed full under the top layer of red and green tissue paper. Inside were a set of leather touchscreen-compatible gloves, a matching scarf and hat in a burgundy that Rowan had been assured looked good on him, and finally a brown leather messenger bag with a "handmade in BC" label and his initials stamped in the bottom corner of the flap.

"Jordy," Rowan choked. There was no way Jordy had purchased this in the past forty-eight hours. He'd bought this for Rowan his friend, not his lover. Rowan ran his hands over the leather, then flipped it open to find pockets of varying sizes and uses tucked everywhere. Damn.

"I figured anyone working at a library or a college needed a good leather bag."

"It's a university, you heathen," Rowan bitched, mostly so he wouldn't give in to the tears threatening. "Thank you. I love it. I love you," he added impulsively and kissed Jordy in thanks.

"My turn," Jordy said breathlessly once Rowan finally released him.

"It's a bit of a letdown after this." Rowan didn't have the funds to spend what was probably a good thousand dollars—the bag alone could cost that much, and Rowan was pretty sure the hat and scarf were cashmere.

Jordy gave Rowan an unimpressed look, then unwrapped the small flat box. Rowan had agonized for the past three weeks what to get his friend/employer/unrequited love and had finally settled on something that would help him build happy memories with Kaira—a family pass to the science museum.

"I got the one for two adults, since I'm sure you'll want to add the new nanny—"

Jordy cut him off with his lips.

"It's perfect," he said, and well, Rowan had to agree. Perfect was definitely the best way to sum up the day.

Boxing Day went marginally better in that Kaira had enough energy to open the rest of her presents and didn't vomit on anyone or anything, but she still spent the day eating soup, drinking as much Pedialyte as they could force into her, and watching Christmas movies.

Jordy went back to work on the twenty-seventh, but since it was an away game in Seattle, he was hardly gone much longer than if it had been a home game.

Then Kaira was feeling well enough to leave the house, and they filled their days with family activities in between Jordy's practices and games.

By some miracle the Orcas weren't playing on the thirtieth or thirty-first, though they had a New Year's Day matinee. The two days off inspired Ryan to extend two invitations—a team New Year's Eve party on the thirty-first and free babysitting the day before.

Or as the text he sent Jordy put it, *Bro, let the hubby and me watch the kid while you take your boo out to dinner. He deserves to be wined and dined after taking your kid on a transcontinental flight.*

That was the least of what Rowan deserved, but Jordy hardly had time to whisk him away for a romantic weekend in Whistler, and even if he had, it wasn't as though Jordy could've skied or snowboarded. Besides, he couldn't justify spending a whole night away from Kaira when he'd just gotten her back in his time zone.

Instead, he settled for a chilly romantic walk through VanDusen Park to see the light displays, and then a nice dinner out.

Or—he tried to settle for that, but as soon as they took their seats at the second-floor table Jordy had reserved at Tap & Barrel, Rowan looked at him, their knees brushed under the table, and Jordy watched in real time as the same spark that went up his spine went up Rowan's.

Rowan licked his lips and cleared his throat. "We could have a pizza delivered," he suggested, and that suddenly sounded perfect.

Jordy gave his apologies to their bemused server, left a hundred-dollar tip, and bundled Rowan right back into the car.

Jordy's knees were too old for any kind of "lovemaking on a rug by the fireside" nonsense. Fortunately there was also a gas fireplace in the master bedroom, so they could have all the ambiance with none of the protesting joints. They made thorough messes of each other—Jordy unrepentantly left a hickey on the side of Rowan's neck that he'd be explaining away at work for weeks—and only dragged themselves out of bed when the pizza arrived so that it didn't freeze to the doorstep.

They ate tangled up together on the couch, too hungry to bother with plates, catching stray dribs of cheese with paper towels.

"This was definitely a better idea than dinner out," Jordy admitted as Rowan stretched out a leg. Jordy lifted his thigh so Rowan could tuck his foot under.

Rowan sucked a glob of sauce from his thumb. "I am a genius."

Jordy still wanted to wine and dine him, of course. Rowan deserved that. But that would've meant sharing him, and Jordy would only get to have this for a few more days.

When he thought about it too much, it put a knot in the pit of his stomach. Couldn't Rowan be a librarian anywhere? Wouldn't he want to do that here, with Jordy and Kaira, if he loved them as much as he claimed to? But then, he'd worked hard for his job, and Jordy wasn't about to give up the life he'd worked for either.

"Hey." Rowan flexed his toes under Jordy's leg. "Happy thoughts only, mister."

Jordy made a face at him and almost lost a string of cheese to gravity because he wasn't paying attention. "Do you remember that charity fundraiser dinner?"

"The one where you were trying to hide in the bathroom?" Rowan smiled. "No, I've completely forgot. Jordy, I still have dreams about that suit."

One last bite and then Jordy wiped his greasy hands with a napkin. "You were the best thing about that night."

He wasn't quite brave enough to look at Rowan while he said it, but he glanced over afterward and was rewarded with a tender, open expression. "I don't have any regrets," Rowan promised.

Jordy did. He wished he'd pulled his head out of his ass sooner. But he wasn't allowed to say that out loud or even think it too loud, apparently, so he made a joke instead. "No? You could've had the fourth-richest man in Toronto."

Rowan cackled. "God! I should send him a picture of the two of us together. That'll give him a real thrill."

"Don't you dare." Jordy laughed. "He'll probably frame it and put it on his nightstand."

"Nah." Rowan waggled his eyebrows. "Gotta keep that kind of thing under the mattress."

They collapsed into horrified giggles, but eventually those subsided too, leaving them in a warm, aching kind of silence.

"What are you thinking right now?" Rowan asked after a moment.

"Wondering if I'd be a terrible boyfriend if I wanted to pick Kaira up early," Jordy admitted.

The foot wriggled out from under his butt. "Thank God," Rowan said. "I thought I was going to have to suggest it. I miss that little nugget. Let's go."

The little nugget barely woke up—apparently she'd been subjected to hours of board games *and* classic Disney movies—but that didn't stop Jordy from enjoying the quiet drive home with her in the back seat and Rowan sitting next to him, where he belonged.

Still, it didn't surprise Jordy when he woke up in the wee hours of the morning to find Kaira standing beside the bed.

She hadn't had any bedwetting issues since the move to Vancouver—actually since Rowan had agreed to be the one to take her—but Jordy prepared to get up anyway. "Hi, peanut. What are you doing up?"

"I had a scary dream. Can I sleep with you and Rowan?"

Soon she'd be too old for this, Jordy thought to himself as he scooped her up and plopped her in the middle. If she thought it was strange he was sharing with Rowan, she didn't mention it.

"Better?" Jordy asked, kissing her hair.

"Uh-huh. Night, Daddy. Night, Rowan."

Jordy would've sworn Rowan was still dead to the world, but he mumbled, "Nigh', poppet," and gave her a little snuggle before subsiding into sleep.

New Year's Eve was Rowan's last full day in Vancouver, which meant lots to do. Kaira had already been introduced to her new nanny via FaceTime—a teammate whose kids had grown out of needing one had recommended her—but her stomach flu had prevented an in-person meeting. But with Rowan leaving, formal introductions could wait no longer.

But neither Rowan nor Jordy wanted to give up any more time with Kaira than they had to, so they decided to make use of Rowan's Christmas gift and take a trip to Science World. That would give Sandy and Kaira a fun atmosphere to get to know each other, and Sandy could take the lead without Jordy sacrificing Kaira time.

He felt a little wistful about it, hanging back and holding hands with Rowan as Kaira and Sandy did most of the exploring, but Sandy's patience and Kaira's enthusiasm assured him he was doing the right thing.

"How are you so chill right now?" Rowan asked quietly when Kaira and Sandy were challenging each other to make the letter T out of different shapes. "*I'm* not chill. I want to push her out of the way and bare my teeth, and she's *lovely.*"

"Mostly I just don't want to get arrested," Jordy joked. Sandy was five foot three and maybe a hundred and five pounds. "No, but… it's a reality of my life. I can't be here all the time. Kaira deserves someone she likes to hang out with when I'm not. So that makes it easier, if not exactly easy."

It was probably worse for Rowan because he was leaving. Soon he wouldn't get to spend any time with Kaira at all.

Or Jordy, for that matter.

But Jordy wasn't allowed to say that. "Anyway," he went on, "just keep holding my hand so I don't punch her."

Rowan checked his shoulder. Jordy pretended to let it push him.

That evening, they headed to Ryan and Nico's family-friendly party. They'd enlisted the help of teammates to have supervision for the kids while the parents ate and drank. The spread was extensive and, according to Ryan, catered, because fuck no, he was not cooking that much food for you losers. He did take credit for the large vat of mulled wine—or "glue vine" as Nico called it—and the somewhat baffling pot of something called *Feuerzangenbowle* ("foyer song in bowl ah"?), which Nico lit on fire with the same flair Jordy might give adding ice to a glass of whiskey.

They stayed long enough to eat and enjoy a drink each, but by that point Kaira was wilting, still not yet fully recovered from her flu. Jordy used his napping daughter as a convenient excuse to make an early exit. Ryan and Nico all but waved them out the door and didn't make a single snippy comment about Jordy being a lame old man.

At home, with Kaira back in bed, Rowan and Jordy followed suit. They made love in Jordy's bed, pressed close together, hands clasped, while Jordy moved inside Rowan as slowly as he could, trying to make the moment last, to remember every second of Rowan's mouth, his skin, his gasps and groans. Why didn't Jordy get to keep this?

As they lay tangled together in the sheets, catching their breath, Jordy wished he could beg Rowan to stay. But that wasn't allowed, so he kissed him and then suggested they raid the fridge for leftovers.

They welcomed in the New Year standing half-naked in Jordy's kitchen, eating cold slices of pizza and leftover Christmas chocolate.

"Happy New Year," Rowan said and leaned in for a sweet, hazelnut-flavored kiss.

Jordy kissed him back with all the love and wanting he had in him. "Happy New Year."

Whatever you're doing at midnight, you'll be doing all year.

Or so people said.

If only it were actually true.

ROWAN DIDN'T want to get out of bed. Once he got out of bed, he'd have to eat breakfast, say goodbye to Jordy and Kaira, then go to the airport and fly away from the first family who had ever really loved him.

In other words, getting out of bed meant breaking his own heart.

Breaking his own heart only to go home to listen to "I Will Always Love You" a billion times on repeat and cry into tubs of ice cream.

Because no matter how much he loved Jordy, it didn't change logistics. Relationships were about building a life together, not about... about chocolate-sweet kisses at midnight.

So Rowan should stop lying here with his eyes closed like hiding under the covers would change anything.

Jordy was already up and out of bed, so bed was missing its main attraction anyway.

In the kitchen, he found Jordy and Kaira at the breakfast table eating pancakes. Despite Jordy's clear attempt at a fun breakfast, the mood in the kitchen was kind of a downer.

"Why does Rowan have to go back to Tronno?" Kaira asked as Rowan was trying to stomach his own delicious breakfast.

"Because that's where he lives, where his job is."

Kaira frowned. "But Rowan lives with us."

"He did for a while, but remember, we talked about him moving into his own apartment." Jordy's voice was gentle and patient and only sounded a little like each word hurt to say.

Kaira scowled at her plate. "Rowan, when are you coming back to 'Couver?"

God, Rowan was going to miss hearing her say "'Couver" in her adorable kid voice. And he would miss the day she started calling the city Vancouver and made her dad misty-eyed about her growing up too fast.

"Um, I don't—don't have any plans to come back." Coming back for a visit would be stupid. It would tie him and Jordy to a half-dead relationship, keep it on life support instead of letting it go. Rowan couldn't bear the thought of Jordy growing bitter and resentful toward him. So no, Rowan wouldn't be coming back.

Kaira cried and clung when Rowan's Uber arrived. Rowan and Jordy barely got to say goodbye, let alone make it tender, since Jordy's hands were full with Kaira.

If he cried all the way to the airport, no one had to know but him and the Uber driver.

At least he didn't have any luggage to check this time around, since he'd used his checked luggage on the way here for Kaira's stuff, which kept things simple.

Once through security—which was always the worst; the less said about it the better—Rowan slouched into a seat and prepared to wait.

He texted Gem. *Please have biggest bottle of wine and tub of salted caramel ice cream ready.*

For goodness sake, came Gem's answer. *What now?*

Rowan swallowed hard and risked the inevitable I-told-you-so. *I love them.*

Because it really was about both of them. Rowan loved Jordy with a passion he'd never known, but he'd been equally blindsided by the depth of his affection for Kaira.

Yes, and?

Rowan could practically hear her talons impatiently drumming on a table.

And leaving them hurts.

A few interminable seconds ticked by before Gem's reply appeared. *So why are you doing it?*

Rowan huffed and shoved his phone back into his bag—his new leather messenger bag—and glared out the airport window. Didn't Gem think Rowan wanted to stay? But it wasn't that simple. Rowan had a life in Toronto—friends, Gem, a dream job he'd only just started. What was he going to do, just say fuck it and move in with Jordy? Play house with him and his kid and do… what?

He couldn't give up the stability that he'd worked so hard for just for the sake of maybes. He couldn't run away from reality to live on love. That wasn't a thing. His job was real, was safe, and Jordy and Kaira were just a—a *fantasy*.

God, Rowan probably could have dreamt them into existence. A single dad with a half-desi baby and the ability to fuck Rowan into the wall? The stuff of Rowan's fantasies.

All of it was…

Like trips to the museum and adorable hockey jerseys and—

Vomit at five a.m.… Jordy freaking out thousands of miles away. Footprints in the snow. Failed love confessions in dark kitchens. No nannies. Temper tantrums and wet beds.

Okay, all of that had been real, but it wasn't glamorous and wasn't exactly points for the win column.

Was it?

He thought about Christmas, about waking up to literal vomit and sending a half-asleep Jordy out to a drugstore twenty minutes away for emergency supplies, about sitting snuggled on the couch for most of the day, and their holiday feast of chicken soup.

It was the best holiday he'd ever had. Bar none. None of the extravagant lonely holidays of his childhood or the performative parties his parents had put on for friends could compete. Nor could any of the poor holidays he'd stumbled through with friends or Gem after he left home.

One week ago was the best family holiday of his life, puke and all. Maybe even because of it, because it was so, so real and not a fantasy, and holy crap—

"What the fuck am I doing?"

The family sitting across from him jerked in surprise; the parents glared, but the two preteens smiled at Rowan in delight.

The older one snapped her gum and shrugged. "I don't know, man, what the fuck *are* you doing?"

"Casey," their father reprimanded.

Rowan laughed. "Making the biggest mistake of my life." He stood and saluted the kids. "Happy traveling, folks." Then he headed for the exit.

JORDY GOT through the pregame meeting on autopilot because he had a decade of experience. His heart wasn't in it.

His heart was in pieces—one across town with her nanny, one probably somewhere over the Rockies by now.

But he'd heal. Right? His heart had been broken before. Hell, he was divorced. Surely his divorce had been worse than this.

Except it hadn't. That had ended amicably. He'd been sad but not devastated. Not—

"Chin up, Shaw." Ryan nudged his skate. "You can mope after we win the game. Let's get on the ice."

Jordy let his D-partner pull him to his feet and headed down the tunnel. Exercise would take his mind off it.

The scent of the ice didn't cure everything, but it loosened something in his chest. Jordy's legs carried him forward. The echo of skates on ice settled something in his head. He made a loop around the ice, let the speed of it whip his hair back. The cold helped. It hurt, but he could—

He was crossing behind the Orcas' net, reaching out to snag a puck from the pile, when he saw the sign.

Home Team's New #1 Fan

Jordy knew that writing. He'd seen it on his grocery list.

He raised his eyes.

Rowan stood on the other side of the glass, wearing his jersey and the cashmere hat Jordy had bought him for Christmas.

His feet stopped moving. His hand moved toward the glass without his conscious input.

On the other side of the glass, Rowan's moved too.

He was supposed to be halfway to Toronto. He was supposed to be gone.

Home Team's New #1 Fan

The scattered pieces of Jordy's heart rushed back to his chest and thudded loudly. He could hardly breathe.

Rowan was biting down on what Jordy desperately hoped was a smile.

Someone snowed to a stop next to him and checked his shoulder. "Hey. You warm enough yet?"

Right, he had a job to do. "Can we…?" he started.

Nico clapped his helmet and nudged him back toward the drills. "After warmups," he said. "Ryan's sending someone for him."

Jordy could only imagine he looked like an idiot for the rest of warmups. He couldn't keep his eyes off Rowan. Every time he glanced over, he found Rowan's gaze on him. He was really here. He hadn't left.

"Oh my God, you've forgotten where the net is," said his D-partner. He gave Jordy an admittedly deserved facewash.

He didn't seem particularly upset about it.

Finally they were called off the ice. Jordy practically tossed his stick into the rack and sprinted down the tunnel toward the locker room.

For a second, he was convinced he'd imagined the whole thing. And then Rowan stepped out of the hallway past the dressing room and suddenly it was the rest of the world that wasn't quite real.

"Hi," Rowan said shyly. The sign had disappeared, along with most of Jordy's sense.

"Hi," he said back, feeling stupid. "What, uh. What are you doing here?"

Rowan tugged at his earlobe and cleared his throat. "Well, you know, I thought—I've heard rent in Vancouver is very expensive—"

Jordy stared at him.

Rowan snapped his mouth shut and changed tack. "I have spent my entire adult life trying to build myself a home." He took a step forward. Jordy's hands itched to take his, but he couldn't move. "I saved and I sacrificed and I finally got a job that I love and an apartment that I still haven't slept in, and it was supposed to make me happy."

Surely he didn't miss his flight to tell Jordy he was still leaving? He wouldn't be so cruel.

"And it did," Rowan said. He was smiling a little now. His hands found Jordy's. "When I quit it."

Jordy's mouth went dry.

"I spent so much time and energy trying to build a home. But home's not a place, it's people. It's you and Kaira and—and me, if you'll have me."

Jordy dropped his hands and pulled him into a kiss by his face.

It didn't go further than that, not with the game in twenty minutes and Jordy's teammates just around the corner. But it felt good, right, to kiss Rowan like this here and finally make a public statement of what he'd been feeling for months. As indulgent as his teammates were, Jordy knew his coach would give him only so much leeway.

"So," Rowan panted when the kiss broke, "that's a yes?"

"That's a yes," Jordy confirmed.

"Oh good," Rowan said breathlessly. "'Cause once I break my lease, I am going to be super broke."

IF POSSIBLE, Rowan took in even less of this hockey game than he had any of the previous ones. He also enjoyed it the most. Quite possibly every other fan in the building thought he was deranged because he couldn't stop smiling, even when the Orcas allowed a goal against, but he consoled himself that they would've been grinning like a fool too if the love of their life had just snogged the daylights out of them in the bowels of a hockey arena.

When the game ended, a team employee fetched Rowan from the stands and led him back down to the dressing room, and Jordy drove them home.

Home. Where their room was, and the throw blanket Jordy had bought for Rowan in New York City, and Kaira.

His family.

But when they turned onto Jordy's street, Rowan's stomach twisted into knots. "What if she's still upset? What if she thinks I'm going to leave again?"

Jordy's hand covered his on the center console. "Then we'll prove you aren't."

Sure. No problem.

Jordy squeezed his fingers. "Rowan, she loves you. It's going to be okay. Remember how upset she was you were leaving? She'll be just as excited knowing you're going to stay."

Rowan tried to believe him, but his nervous heart wouldn't be convinced—not until Jordy opened the door to the house and said, "Kaira? There's someone here to see you."

"Who?" Kaira demanded from out of sight.

"Come see," Jordy laughed, though Kaira's dramatic sigh was still loud enough to be heard.

"Rowan!" she screamed when she rounded the corner and came into view. She didn't hesitate but ran full tilt toward him. "Rowan!"

He crouched and caught her, pulling her close and burying his face into her tangled hair. "Hello, poppet."

"Rowan, Rowan, Rowan," she gasped and clutched him. "You're here. You didn't leave."

"No, I didn't. And I'm not ever going to."

Kaira pulled back and looked him squarely in the eye. "Promise?"

"Promise," he choked out, but then couldn't force out anything else.

"Promise," Jordy said, crouching next to them. "Rowan is staying here. He's going to live with us. Be a family with us."

Kaira pondered this. "Does that mean he's going to be my papa for real?"

Rowan's brain record scratched to a halt.

"For real?" Jordy asked curiously.

Kaira nodded. "People keep calling him my daddy, but I tell them he's not my daddy, you are. Ms. Jansen asked if he was Papa then, but I said he's just Rowan." She sighed like adults were confusing.

"But you liked the idea of Rowan being Papa?" Jordy didn't sound pressuring, only deeply curious about her own feelings. Rowan wished Jordy would give him a clue.

"Yeah, Then I'd have two parents like other kids, and Rowan is a good dad. He's better at reading stories than you, Daddy."

"Well," Jordy said grinning, "if he's better at story time...." He caught Rowan's eye, radiating joy and satisfaction.

And maybe his own surging joy and adrenaline were to blame for what he said next. "You know, the Urdu word for daddy is *baba*."

"Baba," Kaira said, testing it out.

Rowan wanted to melt into a puddle on the floor.

"I think it suits him, don't you, Kaira?"

She nodded and planted a smacking kiss to his cheek. "You're a perfect baba."

"Guess it's good I'm sticking around, then. And will have lots of free time for the next few weeks, because I don't have a job or money or even enough clothes to last me beyond a week."

"That's okay." Jordy shrugged and helped them both off the floor. Kaira refused to loosen her grip on Rowan's neck, so he balanced her on his hip. "You can take your time finding a job, or just stay home all day and buy new clothes using my credit card. I've got money to share."

"You better," Rowan said, suddenly sounding way more serious than he intended. "Share, that is. I'm trusting you to keep me safe here."

"Always," Jordy vowed. "There's nothing I want more than to keep you both happy and safe and loved."

Rowan was not going to cry. Again. "Sap."

Jordy kissed him softly, sweetly. "Proudly."

For several long beats, they just stood in the hallway, basking in the love and satisfaction of finally officially being a family. Naturally Kaira broke the silence.

"Baba, can we make cookies?"

"Can we make cookies. Poppet, we can always make cookies." Rowan set her down on the floor and happily let her drag him into the kitchen, laughing as she described the cookies she wanted to make. Something about chocolate unicorn sparkles?

There was so much that needed doing, planning. They would have to call Gem to get the packing and shipping sorted, and the house in Toronto needed selling, not to mention figuring out what Sandy's new duties and schedule would look like—though Rowan could already hear Jordy holding back to reassure her that her contract wasn't being canceled or her salary changed, the same promise he'd made Rowan on the drive home—but for now, Rowan just wanted to be a family and have fun with his Kaira.

They'd pulled out all the ingredients for chocolate chip cookies and set them on the counter when Jordy joined them. He watched as they measured the flour, then suddenly said, "You know, there's one easy way to keep you both safe and happy no matter what life brings at us, trades and all."

"Oh?"

"We should get married."

Rowan dropped the measuring cup full of flour onto the floor.

Then he kissed Jordy's dumb beautiful face while Kaira collapsed into giggles.

Postgame

Shaw's New Chapter

Jordy Shaw got married but only wants to talk about libraries.

Jordy Shaw became the talk of the internet earlier this week after fans spotted the brand-new gold band on his ring finger, just ten weeks after the appearance of viral photos of his rumored-to-be boyfriend attending an Orcas game with a sign proclaiming to be the team's newest fan.

The boyfriend, Rowan no previous surname name given, is not a fellow hockey player for a change and in fact isn't even a hockey fan, and his only claim to internet fame is being spotted with or near Shaw in posted photos. (See gallery of photos here.)

When asked during a postpractice media scrum about the new jewelry, Shaw grinned and confirmed that he and his partner got married last week, but offered little by way of details when pressed. The ceremony was small and private, and everyone in their lives is happy for them, he said.

Shaw did offer up one detail about his new spouse, beyond his married name of Rowan Shaw, that is—they met at the library.

"Rowan's a librarian, and he was working at the branch in Toronto where I brought my daughter. The two of them hit it off immediately."

This announcement ended Shaw's reminiscence about his new marriage and his husband.

"Did you know that libraries are an integral part of our society? They're amazing places that bring so much more to communities than just books—though bringing books is a very important service."

His passionate defense of public libraries drew in listeners and refocused the conversation, though the discussion did not read like a manipulation to distract so much as an enthusiastic interest.

"He'll probably get the whole team talked into some sort of outreach or charitable campaign. I can't wait," Captain Ryan Wright agreed when asked about his thoughts on the benefits of public library systems. "Maybe another player will find a future spouse there to check out," he added cheekily.

Though Rowan Shaw might be a husband of mystery, the couple's mutual love of learning and community clearly isn't.

Keep reading for Jordy Shaw's impassioned manifesto concerning libraries and all the reasons you should visit your local branch.

ASHLYN KANE likes to think she can do it all, but her follow-through often proves her undoing. Her house is as full of half-finished projects as her writing folder. With the help of her ADHD meds, she gets by.

An early reader and talker, Ashlyn has always had a flair for language and storytelling. As an eight-year-old, she attended her first writers' workshop. As a teenager, she won an amateur poetry competition. As an adult, she received a starred review in *Publishers Weekly* for her novel *Fake Dating the Prince*. There were quite a few years in the middle there, but who's counting?

Her hobbies include DIY home decor, container gardening (no pulling weeds), music, and spending time with her enormous chocolate lapdog. She is the fortunate wife of a wonderful man, the daughter of two sets of great parents, and the proud older sister/sister-in-law of the world's biggest nerds.

Sign up for her newsletter at www.ashlynkane.ca/newsletter/
Website: www.ashlynkane.ca

MORGAN JAMES is a clueless (older) millennial who's still trying to figure out what they'll be when they grow up and enjoying the journey to get there. Now, with a couple of degrees, a few stints in Europe, and more than one false start to a career, they eagerly wait to see what's next. James started writing fiction before they could spell and wrote their first (unpublished) novel in middle school. They haven't stopped since. Geek, artist, archer, and fanatic, Morgan passes their free hours in imaginary worlds, with people on pages and screens—it's an addiction, as is their love of coffee and tea. They live in Canada with their massive collection of unread books and where they are the personal servant of too many four-legged creatures.

Twitter: @MorganJames71
Facebook:www.facebook.com/morganjames007

WINGING IT

Falling for his
teammate wasn't in
the game plan....

ASHLYN KANE
MORGAN JAMES

Hockey Ever After: Book One

Hockey is Gabe Martin's life. Dante Baltierra just wants to have some fun on his way to the Hockey Hall of Fame. Falling for a teammate isn't in either game plan.

But plans change.

When Gabe gets outed, it turns his careful life upside-down. The chaos messes with his game and sends his team headlong into a losing streak. The last person he expects to pull him through it is Dante.

This season isn't going the way Dante thought it would. Gabe's sexuality doesn't faze him, but his own does. Dante's always been a "what you see is what you get" kind of guy, and having to hide his attraction to Gabe sucks. But so does losing, and his teammate needs him, so he puts in the effort to snap Gabe out of his funk.

He doesn't mean to fall in love with the guy.

Getting involved with a teammate is a bad idea, but Dante is shameless, funny, and brilliant at hockey. Gabe can't resist. Unfortunately, he struggles to share part of himself that he's hidden for years, and Dante chafes at hiding their relationship. Can they find their feet before the ice slips out from under them?

Scan the QR code below to order

HOCKEY EVER AFTER BOOK 1.5

THE WINGING IT HOLIDAY SPECIAL

ASHLYN KANE
MORGAN JAMES

Hockey Ever After: Book 1.5

Hockey's started, holidays are looming, and NHL player Dante Baltierra's husband is keeping secrets.

Of course, secrets aren't unusual this time of year, but Dante is pretty sure Gabe isn't being squirrelly about a new flat-screen or tickets for a second honeymoon. Whatever is eating Gabe is more serious than a surprise under the tree. But as much as Dante wants to help, asking about it would be fruitless. Besides, he has a theory about the problem—and the solution.

He's just not sure Santa has the power to deliver what Gabe really wants this Christmas.

Scan the QR code below to order

HOCKEY EVER AFTER BOOK TWO

SCORING POSITION

You miss
100 percent of
the shots you
don't take.

ASHLYN KANE
MORGAN JAMES

Hockey Ever After: Book Two

Ryan Wright's new hockey team is a dumpster fire. He expects to lose games—not his heart.

Ryan's laid-back attitude should be an advantage in Indianapolis. Even if he doesn't accomplish much on the ice, he can help his burned-out teammates off it. And no one needs a friend—or a hug—more than Nico Kirschbaum, the team's struggling would-be superstar.

Nico doesn't appreciate that management traded for another openly gay player and told them to make friends. Maybe he doesn't know what his problem is, but he'll solve it with hard work, not by bonding with the class clown.

It's obvious to Ryan that Nico's lonely, gifted, and cracking under pressure. No amount of physical practice will fix his mental game. But convincing Nico to let Ryan help means getting closer than is wise for Ryan's heart—especially once he unearths Nico's sense of humor.

Will Nico and Ryan risk making a pass, or will they keep missing 100 percent of the shots they don't take?

Scan the QR code below to order

UNRIVALED

Love
doesn't
pull its
punches.

ASHLYN KANE
MORGAN JAMES

IPG WORK ORDER

Job Number: 9955766

Due Date: 2025-01-17T00:00:00

ISBN Number: 9781641087322

PO#: 47296

Title: Textbook Defense (9781641087322)

Type: POD

Qty: Job 1 Batched 2 Copies 2

Trim Size: 6.00 x 9.00

Paper Stock: 50# White

Cover Stock: 50# White

BW Pages: 312

Color Pages: 0

Laminate: GLOSS

Number of Pages: 312

Finishing: Perfect Bound

Spine Bulk Fraction: 0.625

Production Notes: